One Summer in Italy

Sue Moorcroft

AVON

A division of HarperCollins*Publishers*
1 London Bridge Street,
London SE1 9GF

www.harpercollins.co.uk

A Paperback Original 2018

1

First published in Great Britain by
HarperCollins*Publishers* 2018

Copyright © Sue Moorcroft 2018

Sue Moorcroft asserts the moral right to be identified as the author of this work

A catalogue record for this book is available from the British Library

ISBN-13: 978-0-00-826004-0

Typeset in Sabon LT Std by Palimpsest Book Production Ltd, Falkirk, Stirlingshire

Printed and bound in Great Britain by CPI Group (UK) Ltd, Croydon CR0 4YY

MIX
Paper from
responsible sources
FSC **FSC® C007454**
www.fsc.org

For all my lovely readers.
If you enjoy my books, you bring me joy.

Prologue

July

'Don't mope, Sofia. *Non frignare.*'

Sofia jumped out of her reverie. She hadn't realised her dad, Aldo, was awake. His eyes had been closed for ages, the steady hiss of oxygen a contrast to his ragged breathing.

She edged her chair closer, glad to see a twinkle in Aldo's dark eyes. 'I'm not moping. I'm a bit worried about you, that's all. We worry about each other, don't we? That's how it works.'

He met her smile with one of his own. Aldo had a beautiful, mischievous smile, spoiled now by the odd colour of his lips as his heart failed. 'I don't mean now. I want you to promise you won't mope when I'm not here.' His voice still sang with the rhythms of Italy, but his English was fluent after living in the UK for more than thirty years. Sofia was so used to hearing both languages from him that she sometimes scarcely noticed which he was speaking. It had brought him comfort in these last few years to roll Italian lovingly around his mouth, as well as

1

allowing her to practise her grasp of one half of her family's mother tongue. Not that she'd met any of her family, on either side, apart from her parents.

The smile she'd summoned up for him wavered.

'Promise,' he insisted gently.

It was obviously so important to him that she nodded. 'I'll try.'

'No. You must promise. You've given up so many years to being my carer. I don't want you to be trapped in this house any more.'

She swallowed the fruitless urge to demand that he live for ever. 'OK. I promise.' Leaving the house in Bedford, the only home she'd ever known, would be taken out of her hands anyway. She hadn't stressed Aldo by telling him about the builder who'd inspected the big crack running up the dining-room wall and into Sofia's bedroom above. The builder had recommended an engineer's report. He thought the house had subsidence, and Sofia already knew that it needed a new roof and had woodworm. When Aldo's health had taken this recent grave turn, she'd been nerving herself to reveal that they needed to put the house on the market in the hope that a developer would buy it as a project and she and Aldo would receive only a proportion of what they considered its worth. Money had become the least of her worries.

He gave a slow, satisfied nod, his gaze unwavering. 'And promise me you'll get out and do all the things young single women do. Travel. You've always wanted to travel and instead you've stayed to help me. Go and have fun.'

'Dad, I don't want you to feel—'

'I don't feel anything you don't want me to feel,' he assured her with a dismissive wave. He made a mock reproving face. 'But this is the dying wish of your papà. You must promise.'

She'd often shared with him her fantasy of getting on the plane from Stansted Airport for breakfast and arriving at a pavement café in Italy in time for lunch, even before his health had made such an adventure impossible. Sofia grinned, though her eyes swam. Half her life he'd cared for her and half her life she'd cared for him, latterly in his hospital-style bed in the front room with the oxygen cylinders located behind it. 'OK, if you'll stoop to emotional blackmail, you old fox, I promise.'

Aldo's laugh creaked out into his oxygen mask, fogging it up. 'Promise me you'll visit Montelibertà. As you have no family in England I'd like you to see the town where I was born. Lay flowers for your grandparents.' He sighed. His breathing hitched. Faltered. Began again.

A tear leaked onto Sofia's cheek but she fell back on black humour, their coping mechanism through all the operations and treatments that had bought them time. Till now. 'Just how many dying wishes does one papà get?'

His eyes closed but his smile flickered. '*Molti, molti*. I wish you could have met your Italian family.'

Despite Aldo's condition, Sofia's interest stirred. He was always happy to talk about Italy but much less forthcoming on the subject of his family. 'I wish that too. I wish I knew more about them,' she said.

Aldo's forehead puckered. 'It was all such a mess. I thought I was doing the right thing, coming here. But my parents . . . they were in the middle. There were many emotional letters and phone calls between us when you were young. "Come to England to visit us," I said. But they would always reply, "Come home to visit *us*." They were convinced we could patch things up if I went home.

3

It would only make things worse. I told them, "How can I take Dawn and Sofia to Montelibertà? It will be so painful."'

Sofia leaned forward intently, the blood thudding in her ears. 'Why, Dad? Why wouldn't you take Mum and me? Or me, after Mum died? What did you need to patch up? What were they in the middle of?' Was Aldo at long last ready to tell her the story that had intrigued her, growing up, of how and why he'd abandoned his homeland? Till now he'd avoided revealing more than the bare facts: that he'd left his parents and brother behind in Italy thirty-two years ago to marry Sofia's mother, Dawn. His Italian family hadn't been at the wedding. Dawn had died when Sofia was five, and his parents, in a road accident, two years later. He'd always parried Sofia's eager quest for more information with *It's all too sad to talk about. I don't want to make you sad*. Then he'd stroke her hair and change the subject.

Now Aldo opened his eyes and continued as if he hadn't heard her questions. 'Go to Montelibertà and drink Orvieto Classico as it's meant to be drunk – designed for the Italian palate, not the British one.' He paused. His breathing paused, too. Restarted. 'If you see your Uncle Gianni, tell him I'm sorry.'

She used the heels of her hands to wipe her tears away. It was frustrating that her father was dodging her questions once again, but he was so gravely ill now that it would be unkind to press him on why he wanted to apologise to the brother he'd been estranged from for decades. 'I will.' She took his hand.

Aldo's smile was so faint she almost missed it. 'The last promise then. Be happy, Sofia. Be happy.'

'I promise,' she whispered.

Chapter One

The following year, as tourist season begins
Promises #1, #2 and #3: Don't Mope. Do all the things
single women do. Visit Montelibertà.

Sofia could see what Davide was up to. Threading between the black iron tables of Il Giardino he was deliberately brushing against Amy, apparently irresistibly drawn to her blonde-haired, blue-eyed prettiness.

Like Sofia, Amy had only been working at the hotel Casa Felice for ten days. As Davide had been away on a course, this was the first time their duties had brought them all together yet Sofia had heard Davide ask Amy for a date within ten minutes of the start of the shift. Not visibly rebuffed by her gasp of dismay and embarrassed head-shake, he'd then proceeded to behave like a Jack Russell in heat.

Sofia's protective instincts were roused by her friend's obvious distress. Amy was eighteen and this was her first summer job, for crying out loud! Davide was at least a decade her senior and the son of the owner. Sofia timed her next run to the kitchen hatch to coincide with Amy's. 'Are you OK?' she whispered.

Amy's eyes sparkled with angry tears as she balanced two pâté boards and an order of truffles on her tray. 'Davide's being a creep.'

'He certainly is. I'm just checking you're aware he's Benedetta's son—'

'Don't care! I'm not putting up with him rubbing his yucky "bits" on my bum.' Amy spun on her heel with a swish of her blonde ponytail and made for a table of three middle-aged Englishwomen who'd whiled away the wait for food with a couple of bottles of prosecco.

Powerless to help, Sofia continued to run food and drink to her own tables, swinging fully laden trays up onto her flattened hand. It was hard work in the midday sun and the mercury was soaring even at the beginning of June. She watched her section, whipping out pen and pad to take orders then running the food and drink to the appropriate table. Quick, brisk, hurry. Smile, smile, smile. Take money. Clear tables; sanitise. Ignore burning feet and aching back . . .

'YAH! *Ungh*!'

Sofia halted, sanitising spray poised as her eyes hunted out the origin of the strangled cries. In front of the corner of the bar Davide was doubled over, eyes bulging.

Nearby, a flushed Amy swung an empty tray. 'Sorry. You startled me and my tray slipped.' Then she loaded her next order of drinks and glided rapidly away without troubling to hide a triumphant grin.

Sofia smiled back uneasily, not missing the malevolent glare Davide directed at Amy's rear view. 'Keep an eye on him now,' Sofia murmured when she contrived to make their paths converge at the bar. 'What did you do?' She cast a glance at Davide, who'd managed to straighten up and was taking an order from an Italian family.

'Hit him in the 'nads with my tray. He might keep them further away from me in future.' But the first flush of victory was obviously fading and Amy was beginning to look apprehensive as she slid four coffees onto the tray-slash-weapon.

Sofia wiped her hands on her apron and arranged her own tray so that it balanced before following in Amy's wake. Amy was evidently given to impetuous action when threatened, but Sofia knew Davide's type. He might not take long to strike back.

Smiling through the familiar routine of 'Whose is the Cappuccino? And the Americano?' with her customers, Sofia watched with a sinking sense of inevitability as Davide slunk up behind Amy at the table of the prosecco ladies just as she began the rotation of the wrist that would arc a tray full of steaming coffee cups from her shoulder to the table.

All it took was for Davide to shoot out a furtive arm.

The tray flipped off Amy's hand . . . slap into the lap of one of the customers.

'Ow, ow, ow!' The woman leaped to her feet, dragging steaming fabric away from her legs. 'You stupid girl! My best white linen trousers! How could you be so clumsy?'

'I'm sorry!' Amy, pale and shocked, glanced frantically behind her, obviously suspecting the tray had had some help in its flight. But Davide had lost no time in gliding away and was already watching from the shady doorway that led to reception.

'Excuse me!' Sofia plonked down the final Americano and raced between the craning guests, whipping off her apron. Reaching the unfortunate customer, she dunked the white cotton into the meltwater surrounding upended prosecco bottles in the ice bucket. 'If you'd like to sit down I'll put this over your legs in case you've been scalded. It'll dilute the coffee, too. I know it's not comfortable but I'm sure Casa Felice will pay for cleaning. Amy's right to apologise, but I do think she was jostled.'

'I was.' Amy's bottom lip began to quiver. 'I'm very sorry – but the tray just seemed to leap off my hand.'

'Oh, yes, trays are full of tricks like that,' Mrs Coffee Trousers retorted. But then, seeing everyone staring at her, sat down and let Sofia lay the cold cloth across her thighs.

'It'll soon dry in this heat,' remarked one of her companions from the comfortable position of not having been bathed in near-boiling liquid. She smiled at Amy. 'Don't you worry, darlin'. Worse things happen at sea.'

Sofia was just about to suggest Amy return to the bar to ask for the coffee order to be repeated when Benedetta barrelled out through the double doors of the hotel with Davide a few steps behind. Sofia's heart dropped. Benedetta Morbidelli, an impressive mix of immaculate and statuesque, owned all of hotel Casa Felice and its café, Il Giardino. By the look of Davide's smirk, he'd lit his mother's blue touch paper and was now intending to watch her explode.

'Sacked! Go, you!' Benedetta yelled at Amy, her dark 'updo' quivering as she made extravagant shooing motions with her hands.

Amy's lip quivered harder. 'But it wasn't my fault—'

'Pack! Go!' Benedetta thundered up to the table and gave Amy a little shove with her well-manicured fingertips.

'But it wasn't her fault,' protested Sofia. She turned to give Davide a pointed stare, raising her voice over the sound of a motorbike arriving in the hotel car park beyond a row of flower tubs. '*Someone* knocked her.'

'There was a young man nearby,' said the same prosecco lady who'd tried to calm things before.

'*Go!*' Benedetta shouted in Amy's face.

Amy took a frightened step back, stuttering piteously. 'I h-haven't got anywhere to go. I'm supposed to stay here till S-September.'

'Look! Look what you do to my customer!' Benedetta lifted the wetted apron off the maltreated prosecco lady's legs.

Mrs Coffee Trousers was beginning to look discomfited. 'You shouldn't sack her. Even if she wasn't jostled it was an accident and you've got no call to push her around, neither. You could get sued for that.'

'I'll pay for the cleaning,' Amy quavered, before adding, wretchedly. 'Once I've had some wages.'

'*Wages?*' Benedetta began shouting again at Amy, this time in Italian, that she would get no wages, she must go this very minute and pack her bags, then leave Casa Felice and never return.

The English tourists were obviously not following shrieked Italian but they all blinked as Benedetta shoved Amy again, presumably to encourage her to her room to pack. Amy, not understanding, began to cry.

Sofia lifted her voice. 'Maybe we could discuss this indoors in private, Benedetta?' When ignored, she repeated the suggestion in Italian.

Benedetta turned her wrath down a notch, perhaps seeing in Sofia an experienced hand. 'She's too young for this job. I need to get someone new from the website,' she explained in the same language.

Sofia took a deep breath. 'Actually, it was Davide. He

made a nuisance of himself and when Amy put a stop to it he got his revenge by bumping her tray. I'm afraid I saw him do it.'

Davide stopped smirking and began to protest 'Eh, eh!' as Italian-speaking customers turned to gaze reproachfully at him.

'What's that you're saying?' demanded Mrs Coffee Trousers.

Sofia, despite a growing feeling that crossing the excitable Benedetta might result in her soon joining Amy in clearing her room, repeated her accusation in English. The English-speaking customers swivelled suspicious gazes towards Davide too.

'No!' remonstrated Benedetta with an air of injured reproach. 'Not Davide.'

Then a man appeared beside the group, raking back fair hair damp with perspiration. In his thirties, he carried a red crash helmet and a black biker jacket, his lower half encased in protective gear. 'She's right. I saw this waiter do it.' He turned a fierce glare on Davide. 'You should be ashamed of yourself, getting this young girl in bother and then grinning about it.'

'Eh, eh!' protested Davide again. 'She dropped it. She is clumsy. It's not my fault.'

'She did not drop it!' Sofia glanced at Biker Man, hopeful that this English tourist would continue to support her. 'You've been brushing your . . . the front of your trousers against her and when she hit you with her tray, you got your revenge. *And* you went in and told tales to your mother.' For Benedetta's benefit, she repeated her allegation in Italian. Biker Man nodded, arms folded, interposing at intervals, 'That's absolutely right!' even at the Italian bits.

Benedetta, visibly dismayed by the way things were going, dropped her voice to a confidential murmur. 'We talk indoors, Amy.' Rounding on Davide she snapped at him in Italian to give Mrs Coffee Trousers and her coterie their drinks on the house in lieu of paying the cleaning bill and then take over Amy's tables as well as his own.

She made to usher Amy inside but Biker Man began to follow. 'I'm here to check into the hotel, but I won't be doing so until I have your assurance that this young girl still has a job.'

Sofia felt her mouth drop open. Biker Man was certainly taking his support of Amy seriously. What was it about blondes? Men all seemed to act like fools where they were concerned.

Benedetta hurriedly backtracked to pat Amy's arm and turn her in the direction of her tables. 'You stay. It's OK. You work. I 'pologise for my son.' She turned a smile on Biker Man. 'You are a hotel guest? Welcome to Casa Felice. Please follow me.' Glaring at Davide as she passed, she ushered Biker Man towards the cool interior of the hotel.

Just before he disappeared, the man turned and gave Sofia a grin and a wink.

She gazed after him, lips parting in astonishment.

A scowling Davide silently cleared up the mess of spilled coffee and broken crockery and Sofia gave Amy's arm a quick pat. 'How about you pop and get these lovely ladies cake to go with their fresh coffees. Signora Morbidelli said it was on the house.'

'That's very good of you,' the prosecco ladies said to Sofia, and 'Isn't that good of her?' to each other.

'*Thank* you,' Amy whispered as they both headed to the bar. She was clinging to Sofia's arm as if she were even younger than her eighteen years. 'I don't know what

I would've done if she'd sacked me. That man turned up just at the right time.'

'Yes, it was lucky the guest saw everything.' Sofia placed a slight emphasis on the word *guest*, but decided that now was not the time to point out more clearly that the residents of the hotel were always referred to respectfully. 'If you want to clear tables for a bit I can take orders from your section until you're feeling better.' Or feeling a bit less Jekyll and Hyde. She would never have suspected Amy of being capable of swinging so rapidly from sweet and mild to angry and vengeful if she hadn't witnessed it.

A few minutes later, encountering Davide at the kitchen hatch, Sofia treated him to her widest smile. 'Shall we forget that all happened and just be friends?'

Davide spat out a word Aldo had told Sofia never to use, prompting the dad of a nearby Italian family to berate him for his language.

'So that's a "no" then.' Sofia turned briskly and headed off towards a new table of red-faced, sweaty tourists to fulfil their urgent requests for cold drinks.

Levi left the storm in a teacup behind him and followed the woman indoors to the reception desk, bemused by her speedy change of mood – only seconds ago she'd been bandying about threats of the sack but now she was beaming benevolently as she indicated the well-groomed young woman behind the reception desk. 'My daughter Aurora will be delighted to check you in.'

Aurora, looking to be in her twenties and oozing Italian chic – or whatever the Italian for chic was – smiled at Levi as if nothing would give her greater pleasure. 'May I take your name?'

'Levi Gunn.' He was glad the personnel at the hotel

spoke English as he'd had no opportunity to brush up on even a few Italian phrases before rushing off on this trip. While Aurora took him through the check-in process, he planted his Joe Rocket textile jacket and unpleasantly sweaty crash helmet on the desk. The armour in both jacket and his bike pants was essential for the road but less suitable for the blazing sun at a journey's end. At his last stop-off, near Verona, he'd wrung his T-shirt out in cold water before putting it on beneath his bike jacket, but he still felt like a steamed fish.

Or was he just hot with anger at the scene he'd witnessed? His instinct to help the sobbing girl had seized him like a giant hand. Supporting the protests of the other waitress had done the trick. The blonde waitress's job seemed saved and the dark-haired one had smiled at him, even though her eyes had been alive with curiosity.

Aurora finished tapping at her computer keyboard and took a printout from the printer tray. 'You have room 303, which has a balcony looking over the town of Montelibertà. Hotel residents have use of the terrace at the rear of the hotel, with a fantastic view across the valley and of other peaks in the Umbrian mountains. The terrace leads from the dining room on the lower level and many guests choose to take their breakfast there.'

'Sounds great. I like to paint landscapes so the terrace sounds wonderful.'

Aurora smiled as she turned the printout towards him and passed him a pen. 'You will find many beautiful views to paint here. Please, if you need information or recommendations, let me know. Casa Felice is a family concern. My mother expects us all to work hard at pleasing our guests.'

'I'm sure she always puts the guests first,' Levi said

dryly, thinking again of the crying waitress. Once he'd been given a key card he reluctantly closed his ears to the call of a frosty beer in Il Giardino and clumped across the small lobby in his biking boots, back out into the sun that blazed down on his fair English head. In the car park his Ducati Diavel, black with a red sub-frame and flashes, still radiated heat from the long trek across England, France, Germany, Austria and Italy in three days of hard riding. He didn't hang around as he transferred tightly rolled underwear, T-shirts and shorts out of his panniers, the nearest things to luggage compartments on a bike, and into the cotton sack he kept for the purpose. All the while, he kept an eye on Il Giardino and the staff weaving their way between busy tables.

The teenage girl – Amy, the owner had called her – although appearing in danger of buckling under the weight of a well-laden tray, moved briskly, her face pink with exertion. After watching her for another few moments and deciding she was fundamentally OK, Levi checked out Davide, who, as he swept tables clear with angry movements, didn't seem to be able to make up his mind which of the waitresses to glare daggers at. A man who'd sexually harass a younger colleague found no favour with Levi and that he'd proved to be the owner's son made it worse. Little shit. Levi was usually a live-and-let-live kind of guy but his old man, 'Bullet' Gunn, had run a repair garage all Levi's life and treated his workers with friendly respect. Levi had followed his dad's example when it came to his own business.

Emptying the second pannier, he glanced at the dark waitress, her upswept hair glossy beneath the sun. She looked about thirty to his thirty-five. A crisp black dress emphasised her shape and a white apron hugged her hips.

As he watched, she paused to speak with Amy, tray of empties aloft. She seemed to have the younger girl's back, judging by the way she'd launched into battle in – impressively – both Italian and English. After watching for another second, he locked his panniers, grabbed his paintbox from the bungees securing it and took himself indoors.

Now he had the opportunity to study Casa Felice as he returned to the cool of the reception area, he found it charming. Where the walls were plastered they were painted white, but large areas of craggy russet stone had been left exposed, a contrast to the dark grey marble of floor and front desk. A wooden banister curved up alongside the stairs.

Room 303 proved as pleasant a surprise as the foyer had been, though oddly shaped. It held a modern bed and an eclectic mix of graceful furniture, and the bathroom was up to date and clean. Levi had booked a 'superior' room, all that was available at short notice, so was glad to see something for his extra seventy euros a night, especially the balcony that gazed over tiers of tilted terracotta roofs and the road curving down the hill into a jumble of buildings.

Montelibertà was a select but significant tourist destination, much of it made from the same rock it perched upon, like a little brother of the city of Orvieto to the north. Casa Felice stood on the edge of the town, secluded in its own grounds yet only a ten-minute walk from the centre. According to the website it boasted fifty guest bedrooms over three floors. The road outside, Via Virgilio, led out of town to an extensive country park. Il Giardino, he reflected, was neatly positioned to tempt those who'd worked up thirst and hunger with a country walk.

The ground fell away from the hotel at the back too, and he paused to drink in the view over the shrubs and lavender of the gardens below the terrace where the valley steepened. Large tracts of the slopes were darkly clothed with trees below the hazy purple peaks, some with other towns on the summit. He itched to get out the watercolour paints that had provided his major means of relaxation since his school days. Instead, conscious of his rumbling stomach, he returned to the cool indoors to take a shower and make his way downstairs to seek refreshment.

Half an hour later he was seated beneath the shade of one of Il Giardino's off-white parasols. He had no trouble finding a vacant table. It was now three o'clock so perhaps many tourists had lunched already. Both waitresses were still working and the dark one appeared before him, producing her pad and pen from her apron pocket.

'*Buon giorno*,' she greeted him brightly. 'Would you like to order?' Her eyes were brown and her skin golden. If he hadn't heard her speaking English he would have taken her for Italian.

'*Buon giorno*.' He ordered a large beer and an arancino rice ball stuffed with ragù.

'Coming right up.' She returned in a couple of minutes bearing a tall glass of pale beer and deposited it on the table. 'Your arancino will be ready shortly.' She shot a swift glance around and then lowered her voice. 'Thanks for your help earlier. It made things a lot easier.'

'It felt like the right thing to do.' He took a long, satisfying draught of his beer, the chill liquid cutting through any remaining journey dust in his throat. As she'd raised the subject he asked, 'Is the other waitress OK?'

'I think so.' Her eyes smiled. 'I'm not sure how you saw the incident when you and your motorbike didn't arrive until after it had taken place but I'm grateful, and I know Amy is.'

Levi shrugged off the first part of her sentence. 'That guy – Davide? He's not around right now?'

She grinned, her teeth white and even. 'Benedetta thought it was a good idea to send him on his break.'

He chuckled. 'I suppose Casa Felice's not like one of those massive places where it's easy to assign staff members to opposite ends of the building and know they'd be unlikely to see each other.'

She nodded. 'Especially as Amy and I live in at Casa Felice.'

'Do all the staff?'

'No, most of the kitchen and housekeeping staff are local and many of the wait staff are too, but Benedetta likes some native English speakers for the tourists. Amy speaks German as well.'

'Remarkable,' he said. 'What time does your shift end?'

Her smile faltered. 'I'd better get back to work.' She turned smartly away.

Watching her glide off to a nearby table and begin to clear, he realised that she'd taken his question as a prelude to asking her to join him once she'd finished for the day.

He hid a rueful grin as he lifted his beer glass. Her hasty evasion had certainly put him in his place.

Chapter Two

Promise #4: Lay flowers for your grandparents

It was Monday before Sofia got a break after seven straight days on duty.

It was a shame that, as long as Sofia and Amy both worked in Il Giardino, their time off together would be limited. They'd bonded right from their first evening when Sofia, thinking Amy looked a bit lost, had suggested eating together. Over pasta, Amy had been wide-eyed to hear about the string of waitressing jobs Sofia had fitted around caring for her dad. In turn, Sofia had been green with envy over Amy's tales of living in Germany with her expat British family.

The evening had ended in giggles as they pored over the list of rules that had awaited them in their rooms, Benedetta's name printed in capitals at the foot. 'Wow,' Sofia had commented. '*Staff are required not to* go here, wear that, do the other. We'll be sacked for sure.'

They'd each managed not to transgress so far.

Benedetta had given Amy the weekend off as Amy was

used to handling euros, but her Italian was sketchy so she needed to concentrate hard when serving the locals. Also, she was visibly exhausted by long shifts on her feet in the bright sun or late into the evening.

Sofia hadn't minded waiting until training was over and she was established on the staff rota for her precious two days off – and now they were here. She could catch up on laundry in the staff kitchen-cum-utility-room this evening but this morning, after a couple of extra hours in bed, she meant to embark on the fulfilment of another promise to Aldo, one that had felt too important to be squeezed into the few off-duty hours she'd enjoyed so far.

It meant flouting Benedetta's rule that staff should avoid any area of the hotel where their duties did not take them, especially when not in uniform. However, Sofia risked entering the coolness of the reception area when she saw Aurora on duty because she was thought Aurora would be less wedded to the rules than Benedetta. Sofia had learned to like Aurora as readily as she'd learned to dislike her brother Davide, who seemed to go through every day resenting working for his mum and serving food to pink-faced tourists.

In contrast, Aurora obviously loved working in Casa Felice and had the happy knack of getting on with everyone. Like many Italian women, she had an air of effortless glamour. Her nails were immaculately crimson, her makeup pristine and her not-a-hair-out-of-place plait hung dead centre down the back of her smart black jacket. She beamed when she saw Sofia. 'Now you have some time to explore Montelibertà?'

'I can't wait,' Sofia returned frankly. 'Is there somewhere in town I can buy a map?'

19

Aurora opened a drawer. 'Of Montelibertà? *Informazioni turistiche* gives to us their maps.' She brought out a neatly folded rectangle and shook it out to display a colourful street plan. 'See, here is Casa Felice.' She tapped with a perfect fingernail. 'Follow Via Virgilio down the hill and into the town and you see the church, many restaurants and museums. Here for good Italian ice-cream.' She tapped a different point on the map. 'Gelateria Fernando – my favourite.'

'I'd like to find the cemetery.' Sofia tried to sound as if this destination was on the 'must see' list of every seasonal worker.

Aurora's wide eyes and flipped-up eyebrows suggested interest. 'Your family name, Bianchi, it is unusual for Umbria. But there *are* others in Montelibertà.' Her expectant pause invited Sofia to fill in any blanks.

Sofia saw no reason to be secretive. 'My father was from Montelibertà. I promised I'd put flowers on his parents' graves. He was ill for a long time before he died so hadn't been able to return to Italy.'

The corners of Aurora's mouth turned down. 'I'm sorry you have lost your papà.'

Sofia tried to smile but it didn't quite come off, though the memory of Aldo's breathlessly cajoling '*Non frignare, Sofia,*' reverberated in her mind. It was hard not to mope when, as now, grief gripped her like a fist around her lungs. Sofia swallowed hard and forced her voice not to tremble. 'Thank you. He'd be glad I'm here.'

Aurora switched her smile back on. 'It is a large cemetery. Did your grandparents die long ago?'

'In 1994. They were together in a car accident between here and Turin.'

'Many people from the villages around this town also

rest there. It will be necessary to find exactly where are your grandparents.'

Sofia sighed. She'd hoped the cemetery would be of a size she could stroll around and chance across the names of Agnello and Maria Bianchi. 'Dad said I should ask at Santa Lucia church, but I wonder if the records are available to the public online?'

Aurora nodded. 'Of their passing, yes, but I agree with your papà. It will be better to ask Ernesto Milani at Santa Lucia. He is the one who writes down every funeral. He will find it for you.'

Sofia's stomach did a loop-the-loop at Aurora's matter-of-factness. It made the prospect of making this connection to her unknown family excitingly real. 'Is Ernesto the parish clerk?'

'*Si, è il responsabile del registro.*' Aurora was already reaching for the telephone, her plait swishing with her movements. She looked up something on the computer on the reception desk, dialled a number and began speaking into the phone in rapid Italian.

Sofia listened, noting unfamiliar vocabulary relating to the function of record keeping and registries. By the time Aurora put down the phone she didn't need much additional information. 'Ernesto has agreed to meet me? Today?' It was that easy?

'Yes, at the church. There is no service until evening so you can find him now in the rooms at the back.' She marked the church on the map, although Sofia already knew it was on Piazza Santa Lucia, one of the two major squares in town, because Aldo had taken her on imaginary walks through Montelibertà so many times. On a sheet of paper, Aurora wrote Ernesto's name and drew a diagram of where Sofia would find the rear door.

21

'Thank you.' Gratefully, Sofia folded up the map, smooth and flimsy beneath her fingers. '*Ciao.*'

As she turned away, she caught sight of the guest she'd mentally christened Biker Man across reception. He'd adopted a more orthodox approach to holiday wear now, black cargo shorts and a T-shirt that stretched across his chest. He was starting to tan even after a couple of days, she noticed.

Then, realising the reason he was staring at her was probably because she was staring at him, she smiled briefly and set off towards the door. She shouldn't 'notice' a male guest, even one with ruffled hair and bright blue eyes, even one who'd asked when she got off shift. Because he'd asked the question where she could be easily overheard, she hadn't confided that one of Benedetta's rules – printed in bold – was that staff should not have relationships with guests. Shame, as one of her promises to Aldo had been that she'd do all the things she hadn't been able to do in the years of caring for him, and that, she'd promised herself, would include men.

Boyfriends had been few. The last had been Jamie, whose financial situation had made him happy that 'dates' had consisted mainly of staying home with Aldo. Jamie had been good at hugs, and sometimes she'd needed them, but she was pretty sure the sex could have been better, even allowing for the fact that she'd never felt at ease up in her room with Jamie while Aldo slept on the ground floor.

Though she had every intention of steering clear of actual *boyfriends* for a good long while, Biker Man, a tourist, was unlikely to stick around long enough to qualify. She was single. She'd never had a one-night stand and had placed it high on her list as something a single woman might do.

She braked to a sudden halt as Biker Man, as if divining her thoughts, stepped into her path.

'Hi.' He flashed her an easy smile.

'Hi.' She produced what she hoped was a suitably staff-to-guest smile back.

'I didn't get your name last time we spoke.' He lifted an encouraging eyebrow.

'Sofia.' She imagined Aurora's ears coming out of her head on stalks in an effort to listen across the reception area.

'I'm Levi. I was just wondering . . .' He hesitated.

Sofia held her breath, trying to decide how to side-step any further interest in her off-duty time. She was going to meet someone – which was true: Ernesto Milani. It was just such a *waste*! Biker Man Levi's eyes were mesmeric and he looked to have a hell of a bod beneath his T-shirt.

'. . . if Amy's all right,' he finished.

Sofia snapped back to reality. 'You wondered whether Amy's all right?' she repeated, feeling slightly foolish for suspecting him of angling for a date.

He flushed at the surprise in her voice. 'I haven't seen her for a couple of days and, with what happened, I wondered if she'd lost her job after all. I hope you don't mind me asking, but you're obviously friendly.'

Sofia summoned a smile. 'She's fine. It was just her turn for time off. Enjoy your day.' She made a show of checking her watch, then stepped around him and out through the door, trying not to feel ruffled. But, really? Did Levi think a teenage girl like Amy would be interested in him? Levi looked well over thirty, and Sofia had thought Davide, in his late twenties, too old for Amy!

Resolutely, she put Biker Man and his smile out of her

mind. She had to get into town and locate the church of Santa Lucia.

Via Virgilio was busy with cars, vans, the occasional lorry and a swarm of motorbikes and scooters. Sofia didn't rush down the hill towards the centre. Apart from the sun already being a significant presence at just turned eleven o'clock there were enough pedestrians occupying the pavements to make hurrying an effort and she enjoyed gazing around at the buildings, stone or rendered and painted. She'd seen a little of the town in whatever part of each day she wasn't on shift but it was surprising how much of the past two weeks had been taken up with settling in. Her first couple of days had passed in a whirl of unpacking, orientation, getting sorted with uniform and a hunt for toiletries at a nearby kiosk that seemed to sell everything. Sofia had also found herself helping Amy through orientation and uniform. Sofia had missed out on siblings and was enjoying the novelty of the big-sister role in which Amy seemed to have cast her.

But, right now, with two joyous days of freedom to enjoy in Montelibertà, she was seized by a ridiculous urge to jig around singing, 'I'm here, I'm here, I'm really here!'

Instead, she strolled decorously past shops that sold shiny ceramics decorated with splashy yellow sunflowers and succulent purple grapes. In between the shops came pavement cafés, their parasols the same shade of ivory as those at Il Giardino. On this upper part of the hill the commercial ventures were interspersed with houses and apartments, lavishly ornamented with window boxes in full flower and lavender tumbling from the tops of garden walls. She thought the scent of lavender would everonwards remind her of her feeling of euphoria.

24

Nearer the town centre the residences petered out and the road became lined with shops and eating places, until Via Virgilio widened into Piazza Roma. Here the buildings were three or even four storeys, painted in earthy tones from ivory to apricot and umber, creating shade for the people passing by or sitting on benches along the way. A giant cartwheel sat in the centre with an old water pump and a profusion of flowers. The cobbles were laid in fan shapes, old and uneven enough to bear witness to a million treading feet.

One building of honey-coloured stone had a sweeping ornamental arch built into it and when Sofia stopped gazing up at cornices, wrought iron and shutters long enough to walk through, she found herself in Piazza Santa Lucia, faced with the gracefully imposing building that was Santa Lucia church.

The Palladian front was rendered and painted palest lemon with white raised plasterwork surrounding the circular windows and forming mock columns and niches. Both of the huge carved wooden doors were closed but the door-within-a-door in the one on the left stood slightly open as if to reassure the parishioners that they could visit any time. The upper storey curved and narrowed until it met the triangular gable.

Her father had been raised a Catholic; her mother had not. Sofia hadn't been baptised or even attended church very often, but she thought she'd be OK to enter as her shorts were bermudas and her top wasn't low-cut. Following Aurora's directions, she made her way around the outside of the church, where the walls were of unrendered stone, to a plain door.

After hovering a moment, she knocked and entered a tall, cool, silent foyer that smelt of dust and incense. The door snapped to behind her, shutting out the sunlight.

25

A man in his sixties emerged from a nearby doorway, his smile lifting the ends of his big grey moustache. His fulsome eyebrows grew as if they'd been blown up and back by a strong wind. 'Are you Miss Sofia Bianchi? I am Ernesto Milani.'

As he spoke in English, Sofia followed suit, shaking his hand and thanking him for sparing her his time.

'Please, come this way,' he rumbled as he turned towards the room from which he'd emerged. 'I have looked at the register since Aurora Morbidelli speaks to me on the telephone and have information for you.' His English was accented and far from faultless but it flowed musically from beneath the moustache.

'Thank you!' Eagerly, Sofia followed him into a little office of glass-fronted cabinets and piles of papers. A window stood open to catch the breeze and a large book lay open on the table. Ernesto seated himself at one side and Sofia took the chair at right angles.

Ernesto fished a pair of glasses from his top pocket, put them on and regarded Sofia over their rim. 'Our current records we make on the computer but in 1997 we still record the events of our church in this book.' He looked at her for a few moments more, his eyes brown and knowledgeable, then he took his glasses off again.

Wondering if he was waiting for her full attention before he went on – she had been trying to decipher the register from the corner of one eye – Sofia nodded. 'I understand.'

'Forgive me, but I must ask.' A smile tried again to shift the weight of his moustache. 'You are the daughter of Aldo Agnello Bianchi, yes?'

Surprise made her sit back. 'Yes. But it wasn't my dad who died in Italy in 1997. It was my grandparents, Agnello and Maria.'

He sighed pensively. 'We were friends, Aldo and me, at school here in Montelibertà. I knew your grandparents also. I played in their garden and your grandmother made us a delicious drink from lemons. The family had their house in Via Salvatore.' He gestured vaguely behind him, as if pointing the street out. 'I remember very well. The Bianchi family and the Milani family, they attend this church, so we know each other.'

It was several seconds before Sofia could find her voice. The grandparents she'd never met and that her father had rarely spoken of leaped into focus as real people. Unexpectedly, her throat grew tight. 'I never knew them. They died when I was seven. This is the first time I've visited Italy.' She couldn't help adding, because she'd really like someone to put some meat on the bare bones of what Aldo had confided, 'And they never visited us in England.'

But Ernesto didn't offer insight. Instead, his eyes grew expectant. 'And Aldo . . .?' His pause invited her to fill the silence.

Throat constricting, Sofia shook her head. 'He died last summer.' Briefly, she outlined Aldo's history of heart trouble. 'I never thought I'd meet anybody who'd remember him. He was a young man when he left Montelibertà.'

'He was, he was,' Ernesto sighed, eyes closing for a moment as he crossed himself. 'I did not know. I am sorry for your loss. And for my own, though I had not seen Aldo for many years. When he met your mother—'

'Did you know my *mother*?' Sofia's heart almost leaped from her chest. 'I've never met anybody but Dad who knew my mother! She seems to have had no family, and she died when I was five.'

His eyes were soft with sadness. 'Yes, I knew her and of her passing. I knew from your family here.'

'From my family here?' Sofia repeated blankly. 'How?'

Shaking his head as if still trying to comprehend the loss of his old friend, Ernesto drew the big register closer. 'We said a mass,' he observed, as if that settled the matter. 'Now I show to you the names of your grandparents.' He turned the big faded book so she could see line after line of entries in ornate inked script. Thanks to his pointing finger she was able to pick out the names Agnello Francesco Ricardo and Maria Vittoria Bianchi. Her eyes burned at this further link with the family she'd never known. A frustrating link because it came to a dead end – literally.

'The funeral, it was here at Santa Lucia, one funeral for both. And here—' Ernest pointed to a reference made up of letters and numbers '—here is a record of their place in the cemetery.' He took out his phone and took a photo of the reference, an incongruously up-to-date way to make a note from the old ledger. 'I will show you in a little while. But talking makes me thirsty. Will you join me to drink coffee in the piazza?'

'That would be lovely,' she replied with automatic courtesy and followed him out of the office, mind whirling with her good fortune at meeting someone who'd known Aldo well. And her mother! Aldo telling her to come to the church of Santa Lucia began to make a new kind of sense – he'd known that directing her there would increase her chances of falling into friendly hands.

For the millionth time she wondered why he hadn't had more to do with his family yet had so wanted her to visit Montelibertà. She managed to stem her flow of questions until they'd rounded the front of the church and strolled over the cobbles to a café up a tiny street off the piazza, its situation ensuring shade from the strengthening midday sun. The shiny aluminium tables were incongruously

28

modern in her opinion but Ernesto selected one on at the edges of the group. A waiter arrived promptly, asking after Ernesto's health in rapid Italian. Ernesto ordered espresso and Sofia Americano and the waiter beamed and bustled off. The waiting staff wore dark green waistcoats with their white shirts and black trousers. Sofia preferred Casa Felice's all black and white look.

She turned to Ernesto. 'So do you know—'

Ernesto held up one finger. 'I tell you everything I remember.' He launched into his first memories of Aldo at school, portraying him as a loveable scamp who'd played sport with far more zeal than he applied to lessons. 'But the teachers always smiled when they said his name.' Coffee arrived. Sofia scarcely noticed, fascinated by Ernesto's memories of Aldo in his youth, apparently clear and bright despite their travelling more than fifty years through the hot Umbrian air.

'And then your mother arrived in Montelibertà,' he related. His eyebrows flicked up and down. 'She was very modern, Dawn. With trousers this wide.' He made an exaggerated shape with his hands. 'And big shoes. Here.' He pointed to the sole of his sandal.

'Platforms?' she hazarded, hardly able to believe her luck that this man could remember such a level of detail about the woman Sofia sometimes thought she would have nothing of if it weren't for photographs. Her memories were made up of a hazy sensation of presence and a laughing, excited voice.

Ernesto nodded. 'Her hair was blonde and her eyes blue. All the young men fell in love with her but she chose Aldo. In the end. There was *gelosia*. Jealousy.' He cleared his throat and turned to raise a hand in the direction of a waiter. 'We should eat. Two o'clock has passed.'

The waiter returned and took their order for hot pastries and cold beer.

The afternoon wore on. They ordered more beer and still Ernesto talked about Aldo and how he'd had eyes for no one but Dawn from the moment they met. And how Agnello and Maria had been worried and upset by the relationship.

'And that's why they left Montelibertà,' Sofia finished for him, thinking that she knew this part of the story.

'Well—' Ernesto gave an eloquent shrug. 'Families. There can be many issues. Aldo never said to me, "Ernesto, I leave for this reason or that reason." He just said, "It is not fair to live here with Dawn, so I go to England, her country."'

'And did you ever hear from my father again?' Sofia swallowed, sensing the past disappointment of this good and genuine man even before he answered.

'At first,' Ernesto sighed. 'But there were difficulties.'

'Difficulties?'

Ernesto hesitated. Then said, 'In not so many years your mother became ill and passed away. I think Aldo had much on his mind, many worries and griefs. Grief upon grief. When your grandparents died I think he finally left Italy behind and embraced England.'

'But when he became very ill he talked about Montelibertà constantly. He asked me to come here. We spoke Italian almost all the time.' Eyes prickling, she grabbed a paper napkin to blow her nose.

Ernesto's eyebrows quirked. 'Ah! *Parli Italiano?*'

At first Sofia only managed a strangled '*Si.*' But when she'd swallowed her tears she told him, in Italian, how much her father had loved his country, even if he'd never been able to return. How she'd once wanted to take a degree in Italian but Aldo's health had never permitted such a commitment. 'My secret wish was to come to Italy to study, but it was so impossible that I never mentioned it to him. Maybe I'll do it some day.'

Ernesto gave his moustache a thorough wipe as if needing time to compose himself. But when he looked up, his eyes were smiling again. 'And you not only speak our language but with the accent of Montelibertà! Now, shall we walk to the cemetery? Or I can fetch my car.'

Sofia jumped up. 'Let's walk. Dad wanted me to take flowers.'

Ernesto made an expansive gesture. 'There is a little cart at the cemetery gates. There you can buy.' They left behind the aroma of coffee and set off diagonally across the piazza.

On leaving the square they took the shady side of a street that snaked uphill in the opposite direction to Casa Felice. Sofia broached the other subject on her mind. 'I noticed you didn't mention my father's brother, Gianni Bianchi. Did you know him too?'

For several seconds, Ernesto was silent. Then he said, 'I know him still. He lives here in Montelibertà.'

Chapter Three

Promise #5: Drink Orvieto Classico in Montelibertà.

Sofia stopped short in excitement. 'He still lives here? I know so little about him. For a long time the only family members Dad mentioned were his grandparents. Then one day he was feeling melancholy and said, "I should tell you about your Uncle Gianni."'

Ernesto turned to wait for her, great eyebrows lifting. 'And what did he tell you?'

Sofia's breath came quicker as the slope steepened. 'Just that Gianni existed, really. I was intrigued – I suppose I'd always assumed he would have mentioned siblings long ago if he had any. I asked a lot of questions but he just said Gianni was younger than him.'

'*Si*. Two years, I think.'

'Two years isn't much. I thought it would be a lot more, that maybe they hadn't kept in touch because they had nothing in common.'

'They had much.' Then Ernesto began to comment on the streets they were passing through, slanting ever upward.

'In summer the town is full of sun. In winter, full of snow. This hill, like all the hills, becomes very difficult. We are surrounded by the mountain with only one piece going down. In the past, it was easy to defend. It is an old town, Montelibertà. We have less than ten thousand residents.'

'But lots of tourists? You're about midway between the airports at Perugia and Rome here, aren't you?'

He nodded. 'Many tourists, but often for short visits or day trips. There is not so much—' He paused, clicking his fingers as if to summon up a word. 'Entertainment,' he selected, in the end.

Sofia replied in Italian to give him a break from speaking English and his smiles became ever more frequent as he chatted about the town with the knowledge and affection that came from lifelong citizenship. It was half an hour before they reached a cemetery so steep that the gravestones looked as if they had ranked to watch over the town, but to Sofia it seemed to whizz by.

She bought a bunch of yellow roses at the gates and Ernesto led her up several pathways until they reached a particular marker set in the floor. 'This row, plot E54. We must search because the lines are long and the marks are old.'

He was right. It took them a good fifteen minutes of following row E, which wavered and wandered around trees and occasional outcroppings of rock, before they met with success.

In the end, it was Sofia's eye that was caught by the sight of her own surname on a small squared-off column of black marble with a white marble angel on top. '*Agnello Francesco Ricardo Bianchi, nato Dicembre 2 1938, morto Aprile 29 1997. Maria Vittoria Bianchi, nata Gennaio 21 1940, morta Aprile 29 1997*,' she read. Agnello born in December, Maria in January, and they'd died together in their fifties.

She lowered herself before the column, not as a mark of respect but because her knees felt as if someone had whipped them away.

There were two ovals of porcelain affixed to the column and on them were photos of her grandparents.

To suddenly know what her grandparents looked like gave her a strange, fizzing feeling. Aldo hadn't brought family photographs away from Italy with him, and if anybody had sent him any Sofia had never seen them.

She gazed at the ceramic likenesses. Agnello's strong straight nose reminded her of her father's – and for that matter of her own, though she was glad to have a more ladylike, less beaky version. Maria's face bore a smile both mischievous and sweet, a smile Aldo had inherited. Instead of merely being names, her grandparents became *people*. People she would have known as Nonno and Nonna . . . if she'd known them. But if they'd wanted to know her, wouldn't they have travelled to the UK even if Aldo had been unable or unwilling to travel here?

Finally, becoming aware of minutes passing and Ernesto waiting in silence, Sofia glanced uncertainly at the flowers in her hands. There was a pot at the base of the black marble column containing a collection of crumbling lavender spikes. Would she cause offence to someone – perhaps her uncle Gianni – if her roses supplanted them? Finally deciding she'd cross that bridge if she ever reached it, she removed the dying spikes and, fingers trembling, arranged the roses in their stead.

Then, clearing her throat, she spoke to the photos. 'Aldo was a very good man,' she said in Italian. 'He looked after me and I looked after him. At the end of his life he was sorry he'd lost you before he could rebuild your relationship, but he always loved you.'

She stood up and dusted off her hands, sending Ernesto a tentative smile. 'Do you think that was OK?'

He made a movement of his fulsome eyebrows and the moustache twitched. '*Perfetto*.' Perfect.

They ambled back down the hill together, Sofia beginning to wish she'd brought a bottle of water. At least the view as they trekked back down provided distraction. She could see clearly how Montelibertà lay in a bowl on three sides, the fourth plunging down to the valley. The distant peaks rising beyond were like giants wearing lilac bonnets and cloaks of grey-green woodland.

Shifting her gaze to the town, Sofia picked out Casa Felice and the roof of the church of Santa Lucia. Ernesto pointed out a couple of smaller churches, the library and the town hall. Skyscrapers had never come to the historic town and she saw not a single ugly building amongst the orange-brown roofs and shuttered windows.

Now she could tick off one promise from her list, but another was crowding to the forefront of her mind. 'If you know my Uncle Gianni, do you know whether he has children? Cousins of mine?'

'Yes, you have a cousin. I do not remember her name. And you have an aunt, of course – Gianni's wife is called Mia.'

'Wow.' Sofia laughed, almost giving a little skip of excitement. 'I feel as if my head's going to explode, trying to take it all in. Do you know where I can find my uncle? My father left him a message.'

Ernesto wiped his sweating forehead on the sleeve of his shirt. 'A message?' He gazed at the distant peaks and his steps slowed as if with the weight of his thoughts. Eventually he offered, 'I don't have his address in my head but I'll see him on Sunday, I think, because we attend the same mass. If you wish, I'll tell him where you're living and then he'll find you for himself.'

'OK.' The urge to skip faded. Ernesto seemed to be picking his words. Maybe he thought Gianni might not want to meet her? It was fair enough that he be given the choice, she acknowledged reluctantly, quashing a tiny wriggle of hurt. She'd known for months she was going to make this trip but Gianni might want time to digest the fact of her presence – even her existence – before they came face to face. Several times she'd thought of trying to locate him and sending a letter or email before her visit, but she hadn't known where to start and it had seemed one task too many in the tedium of tying up Aldo's affairs. 'Yes, please,' she answered eventually. 'But is it possible to leave it to me to tell him about Dad dying? I think that was what he wanted. My uncle can leave me a message at Casa Felice on Via Virgilio . . . if he wants to.'

Back on the edges of town again, they found shade to walk in. Ernesto asked about Sofia's job and her plans to travel for at least two years.

'You are an independent young woman.' He smiled as they once again entered the Piazza Santa Lucia.

'In practical ways,' she agreed cautiously. 'I've spent so many years feeling as if the world was passing me by. Even after Dad died—' her voice quavered for an instant '—I had to arrange the funeral, deal with his estate and sell the house in time to get out here for the summer season. I need to have fun. To experience the world.' Then, to cheer herself up, she asked Ernesto for suggestions for what to see in Umbria and left the emotion behind in the excitement of talking about Lake Trasimeno and 'Il Duomo', the cathedral in Orvieto.

It was nearly six o'clock by the time they kissed cheeks, called '*Ciao*!' and went their separate ways. Sofia had an overwhelming desire for a glass or three of cold wine. As she trailed through the arch to Piazza Roma, legs heavy from the walk, she almost flopped down at the nearest shady café. But she would enjoy it so much more after a shower and a change, she told herself, and there was no rule to prevent her drinking in Il Giardino as a paying customer. Amy was scheduled to be serving there this evening. Would Davide have been given the same duty?

His English was good, which was one of the reasons his mother liked him out there, and so he'd returned to Il Giardino, practising the fine art of throwing his weight around while simultaneously avoiding work himself.

Sofia bought a bottle of cold water and began climbing the hill, taking her mind off her burning calves by checking out bars and cafés that might provide the kind of nightlife she thought a young single woman ought to be sampling.

Finally she reached Casa Felice, intending to skirt Il Giardino and cross the car park to the utility yard where bins and crates were stored and deliveries received, and staff could access the hotel. Glancing over the greenery that marked the division between pavement and Il Giardino she saw Davide was indeed threading between tables, tray high. Amy was at the bar, balancing an order of drinks on her own tray, and another waiter Sofia had shared a shift with a couple of times, Thomas, was picking up food from the kitchen hatch.

As she watched, Davide called something to Amy, who cast him a sullen look in reply.

Hmm. Picking up her pace, Sofia whisked through the utility yard and out the other side, taking the steps down to the low, staff-only gate that led to the strip of garden overrun by vine that disguised what Benedetta grandly termed the two 'apartments' beneath the terrace for the live-in staff. Hotel guests wandering about the sloping gardens below the terrace would have to approach almost up to the fence of the utility yard in order to stumble upon the gate. The Morbidellis shared an apartment up in the eaves of the hotel and Sofia suspected it was not the kind best hidden behind a garden filled with rampaging vine.

Once through the gate, Amy's accommodation lay behind the first faded green door and Sofia's behind the second. She let herself into her room and breathed a sigh of relief at the drop in temperature that came along with stone walls, tiled floor and only one window. Despite it being furnished economically, Sofia liked her room. The white walls made it airy, the bedclothes were pretty but simple in blue and white. There was enough room for the clothes she'd brought with her and the chest of drawers provided somewhere for her box of costume jewellery and makeup bag.

She stripped, left her clothes in a heap and stepped into the small shower room. The lukewarm water felt fantastic as it sluiced down her body and, defying Benedetta's warnings about not wasting water, even though Umbria received more rainfall than most of Italy, she gave herself up to the pleasure of being cool for several blissful minutes. Finally, she stirred herself to wash. When dry, she teamed a white dress with shiny black flip-flops, then brushed her hair into a high ponytail and picked up her purse.

After retracing her route to the front of the hotel she

cut across the car park to Il Giardino. From there she could see Amy hurrying through the tables wearing a set expression while Davide grinned slyly at her rear view. It looked as if Davide had bagged the centre section again and as the only empty table in the place was in that area, Sofia headed towards it.

She noticed two things simultaneously. A group of tourists was racing her for the table; and a neighbouring table had just one occupant: Levi the Biker Man. Sofia paused.

Davide spotted what was happening and indicated, by pointing rapidly between the tourists and the empty table, that the two were destined to be together.

Sofia nodded, quite understanding that the tourists had the greater revenue potential, and pointed to herself and the vacant seat at Levi's table. Benedetta couldn't complain about her mixing socially with a guest in this circumstance and she had an urge to learn a little more of what this particular guest was up to.

Decision made, she headed towards Levi. 'Would you mind if I shared your table?'

He'd been engrossed with his phone but glanced up at the sound of her voice, his hair lifting in the early evening breeze. 'I'd count it as a bonus.' His smile was slow and interested.

Knowing she'd probably have sent an equally interested smile back if she a) wasn't banned from cosying up to guests and b) didn't suspect him of making a goon of himself over a girl half his age, Sofia pulled out the chair. 'Thanks.'

Levi put down his phone and turned to catch Davide's eye. 'I was just about to order.'

Approving of his discreet getting-the-attention-of-the-waiter etiquette – she had a hatred of finger clickers and, even worse, those who thought it OK to *whistle* – Sofia watched as Davide jettisoned a tray of empty glasses at the bar and arrived with a smile that didn't reach his eyes. '*Buonasera.*'

Not certain whether he'd been so prompt because he was watching her with a guest, Sofia replied, '*Buonasera.*' And, when Levi made a courteous gesture that she should order first: '*Un bicchiere grande di Orvieto Classico, per favore.*'

Levi's eyebrows flipped up. They, and his eyelashes, were darker than the tawny locks on his head. His eyes gleamed silvery blue in the twilight. 'What did you ask for?'

'A large glass of Orvieto Classico. It's an Umbrian white wine.'

Levi switched his gaze to Davide. 'Make that a bottle and two glasses, please, with a cooler.'

Sofia sent him a mock-reproving look as Davide ambled off. 'My dad told me good white wine shouldn't be served too cold because it "destroys the bouquet."'

'Blame it on my Englishness.' He smiled that slow smile again, causing Sofia to heave an inner sigh that he was out of bounds. 'Are you enjoying your day off?' he asked.

She was about to answer, but then his gaze flickered to Amy, and Sofia had to refrain from snorting, 'She's too freakin' young for you!'

'Yes, thank you,' she murmured instead. She caught Amy's eye and sent her a smile as the younger woman charged up the aisle in their direction, tray piled high with dirty crocks. 'All right?' Sofia mouthed, indicating Davide with a tiny movement of her head.

Amy answered with an enormous tragic-teenager roll of her eyes, making Sofia smile sympathetically, though she would be angry if Amy was still being harassed. What was it about her that was getting her attention from older guys? Her pale blonde hair? Her air of youthful naïveté? The slender, boyish figure Amy made as she paused beside their table?

Sofia patted her arm. 'Are you on at eleven tomorrow?' Amy currently got all her seven-hour shifts in Il Giardino beginning at either 11 a.m. or 6 p.m. Benedetta didn't yet consider her up to serving in the more formal residents' dining room, nor to taking the 8 a.m. shift serving coffee and snacks in Il Giardino. The latter, though a popular duty with those servers who enjoyed having their day's work over at three in the afternoon, was a solo shift only given to the experienced, such as Sofia herself.

Amy made a face. 'No, I'm on at six again.' Il Giardino shut at midnight but the shift went on another hour to allow for the departure of stragglers and the clean-down. Sofia had an unpleasant vision of a weary Amy being circled by Davide as the lights went down and witnesses to his actions became fewer.

Casting a quick look his way to check he hadn't noticed Amy chatting, Sofia asked, 'Are you doing anything for lunch tomorrow? If not, we could go into town together.'

A smile lit Amy's face. 'That would be wicked. I haven't been away from the hotel enough.'

If at all, Sofia added silently, strongly suspecting that Amy was feeling isolated and out of her depth in Italy. Almost every time Sofia sought her own quarters when Amy was off duty, the younger girl would be hunched on a past-its-best bench outside her room so as to get a signal for her phone.

Although Amy seemed to be trying valiantly to learn the waitressing ropes, Sofia would never have picked her out as the type of teenager to leave her home to travel to another country in search of a summer job. Apart from the flash of spirit that had seen Amy wielding a tray as a weapon, she frequently looked lost and uncertain.

Sofia's own late teens were fresh enough in her memory for her to acknowledge how patronising sympathy could feel, though, so she kept her voice upbeat and friendly. 'Great. I'll tap on your door at about twelve.'

'Cool!' Amy gave Sofia a quick smile, then turned her attention politely to Levi, probably realising he'd been excluded from the conversation. 'Are you enjoying your holiday?'

Levi returned her smile. 'Enormously. I hadn't realised how beautiful Umbria is. I paint landscapes for relaxation and Montelibertà has fabulous views. Do you like it here?'

'Mostly.' Amy cut her gaze meaningfully towards Davide. 'But not entirely.' She flashed them both a quick smile before beetling off to the kitchen hatch to dump her full tray.

The brief exchange between Amy and Levi was so unexceptional that suddenly Sofia wondered if she'd imagined he'd been showing too much interest in Amy before. Levi hadn't taken the opportunity to flirt or even to hold Amy's attention by delaying her from going about her duties. Experimentally, she tested his reaction to being asked about himself. 'Are you a family man? Wife and kiddies waiting for you at home while you roar around Europe on your motorbike?'

He showed no inclination to avoid the question. 'No wife or current life partner.' He paused while he took another sip of wine. 'One daughter.'

'A daughter?' Reassured, Sofia resisted the temptation to ask whether she was older or younger than Amy. 'Are you close to her?'

His eyebrows rose slowly, as if processing the question. 'Depends how you look at it. How about you?'

'Footloose and fancy free,' she replied flippantly as Davide arrived at their table with an ice bucket, a bottle of wine and two glasses. Opening the wine with a flourish, he hovered the mouth of the bottle over Levi's glass. 'Would you like to taste the wine?'

Levi began shaking his head but Sofia said, '*Sì, grazie*,' and when Davide poured a small amount in her glass, sipped appreciatively. '*Bellissimo*,' she said, which earned her a nod before Davide half-filled both glasses and departed for tables new.

'Is that performance obligatory?' Levi lifted his glass.

Sofia wrinkled her nose. 'Not unless you're a member of the owner's family showing off in front of "the help", or a waitress who recognises the value of kissing up by playing along.'

He laughed and took a sip of his wine. He paused, looked into the contents of his glass, then took several more sips. 'This is fantastic.'

'Dad said I'd have to visit Umbria for the real thing. We used to buy it from the supermarket at home but he'd always wrinkle his nose and say it wasn't the same.' Sofia took a sip and let it roll around her mouth, giving herself a moment to absorb the pain at the memory, then let it go, content for the evening to pass comfortably over wine, a large shared pizza and casual conversation. Sofia discovered Levi lived in Cambridgeshire and ran some kind of website. She didn't ask for details. When Aldo had been alive she'd depended far too much on the internet for entertainment and human communication and now she wanted to concentrate on reality and flesh-and-blood people.

Levi was good company. He made her laugh, his smile was the kind to make her tummy turn over and, in other circumstances, he would have crossed her mind about once every minute as a candidate to be her first ever – hopefully wild – one-night stand.

It would be exciting to see what developed from the expression in his eyes when they rested on her. He looked . . . hungry. It made her feel fizzy inside, even though she kept fighting down the attraction.

But he was a hotel guest and though Sofia let him draw her out about her dad, her promises, her intention to travel for at least a couple of years, her grandparents and the exciting knowledge that she apparently had living relatives in this very town, she made certain not to let her gaze linger too long on the way his body filled his clothes.

It was Levi who made the move, as Il Giardino began to empty. He let a finger rest softly on Sofia's wrist. 'Can I persuade you to go on somewhere? Maybe down into the town?' And then he turned and took a good long look at Amy before checking out Davide, for all the world as if making sure Davide wasn't making any progress before he left. Davide turned and obviously caught the look. After an initial start of surprise, he stared right back. Levi's gaze didn't waver.

What? Were they doing the alpha-male confrontation thing over Amy?

Infuriated that she'd obviously been totally wrong to give Levi the benefit of the doubt over Amy, Sofia didn't see a need to explain that staff weren't to mix too closely with guests. Her manners deserted her. 'I don't think that would be a good idea. At *all*,' she snapped.

Levi turned back, blinking. Encountering her glare, he took back his hand. 'I see.' He waited, as if he thought he might get an explanation for the sudden frost in the air. When none was forthcoming he glanced around at Davide again, this time with the international gesture of pretending to write on his palm to indicate his readiness to pay.

Davide came straight over – waiters hardly ever failed to notice a customer ready to settle up, especially when it was late and they were grateful one more punter was ready to leave. Perhaps he was particularly glad to see this one leave.

Sofia paid her half of the bill in stiff silence.

Levi rose, his mouth set. 'I take it you're not going to invite me to your place for coffee either,' he said sarcastically.

Sofia remained in her seat. 'I'm going to hang around and help clear tables so Amy will have female company on the walk back to the staff accommodation. I think she could do with someone around.'

Levi nodded curtly. 'I think so too.' Then he spun on his heel and strode towards the front doors into Casa Felice.

Sofia stared after him. 'You don't have the moral high ground here, mate,' she muttered to herself. Then she tossed back her last mouthful of wine and jumped up to grab a tray and help clear tables.

Chapter Four

Amy couldn't believe how much she was looking forward to lunch with Sofia. 'Going out to lunch' was something her mum did with her colleagues from work on a Saturday. Amy and her friends ate when they were hungry, grazing throughout the day according to their euro supply or at whose house they were hanging out.

She was hit by a sudden wave of homesickness for Della and Maddalyn and her other friends in Germany. As it wasn't yet time for Sofia to knock on her door she went out to the bench outside, where the rampant vine overhead made everything look green, to get a signal and look on Della and Maddalyn's social media pages. Maddalyn's last Instagram post showed a picture of the lush green park near her house in Neufahrn bei Freising, north of Munich, and read:

Holidays! No work. ☺ ☺ ☺

Amy rolled her eyes and clicked on the speech bubble so she could reply.

I'm working my arse off! ☹ ☹ ☹

Della's Snapchat showed her on a beach in France, to which she'd added dog ears and bunny teeth and the label *Hangin'*!

Swallowing hard, Amy went onto her brother Kris's Instagram and watched several live videos from the playing fields near their house; she blinked back her tears because her mascara wasn't waterproof, and clicked to reply:

Take it mum doesn't know ur smoking down the fields dummkopf

Kris was the elder of her brothers but he wasn't quite sixteen and still thought smoking made you look cool.

Then she went onto Louis's Instagram but all her younger brother had put up since the last time she looked was a stupid picture of him stuffing a torch in his mouth and blowing his cheeks up so they shone red. Even with the blown-up cheeks, Louis's eyes laughed out of the picture, making her heart heavy. At twelve, Louis was the baby of the family, the only one who remembered no home other than theirs in Neufahrn because the family had moved there from England when he was two.

Improvement! she added underneath his post, then a collection of emojis, laughing, smiling, making heart eyes or scratching their heads, because Louis liked emojis better than actual words, judging by his text messages and social media updates.

Then, breath quickening and feeling a bit like a stalker, she looked on Facebook at her mum's profile, but there were no recent posts apart from a sad face a week ago with a tear and some of her friends commenting *Big hugs* or *Love you lots xx*. She closed Facebook down, not sure whether it was grief, guilt or anger that suddenly made her feel like throwing up.

Then Sofia stepped out through her door. 'Hey, Amy!'

Amy stuffed her phone in her little Cath Kidston bag, one that Dad had bought her. 'Hey,' she returned, feeling suddenly shy that not only was she 'going out to lunch' but her companion was at least thirty, maybe more, looking hot but cool in a short flowery dress. Her legs were amazing. Amy wished she had skin that tanned instead of the kind you could see through to the veins. Sofia's dark hair was straight and glossy too. Today she'd divided her ponytail into three separate plaits and Amy wished she'd thought of it first.

Sofia grinned cheerfully. She was one of those people who could give you the feeling that there was genuinely no one she'd rather be with. She'd been a real friend, sticking up for Amy against that shit Davide and that cow Benedetta, helping conquer the hollowness Amy had carried in her stomach since she arrived in this Italian town where all the buildings were old and the native language was neither of those she knew. After she'd nearly been sacked she'd toyed briefly with trying to find another job but bailed on the idea almost at once. All well and good if a new place was an improvement on this one but she could easily be jumping out of the frying pan and into the fire – with no Sofia to wield a fire extinguisher.

'Ready for a lovely relaxing lunch before you have to hit the tables again tonight?' Sofia treated Amy to a quick hug. 'Glorious day but it's getting hot. Have you slapped some stuff on?'

It was exactly the kind of question Amy would have resented if her mum had said it, but coming from Sofia it just gave her the warm and fuzzy feeling that someone cared. 'Yep. All done.' On her first day in Il Giardino she'd ended up with scarlet forearms and a peeling nose, and Sofia, although explaining she didn't burn easily because she had the same Mediterranean skin as her Italian father, had helped her locate a pharmacy and buy the once-a-day stuff her mum stocked up with at home every summer.

'Then let's leave Casa Felice behind.' Sofia led the way.

They were soon strolling down the hill into the town, the breeze playing with their hair and cooling their skin. Sofia pointed out things she'd already found out about, as if she'd known Montelibertà for months rather than the same couple of weeks as Amy.

Sofia peered to her right. 'I've seen a place somewhere here I like the look of. It's got a . . . oh, here it is! See what you think.' She disappeared through a pair of open doors beneath a smart black-fringed canopy and a sign saying 'Trattoria del Sole'.

Amy followed Sofia, blinking as they passed straight through the dim interior and the familiar aromas from a pizza oven to another exit, one that gave out onto a terrace much like the one at Casa Felice, with a stupendous view of the valley and the peaks. 'Love it,' she breathed, drinking it in. The near things seemed really near and the faraway things very far, as if the scenery had been built up in layers by a giant hand.

Sofia made a beeline for a vacant table nearest the edge of the terrace. 'It feels a bit as if we're getting one over on Benedetta by occupying a spot so like the one that's "guests only" at Casa Felice, doesn't it?'

Amy felt her spirits lift at Sofia's conspiratorial tone. 'Benedetta's a mega-stress monster.'

They seated themselves on wooden benches warm from

the sun. On the terrace the whirr-whirr and zirr-zirr of the insects around the tubs of flowers was louder than the traffic rolling up and down Via Virgilio.

Briskly, Sofia opened a menu. 'I fancy a nice cold glass of vino.' She paused, eyes wide. 'You are old enough to drink?'

Amy laughed. 'I'm old enough to serve it, so I must be! Do they do shandy in Italy?' Della and Maddalyn called her a lightweight because she'd failed to develop the joy they seemed to find in alcohol and the trouble they got into when it was involved.

'Let's find out.'

A young Italian waiter approached their table, seriously hot, crisply curling hair tucked neatly behind his ears and dark eyes as soulful as a puppy's. Sofia began a rapid conversation about *birra con* something. He nodded, smiling at Amy with a tiny lift of his eyebrows as if noting and returning her interest. In minutes, a tall glass of shandy appeared before her along with a glass of straw-coloured wine for Sofia and a tall, frosty bottle of water between them.

The waiter spoke to Amy in English, probably getting that the Italian was largely flowing over her head. 'The water, it is sparkly, but you can have natural if you prefer it.'

Amy managed to smile back without feeling her cheeks heat up. 'Sparkly's lovely.' It sounded nicer than 'sparkling'.

The waiter moved on to another table. Sofia took a good gulp of wine and sighed contentedly. 'I think you're really brave to leave home for a summer job when you're only eighteen. Look at me! I'm thirty-one and I've only just managed it.'

She laughed, but Amy already knew from earlier chats in the overgrown garden outside their rooms how hard it must have been for Sofia to look after her dad for years. It sounded rubbish. She tried to imagine Mum or Dad . . .

No, don't go there. 'Waitressing's harder than I'd thought,' she confessed. 'I was supposed to go to uni in England and live with my grandparents in Hendon. But, as I told you when we went out before, I wanted a gap year, so I decided to travel.'

What she hadn't confessed was the gut-wrenching shock, Mum's guilty tears, Dad's horror, the screaming match that took place with Amy in the middle, the explanations and apologies that had preceded her sudden determination to do *exactly* what her mum hadn't wanted her to do – miss her final couple of International Baccalaureate exams, making it impossible to be granted the diploma that should have allowed her to take up that university place. It made her feel sick to remember the time, less than three weeks ago, when she'd holed up in her room and, pounding angrily at her laptop, fixed up the job at Casa Felice via a website for seasonal workers.

Looking back on it, she felt a slithering suspicion that she needn't have been so hurtful as to actually exit during the night, leaving a furious note behind her:

I've gone travelling because I need time alone. You don't need to worry about me. I've got a job at a hotel called Casa Felice in Montelibertà, Italy. I'm only telling you so you know I've got everything sorted. I'm 18 and I'm not coming back unless I want to. I'll keep in touch so long as you don't follow me. If you do, I'll move on and you won't hear from me at all. Don't ring or text me either. I'll text you.

She took several sips from her drink before she could continue past what felt like a ball in her throat. 'To be honest, we didn't part on good terms. I talk to my brothers on social media and text Mum every few days to say I'm OK and that's it. Dad's actually my stepdad,' she added, to forestall Sofia asking about him. She hoped it sounded as if she'd coolly put a plan into action rather than simply lashed out to hurt everybody who'd spun her life into the wall and watched it smash down in pieces.

Sofia had paused with her wine glass halfway to her mouth, brows right up at her hairline. 'Wow. Poor you. I can't imagine how falling out with your family feels.' Her eyes brimmed with sympathy. 'Do you want to talk about it? It's fine if you do, but don't feel you have to.'

Amy shook her head.

But then, because Sofia hadn't said anything judgy, she immediately wanted to. 'I found out something. Something Mum knew about and never said. In fact, she lied.' She felt tears gathering hotly behind her eyes. 'I hate my mum at the moment. I don't think I'm ever going home.'

Sofia tilted her head, concern written all over her face. 'That's a big decision,' she said tentatively. 'Don't you think—'

'No.'

Sofia showed no sign of taking offence at the way Amy cut her off. 'OK,' she said softly. 'I don't think I'm going home, either, come to that – well, I don't really have a home as I've sold Dad's house because it was a ruin, but I don't think I want to go back to living in Bedford. I've given myself a couple of years to travel before I even think about doing anything grown-up. Then I *might* do something about getting a degree myself.' She grinned suddenly. 'That makes our plans quite similar, doesn't it?'

All at once, Amy felt loads better. 'Where do you think you'll go after Montelibertà?'

Sofia shrugged, turning her face up to the sun. 'Somewhere I like the look of and I can find a job I fancy. There are a hell of a lot of places that need waiting staff.'

'So you don't have a husband or anything?'

Sofia crossed her eyes. 'Nope. Enjoying the life of the independent woman.' She grinned.

On a sudden surge of excitement Amy said breathlessly, 'Will I be able to go with you?' Almost instantly she wished she hadn't said anything so stupid. *As if Sofia, just about a teenager when you were born, would want you tagging along, all shy and dorky! You just sounded like you had a girl crush on her or something.* She opened her mouth to stutter a red-faced retraction.

But Sofia didn't betray by so much as a blink that she found anything odd in the suggestion. 'Don't see why not. Where do you fancy? North Pole?'

Amy tried to think of something someone older and cooler might say. Someone of about twenty-five. 'Seen enough snow in Germany in winter. I was thinking Spain.'

Sofia's eyes lit up and they swapped ideas about which part of Spain looked most appealing while they ordered salads and more drinks. People came and went from the tables all around, English, American and Italian voices mingling on the air.

'If we pick up a bit of Spanish,' Sofia suggested, 'we could follow the sun to the Canary Islands as autumn comes and central Europe gets cooler.'

Amy didn't know where the Canary Islands were but she nodded enthusiastically. 'Awesome!'

'Or we could travel south through Spain to Gibraltar and cross over to Morocco.'

'Sounds great!' Amy thought that with Sofia's quiet confidence along for the ride, almost anything sounded possible.

53

They sat on, planning ever more adventurous journeys as the sun crossed the afternoon sky, making the colours of the peaks change as it hit from different angles. Sofia switched to drinking coffee, Amy to lemonade. Finally, Amy had to check the time because she knew soon she'd have to return to Casa Felice, put on her black dress and white apron and race around the tables. She sighed.

Sofia's gaze softened. 'Cheer up. Soon be payday.'

Amy's heart hopped. 'Will it?'

'Friday. We'll get paid for the first part-week we worked, then a full week's pay next week – which is when we start getting our share of the tips!' Sofia had popped sunglasses on as the sun moved around. They made her look super-cool, like Selena Gomez or Demi Levato.

'Tips?' Amy had never been on the receiving end of a tip. She was used to her parents paying for meals when they went home to the UK and checking the bill to see whether a tip was included, but in Germany tipping didn't seem so much of a thing.

'Of course!' Sofia fanned herself. 'Haven't you worked as a waitress before? I can give you "Tipping 101" if you like.'

Amy understood what she meant. There were American and Canadian kids at the international school she'd attended and something-101 always meant basic introduction. 'That'd be good.' She'd watched Sofia swerving through her tables and seeming to make customers and staff love her – apart from maybe Davide, who was surly towards Sofia but at least hadn't ever tried it on with her.

'OK.' Sofia pushed her sunglasses up on her hair. 'At Casa Felice most tourists leave tips and locals don't – but that's probably because "gratuity included" is only printed in Italian on the menu! The better the service the better the tips, generally speaking. Make personal connections if you can, remember faces so you can say "hello again!" to show you appreciate their repeat custom. They're incredibly flattered and it loosens the wallets and purses nicely. At Casa Felice, whether they come back to your section isn't important because all the tips go in together and are divided up on payday.' She wrinkled her nose.

'Is that bad?'

'Can be. If you see your own tips you know what you're getting, and that you're getting your due,' Sofia said frankly, dividing the last of the bottled water between their two glasses. 'Smile, even if you hate your job. If you call the men "sir" then call the women "madam", not "love" or "darling". The women often carry handbags and therefore the money, so if they feel they're being condescended to they may indicate their displeasure with a stingy tip.'

Amy threw back her head and laughed. 'You are such an experienced waitress!'

Sofia's smile wavered and she turned her gaze to the peaks across the valley. 'Dad was sick for a long time but he had good patches, especially when I was your age. It had to be casual work so I could leave at short notice when I had to.' She wrinkled her forehead. 'I did once or twice work as a carer, too, but that was a bit samey.'

For several moments, Amy could only stare.

'What?' Sofia demanded.

'You looked after your dad when you were my age?'

'Since I was fifteen. Didn't I mention my age before?' Sofia laughed. 'Don't look so horrified! I would rather have done that than leave him at the mercy of someone else. But you can see why tips were useful, especially if I forgot to declare them to the taxman.'

With only a vague idea what a taxman did, Amy just

stared at Sofia some more. 'It seems like you're never bothered by a thing.'

Sofia shrugged and turned the subject back to Amy. 'Talking of being bothered, how are things with Davide?'

Amy pulled a face. 'He's being a shit person, criticising me in front of customers, but it's better than him being a creep. I don't think he dares to do much now you and Levi have shown him he can't get away with it.'

'Levi?' Sofia sounded as if she didn't know who Amy meant.

'The one you were sitting with last night, who saw Davide tip up that tray of drinks and told Benedetta. Didn't you know his name?'

'I was just checking it was the same Levi. Have you talked to him much?'

Amy smiled, picturing the nice man who'd jumped in on her side when she'd thought she'd got the sack and had no idea what she'd do next. 'I saw him again this morning and he said if Davide keeps bothering me I can leave a message for him at the desk and he'll talk to my boss.'

Sofia made a shape with her mouth like an upside-down smile. 'You can tell me too. If *anyone* bothers you, not just Davide.'

Amy beamed. Now she was settling in, she felt as if she might like Italy. 'Thank you. You're *sooooo* kind.'

Maybe she did have a girl crush. A tiny one.

Chapter Five

Levi was incarcerated in his room, laptop open, while he Skyped Wes.

'So, what the fuck's Dick done?' he demanded irritably, staring at the random blocks of colour and text that were usually the streamlined *Modern Man* page of his equally streamlined website, The Moron Forum. Freelancer Dick liked to be called Richard but they referred privately to him as Dick because sometimes he was one.

Wes's exasperation was obvious. 'Looks like he made a basic error and somehow introduced HTML code along with his content. I'm about to set it all to rights.'

Acutely aware that he'd left Wes alone to deal with things like Dick's latest brain fart, Levi suppressed a sigh. 'I suppose he copied and pasted something over without making certain it was in plain text, lazy git.'

Wes snorted. 'He said it wasn't him. When I pointed out that he was logged on via his username and password when the upload actually took place he said he wasn't putting up with being called a liar and told me to shove his pages. Contract cancelled by mutual consent.'

Levi winced. 'I should have worked with him weeks ago to clean up his procedures. Sorry so much is falling on you.'

Wes laughed. 'Don't worry. I've put on my "in charge" hat and I'm sitting here feeling important. I know you have some serious stuff to sort out.'

'Can't argue with that. But even if there's no one updating the content, we at least need a moderator on that page straightaway. It gets high traffic and we need to be on it to prevent idiots posting inappropriate material. I'll put out an SOS to the other contractors to see if anyone can take it on a temporary basis until we get someone permanent.'

'No need.' Wes sounded smug and Levi didn't need to enable the video camera to picture him swivelling gently on his office chair, red-framed glasses set at a jaunty angle and hair spiking up at the front. 'I've taken on another tech. She recently sent in a fantastic CV so I got onto her as soon as Dick chucked the page. I sent her the contract to look over, she said great, and I issued her with a username and password.'

'Really?' Levi got up to pace, stomach sinking. Wes had logic to the point of geekiness but, somehow, not much common sense. It wasn't usually a problem when Levi was working alongside him – but these were not usual times. He raised his voice so the laptop mic could pick him up. 'But you've had no time to get references.'

'No need,' Wes repeated, sounding smugger than ever. 'It's Octavia.'

Levi halted mid-stride. '*Octavia*?' He hunted fruitlessly through his memory bank for some other Octavia. 'Octavia who?'

'Octavia Hawthorn. The one who found your phone when you lost it the week before you left.'

Freshly irritated just by the memory of the whole episode, Levi paused to absorb the unwelcome information. 'Her? Don't you remember that I told you she made me really uncomfortable, the way she came onto me? Can you call a halt? Please,' he added belatedly.

'Not really. I said if she could take Dick's pages on straightaway she had the job. I can't go back on it. So, she asked you out and you said no. What's the problem?'

After asking Wes to step up while he was away it would be bad management to jump on him for his first decision so Levi kept his voice even. 'It's more about policy than it's a problem. We take references.' He dropped back down in front of his laptop. 'Don't worry, I can do the necessary,' he said smoothly, preparing to gain access to the server he rented from a data centre.

'Whoa, whoa!' Wes laughed, but didn't sound amused. '*You* can't go back on *my* word. That sends the message that you don't trust me.'

Levi's fingers hesitated over the keys.

'And,' Wes went on, sounding his usual mild self again, 'I think she'll be good, and I take responsibility for my decision.'

'I understand that.' Levi let a silence draw out while he quickly ran the situation through his mental filters. He tried switching to inclusive language to make Wes part of the decision-making process. 'We can still ask her to apply formally for Dick's pages. She won't think there's anything odd about us withholding access while we process that.'

'*I'll* think it's odd,' Wes returned promptly, his voice tinny through the laptop speaker. 'I'll think I've offered her those pages and you've reversed my decision. And that would make me look like an idiot. In fact, it would make me think you view me as an idiot – and I'd have to give up my minor shareholder status here and start looking for another job, one where I wasn't asked to take on extra responsibility and then overridden by the major shareholder as soon as I do.'

Alarmed at Wes's reaction, Levi let his hands fall away from the keyboard. 'I'm not overriding you, but—'

'That's great then,' Wes broke in cheerfully. 'Just leave her with me. I think if you refresh the *Modern Man* page now you'll see I've cut the unwanted code out and everything's running as it should. Got to go. See you.' Skype gave its *whoop-whop* 'call ended' tone and Wes was gone.

Levi stared at the screen, shaken at the way Wes had come down on him. He could revoke Octavia's privileges himself but had Wes *really* said that if Levi did anything like that he'd simply walk? Levi wasn't prepared to risk it, especially while he was in Italy. He doubted he'd ever find another Wes, someone so solid, dependable and formidably intelligent. Though the company was 90 per cent Levi's it came from an idea they'd developed together and made a lot of money from and on which future income depended. The Moron Forum was a cult hit. It might be heavily laced with satire and silliness but that didn't stop it being a serious business.

What it came down to was that he wanted to keep Wes even more than he wanted to cut Octavia Hawthorn out of his life.

He cursed the day he lost his phone somewhere in or around the Costa in Bettsbrough where he'd stopped for a caffeine fix.

No sooner had he begun the process of informing his insurance company and speaking to his provider than an email notification, apparently from his own LinkedIn account, dropped into his email inbox. *My name's Octavia and I think I have your phone. I found it on the pavement in High Street. It was signed into LinkedIn so hopefully you'll get this message.*

Relief had swamped him. *You've saved my life! Thank you!* As an afterthought, he'd added: *Intrigued how you got around the passcode though.*

No password protection enabled, she'd replied. It would have been rude to disbelieve her and, sure enough, when he'd met up with her by arrangement in Bettsbrough town centre he'd found the passcode protection box unchecked.

He'd brushed that detail aside as he settled his phone's comforting and familiar weight in his pocket; he'd been so relieved that he'd grinned like an idiot and showered her with thanks. 'I keep my life on that phone! You were in Costa, weren't you? You must've left right after me to find my phone before I got back for it.' He generally noticed well-groomed, attractive women and he remembered seeing her behind him in the queue and then brushing past his table on the way to one nearby.

'Nice to be noticed.' She'd returned the smile coquettishly from behind her curtain of blonde hair. 'You'd better take me out to dinner to express your gratitude.'

He'd been taken aback. But, hey, she *was* an attractive woman and it would have been churlish to refuse – even when she'd laid a well-manicured hand on his arm and steered him straight to a nearby Greek restaurant where she'd become uber-chatty and mega-friendly, even taking his hand when he rested it on the table. That had been the beginning of a crazy week.

He supposed that some men would have been intrigued by her front, or simply gone along with her in the hopes that she'd jump into bed with the same lack of inhibition, but on him she'd had the opposite effect. Uncomfortable with her over-familiarity, only good manners had made him remain until the end of the meal. Then, with cool courtesy, he'd put her in a taxi and said farewell.

Alarm bells had only really begun to sound the next day when she'd texted effusive thanks for 'a fab date' and he knew instantly that he hadn't given her his number so she must have extracted it when she had his phone. An avalanche of texts followed, all suggesting 'another date'. After the first few polite prevarications his phone had begun to buzz with her calls, all of which he'd let go to voicemail. He was grateful she'd returned his phone, but she had 'unwanted admirer', 'cling' or even 'ring' written all over her.

And then he'd been distracted when a sobbing Freya had blasted from the past to lob into his lap a bomb with a short fuse. Octavia's next call had come while he'd been packing his bike to shoot off on the mission that had brought him to Montelibertà. Angry and stressed enough already, he'd blocked her number.

But now she was somehow intruding on his life via his business and his best friend. He rose to pace once more, wandering out onto the sunny balcony, idly watching the aerial view of Il Giardino as his mind circled the problem. Despite the disparity in their company share-holdings he was all too aware that Wes had worked just as hard as Levi to set up The Moron Forum. Levi had simply been the one with the money to put up for the Mac Pro computers and other set-up costs. Between student loans and his girlfriend at the time having expensive tastes, Wes had been broke. His 10 per cent share had been a reward for his work. The benefit was only monetary as Levi kept an ample controlling interest, but it could definitely cause all kinds of issues if Wes followed through on his threat.

His gaze strayed from Il Giardino to the view of Via Virgilio, the engines of the ever-present scooters shrill with the pain of climbing the hill, cars and buses rumbling up in lower gears. His attention was grabbed by two figures sauntering along the pavement and he recognised Amy, with Sofia by her side. As they drew closer, the breeze brought a gust of their laughter to his ears.

The sound redirected his thoughts and he hurried back indoors to gather up his A4 pad of watercolour paper and his paintbox. He wasn't going to worry about Wes and Octavia right now. He was going to paint, as planned.

Chapter Six

Hooray! Davide was on a rest day when Sofia returned to Il Giardino the next day, Wednesday. She and Amy were both on the lunch shift and alongside them was Paolo, a middle-aged man who made ends meet with shifts at Casa Felice on his days off from a bar in town. Paolo was stooped like a man thirty years older and walked as if treading hot coals.

Paolo got section two, which contained one table fewer than either of the other sections. Although Sofia felt a bit mutinous when Davide continually allotted himself section two, she didn't mind Paolo getting it because a bloke who worked seven days a week deserved a break, however meagre. Amy was on section three, nearest the car park, and Sofia section one, close to the clatter of the kitchen hatch.

What made that interesting today was that Levi was crammed in a shady corner of Il Giardino beside the hatch, a board-backed pad propped across his lap and a box of paints and two little jars of water on a stool beside him.

It was hard to see what he was doing because she had no reason to be in the hatch area unless clearing crocks or an order was called for tables one to nineteen, when she'd whizz up to sweep up a tray of food and hurry to deliver it to whichever hungry customers awaited.

'Hello,' she greeted Levi the first time she arrived, conscious of the tetchy end to their last encounter but curious about the paints and pad.

He returned her greeting politely but with no smile.

As the shift progressed she noticed that his smile was definitely in evidence whenever he paused to speak to Amy, paintbrush poised. It was only when she saw him taking photos of Il Giardino on his phone that Sofia addressed him again, unsettled that the camera might be following Amy, who, so far as Sofia knew, hadn't given her permission.

'Why are you taking pics?' she asked bluntly as she arrived to grab a food order for table twelve.

He glanced at his screen before answering briefly, 'Record shots.'

'Of?' She hefted the heavy tray shoulder-high.

Slowly, he fixed his stare on her. 'You're here to wait on tables, aren't you?'

'I am,' she agreed equably. She whisked off to deliver bruschetta to the man and woman on table eight. They'd already told her they were returning home from a sales conference in Perugia and had chosen to break the journey. Sofia, observing covert touches and meaningful smiles, had decided they had a lot more in common than whatever they sold.

'*Grazie mille*,' the man said as Sofia deftly deposited the appetiser and small plates in the centre of their table.

'*Prego*!' She gave them her warmest smile. Then, acting

on impulse, dropped her voice, speaking in Italian so Levi wouldn't be put on his guard if he chanced to hear her above the clatter and chatter of the cafè patrons enjoying the sun. 'Tell reception if the artist in the corner is bothering you by taking photos. I hope he isn't posting on Facebook.' She gave an expressive shrug.

The man and woman exchanged looks of alarm as Sofia wished them *buon appetito* and whisked off to clear table fourteen and take orders from the tourists seated there.

'*Buon giorno*,' she greeted them.

The man, probably the dad of the family, looked apprehensive. '*Solo Inglese*,' he offered doubtfully, probably his only Italian apart from *vino* and *pizza*.

'I speak English,' she confided with a grin.

His look of relief was comical. 'Phew! Is the lasagna good?'

Wondering whether there could possibly be an eatery in Italy that served bad lasagna, Sofia beamed. 'I can recommend it.' She kissed the tips of her fingers.

From the corner of her eye she watched the man from table eight throw down his napkin and stride across Il Giardino towards reception.

Most of the tourist family agreed on lasagna but one little girl stuck out her bottom lip. 'I want pizza with pineapple on.'

The mum looked embarrassed. 'You only want that because someone at the hotel in Orvieto told you that Italian restaurants never serve it. It's an American concoction.'

The lip went out further. 'I want it. I want Hawaiian.'

'No problem,' Sofia assured her cheerfully. 'I can ask the chef.'

The teenage boy of the party snorted with lofty amusement. 'It's tourist pizza. They probably import it frozen from Tesco.'

The girl glared at him and threw down her menu. 'I like it from Tesco!'

'Ours is even better,' Sofia assured the youngster with a wink as she scribbled on her pad. Then she caught sight of the man from table eight emerging from the hotel foyer looking pleased with himself. Though she'd given way to the urge to make things awkward for Levi, now her efforts looked as they were paying off, she felt sudden compunction. Had she overstepped the mark in her wish to support Amy?

Putting in table fourteen's order a minute later, Sofia was afforded a grandstand view of Aurora approaching Levi with an apologetic air.

'I'm so sorry.' Aurora flashed a white smile from between immaculately made-up lips. 'A customer has complained that you're taking photos. I'm afraid it's not possible for you to paint in Il Giardino any longer.'

Levi hurriedly stuffed his phone into his pocket. 'Sorry! I won't get my phone out until I leave.'

But Aurora just smiled more determinedly and repeated more firmly that he could no longer paint here. 'Perhaps the terrace?' she suggested. 'The view, rather than the people.'

Looking disgruntled as Aurora made her way back towards reception, heels tip-tapping on the concrete, Levi laid down his pad. Feeling a shiver of guilt about his obvious embarrassment, Sofia offered him a tentative smile as she turned to whisk off with a new order. When he paused in packing away his things to send her a baleful look she speeded her already brisk pace, pretty sure he'd like to ask her whether she'd somehow arranged his igno-minious ejection. She'd prefer not to have to say yes.

*

When the shift ended at six o'clock, Sofia was about to follow Amy in the direction of the staff quarters when Benedetta intercepted her to discuss the possibility of giving her a few shifts in the residents' dining room and terrace. Liking the idea of working with such a fantastic view across the valley, Sofia happily followed Benedetta down the staircase to the lower level at the back of the hotel to prove that she knew how to lay a table and was willing to learn the menu system.

Benedetta ushered her into a workstation behind the dining room. 'For dinner, a choice from three starters, five mains, three desserts. Seven set menus, one for each day of the week. For lunch the same menu as Il Giardino offers. It makes it easy in the kitchen.' She showed Sofia where the menus were kept in clear plastic pockets on the wall along with a file of laminated sheets detailing the ingredients of each dish so serving staff could reassure diners with dietary requirements. 'Now I'll show you the terrace.'

Sofia suppressed the urge to say, 'A member of staff allowed on the terrace when not strictly on duty? Isn't there a rule about that?' She followed Benedetta out into the slanting evening sunlight, nodding along to her boss's recitation of what she needed to know about the terrace's snacks and drinks menu. She noticed Levi Gunn was seated at one corner, facing the gardens and valley below and painting again.

'And guests can eat from the Il Giardino menu out here at any time?' she said as she saw him look from the view to his page and back again.

'Correct!' Benedetta gazed around with satisfaction at the beautiful terrace of stone pavers and wrought iron, flower tubs frothing in every direction. 'Good. I'll change your shifts around tomorrow and email your new roster to you.' Benedetta began to turn away.

'Thank you.' Sofia hesitated before adding hopefully, 'Amy's learning quickly in Il Giardino.'

Benedetta gave a decisive shake of her head. 'She's not experienced enough to come down into the dining room yet.' She ended the interview with '*Ciao*', which told Sofia she was now on slightly less formal terms with her boss.

'*Ciao*.' Sofia responded. She trained her gaze on the movements of a nearby waiter as if keen to learn, but as soon as Benedetta had bustled back into the hotel she drifted closer to where Levi was making tiny movements of a fine brush, drawn to this handsome biker who also painted Italian landscapes, even if she couldn't shake her doubts about the attention he paid Amy.

Her breath rushed into her lungs. His painting was charming – a couple of wispy white clouds against a blue sky, paler where the sky met the horizon. The furthest peak was mistily dark and flat, whereas the woodland on those closer was brought to impressive 3-D life with cunning brushstrokes picking out a row of tall, thin conifers like punctuation marks. Between the trees tiny details brought groups of terracotta rectangles into focus as hamlets and villages. In the foreground a stem of pearly white petunias from one of the pots that punctuated the railing around the terrace gave perspective to the rest.

As if feeling the weight of her gaze, Levi skewed around in his chair. 'Oh,' he said when he saw her.

Sofia stepped closer, setting aside any antipathy as she gazed on his work. 'That's truly beautiful. I feel as if I could step into your painting.'

'It's a watercolour sketch,' he said. 'I'm getting a feel for my subject before I attempt anything on canvas at home.'

'Right.' She nodded as if she understood the intricacies of watercolour painting. 'Is this how you make your living?'

'No. My day job is in website development. Painting's an escape from spending all day poring over pages of code.' He stuck the brush he'd been using into the darker of the two jars of khaki water beside him, turning on her a challenging gaze. 'And at least nobody here gets me chucked out, making me feel two inches tall in the process.'

Though her face heated up Sofia pinned on her most serene smile as she replied lamely, 'I can't help it if customers don't want to be in your photos.'

'You can help pointing out to them what I'm doing.' Evidently he hadn't been as oblivious to what Sofia had been up to as she'd hoped.

'True,' she acknowledged guiltily, wondering why she couldn't quite get a grip on what kind of man Levi was. Then her eye was drawn to where the early-evening breeze flipped the pages of his pad as if with giant lazy fingers and she caught sight of the view of Il Giardino he must have been working earlier. Centre stage in front of the colourful and busy tables was a slender figure with blonde hair twisted up behind her head and a black dress covered by a white apron. Levi had painted Amy in the act of swooping a tray of drinks down from her shoulder and onto a table. Along with the movement he'd somehow portrayed youth and even Amy's air of reserve.

Though a part of the scene, the figure stood out, as if he'd focused hard on getting it just right. It made Sofia feel something – not jealousy, surely? No, more like envy, because there seemed to be something like affection in the careful brushstrokes.

Gazing at his painting in silence she struggled with herself. She'd been downright rude to Levi last night and then deliberately caused mischief for him today. It couldn't be because her nose had been put out of joint that even as Levi had been asking Sofia out he'd so blatantly 'noticed' Amy? Could it? She knew herself to be naïve when it came to men. Maybe, if he knew her thoughts, Levi would be incredulous that Sofia would mind?

She cast around for an olive branch to extend, one that might even explain her pissy attitude last night. 'You know, I feel a bit like Amy's big sister. If I had a little sister alone in a foreign country I'd want someone to look out for her.'

Levi looked gently mystified by this turn in the conversation. 'I only have a brother, but likewise.' He met her gaze unflinchingly and Sofia suddenly felt he wouldn't be able to look her in the eye like that if whatever he felt for Amy was a threat.

Was Sofia justified in setting herself up as judge and jury? Amy seemed quite at ease with Levi, yet she'd recoiled from Davide from the first, which suggested she had perfectly good instincts. So far as Sofia knew, Levi had never made the least move on Amy.

Further, Sofia admitted to herself, her own experience should tell her that Levi understood the meaning of the word 'no' and could hear it with good grace. She felt uncomfortably guilty of jumping to conclusions.

'I'll leave you to your painting then,' she said, having not the least idea of how to explain her thoughts and feelings to him without making herself look more of an idiot than he probably already thought her.

He smiled politely. 'It would be nice to get the last of the light.'

She smothered a sigh, hyper-aware that she was still missing the wild one-night stand from her single woman's CV. And Levi was so big and firm and golden . . . but out

71

of bounds, even if she hadn't killed any interest from him stone dead. Turning away, she headed for the stairs at the side of the terrace resolving to visit a couple of bars down in the town tonight where some of the thirty-something locals hung out. Maybe her English/Montelibertà accent would seem exotic to them and she could have a bit of an adventure with a Stefano or a Marco or a Tonio.

Once she'd let herself into her room she threw off her uniform and stood under the shower for several minutes, letting the cool water wash away her discomfiture along with the heat of the day. When she got out, she promised herself, she'd wriggle into the tight red dress she'd bought from Autograph last autumn because it was reduced. She'd be daring with her makeup, creating smoky eyes and a kissable mouth. She'd stuff thirty euros in her smallest bag and take herself off down into the town. Other women did it. Maybe by midnight she'd have gone home with the greatest talent she could find.

Ignoring the facts that she was having trouble imagining herself behaving that way, particularly when she was on breakfast shift on the terrace tomorrow, she stepped out of the shower and dried herself before stepping into her prettiest underwear.

But before she could start her makeup she heard a tentative knock on her door. 'Sofia? Are you there? I've got the creeps.'

'Amy?' Covering up with a thin robe, she opened the door. 'Are you OK? What's creeping you out?'

Amy hugged herself, smiling sheepishly as she stepped into Sofia's room. 'I'm going to sound pathetic but I keep thinking someone's tapping on the fly screen on my window.'

Sofia, imagining being eighteen years old, away from home for the first time and building up fearsome scenarios

72

in her mind, replied bracingly. 'I bet it's that damned climber that grows like a Triffid all along this so-called staff garden. Shall we grab scissors from the kitchen and hack it back? Then it won't be able to reach your window.'

Amy's expression relaxed. 'Do you think that's all it is? I feel stupid now. You weren't going out tonight, were you?' she asked belatedly, gazing at Sofia's red dress on its hanger.

Sofia's hand passed over the red dress in favour of a T-shirt and a pair of shorts. 'Not tonight. I've got to be up for the breakfast service tomorrow,' she said, blithely abandoning her plans. It wasn't much of a hardship when her heart hadn't been in them in the first place.

Chapter Seven

On Friday, Levi enjoyed a leisurely lunch in Il Giardino. Amy took his order for cold beer and a small portion of pasta, giving him a friendly grin. 'Having a good day?'

'Great,' Levi answered. 'I plan to paint in the garden this afternoon.'

'Enjoy!' And she whisked off, ripping his order from her pad, looking much more confident about her job than when Levi had first met her. Davide was on duty too but Amy seemed to have taken to ignoring him as much as working together allowed, which seemed an excellent tactic.

Levi enjoyed a second beer then vacated his table to allow a young Italian couple to sit down. He went into the hotel to collect his painting kit and then down the many flights of stairs necessary to reach the garden. The sun was blazing when he settled down, the valley spread out before him. Soon he was absorbed in trying to capture the delicate arc of lavender stems in the foreground of the painting he was working on.

A couple of hours drifted by, until his phone rang. 'I've

got something to tell you,' Wes said as soon as Levi had laid his brush down to answer the call.

'Oh?' Holding his phone to his ear with his left hand he picked up his thinnest brush, mixed up the palest grey he could imagine and touched it down one side of a stem, instantly creating light and depth. He cocked his head to one side to admire the effect. 'What?'

'It's something about Octavia.' Wes sounded as if he was trying to be casual.

Levi's brush froze in midair. 'Oh, shit. What?' He hadn't even checked the website today. Had she screwed it up?

'It's nothing bad,' said Wes stiffly, obviously not appreciating the 'Oh, shit!' part of Levi's response. 'It's nothing I'm obliged to tell you, but I thought I ought to in the interests of transparency and because we're friends.'

'Right.' Levi breathed slightly more easily. 'Sorry, mate, I didn't mean to leap to the conclusion that it was negative. What is it you want to share?'

Silence.

'Wes?'

Wes sounded defensive. 'I thought it would be a good idea to tell you that Octavia and I are a thing.'

'Oh!' All attention now on his conversation, Levi spun the simple sentence around in his mind in an effort to make sense of it. He wanted to snort, 'What? In a couple of days?' But Wes was being weird. Octavia was odd and maybe Wes was catching it. 'Thanks for telling me. How long's this been brewing up?'

'Not long,' Wes answered. After a pause he added, 'I'm sorry if I'm stepping on your toes.'

Levi almost dropped the phone. 'Stepping on my toes?'

Wes cleared his throat. 'Octavia explained you'd been on a date and had been texting.'

75

'But I told you it wasn't a date. Or only in her mind—'

'I phoned to congratulate her about taking on Dick's pages. She said could we meet to talk about it and suggested dinner. We really hit it off but, as I say, I'm sorry if I've trodden on your toes.' Wes hummed and hawed before adding in a rush, 'It sort of turned into dinner and breakfast. And I know what you're going to say,' he hurried on before an astounded Levi could react. 'I know it's not like me. I'm more of your cautious type so far as women are concerned. It just sort of happened. *And*, it was the night of my life, to be honest. The only fly in the ointment was that this morning Octavia did this big sighing thing and said she hoped you wouldn't be hurt. Her version of what happened between you isn't quite the same as yours.'

He paused as if to let Levi speak, but he was so astonished at this development that he couldn't find the words.

'Anyway,' Wes went on. 'I'm saying sorry if I need to say sorry, because Octavia insisted that I should clear the air with you. But, as the saying goes, "we just couldn't help ourselves."'

'Right,' said Levi blankly, watching a fat bee hover indecisively between two lavender heads then sink down to land on the largest. If he could have chosen someone for Wes to take on as a freelance and then jump into bed with, Octavia would have been at the far end of a very long queue. 'You've taken me by surprise,' he admitted, because he felt he had to say something and *What are you THINKING?*, however heartfelt, seemed inappropriate. 'But my feelings aren't hurt. Are you sure—'

'Phew!' Wes laughed. 'I'll be sure to tell Octavia. How's everything going out there? Have you achieved your goal yet?'

Levi gave up. Wes and Octavia were adults and if Wes was as happy as he sounded he probably wouldn't appreciate Levi pointing out that Octavia was lying to him. 'Getting that way. If things go on as they are I'll be able to telephone Freya and tell her Amy's doing OK. But I haven't decided—'

'Gotcha. Speak soon then.' And Wes ended the call.

Levi put away his phone and gazed at his painting, his appetite for it now absent. Was Octavia simply bizarre enough to angle for dinner with every man she met? And then pretend there was more to it?

As he sat uneasily, turning things over in his mind, he became aware of a sound reaching him over the lavender-scented air. It sounded like a woman singing, punctuating her song with loud clicks.

Curiosity aroused, he washed his brush and closed the lid on his palette, then stood to stroll up the slope, past a couple of olive trees, tracking down the sound to one side of the terrace and a shabby wooden gate he hadn't noticed before. On the other side of it he found Sofia, looking very much off-duty in black shorts that clung as if in joy at finding themselves touching such a good part of her. In her ears were earbuds and in her hand a big pair of scissors. A flourishing vine dominated almost every available support in the vicinity and she was making an attempt at taming it, judging from the carpet of clippings beneath her feet and the neatness of the growth where it had been tied to two uprights. As she worked, she sang softly in Italian, insects buzzing companionably around her as if they thought they were her backing group. The slow, gentle song made her voice sound especially sweet. She blinked hard, pausing to wipe a tear from her cheek with the sleeve of her T-shirt.

Though she always seemed inexplicably tetchy where he was concerned – which was a shame – Levi recognised a private moment when he saw one. He was about to creep away when she shifted position and caught sight of him. Visibly startled, she dropped her scissors, which narrowly missed her toes. 'Fu— for crying out loud!' she squeaked, dragging her earbuds from her ears. 'Why are you lurking there?'

Levi lifted his hands to signal he came in peace. 'Sorry! I heard you singing.' And then, because the opportunity to leave unobserved had passed and the evidence of her tears still glistened on her face he felt compelled to put aside her occasional snarkiness. 'Are you OK?'

She lifted the hem of her T-shirt to blot her eyes, affording him a glimpse of a taut abdomen before she let the fabric fall. 'Yes, thank you,' she sniffed, managing a tremulous smile. 'Amy and I began cutting back this monster vine last night and I've worked my shift today so I thought I'd finish off and tidy up. I was listening to an Italian radio station and a song came on that Dad used to sing – *Solo Tu*. Apparently my parents considered it "theirs" and used to smooch to it.'

'Then I'm sorry I interrupted.'

She gave him another watery smile, stooping to pick up the fallen scissors. 'It's OK. I promised not to be sad after he'd gone.'

Because she didn't appear to be doing a great job of keeping that promise, Levi found himself saying, 'I'm on my way to Il Giardino for coffee. Fancy joining me? Maybe a shot of caffeine will help.'

She studied him for a moment before she nodded. 'That's kind of you. Thank you. But off-duty staff aren't meant to hang out with guests so I'll meet you there and conveniently find a vacant seat at your table. I need to wash the green stuff off my hands anyway.'

Waiting for Sofia to join him at a table in Amy's section of Il Giardino he had time to order a bottle of cold water and a couple of glasses. He was just beginning to wonder if Sofia had had one of her lightning changes of mood and wasn't going to turn up when she appeared, cleaned up and changed into a cotton skirt. He rather missed the short-shorts. However changeable she'd been towards him she always looked amazing.

Amy sailed up the aisle between tables, beaming. 'Finished the breakfast shift, Sofia? What can I get you both?'

Sofia ordered cappuccino and Levi Americano and, perhaps to counteract the hot drinks, they also selected an ice-cream each from the cabinet behind the bar. Sofia chose a chocolate-hazelnut combination called *bacio*, which she said meant 'kiss'. Levi chose *limone*, the translation of which he could work out for himself.

'Amy seems a bit happier now,' he observed, when she'd served them with tall glasses of ice-cream and moved on to another table.

Sofia sent him one of her searching looks before glancing at Amy and nodding. Then she turned the conversation. 'So what's going on with you today? More painting? I was impressed with what I saw yesterday.'

He took up his spoon, ready to broach the three scoops of ice-cream with a tube-shaped wafer stuck jauntily in the top. 'I was. Then I was distracted by an awkward phone call.'

She was already digging into her *bacio*. 'Nothing too awful, I hope.'

He watched the way she ate the first taste of ice-cream,

half-closing her eyes as she savoured it. Today she seemed back to the friendly, approachable woman she'd been on Monday evening when she'd asked to share his table – before greeting his suggestion they go on somewhere together like a deadly insult. Curious to see if he could complete a conversation with her without prompting the same result, he decided to try to engage her. 'I'm not sure. Maybe you can give me an objective view? I'm not sure if I'm imagining something that isn't there.'

Her eyebrows lifted. 'Go on.' She took another spoon of ice-cream and did the savouring thing again. It was damned distracting.

Between spoonfuls of his own delicious tart-but-sweet lemon ice-cream Levi recounted the story of Octavia hitting on him so hard then moving on to Wes without, apparently, missing a beat.

Sofia listened, dark brown eyes thoughtful. She finished her *bacio*, wiped her fingers on her paper napkin and sat back. 'Did you know her before she found your phone?'

'Not that I remember. But Bettsbrough's a small town so it's possible. Dad owns a garage and I worked there during the holidays when I was younger. I must have met a lot of his customers over time.'

'But that's not where you work now?'

'Yes and no. My office is above my dad's garage, but it's just rented from Gunn's Motors. My brother Tyrone works for the business itself.'

'You didn't go to the same school?'

'I don't think so. She's several years older than I am, probably early to mid-forties.'

Sofia raised an eyebrow as she reached for the water to top up their glasses. 'So she's a polyamorous techie who doesn't see anything wrong in making her desires known, fancied both of you and so went for it. If everyone concerned is single then she hasn't actually done anything wrong.'

Levi heaved a sigh of relief at her no-nonsense summation. 'Thank you.'

Her eyes began to dance. '*Or* she's a right old bunny-boiler who took one look at you, became violently infatuated and is infiltrating every aspect of your life, even to the extent of granting sexual access to your best friend in an effort to stay close to you and/or make you jealous.'

'Shit.' He contemplated her. 'Do you think it's that?'

She shrugged. 'Not really. If you're positive you've never met until she found your phone I'd say the most likely explanation is that Octavia's simply an oddball who falls suddenly for men and equally suddenly gets over them. Or she's been single too long and is getting a bit desperate to couple up.'

Levi made no reply, mainly because he couldn't think of a polite way of saying 'Yeuch.'

As she cleared tables, the sun hot on her neck, Amy watched Sofia and Levi together. She liked them both. They'd stuck up for her right at the beginning when she hadn't known how to handle creepy Davide. Sofia had even taken charge when Amy had been a wuss last night about the climbing plant tapping at her window in the breeze.

When she'd first arrived in Montelibertà she'd felt such a kid, panicking at an unknown or unfamiliar situation at least twice a day, teetering on the point of packing her bags and running back to Neufahrn bei Freising. Only the unexpected kindness she'd met from Sofia and Levi – and the memory of the mess she'd left behind her at home – had enabled her to stick it out in Italy. Now she was actually beginning to enjoy it. Two new servers had been taken on, Matteo and Noemi, local teens who'd finished their exams, as Amy should have now it was June, the staff growing in line with increasing visitor numbers as the tourist trade moved towards high season.

Brought up in a tourist town, both spoke good English, and they'd invited Amy out tonight to where the local young adults went to chill.

Amy felt as if it had been months rather than weeks since she'd talked properly to someone of her own age group and was really looking forward to it, much as she liked 'doing lunch' with Sofia or stopping for a quick chat with Levi when he turned up in Il Giardino.

She felt a sudden urge to do something for Sofia and Levi, for being so nice to her. Glancing around to check none of her tables seemed in imminent need of her attention, she hurried over to a waiter she liked, Thomas, and whispered that she was going for a comfort break. Thomas nodded and Amy ran down to her accommodation, grabbed a twenty-euro note and hurried back to the staff access to the reception area. There she paused, cracking open the door to check neither Davide nor Benedetta were around and that Aurora wasn't dealing with a guest. Seeing the coast clear she tiptoed across to the reception desk.

'Aurora,' she whispered. 'Do you still have tickets for that thing tonight in town?'

Aurora, who'd raised her eyebrows at seeing Amy in reception when she ought to be serving in Il Giardino, gave a nod, brow clearing. 'The boar roast? Yes, I have five unsold.'

Amy swiftly thrust the twenty euros at her. 'Two please.'

In ten seconds the tickets were in her apron pocket and

she was back in Il Giardino, glad to see that Sofia was still talking to Levi. Grabbing up a tray, she arrived again at their table. Feeling grown up to be doing something nice for someone else, which was something Mum suggested to her a lot, she swept up their coffee cups and ice-cream dishes, then, balancing the tray on the table, dug in the pocket of her apron for the bright yellow tickets and dropped one in front of each of them.

'This is for being so nice to me,' she gabbled, before she could lose her nerve. 'I hope you have a good time.' Then, cheeks scorching, she beamed at the two astonished faces and hurried off to dump her crocks at the kitchen hatch. Mum had been right. Doing something unexpected for someone else gave you a definite case of the warm and fuzzies.

Chapter Eight

Slowly, Sofia picked up one of the pieces of yellow card from the table. 'These are tickets for a boar roast.'

'Tonight,' Levi confirmed, picking up the other.

Catching sight of his expression of amazement, Sofia snorted a giggle. 'Is Amy trying to *fix us up*?'

As Amy could at any moment look around from where she was taking an order at a table near the bar, Sofia clamped her hand over her mouth to prevent more giggles escaping, but the chagrin that Levi must be feeling if he *was* harbouring an age-gap crush on Amy struck her as hysterical. Not to mention that they'd ended yesterday evening by snapping at each other.

'She must be!' Outrage stole across his face. 'Does she think I can't get my own dates?'

Sofia's shoulders shook. 'At least it's not with Octavia,' she gasped.

'That isn't even funny,' he protested, but answering laughter leaped into his eyes.

Sofia saw Amy begin to turn from the customers she'd been serving and yanked her face straight. 'Look, the tickets cost ten euros each. If we don't go, we'll hurt her feelings. But of course it's awkward,' she added, flushing at the flash of surprise in his eyes.

The surprise was swiftly replaced by a spark of challenge. 'It's only awkward if you make it awkward. Shall I call for you or will you call for me?'

'We'll have to meet down the hill,' Sofia said. She was so glad he wasn't making her doubt him again – by sulking that it wasn't Levi and Amy going together – that she took up the challenge. 'Have you noticed that house on the right with all those galvanised buckets full of lavender? Let's meet there, at eight so it doesn't look too obvious that I'm bending Benedetta's staff/guest rule. I want this job . . . for now.' She was hoping, belatedly, that she wouldn't get caught out and find the letter of the rule applied.

Thoughts of her so far unknown uncle fleeted across her mind. She intended to meet him before she left Montelibertà and she felt as if Sunday, when Ernesto hoped to make contact with him on her behalf, would never come. She tucked her ticket into her purse and pulled out enough euros to cover her share of the bill. 'I'll thank Amy when I pass her because I think we were both too stunned to do more than gape.'

'OK.' He picked up his ticket. 'See you later.'

Sofia didn't return to taming the mighty creeper after she'd thanked Amy and been rewarded with a wide smile of delight. Not for anything would she let her friend think Sofia was the least bit nonplussed at being set up with Levi. Nor remind her about Benedetta's rule.

She refused to hurt Amy by not going to the boar roast. She really liked the slight girl and the way she'd toughed out her first couple of weeks in Italy. Sofia would make an effort not to fall out with Levi tonight, even wearing that slinky scarlet number as practice for when she could go out and meet that one-night stand she still hadn't had.

It absolutely wasn't a matter of showing him what he was missing. Obviously.

As Sofia approached the house with the lavender just after eight she could see Levi already waiting, idly watching the passing traffic. Then he glanced up the hill and she knew the moment he picked her out from the other pedestrians, straightening slowly and regarding her with a fixed stare.

Suddenly, Sofia felt acutely self-conscious. It was as if she would stumble out of her sassy medium-heel mules at any moment and her dress felt indecently short and clingy. But it was too late to rue her bold choice of outfit. Forcing herself to keep her head high, she sauntered up as if a man waiting for her was an everyday occurrence.

Levi's golden-brown eyes followed every step.

'Hope you haven't been waiting too long,' she managed, pleased when the greeting emerged neither shrill nor breathless.

His smile was slow. 'No. I came down ten minutes early to make certain your employer had no reason to suspect you of having designs on a resident.'

'Thanks.' At this reminder, she cast back a quick glance as if expecting to see Benedetta rushing down to sack her.

'I checked out Trattoria Bianca, the venue, and it's just off Piazza Roma.'

'Great.' She waited for him to turn around so they could move off in the right direction. Instead, he gazed at her, seemingly lost in thought.

'Piazza Roma's that way.' She pointed behind him.

'Oh. Yes.' He turned swiftly. He still didn't start walking but lifted the elbow closest to her and she realised he was inviting her to take his arm. It was a charming gesture, almost courtly, and she felt acutely aware of him as she placed her hand on his bare skin. She just hoped her hand wouldn't get hot enough to sweat as they fell into step.

Happily, it took only a few minutes to stroll to Trattoria Bianca and within its thick stone walls the temperature was a few degrees cooler. Even better, the boar roast was taking place in a function room with its own shaded courtyard at the rear of the building. They were shown to a table for two on the edges of the courtyard and quickly served with a tall bottle of cold water and a jug of white wine.

Their waiter was a man in his late twenties who treated them to a beaming smile. The event was definitely aimed at tourists and he addressed them in English. 'From nine, the platters of meat will be brought out, and many salads and bread. Please take your plates and our chefs will be happy to serve you. If you would like more water or wine, please let me know.'

Sofia smiled back. '*Grazie mille.*'

He turned his smile directly on her. '*Prego.*' And then whisked away.

'I think you made a hit there.' Levi filled Sofia's wine glass before attending to his own. 'He was dazzled.'

'He was doing his job,' she protested mildly, taking a sip from the wine, which was OK considering it came in a jug. 'Having been on the wrong end of too many surly customers I'm always as pleasant to other servers as humanly possible.' But she glanced at the waiter's retreating back, quite liking the idea that she could dazzle anyone.

She crossed her legs to allow her hem to ride up another inch or two. This being free and adventurous lark was fun.

'There's dazzling,' Levi murmured, his eyes following the movement of her legs, 'and then there's heart attack.'

She smiled serenely. 'I might want to give someone a heart attack. Not a real one, *obviously*,' she amended when his eyes widened. 'I mean figuratively. To get the kind of reaction you read about in books – making someone's heart race, rendering them temporarily speechless. That kind of thing.'

'Thanks for the clarification. It's good to have goals.'

She laughed. 'My dad certainly thought so. He gave me a whole list.' She began to count her promises to Aldo on her fingers. 'Don't mope, do act like a young single woman, visit Montelibertà, lay flowers for my grandparents, search out my uncle with a message and—' she pinned on a bright smile because she could feel her eyes burning as she thought of Aldo '—be happy!'

He listened intently, as if he really wanted to know. 'I know you're finding the one about moping hard. How are you doing with the others?' His eyes didn't look their usual light blue under the strings of lights that had glowed into life as dusk deepened to night – they were several shades darker.

Quelling the sadness that threatened to rise up inside her as she spoke about her father, she said, 'I'm doing my best to enjoy being young and single – I sort of have my own subheadings for that one. And I've taken flowers for my grandparents.' She told him about Ernesto's kindness, concluding, 'So I'm not-very-patiently waiting for my uncle to seek me out. If he doesn't, I suppose I have to try and find out where he lives. I promised Dad I'd pass on a message.'

'Do you think Gianni seriously won't want to meet his own niece?' Levi's brows drew down over his eyes.

'Well—' Sofia took a draught of her wine, because the prospect of her uncle not wanting to even meet her once was pretty damned sad. 'I'll find out, won't I? I've searched for him online but drawn a blank apart from a mention or two connected with the church. I'll just have to hope Ernesto sees him on Sunday. Only another couple of days to wait, I suppose.' Deliberately, she turned the conversation. 'Do you know that Benedetta once had to choose between her husband and Casa Felice – and chose the hotel?'

Levi lounged in his chair as if mirroring, with his body language, her wish to lighten up. 'How intriguing.'

'One of the local staff told me.' Sofia felt herself begin to unwind with the recent wine-hit. 'He wanted her to sell up because he said Casa Felice was slowly killing him. She refused, which I think was pretty gutsy of her, and just worked harder than ever to make up the lack when he left.' She gurgled with laughter. 'Apparently, the consensus is that Aurora inherited her work ethic from her mother – and Davide from his father.'

It wasn't the only thing they laughed about as the evening got into full swing. They laughed about a chef in a tall hat almost filling Sofia's plate with a huge slice of crispy pork, murmuring, '*Bella signorina*',' and giving her a lewd wink. Sofia swapped plates with Levi as soon as the chef turned to the next person.

They laughed at an English lady claiming the centre of the dancefloor to perform an energetic twist when the band began to play, and, in a whisper, Sofia taught Levi the phrase *Signora Turista* for 'Mrs Tourist'. Then, well down their second jug of wine, they joined her in her gyrations and the woman wrapped herself around Levi and tried to persuade him to try the lambada to the energetic Latin dance music, at which Sofia had to sit down to weep with laughter at Levi's expression of dismay.

Eventually Signora Turista good-naturedly gave Levi back. 'Thanks for lending me yer man, my lovely. You can dance with him now.' With total lack of ceremony she hauled Sofia to her feet and shoved her into Levi's arms, whooping with laughter. 'Don't let a handsome man go to waste! Get a grip!' And she grabbed Sofia's hands again and clamped them to Levi's bottom.

Although Sofia stuttered at finding herself plastered so compromisingly against Levi's body, he simply slid his hands down to her buttocks, murmuring, 'I'm beginning to like Signora Turista,' making Sofia blush like a poppy and hastily reposition her hands on his waist.

At midnight, the band announced their last song. It was a 'slowie' and, as they were kind of *in situ*, Sofia and Levi remained on the dancefloor, no longer plastered together but not far apart.

When the final notes died away, not knowing quite how to part company and whether the last dance still ended with a kiss as it had at the school Christmas party, which was possibly the last time she'd been able to stay till the end of something that included dancing, Sofia stepped back to execute a jokey curtsy. 'Thank you, kind sir. I think we've made full use of Amy's twenty euros.'

Levi responded with a deep bow. 'My pleasure.'

The bar was still open and Levi suggested coffee but Sofia shook her head regretfully. 'I could murder a latte but I'm on the residents' breakfast again tomorrow and it begins at six thirty.'

Levi surprised her by taking her hand as they crossed

the corner of Piazza Roma and headed for Via Virgilio, and Sofia found she wasn't quite ready to re-enter real life by freeing herself. The evening air was a pleasant temperature with just enough breeze to lift tendrils of her hair where it escaped from its ponytail.

Levi's gaze was on her. 'I've been racking my brains all evening. What are the sub-headings you've added to the promise you made to behave as a young single person should?'

Taken by surprise at him remembering that throwaway line, Sofia laughed.

He squeezed her hand. 'You can't just giggle knowingly but not spill the beans. It's unkind.'

The wine she'd drunk making her slightly reckless, Sofia arched her brows. 'To be fiercely independent. Not to get tied down. Travel for at least the next two years. Get a tattoo – something delicate and elegant. Have a one-night stand.'

One side of Levi's mouth quirked up. 'I can help you with the last one.'

Sofia sighed. 'I thought about it,' she admitted, knowing already she'd regret her candour in the morning.

His voice dropped. 'We could begin with coffee in my room—'

But Sofia was shaking her head before he could get to the end of his sentence. 'I could get the sack.'

'We could book into another hotel.'

The slight lift at the end of the sentence made it a question rather than an answer. Sofia shook her head again. 'Now you're wandering into the realms of tacky.'

He halted, bringing her around to face him so he could take her other hand. 'You definitely deserve more than tack. You're a beautiful woman, Sofia.' He kissed her

91

knuckles, sending a frisson up her spine, then set her free. 'You go on up the hill so we're not seen arriving back together. I'll follow on.'

Unsure of how to reply to such a fulsome compliment when she'd been so convinced of his interest in Amy, Sofia simply smiled her thanks and fell in with his suggestion. Conscious of his eyes on her rear view she was tempted to rush, but her medium-heel mules had turned to medium hell towards the end of the dancing and she had to be up on those feet for a seven-hour shift before six more hours had passed.

She was pretty sure he'd be watching her behind though.

Chapter Nine

By the time Sunday rolled around Levi was reaching the point where he had to either ask to extend his booking at Casa Felice – which he'd already done once – or go home.

He'd chosen to paint in the lavender garden again. It gave him a slightly different perspective on the aching beauty of the valley vista than from the terrace, but he got fewer people watching over his shoulder, a practice he found conducive to neither painting nor thinking. The latter was taking precedence this afternoon and he was conscious of staring at the view with his brush drying in his hand.

Part of him wanted to go home. He had a strong urge to pick up the reins of his business and try to get a better grasp of what was happening with Wes and Octavia and whether he was spooking at shadows.

But before doing that, he needed to MAKE THE DECISION. That's how he thought of it, hanging in his mind in capital letters, probably bright scarlet and impatient because it was so unlike Levi to dither. He'd wanted to talk to Wes about it last time they'd spoken, but Wes had been in a hurry to get off the phone.

The consequences of making the wrong decision frightened him in a way nothing else ever had.

Added to that, he couldn't stop thinking about Sofia. He dipped his brush into his water jar and touched it to a misty green he'd mixed on his palette, then shook his head, dropped his brush in the jar and dragged his phone out of the pocket of his shorts. What was wrong with him? 'Focus!' he muttered as he pulled up his contacts and tapped the name *Freya Webber*.

Freya answered the call quickly. 'How's it going?'

Recognising the strain in her voice and all too aware that they were only in contact again by circumstance, he wasted no more time on pleasantries than she had. 'No change since I sent you the last lot of photos. I thought I'd just touch base with you to talk about what comes next.' As he spoke, he flipped the pages on his pad to the painting of Il Giardino. It was a shame he'd been interrupted halfway through. From his amateur perspective it was amongst his best work. At least he had the record shots on his phone and would be able to go back to it.

Freya's voice flattened, tinged with disappointment. Probably she'd hoped he was ringing to tell her he'd completed his mission and her daughter would soon be restored to her. 'I'm so worried that if you explain what you're doing there she'll just run off somewhere else and we won't know where she is.'

'Me, too.' He'd hoped she might have more insight to offer by now but it was hope more than expectation.

Stay. Go.

Speak. Remain silent.

He stared at his painting as if it could give him the advice Freya was clearly hesitating over.

'I know you can't stay there for ever,' she conceded.

'That's about as far as I'd got in my thought process too.' Then, wanting to give Freya something positive, 'Amy's a lovely girl. I love her already.'

Freya gave a laugh that was half sob. 'Then I suppose you'll make the right decision.'

So it was all up to him. Levi said goodbye and ended the call, blowing out his lips on a great sigh.

A voice came from behind him, making him swing round on his chair, dropping his pad onto the grass, still open at the painting of Il Giardino. Sofia was gazing at him with a strange expression. Disappointment? Suspicion? Maybe a touch of compassion.

'I think it would probably be better if you threw that particular painting away,' she said levelly. 'And delete all those photos you took of Amy too. You're getting on the wrong side of appropriate.'

Levi picked up the pad and gazed at his watercolour ruefully, the cream parasols over tables full of diners, the figure with tray poised. Amy. 'You're jumping to conclusions,' he tried, noticing the way Sofia played with the end of her plait, passing it through her fingers over and over. It was much like the way he smoothed a dry paintbrush.

A frown grew above her brown eyes. 'She is lovely, Levi. I'm sure a man would have to be blind not to notice and blondes are always eye-catching. But she's eighteen.'

He felt his cheek flush with guilty heat. 'I know how old she is. She was eighteen on the twenty-third of April.'

If there had been a hint of compassion in Sofia's eyes it vanished. He sensed her withdrawal, her suspicion growing into condemnation. 'That you even know that is disturbing.' She paused, obviously selecting her words, the sun shooting amber threads through her dark hair. 'I know it's legal to have a thing about a girl of eighteen but it does you no credit. She could be your daughter.'

With that, she turned and walked quickly away, up the garden and veering left to where he knew she'd vanish under the rampaging vine outside the staff accommodation.

He sighed, tipping back his head and closing his eyes against the sun, too stretched and worn out by the pretence to keep it up any more. He leaped up and raced after Sofia's stiffly retreating back, catching up with her just as she put her hand on the gate to the staff area. Reaching around her, he held the gate closed. 'She is my daughter,' he whispered, fully alive to the fact that Amy could be in her room and within earshot if he spoke at normal volume.

Sofia turned slowly, wearing an expression of ludicrous astonishment, her mouth half open and her eyebrows arched almost into her hair.

'I've only just found out,' he whispered on grimly. 'And Amy doesn't know,' he added, to be crystal clear. 'I came here to protect her, but I don't know whether or when to tell her who I am. She made it abundantly plain to her mother that if anybody comes after her she'll move on and cut contact.' He made himself take a calming breath. 'Now I know her a little and she seems to trust me as a friend – or, ironically, a father figure – I also feel I can't tell her in case it makes her hate me. Somewhat to my surprise, I find the idea of her hating me gut-wrenchingly terrifying.'

Sofia had managed to close her mouth but still looked dumbfounded.

He removed his hand from the gate. 'Can we go somewhere we're less likely to be overheard? Have you finished your shift, or are you just going on?' He checked his watch. He was nearly as familiar with the server shifts as they were themselves.

'Finished.' She blinked as if coming out of a dream. 'Um. How about I get changed and we meet up at the country park? Turn left out of the hotel and follow the road uphill for about a kilometre and you'll see the sign on the left.' She gave him her phone number in case they somehow missed each other.

'See you there,' he agreed gruffly, and strode back down the garden to pack up his pad and paints. His heart was drumming against his ribs, making him feel giddy. Was it because telling Sofia the truth had made it more real?

He was Amy's father. He was a dad, he who'd never seriously thought of having children, probably because he'd never met a woman with whom he'd plan to create a child.

It was half an hour before he met Sofia again. He waited just inside the country park on a bench made from split trunks, where trees met overhead to create cool green light and the path was paved with old leaves and pine needles, their peppery smell rising on the summer air. As he listened to children laughing somewhere deeper into the trees, Sofia appeared at the park entrance in a bright summer dress, its primary colours suiting her dark hair and golden skin. He rose to meet her and by tacit agreement they took the smallest trail. The whippy lower growth of trees jostled right up to the path, making it unlikely they'd be seen together by anyone who might tell her employer.

It was the hottest part of the day but they found a breeze at a sort of lookout point over the valley, higher than Casa Felice. The Umbrian Apennine Mountains could be seen rising in one majestic rank behind another. The road leading down from Montelibertà into the valley looked no more than a carelessly strewn thread. He dropped down onto the dry grass and leaned his back on a smooth rock. Sofia let herself down to sit beside him, her gaze on the view. She left a good two feet of air between them, he noticed.

'What do you want to tell me?' she asked quietly. At least the censure had left her voice.

Marshalling his thoughts, he began the story that he'd so far shared only with Wes. 'I met Amy's mother, Freya, when I was seventeen. It was August and my eighteenth birthday was coming up at the end of the month. A few weeks after that I'd be off to university. Freya was twenty-seven.' He glanced sidelong at Sofia as she made a tiny exclamation. 'Yes, I know. She was nearly ten years older and twenty-seven-year-old women generally couple up with men nearer their age.' He sighed. 'I was a bit smitten and didn't stop to question her motives. She was in Bettsbrough for the hen weekend of a friend who lived in the town and the theme of their nightclub evening was slutty cowgirls. The bride wore a white satin bandit mask with a veil and there were a lot of toy guns and spurs around. Freya looked so hot she glowed in a fringed miniskirt and boots. I knew a couple of the girls in the party so got caught up on the edges of it. I suppose I looked a bit older than I was but I couldn't believe my luck when Freya started to flirt with me. It turned out she and the bride, and several other guests, were flight attendants. She had her own hotel room! Could life get any more glamorous and sophisticated?' He laughed at his naïve younger self. 'We spent the rest of the weekend together. I was still so young that I lied to my parents and said I was staying with a mate.'

Sofia let out a breath. 'Wow. And you got her pregnant?'

'Apparently. But I've only just found out.' He turned to face her and though touched by the memories of those heady days of calf love he retained sufficient grip on the present to be glad that she wasn't looking disappointed in him any more. 'Freya said she was on the pill and I was immature enough not to use condoms as backup. On Sunday afternoon, she said she wasn't coming back to Bettsbrough for the wedding because of her duty roster, packed her stylish flight attendant rolling luggage and kissed me goodbye. She jumped into her hot hatchback to drive out of my life. A whole lot more experienced than at the beginning of the weekend, I wafted home on a cloud of joy.'

'Do you think she got pregnant on purpose?' Sofia's voice jumped up an octave in shock.

He shook his head. 'On the contrary. It was a particularly disastrous contraception failure for her because a detail she'd failed to share with me was that she was engaged to someone else – the husband she's still with, Stephen. I suppose I was her final fling.'

'Holy crap,' Sofia exclaimed softly.

'Yeah.' He picked a sprig off a tiny blue flower growing nearby and rolled the stem between finger and thumb, releasing its acrid scent. 'I think I carried a torch for her for a couple of months, but then I went off to uni and had other things to think about, other fun to have. Other girls to meet.'

'So how on earth did she get in touch with you after

so long?' Sofia had turned towards him now, her shoulder against the wall and her knees drawn up to support her arms.

He screwed up his eyes against the afternoon sun. 'Through my family's business. The night we met, someone was laughing about having a run-in with my dad. Gunn's Motors stands on a corner of the road leading to Market Square in the town centre and he's always been known as "Bullet" Gunn because if kids dared to take a shortcut over the forecourt he would shoot out and tell them to stick to the path. As we walked to her hotel we passed the garage and she stepped on the forecourt to see if Bullet Gunn would appear. As it was three in the morning he didn't, obviously, but the name of the garage must have stuck in her mind. She got the phone number from the website and rang, terming herself "an old friend trying to get in contact with Levi". Someone gave her the name of my website so she went there and filled in the contact form, asking me to get in touch.'

'You remembered her?' A big iridescent green bug fluttered around Sofia's head. Impatiently, she wafted it away.

It seemed typical of her not to squeal or squawk just because a buzzy thing came to take a look at her. 'Of course. For the few years after our encounter the girls I met were students. Students don't have much money for nicely appointed hotel rooms and Freya's glossy grooming was a contrast to their dressed-by-Oxfam look. She lived on in my fantasies for ages.' He felt bashful at this illumination of a more youthful Levi.

'So what did you think when you got her message?'

'Initially I just noticed her first name and smiled at the memory of the "sophisticated older woman" I'd once had a weekend thing with. Her married surname, Webber, didn't mean anything to me so I was astonished when I realised that it really was the same Freya. I replied from my private email address and she asked for a phone number as she felt we "ought to speak directly". The penny still didn't drop.' He pulled up a couple of blades of dry grass and let them loose on the breeze. 'Then came the phone call. Man! Talk about a bolt from the blue! She was crying, which made it even harder for me to grasp what was going on but eventually I realised that she was giving me the news that she'd realised she was pregnant a couple of months after our time together and had gambled on Amy being Stephen's. The truth came out through something so commonplace that it completely caught her on the hop.'

He paused to wipe his forehead, reliving the shock and turmoil, his sense of surrealism. 'Amy and her friends developed social consciences and decided that as they were now eighteen, they'd give blood. Amy was the last because she barely reached the weight requirement, but when she received her donor card it gave her blood type as A-positive. Stephen's a medical guy, working in research, and he took one look and said, "How can two O-positive parents have an A-positive child?" Freya couldn't think of an answer. She realised what it must mean, but she'd been ignoring the possibility for over eighteen years. Amy—' he blew out suddenly, feeling winded anew at the memory of Freya's half-hysterical words and the painful visions they conjured up '—Amy was there. Witnessed the horror, the anger, the screaming, the tears. Had the dad she'd loved all her life ripped from her family tree. It's no wonder the poor girl reacted by running off.'

Sofia covered his hand with hers. It was hot, like the sunlight pouring down. 'Poor Stephen. Poor Amy. Poor you.'

'Poor them, yes. Not poor me. I don't have a significant other to upset or other children to shock. And now that I know Amy . . . how could I feel sorry for myself that I helped make her?' Levi took a deep breath before he carried on. 'Freya said it was both a catastrophe and a relief to have everything out in the open, not to occasionally worry why her eldest child's blonde when she and Stephen are dark.'

'But she wasn't really prepared for the fallout when the truth came out?'

'I'm not sure how you would prepare for that. Stephen was distraught and demanded every detail. She had to confess about taking off her engagement ring for the hen weekend. As Freya was from out of town only the bride knew the truth – and she was notorious for likening relationships to a chocolate box and saying every woman liked variety. By the time Freya realised she was pregnant it was only a few weeks to her own wedding and the odds were that the baby belonged to Stephen. They later had two more children, both boys, and moved to Germany with Stephen's job in a lab in Munich. Everything was rosy until May, when it all unravelled.'

'Wow.' Sofia's eyes were soft with sympathy. 'I can only imagine.'

He nodded sombrely. Distantly he could hear the sound of church bells from Montelibertà signalling a Sunday afternoon mass. A hot breeze blew up from the valley, lifting his hair out of his eyes. 'Freya was under attack. Stephen was gutted and betrayed. Unfortunately, while they were focused on their own disaster, Amy was making plans. She packed her bags and left, leaving a note that began, "Dear Mum and Stephen" – which was horrible for him – explaining she was coming here and threatening to cut them off if anyone followed.'

He swallowed, wishing he'd thought to bring a bottle of water to ease his constricted throat. 'Stephen's feeling horribly remorseful because he should have reassured Amy that his love for her was unchanged despite his own pain. Freya's drowning in guilt. Relations between them are icy but their boys are twelve and sixteen so they're letting things settle down before deciding where to go next.'

Sofia squeezed his hand. 'Was it your idea to come here?'

He laughed shortly. 'Freya's. That's why she got in touch, to enlist me to come here and make sure Amy was OK. I fell in with it because despite not knowing which way was up I could understand her desperation that someone be on the spot to provide help if Amy needed it. And, although I feel as if I'm in a dream, I am her father.'

'Wow.' Sofia's eyes crinkled in a smile, catching the sunlight, the pupils contracting. 'That's a bit of a sudden responsibility.'

He rubbed his face. 'No kidding. I've always enjoyed being single and haven't really had a yen to settle down and be a family man. Other than being an uncle, anyway. That's quite fun.' He paused to picture his two mischievous nieces and the way his brother Tyrone's face always lit up when they were around. 'Wes and I have ridden around Europe quite a bit on holiday so I jumped on my motorbike and headed for Munich to talk through Freya's plan. She and Stephen were so distraught and scared, so emphatic that Amy isn't a particularly mature eighteen-year-old, that I didn't take much persuading to carry on to Montelibertà. And—' his voice cracked and he had to swallow again '—and how could I not want to see my daughter for the first time?'

'And you arrived just as she was about to be sacked,' Sofia supplied.

He winced at the memory. 'Thank goodness you were standing up for her. If she'd got the sack she might have headed home – but what if she hadn't? What if I'd been too late and she'd gone off somewhere, homeless and jobless, trying to find a way to survive?'

Sofia gave a shiver. 'I don't want to even think about that. She's a lovely kid but I agree she's not worldly wise. This whole episode must seem unreal to you.'

Croakily, he laughed. 'For the last two weeks my life has felt like something you'd read about happening to someone else. I don't feel like a parent. Or, at least, I don't think I do but I can't be sure, never having been one. But I do feel protective of Amy. I'm proud of her surviving a bombshell exploding in her life. Freya sent pictures to my phone so I could identify her but it still didn't seem true then. When I saw her in reality I felt this big rush of . . . I don't know what else to call it but love.'

Sofia grinned. Her plait was hanging over one shoulder, fat and glossy. '*Now* I can see why you've stuck around, watching her all the time.'

'I hadn't realised I'd been so obvious. The fact that this person wouldn't be on the planet if not for me fascinates me. I have a strong urge to be near her, so I can understand why you thought I was some old letch.'

Her grin faded. 'Now I know the whole story I know you never were acting like a letch. I think you might be acting like a parent.'

His heart leaped like a fish on a line. 'I don't feel nearly grown-up enough to be that.'

She laughed. 'I wonder if anyone ever does?'

They fell silent. Insects buzzed around the tiny blue flowers, flitted through the wiry grass and occasionally fluttered against his skin. Even the breeze was hot as it brushed tendrils of Sofia's hair across her cheek and rustled the trees behind them. Distant voices elsewhere in the park were the only indications that they were not alone on the planet. The world had seemed to shrink to this clearing as he'd relived his story but now he focused on the peaks and valleys laid out before him, half surprised to remember they were there.

Sofia shifted her position, releasing his hand as if she too had just remembered where she was. 'Do you see yourself in her? Or is she like her mother?'

He laughed. 'I don't know Freya very well but when I first met Amy I thought that's where she got her impulsiveness. I'm not afraid to act when I think it's necessary, but not in the act-first-think-later manner of Amy and Freya. Amy certainly has the courage of her convictions.'

She nodded thoughtfully. 'So what about your life in England? You say there aren't any baby Gunns or a Mrs Gunn at home, but isn't there a business you should be running?'

'There are three Mrs Gunns – Mum, Gran and my sister-in-law Beth. But you're right about the business and I'm already worried about that. I can manage some actual work from my room, though the signal's too in-and-out for my input to be reliable because I keep dropping the connection to the server. Wes's managing the remote workers and until now he's been the most even-tempered and predictable guy I've ever known. Now he's being awkward and defensive. It's thrown me a bit. I could seriously do without the whole Octavia situation.'

She stretched her legs and eased her back, making her

top cling. 'What kind of website business do you run? All I ever see you do is paint.'

He pulled his gaze away from the roundness of her breasts before she caught him sneaking a look. 'I like to paint but it's a hobby – and also supposedly the reason I'm here in Umbria, as Amy couldn't be allowed to suspect that her mum had sent me.' He took a breath because he always felt slightly odd at confessing the truth about his site. People tended to react in one of three ways – they'd never heard of it, which made him feel he'd made too much of an announcement; they disbelieved him, which made him feel annoyed; or they began to treat him differently, as if he had the money of Bill Gates or Mark Zuckerberg. He was doing more than OK but he was not one of the super-rich. 'My business is The Moron Forum.'

'The Moron Forum? Seriously? But that's huge!' Her eyes sparkled as if she was genuinely pleased for him. 'There are links to The Moron Forum on social media every day. I used to read some of the funnier posts out to Dad.'

He felt himself relax as he realised she was going to be one of the rare people who would just take an intelligent interest. He was beginning to think Sofia was the most pragmatic person he'd met. 'It began as a joke, a spoof of forums like Yahoo Answers where someone poses a question and others share their knowledge or experience. Wes and I developed websites in our day jobs. Sites like News Thump, which is full of parodies and satire, were doing really well, so we set out to appeal to people who like that kind of humour. People started signing up and chipping in with stupid answers. Social media loved it. It snowballed. We began taking The Moron Forum seriously as a second job. We developed an app for mobile devices and as well as the original "ask a stupid question, get a stupid answer" section we created areas for asking serious questions and getting stupid answers – where the knack is to make stupid answers *look* serious when they're not. Then came "ask a stupid question get a sarcastic answer". Some are so witty the site has a huge following. People log on via their phones at lunchtime or on their train commute just to have a bit of a smile during their day. We began to get content providers to write articles to begin conversational threads like the site How to Geek, so soon we had a whole bank of freelancers writing and moderating. We left our day jobs five years ago.'

'Go you,' she said admiringly. 'I'm not surprised you're wondering whether you're grown-up enough to be a parent. How does this joking around make you money?'

'Same as any site. Advertising. You get traffic, you get people paying to put their stuff in front of that traffic. Also, the online shop selling The Moron Forum merchandise is booming.'

'And it makes you enough to *live* on?'

As she sounded as if she were having trouble grasping the magnitude of money to be made, he searched for a measure for his success, something easy to relate to. 'I could probably retire now if I wanted to.'

'*Really*?' She gazed at him thoughtfully. Her dark eyes were sprinkled with bronze flecks, her hair glowing in the sunlight. With her golden skin it was no wonder he'd thought her a local when he'd first seen her – especially as she'd been speaking Italian with every bit as much hand-waving as Benedetta. She toyed with the end of her plait as she regarded him and he had to drag his gaze away from her stroking fingers because it made him wonder how they'd feel stroking him. Like most men, he preferred not to get caught with an erection except in precisely the right circumstances. Like if Sofia had taken him up on his willingness to be her first one-night stand—

'I'm impressed all this comes from two techies sitting in a room over your dad's garage,' she went on, giving him something else to think about.

'Developers.' He drew up the knee closest to him to casually rest an arm on it and incidentally block her view of any visible excitement. 'It does come from us but it involves remote workers all over the place. Media manager, forum moderators, designers to make stuff pretty, and several people handling the on-site advertising. And there's the legal adviser we call on if we think a post might be a bit dodgy. We ask if a post is "too satirical" but we mean "Can we get sued?" And Mary, the bookkeeper—'

She took her hand away from her plait to make a *halt* gesture. 'You're frying my brain. You've spent a couple of weeks lazing around painting pretty pictures and ordering coffees from me, and now in the last hour you've sprung on me that you're Amy's dad and a dot-com mogul. Any other bombshells?'

He grinned and shrugged. 'I'll let you know if I think of one.' But then an uncomfortable feeling took possession of his insides. 'Erm . . . it's never fair to share information with someone and then ask them afterwards not to pass it on to others but I really would prefer that I carry on being just a holidaymaker with a paintbox. It doesn't matter about The Moron Forum but Amy . . . I'd hate her to find out about our relationship the wrong way.'

All levity left Sofia's expression. 'Of course. How on earth are you going to tell her in the end?'

His stomach dropped. 'I'm lying awake at nights

worrying about it. I'm scared that if I tell her she might take off, knowing her mother must have sent me.'

'I can see that's a concern.' Sofia wrinkled her nose.

'I'm more use as a confidant than as a parent, someone to give her a few clues about dealing with pests like Davide.'

Sofia moved closer, laying her hand on his arm, making all the tiny hairs lift from his skin. 'A dad can fulfil a lot of roles: confidant, mentor, shoulder and friend.'

He glanced at her hand, the slim fingers and clean nails. 'OK. But at what point do I mention that I've been tricking her all the time? I've done what I thought best but whichever way you cut it I've been dishonest. Like her mum.'

She sighed. 'There is that. She told me a little bit about being at loggerheads with her family and it's obvious her feelings have been hurt. Now I know the whole tale I can understand what a horrible shock it was and why she feels betrayed.'

'Yeah.' He let his head tip back, eyes closing tiredly. 'And Freya told me not to underestimate her and what she'll do if pushed. Stephen said she's like a firework – quietly fizzing until you get to that point of thinking nothing's going to happen . . . but then she goes off with a bang.'

Sofia gave a soft laugh. 'Certainly fits with what I've seen of her so far.' She wriggled around so she could let herself down to lie full length on the grass.

Levi edged down to lie alongside her, throwing an arm across his forehead to create shade for his eyes. 'There's a very real chance that the time will never be right to tell her who I am, and that she might never know feels like a jab in the guts too. I've got myself in a bit of a corner.'

'You have.' Sofia hauled herself up on her elbow to look

down into his face. He had to close one eye against the sun to look back at her. 'One day she might decide she wants to know who her biological father is. What if Freya tells her? Or Stephen? Or she hires some agency to help her?'

His stomach lurched. 'Those are all dangers too,' he admitted. 'I only booked into Casa Felice for a week originally and I've already been here ten days. Now I'm thinking that if I stay a bit longer the right situation will miraculously present itself. Maybe she'll trust me and accept I had no choice but not to identify myself straightaway.'

Sofia rolled back onto the grass. 'Maybe.'

He sighed so hard it tugged at his chest. Or maybe it was something to do with his heart. He'd heard that your child could have all kinds of extraordinary effects on that. 'I'm in limbo. I can't afford to tell her but can't afford not to.'

Sofia didn't offer any useful insight. Before much longer she checked her watch and said she had to get back to do laundry because she had no clean uniform ready for Monday. 'And there's always the chance that my uncle will turn up. Ernesto was expecting to see him at Sunday mass today.' She sounded wistful, though she smiled.

Smiling through adversity seemed one of her things. Levi gave her hand a sympathetic squeeze. 'Sorry. All I've done is witter on about my own worries. I hope that your uncle will show up soon and everything will be OK.'

She just rolled her eyes and grinned before tossing back her plait and turning to leave.

To pass the time that Sofia needed to get back to Casa Felice, Levi wandered through the park, enjoying the dappled shade as he followed the trails between the trees and the occasional glimpse of a peak to his right. The air smelled of pine, and families or serious hikers in walking boots smiled at him as they passed.

Eventually he found the entrance again and made his way down the hill. Then, acknowledging that his conversation with Sofia had at least crystallised in his mind that he couldn't leave Amy yet, he went in to enquire at reception whether he could extend his stay when the current week ended.

A man served him whom he hadn't encountered before, an older guy with slicked-back hair and black-rimmed glasses. He clicked his tongue and inspected his computer screen. 'For one week, sir? I cannot offer you a superior room, as you presently have. It will be on the other side of the hotel, much smaller and with no balcony.'

Levi was glad to get a room at all in mid-June. 'That's fine,' he said gratefully. 'At least it'll be less expensive.'

The man shook his head. 'I'm sorry, sir. When you booked online you received our advanced booking room rate. But now . . .' He spread his hands. 'I regret that it will be more expensive.'

Levi accepted the situation, getting out his credit card without demur. Money was the least of his problems.

Chapter Ten

Sofia wasn't unhappy to be back in Il Giardino for Monday's and Tuesday's evening shifts, though she found herself on edge in case her uncle made himself known.

He didn't.

Wednesday and Thursday were her rest days this week. On Wednesday she jumped on the train to Orvieto to see the splendid white and black cathedral first hand, and as Amy finished work at six on Thursday they arranged a catch-up at Trattoria del Sole where they'd lunched last Tuesday. As it happened, Amy mentioned the arrangement in Levi's hearing so Sofia took no responsibility when he turned up shortly after them and, citing a lack of free tables, asked if he could pull up a chair.

'Why not?' said Sofia cordially, happy to help further this odd father-daughter relationship. Poor Levi obviously felt a fish out of water so far as parenting went, and surely she and Amy were chaperoning each other, so no fraternisation rules were being flouted.

Amy was chatty and animated. Sofia gradually let Levi take a larger and larger part in the conversation, enjoying the expression in his eyes as he talked to his daughter about something other than what he'd like for lunch and whether Davide was being a nuisance. She had to take a large gulp of wine to wash away a lump in her throat when she remembered the same love in Aldo's eyes when he used to look at her. She almost expected Amy to notice it too.

It was nearly ten when Amy checked the time with an exclamation. 'Supposed to be meeting Noemi in town! Laters!' Then she jumped up and disappeared through the door to the bar and thereafter the street.

Sofia laughed at the suddenness of it. 'We're dumped.'

Levi grinned, clinking his glass against hers in ironic celebration, the wine glittering with the reflection of the tiny lights wound around the terrace railings. 'Young people today.'

Sofia stayed long enough to finish her glass of wine then said goodnight and strolled back up to Casa Felice, enjoying the stillness of the warm evening and letting thoughts drift gently into her mind. The thought that refused to drift out again was that now she knew the truth about Levi's interest in Amy, she could admit to herself the truth about *her* interest in Levi.

He was hot.

She liked him a lot.

If only there wasn't that guest/staff rule . . . It wouldn't be sensible to risk her job for a one-night stand – certainly not until she'd located her uncle.

It was the next morning, Friday, when she reported to begin her 11 a.m. shift in Il Giardino that she found Davide waiting to pass on a message as he put up the table parasols. 'My mother wants to see you in her office.'

Sofia paused in the act of posting her pad and pen into her apron pocket. 'Now?'

Davide nodded and moved on to the next parasol.

'OK,' Sofia said to his back. She smoothed her hair and straightened her apron before entering the cool of the foyer. From the reception desk Aurora directed Sofia to Benedetta's office through the door marked *Solo staff*. She followed Aurora's directions and tapped and entered. The room held a gigantic desk for Benedetta and a frosty reception for Sofia.

'Close the door,' Benedetta instructed. 'Is it true you were out on a date with a hotel guest last night?'

Wrong-footed and alarmed, Sofia made a mistake. Instead of offering a simple explanation, she demanded, 'Who saw us?'

'That's irrelevant.' Benedetta's manicured fingernails tapped on the desk. 'You know that staff members should not form relationships with guests. Hotels that allow that get . . . a certain reputation.' She made a prim shape with her mouth as she uttered the last three words.

Unease growing, Sofia took a breath as she belatedly prepared her defence. 'I went out with Amy and the guest asked to share our table as there were no others vacant. Amy and I were together. It was obvious neither of us was on a date with the guest.'

Benedetta gazed at her keenly. 'You were seen – not Amy.'

'Oh.' Sofia felt her face heat up, wishing she'd thought to forestall this eventuality. 'Amy went to meet Noemi at about ten and I did finish my glass of wine before leaving the guest and coming back here. *Alone.*'

After several more seconds of keen scrutiny, Benedetta nodded. 'I accept your explanation. But I must ask you not to mix socially with the guests. I couldn't countenance staff members in the rooms of guests or guests in staff accommodation. We'll call this an official warning.'

Sofia did *not* enjoy being reprimanded. She almost retorted that actually she fancied the pants off the guest but had made a huge effort and kept everything professional. So *there*. But it seemed a quick route to being dismissed, and there was the hope of her uncle seeking her out at Casa Felice to consider, apart from the inconvenience of having to find somewhere else to work and live. 'Of course,' she replied, as if no other thought had ever crossed her mind. Then she went off to begin her shift feeling a lot less calm than she let her outward appearance betray.

It seemed particularly hot outside. There was no breath of breeze and the heavy road traffic generated its own heat to add to that of the sun. Thomas was working section three and Davide, as usual, had allocated himself section two in the centre. His gaze was trained on the door as Sofia stepped outside and he paused in the middle of sanitising a table to send her a knowing smirk. Temper fraying as she realised the probable identity of Benedetta's informer, she marched over to him. 'Been chatting to your mum about me, Davide?'

He held up his hands with a protesting 'Eh, eh,' and shook his head. But the smirk broadened to a satisfied grin.

'*Nessuno ama uno sneak,*' she hissed, unable to think of a more authentically Italian way of telling him that nobody likes a sneak.

Davide shrugged, evidently unmoved by this information. 'You have section one. And a person is waiting for you. Table twelve.' He pointed with the sanitising spray.

Sofia followed with her gaze and saw a man she almost felt as if she recognised, even though she knew she'd never seen him before. A man who made her aware of what Aldo could have looked like if his heart hadn't begun to spring leaks so many years ago.

Her stomach plunged. Of course she knew it wasn't Aldo, could clearly see that a resemblance was all there was, especially as the man wasn't smiling, as her father so often had. But she couldn't look away.

The man stared straight back.

Licking suddenly dry lips, she approached table twelve. She wasn't sure of the proper greeting. '*Buon giorno*' seemed too formal but '*Ciao*' not formal enough. As she drew near the man, he pushed out a chair as if suggesting she sit down.

'I'm working.' She wasn't sure why her voice shook. It wasn't because she was frightened, but it felt wrong that there was no softening of the half-familiar features.

'I am your uncle, Gianni Bianchi,' the man said, as if that fact trumped any obligation to her employer.

She found that it did, but only because her knees suddenly lost the power to support her in the presence of the person who was her closest living relative, and she had to drop into the chair opposite his. A tremulous smile took charge of her lips. 'You look a lot like my father,' she said huskily.

He nodded.

Now she saw that his eyes, so dark they were almost black, were moist. It encouraged her to add, 'Thank you so much for coming here. I've been longing to meet you.'

Gianni nodded again. His throat worked. 'You remind me of your mother.'

The world took a giant swoop, as if Sofia had had too

116

much sun. 'You knew my mum? I barely remember her. I have photos but I've never noticed that I'm like her. I have Dad's colouring so I thought I took after him.'

'The smile. The shape of your head.'

Sofia's heart began to speed. Any lingering compulsion to begin her day's duties vanished. 'You may know that my mother died a long time ago—'

Pain flashed across Gianni's face.

Sofia halted, confused. Then, when Gianni made no comment, continued hesitantly, 'Dad died last year.'

Gianni drew in a long, slow breath. 'I am sorry. When I heard you were asking for me and appeared to be alone, I wondered.'

'He asked me to give you a message,' Sofia went on, when Gianni asked no questions.

Impassive once again, he nodded. 'Ernesto said this.'

This meeting wasn't going the way Sofia had hoped. The air between her and her uncle prickled with tension and he wasn't interacting with her in any of the ways she'd imagined, greeting the news of his brother's death almost without expression. Confused, she fell silent.

His voice had hardened when he spoke again. 'You're certain your mother is dead?'

Shock made Sofia shrink back. '*Certain*? Of course! What the hell do you mean?'

He shrugged. 'Maybe she left and Aldo did not want to admit it.'

Sofia simply stared, dumbfounded. 'She got meningitis and developed septicaemia. It was over in a few hours. My father had a marble headstone erected at her grave in our local cemetery in Bedford. I can't imagine the authorities allowing that if she wasn't there. Can you?'

He flushed at her sarcasm. 'And the message?' he asked stonily.

She stared at him, completely at sea. Were her uncle's emotions badly wired? Had she unwittingly offended him? 'Aldo asked me to tell you he was sorry,' she said stiffly. 'I'm not completely sure about what. It might be that he never saw your parents again before they died. I know he felt a lot of guilt and sorrow over that—'

'Phhtt!'

The scornful noise made Sofia pause, gazing at the greying man, her temper beginning to simmer at his air of scorn.

Gianni rose.

Silently, Sofia followed suit.

Her uncle drew himself up. 'You think you get Aldo's share of the money from our parents? I tell you something. He had it already.'

'I know that! It helped us for a long time, when he was ill, but it gradually dwindled away,' she said slowly, before adding, 'Surely you don't mind that he accepted his share? That wasn't what his apology was about, was it?'

Gianni glowered darkly. 'I did not expect a single thing from him! And if his money has gone, it has gone. I hope you don't think I have money to give you.' He began to turn away.

Sofia's temper boiled over. '*Non voglio i tuoi cazzo di soldi.*'

Dimly she heard Davide protesting, 'Eh, eh, Sofia!' but she tuned him out. She'd apologise later for yelling at Gianni that she didn't want his fucking money.

Gianni swung back, looking stunned. '*Tu parli italiano.*'

Sofia knew the satisfaction of wrong-footing him. 'Yes. My father and I spoke Italian often. He was wonderful and I loved and admired him. I don't know why he asked me to convey an apology to you, but it was *not* so I could beg money from you! He couldn't have known you'd become the kind of man who'd speak to your niece this way. Now I know why he never contacted his family for help and let me care for him alone for all those years. I'm ashamed to be related to you and you can safely forget I exist.' She flung herself away, intent on putting space between herself and her inexplicably insulting and hostile uncle, not realising until it was too late that Davide was now close behind her.

His tray of crocks did a graceful half-turn in mid-air and emptied slops of drinks and smears of cream down the front of her uniform. 'Shit!' Sophia exclaimed.

Then she saw Benedetta step out from behind her son, quivering with fury. 'Oh, *shit*,' she groaned.

Benedetta snorted like an angry bull. 'My office, Sofia,' before apologising fulsomely to the faces that had turned at the commotion.

The blood singing in her ears, Sofia stalked out of Il Giardino and across reception, aware of beer and milkshake seeping into her clothes as she slammed through the door marked *Solo staff*. She could hear the furious tap of Benedetta's heels as she followed but it wasn't until she reached the office that she realised someone else was padding along behind, too. Levi.

'What are you doing here?' she demanded. He seemed to have appeared out of nowhere, his casual hands-in-pockets slouch at odds with the set of his jaw.

Benedetta obviously shared Sofia's confusion as she held the office door wide to give Levi plenty of room to pass back the way he'd come. 'Please. This is private.'

Levi simply let himself down into a chair. 'As you arrived

only at the end of the scene and I was at a nearby table throughout, I thought you might welcome my insight into events.'

Sofia didn't know whether to be grateful that he was evidently preparing to go in to bat for her or irritated that he might think she couldn't handle this herself.

Judging by the sour look on her face, Benedetta certainly felt no gratitude. She instantly found another way to exclude him from events by addressing Sofia in Italian. 'Who is this man?' She flapped her hand in Levi's direction. 'He's always conveniently around to stick up for the English. Is he a hired witness? Or do you have a relationship with him, despite your protests at our meeting of less than half an hour ago? And do I understand that you're Gianni Bianci's *niece*? Are you here to spy?' Her voice rose along with her colour.

'Spy? Why should I spy for an uncle who has just been offensive and unpleasant to me? And why should I spy on your pisspot operation anyway?' Sofia switched to English. 'There's probably no point talking to her, Levi. Signora Morbidelli's already made up her mind.'

Benedetta stuck to Italian. 'You're rude to a customer, you use bad language and you're rude to me. I can no longer employ you. Go! Clear your room.'

'What kind of employer are you not to even ask for my side of the story?' Sofia ripped off her soiled apron and hurled it onto the desk, finding a savage satisfaction in Benedetta drawing back from the milkshake smears on the polished wood. Then she whirled and marched through the door.

Levi followed her, protesting: 'Has she sacked you? She can't do that. You have a right to be heard and your uncle was obnoxious.'

'Who cares? She says I have to clear my room so that's me gone.' Trembling with rage at Benedetta and disappointment in her uncle, Sofia stormed out into reception, down the stairs and, strictly against Benedetta's rules, across the terrace where residents were enjoying late elevenses or early lunch. She marched down the next set of steps from the side of the terrace and slammed in through the gate to the staff quarters.

Amy, curled up in the dappled sunlight on the bench outside her room with her phone, jumped visibly at Sofia's tempestuous entrance. 'What's up?'

'Benedetta's sacked me,' Sofia snapped. Then she slammed on her brakes, wishing she'd conveyed the news more gently, especially when she heard an indrawn breath from Levi, who she realised belatedly, had stuck with her in her headlong flight.

Amy uncurled herself and climbed to her feet, face pale, eyes wide and panicked as she gazed at the state of Sofia's black uniform. Her voice trembled. 'Does this mean you're leaving, Sofia? Please don't!'

Remorse pounced on Sofia. Horrified at the way she'd let her anger take over, she tried to manufacture a smile as she slid her arm around Amy's slight shoulders. 'I'm sorry, hun. I'm so upset and angry that I don't know what I'm doing or saying. If I hadn't got away from Benedetta I might have yanked her across the desk! So I threw in the towel. Or rather the apron.' Nobody laughed.

In the silence, Amy's phone began to ring in her hand. She frowned down at its screen. 'It's Aurora.'

'Maybe she wants you to do my shift. At least you'll get a few more euros because they'd have to pay you more for working on what's supposed to be your day off.' Feeling

121

suddenly miserable at how badly she was letting her young friend down, Sofia tailed off.

Levi stepped into the breach, giving Amy a reassuring pat on the arm. 'There's no point you being in trouble too. Answer the call. Sofia needs a bit of time before she decides on her next step but I promise I won't let her leave Montelibertà just yet. OK?'

Blinking, two perfect tears trembling on her eyelashes, Amy nodded. Then she answered the phone with a discouraging 'Yeah?'

As she began to nod dolefully along to the conversation Levi muttered to Sofia, 'Sorry to jump in.'

'No, I'm grateful you did. I didn't give any thought to how she'd take it.' She was suddenly realising that Levi had found himself watching Sofia make his daughter cry.

By the time a woeful-looking Amy had finished her call, Sofia had summoned up a smile and some semblance of her usual calm. 'Don't worry. I won't go before we've talked again. At least,' she added, realising that she'd just made a promise she had no idea whether she could keep, as Benedetta might have her marched from the premises, 'if I *have* to leave the hotel I'll—' she floundered to a halt as it dawned on her that she had nowhere to sleep tonight '—text you,' she ended feebly.

More tears eased from Amy's eyes but she managed a tremulous smile. 'Can we go on together to Spain, like we said?'

Sofia's own eyes began to boil as she realised with a jolt how much Amy had grown to depend upon her support, and that this must feel to the youngster like another disaster. She pinned on a smile but couldn't swallow the lump in her throat to offer actual words.

With a last disappointed glance from heart-wrenchingly

mournful eyes, Amy slipped through the door into her room. 'I have to get changed.'

Sofia plumped down onto the bench and Levi settled himself beside her. 'Sorry,' she whispered. 'Why are families so weird? My uncle's decided not to like me without getting to know me.'

Levi slipped a comforting arm around her. 'I don't think he dislikes you. He was too emotional for that.'

'Dislike's an emotion.'

'I think there's more to it.' He hesitated. 'He was in reception when you charged out of Benedetta's office and looked as if he was going to set off after you. Then Benedetta came out and he began snapping at her. As I don't speak Italian I can't guess what he said but he was just as stiff and surly with her.'

'He was probably making certain I got the boot.'

Before Levi could respond Amy emerged from her room in her black dress, tying on her white apron. Sofia jumped up and gave her a big hug. 'I'm sorry.'

Amy's arms closed hotly around Sofia. 'Promise you'll still be around at six when I come off shift?' Her voice was so small and sad that it wrung Sofia's heart.

'Totally, absolutely promise,' she vowed.

'OK then.' Amy gave a watery smile and disengaged herself. Then she looked at Levi, who'd risen to his feet along with Sofia and now stood watching. Tentatively, Amy opened her arms in his direction.

Looking stunned, Levi stepped slowly into her hug. Sofia's eyes swam when she saw, over Amy's shoulder, his expression of wonderment.

Sofia wasn't sure she'd ever seen anything more moving than a father hugging his child for the first time.

He was the one to break the embrace. 'Go earn some

extra dosh from Benedetta,' he suggested bracingly, if a little hoarsely. 'It might make Sofia feel better.'

Amy managed a wan smile before she hurried out of the gate and turned right, taking the staff route to Il Giardino.

Flopping down onto the bench Sofia tipped back her head and clenched her eyes with a groan. 'I feel awful for not breaking it to her gently. Thanks for helping smooth over my crappiness.'

He dropped down beside her. 'Holy shit. That was intense.'

She turned her face towards him and opened an eye. He looked shell-shocked. As she had nothing to useful to say, she shut the eye again and gave herself up to the sound of the vine leaves rustling all around them while she tried to process the emotions having a wrestling match inside her.

It was he who eventually broke the silence. 'Do you plan to just sit here till Amy comes back?'

'Thinking about it.'

'The thing is . . .' He hesitated delicately.

When the pause had drawn out for what seemed like ages, Sofia sighed and opened her eyes. 'The thing is . . . you want whatever I do next not to hurt or upset Amy but you don't know how to say it. And you absolutely don't think now's the time to explain to Amy about who you are.'

'Yes. Sorry, but yes. It's not just that she seems—' again a hesitation, as if what he was trying to say was so vitally important that he couldn't risk even one wrong word '—young and vulnerable. It's that the slenderest of threads connects us right now and if I let that thread break I might never know where she falls or how badly she's hurt. And

. . . it seems as if that thread passes through your hands. You're the person she trusts here.'

Sofia felt her heart stretch. 'As if I didn't have enough shit of my own to deal with,' she muttered.

'Sorry.' He sat up. 'I can help with your immediate problem by moving your stuff into my room temporarily. It will give you a few hours to take stock.'

Slowly she opened both eyes to look at him, grateful he'd identified the most pressing issue and found a way to deal with it. 'That would really help because I don't know if I can find a room for tonight in Montelibertà. I need to stay local because I promised Amy but I don't want Benedetta to have another reason to shriek at me if she finds I'm still occupying my staff quarters.'

Unexpectedly he planted a kiss in the centre of her forehead. 'It's all a plan to get you into my room,' he said, a teasing note filtering into his voice.

Sofia tried to match his attempt at levity. 'Ha! As I've been canned, I suppose I might as well.' Then everything seemed to pause as they stopped and gazed at each other as if each examining the thought that now none of Benedetta's rules applied to Sofia. And, even if it had come about as an emergency measure, they *would* be sharing a room.

Heart stepping up its pace, she turned towards her accommodation. 'I'd better get started.'

Chapter Eleven

Sofia opened every drawer in the room and tipped the contents into her cases, muttering beneath her breath about 'that *bastard* thinking I'm after money!', then grabbed the clothes hanging on the clothes rail and folded them roughly on top. Levi went round disengaging chargers and adaptors from sockets and winding up the leads, then swept her personal effects into the cheery green lightweight backpack she'd brought over as hand baggage.

'That it?' He zipped the backpack with a brisk *zzzzzzp*.

Sofia checked the bathroom and grabbed her robe from behind the door to shove in the top of one of her cases before slapping it shut. 'That's it.'

He halted her when she would have grabbed the suitcase's handle. 'If Benedetta sees you carting your stuff up to the guest rooms she'll want to know what's going on and might throw both of us out. I suggest you let me go first with this lot, then you follow. It's room 202. I've only got one key card so you'll have to knock when you arrive.'

'Good plan,' she agreed, suppressing a sigh of exasperation at the situation she found herself in. 'I'll give you ten minutes then go through the yard and the staff entrance to use the service lift.'

Levi opened the door and took a case in each hand, then Sofia saw his head bobbing past the window and he was gone.

The room was quiet apart from the sound of seconds dragging by. Then, at last, ten minutes were up. She shouldered her backpack, set off briskly up the steps to the yard and reached the service lift unchallenged.

It was only when the doors shut that, perhaps as a consequence of Benedetta not feeling it necessary to go to the expense of air conditioning in a lift that only the staff would use, she realised she smelled disgustingly of beer and coffee and milkshake. She'd almost forgotten about coming into violent contact with Davide's tray. Yuck.

When Levi let her into his room she asked, 'Do you mind if I use your shower? I've begun to smell like the slops tray.'

He grinned as he made a 'be my guest' gesture towards the bathroom door. 'Not just begun, to be honest.'

'Why didn't you tell me?' She made an embarrassed dive towards the bathroom, shut the door and threw off her clothes. The shower, being for guests rather than for lowly staff, flowed beautifully. She piled her hair up on top of her head and stood beneath the soothing spray for several minutes, trying to encourage her resentment to wash down the drain along with the soapy water.

So what if her uncle didn't want to get to know her? So what if her job had ended ahead of schedule? Changing plans was doable for the independent, travelling, single person. Thanks to the sale of the home she'd shared with Aldo she wouldn't starve, even if she didn't get a job for a month. Six months. More. She'd been saving that money for if she ever wanted to return to the UK and get herself a degree but that could wait. She'd done OK without one so far.

She felt better when she finally turned off the water and took a towel from a rail. She was clean and fresh and if necessary she'd sleep on Amy's floor tonight . . . except, damn, that had the potential to get Amy into trouble. But she could scarcely ask for help from her Uncle Gianni, she reflected bitterly.

After getting out of the shower and drying herself, she woke up to the fact that her clothes were in her suitcases in Levi's room. She wrapped the towel around herself, opened the door and peeped round. Levi was propped up against the head of his bed doing something on his laptop. 'Um, I need to get some clothes,' she murmured.

He glanced up. 'Sure.' Then his gaze returned to her for a more leisurely perusal, making her wonder whether the towel was quite so all-enveloping as she'd thought. From the sharpening of his gaze she felt as if he could see right through it.

She crouched down, trying to keep her towel in place with her chin as she fumbled with the zip of her case. Hearing the sound of his laptop snapping shut she peeped from the corner of her eye, only to see that he was now openly watching. Scrabbling through her case because it was really hard to find anything in the heap, she felt her face scalding as first she located knickers and a bra then, fumbling, dropped them onto the floor and had to snatch them up.

Levi laughed, low and deep in his throat. 'You're being coy for a woman who's hinted that if things had been different I would have been a candidate for her first one-night stand.'

Sofia froze in the act of trying to hide her non-matching underwear inside the dress she'd selected because it was near the top of the heap. Heat swept over her from top to toe.

'I could turn my back or leave the room while you dress,' he went on, his voice making the back of Sofia's neck prickle. 'Or, if I'm making you that uncomfortable, I'm prepared to try and book you a room somewhere. But before doing any of that, I really do want to point out—' his pause grew long before he finished softly '—that things *are* different now.'

Slowly, Sofia straightened up, her clothes scattering around her feet. Though the damp towel was cooling, her temperature was climbing. He was right. She was no longer a member of staff. Her mouth went dry at the possibilities that flashed into her mind.

When she didn't speak and didn't move, Levi waited. And waited. Making it obvious that it was her decision. All down to her.

Slowly, clutching the towel, she took a step towards him. Two.

In moments Levi had dumped his laptop, swung his feet to the floor and was there, the clean scent of him reaching out to her. Her heart went crazy, launching itself around her ribcage and bouncing all the air out of her lungs. She looked up at him and, slowly, he smiled, as if her eyes had already said what her voice hadn't.

Because he was closing in to kiss her.

As the blood pounded in her ears, his lips found hers and she angled her head, noticing how well, how easily, they fitted together. He made a hoarse noise in the back of his throat and his arms dropped around her to scoop her up against the hardness of his body.

Sofia could scarcely control her breathing. Groaning, she pressed against him, finding the ridge of his arousal, rising up on tiptoe, savouring the feel of him, of his tongue stroking hers, getting every last atom of pleasure out of the kiss and only dimly aware of her towel slipping.

Levi's hands began travelling over the skin the departing towel exposed, learning the curve of her spine and then the roundness of her buttocks. She gasped. It was as if the whole world had gone away but, before it left, set every one of her nerve endings on fire.

If she'd ever thought a one-night stand – or even one-afternoon stand – would be hurried and shallow, it seemed as if Levi was setting out to prove her wrong. Every movement was slow – except when he pulled away to ditch his T-shirt in a single rapid movement.

She slid her hands over his naked back, gasping as her breasts went skin-on-skin against his chest, hearing him breathe her name.

'Take down your hair,' he muttered hoarsely. 'I've never seen it loose.'

With shaking hands she located the band and clips and pulled them out. Her hair slithered free over her shoulders and down her back.

'You're beautiful.' His fingers threaded their way slowly through the mass as he nibbled her lips, her neck. She let her head tip back, sliding tentative fingers into his waistband, locating the button and zip.

'Go on,' he groaned. He was flushed, eyes glittering, obviously completely into the slow, erotic foreplay of undressing one another.

Breathlessly, she laughed. 'Going to.'

Taking her time, she watched her fingers slowly undo the fastenings, test the texture of the skin beneath. Apart from the rapid rise and fall of his chest he was motionless, letting her take the lead.

She hooked her thumbs in his waistband and drew his cargo shorts and boxers down together until he sprang free and she could hold him against her, savouring his incredible heat as she rubbed him against the sensitive skin of her belly.

Levi shook his feet free of his clothes. Somewhere along the way her towel had hit the floor, she realised giddily as he swung her from her feet and headed for the bed. He laid her down and she had an instant's awareness of the cool, crisp cotton of the sheet and then Levi was on her and it was his firm hot flesh that took all of her attention.

His mouth burned trails across the slope of her breasts. Her breath caught, her fingers in his hair as he gave her all of his focus, stoking her excitement with his tongue, his lips, his hands.

He'd settled himself between her legs and she thought she'd go mad with frustration as he pressed against her but didn't enter. Tilting her pelvis, she reached down for him.

'Sloooooooow down, Sofia. Let's make it intense,' he whispered, his breath cooling her skin where he'd just licked it. He rocked gently, maddeningly against her, not leaving room for her hand to slip between them again. 'I've barely started exploring. We've got until six o'clock.' He consulted a small clock on the bedside. 'And it's only one.'

Sucked into this world of sensation, she gave herself up to the feel of Levi's body on hers, his teeth raking gently down her neck or pulling at her earlobe while she embarked upon an exploration of her own, enjoying the hard planes of his body, the silky hair that dusted his skin. Now she'd slowed down to his satisfaction, he gave her full access, groaning when she made him twitch in her hands, his eyes all but rolling back in his head when she pushed him onto his back so she could take him in her mouth.

Finally, he leaned over to drag a bag from beneath the bedside table and fumble until he found a condom. He rolled it on and brought her over on top of him. 'Now,' he murmured and finally, slowly, she slid him inside her.

And then they stopped the slow stuff and raced for the line.

Afterwards, while her breathing returned to normal, Sofia lay half on Levi and half tangled in the sheets, boneless, heavy, damp, her cheek against his chest as she listened to his still-hurrying heart. Her hair was sticking to her skin and to his. She scooped it up and tucked it back behind her shoulder.

He lay on his back, one arm about her and his hand cupping her buttock as he nestled her closer. 'You know we have to do this all again soon?'

'Sounds good, but why?' she murmured, eyes closed.

'Because I want to be your one-night stand but it's only—' he turned his head towards the clock '—four-thirty. A one-afternoon stand doesn't count.'

She laughed, a tingle walking slowly down her spine. 'But I've got to talk to Amy when she comes off shift at six,' she reminded him. 'I've no idea what to say to her.'

Instantly, he sobered. 'What did she mean when she mentioned Spain?' Dropping a kiss on her hair he disentangled himself enough to half-roll out of bed and reach a door beneath the dressing table that proved to be a mini fridge stocked with several bottles of cold water. He handed her one and they rearranged themselves so they could drink.

Sofia gave a 'Mmm' as the chilly liquid slid silkily down her throat. 'To be honest, I thought going on to Spain together was just one of those subjects you play with over a glass of wine.' Then her phone began to ring. 'Hang on.' She abandoned the conversation to swing her legs over the side of the bed and search for her handbag amidst the mess on the floor.

He let his hand trail down her back. 'Do you think she knew that?'

Sofia sighed. 'I thought so, but . . .' She located her bag beneath the open lid of her case, fished out her phone, stared at the lit screen and pulled a face. 'It's Benedetta. Whatever she wants can wait.' She didn't intend to let their afterglow be dimmed by Benedetta's latest gripe. The ringtone ceased and the screen gradually dimmed as she rolled back into bed, settling against Levi to enjoy the feel of his skin. 'If Amy thinks the plans we made were in earnest then it'll be horrible for her if I leave alone.' Though, right this second, still boneless from Levi's love-making, she shied away from making plans to go at all. Trying to find another job in Montelibertà was a possibility but saying it out loud might make Levi think she was making today something it wasn't, especially as his life was far away from here in a small town in the middle of England. 'I take it you're not ready to come clean with Amy?'

He breathed in sharply, his chest inflating and his stomach hollowing beneath its scattering of golden hair. 'I didn't think the decision could get any harder – but what if you two go off? Can I let her go without telling her? On the other hand, will she fly off the handle and vanish somewhere on her own if I do? My biggest fear is her encountering someone who's even more of a creep than Davide and not having friends around her . . .' He kicked restlessly at the sheet. 'Maybe I should ring Freya and Stephen again, but they don't seem to see the way through this any more clearly than I do. None of us has experience of the situation.'

Sofia's heart lurched. 'I suppose I could hang on for a few days but that's only putting off—'

Her phone began to ring again, *Benedetta* flashing on the screen. Mentally girding her loins, she grabbed it from the bed, pressed the green phone icon and lifted the handset to her ear. '*Pronto.*' Sofia had no problem with Italian on the phone. She'd got used to conversations with Aldo while she cooked in the kitchen, unable to see the movement of his lips or pick up clues from his expression while he lay in the dining room they'd made into a bedroom.

Benedetta sounded formal and wary. 'I would like to talk to you. Please come to my office.'

Surprised, Sofia took a swig from her water bottle. 'If you just want to scream at me again, then no thanks. I've cleared my room. You can calculate my remaining wages and put the money in my account.'

Benedetta made an impatient noise. 'I have something to offer you but I'd prefer to do it in a civilised way, in person.'

Although intrigued now, Sofia made herself sound offhand. 'I suppose that would be OK. I could be in your office in half an hour but I need to be free at six.'

'Fine.' Benedetta's voice was clipped but she ended the call with no further objections.

Sofia relayed an English version of the conversation to Levi. 'I think she was a bit irked that I didn't rush straight down to hang on her every word. But I need another shower.'

Instantly, the slight frown he'd been wearing vanished as a lazy smile took over his face. 'You don't think the just-got-out-of-bed-after-an-afternoon-of-fantastic-sex look will be helpful?'

She laughed as she made for the bathroom but she felt a tingle of something down her spine at the word 'fantastic'. So it wasn't just her who'd thought so.

Chapter Twelve

For Amy the afternoon dragged. She was awarded an extension to her half-hour break as she'd had no opportunity to organise anything to eat around her shift and, feeling the need for solitude, she used it to wander down the hill to buy a vegetable calzone from the little kiosk then perch on a wall in a patch of shade to eat it.

If Sofia was leaving, Amy was leaving, she decided, though her heart thumped at the idea of beginning somewhere new when she was almost settled in Italy. But Amy didn't want to be here without Sofia; Davide was a weirdo and Benedetta was a rules freak.

An unexpected wave of homesickness swept over her, but when she tried to imagine returning home to Germany all she felt was misery. Losing her appetite, she threw the rest of the calzone to a hungry-looking brown dog in a nearby garden. The dog sniffed it then looked at her with a *what is THIS?* expression.

'Sorry, I would have bought chicken if I'd known I was going to give it to you.' She slid off the wall and dusted the back of her dress.

The dog gave a forgiving wag of its tail and settled down to trying to eat the cheese and spit out the veg.

'Eat up, little dog. You look too thin.' Then Amy felt sorry for saying that because people often told her she was 'too thin', as if she could help it. She thought of all the times her dad – Stephen – had put his arms round her and said, 'Don't take any notice. You're exactly right as you are.' Which made tears fill her eyes to remember the last time she'd seen him and her mum, everyone mouldy and angry at each other, and Amy screaming and crackling and banging so no one could get near.

The dog was just sniffing the spat-out vegetables as if checking it hadn't left anything edible behind when a woman came out of the house and noticed the mess on her garden path. She planted her hands on her hips and demanded something of the dog and then of Amy, in tones of outrage.

'*Scusi. Inglese*,' Amy muttered as she backed off. The dog put its head down and slunk into the house and Amy, assuming much the same demeanour, stole off up the hill back to Casa Felice.

When six o'clock finally came around she could hardly wait for Matteo to arrive to take over her section before dragging off her apron, so keyed up was she in case Sofia hadn't kept her word and had cleared her stuff and gone. She skirted the car park and crossed the utility yard, holding her breath because of the whiff from the bins.

But relief broke over her as she cleared the yard gate and found Sofia sitting on the grass outside the staff garden. She was talking to Levi, who lounged on the grass beside her, but she got up when she saw Amy, brushing dry grass stalks from her blue and gold summer dress.

'Hiya.' Sofia gave her a big smile. Her hair was loose

and hung down her back. 'Do you have plans tonight? Or do you fancy dinner with us down in the town?'

Amy actually did have plans to meet Noemi but she could easily text her and push them back. She didn't want Sofia leaving Montelibertà without her. 'Have I got time to change?'

'Of course.' Sofia seemed very smiley for somebody who'd been given the boot. Her earlier, red-faced, flashing-eyed anger had completely vanished.

Levi just stood, thumbs hooked lightly in his pockets, smiling slightly. Amy gave him a shy smile and rushed off to her room to change. She liked Levi and didn't mind that he seemed to be included in the dinner thing.

Quarter of an hour later she felt much cooler in a blue polka dot playsuit and could enjoy the walk down into Montelibertà, the worst of the heat having gone out of the sun. Levi knew a restaurant that wasn't too expensive, which was good, because Amy was still getting used to not having parents around to pay for her. Levi offered but Amy, following Sofia's lead, opted to pay her own way.

Sofia said the place was a *tavola calda*. You queued up at a cabinet full of food and decided how many things you wanted. The server wrote it down, tore the order from her pad and you took it to pay at a till, then took the receipt back to claim your food. It seemed remarkably easy on the servers compared with charging about Il Giardino with a heavy tray up on your shoulder.

Once you had your food, if you were Italian, it seemed, you stayed indoors where there was air conditioning. If you were British or American you carried your tray outside and sat in the garden under a cane parasol and did battle with the heat and the flies.

Sofia, though half Italian, headed out into the garden.

Once they'd unloaded their trays – beer and pizza for Levi, white wine and pasta with salad for Sofia, Aperol Spritz and lasagna for Amy – they sat down to eat.

Unable to contain her impatience, Amy launched her first question before she'd even tasted her lasagna. 'So what's been going on? Are you sacked? What was it about, anyway?'

Sofia chewed and swallowed a mouthful of pasta. 'I was sacked for swearing loudly at my uncle in Il Giardino.' Between mouthfuls, Sofia regaled her with the story of what her uncle had said to make Sofia lose her temper.

Amy could hardly believe it. 'And you were looking forward to meeting him as well! What a shit,' she declared hotly.

Sofia tilted her head. 'True. But it turns out that he's a shit with a hotel of his own. Have you noticed that large white building on the other side of town? You can see it from Casa Felice. That's Hotel Alba, owned by Gianni Bianchi, and it seems that Benedetta and he are at daggers drawn. She's decided that employing me will piss him off so she's not only unsacked me—' she paused impressively '—she's offered me training and promotion.'

'Get off it!' Amy gasped, fork dangling unheeded from her fingers.

'All true. I'd start by shadowing Aurora on reception, learning the booking system, room allocation and admin, handling complaints and guest requests, then go solo when I've learned the ropes. Shifts are seven till three or three till eleven, so eight hours instead of seven, but I'd never have to start as early as breakfast in the residents' dining room or stay so late as the evening shift in Il Giardino.'

'Awesome!' Amy could have cheered. Sofia was staying!

Then, realising Sofia hadn't said that, Amy tagged on apprehensively, 'You're taking it, aren't you?'

Sofia sipped her wine, eyes thoughtful above the rim of her glass. 'I've agreed to tell Benedetta my decision at noon tomorrow.'

'But it means you'd stay.' Amy almost wailed in panic. 'Take it, Sofia!'

Levi, who had eaten his way methodically through his pizza, glanced sidelong at Sofia.

Sofia returned her glass to the table and turned it in precise little circles, a tiny V between her eyebrows. 'True.' Her eyes were full of warmth and understanding but also a hint of warning. 'Thank you for wanting me to stay, but Benedetta's not the most consistent of employers, is she? She's sacked both of us at different times and gone back on it, and it seems she's only offered me this opportunity to spite my uncle. If I take the job it means more money and a different uniform and a chance to get some training that could stand me in good stead in the future. It also means I can leave on my own terms when the time comes, rather than having to make a decision in reaction to one of her fleeting rages. But it also leaves me open to being in the same situation all over again.'

'Oh.' To hide her disappointment, Amy fell to picking over her lasagna with waning enthusiasm. Sofia didn't seem to want to be rushed into anything. Amy could almost hear her mum's voice saying *your trouble is you always want everything to just be all right, Amy Webber. Instead of just grabbing at what you think's the simplest solution, why not think the situation through? Think about consequences.* Not that her mum had appeared to have thought too deeply when she had sex with Amy's father. Amy was the living, breathing consequence.

Again that hollow tug of homesickness for her family and their tall house with its steep roof and mustard-painted walls. Familiar. Safe. She wondered how long it would be before her family stopped expecting her to come home. They might let Kris have her room because it was the biggest and had an en suite, or turn it into a guest room for when Gran and Granddad visited. She'd been on Louis and Kris's Instagrams this morning and shed hot, silent tears at pictures of them playing football in the garden and hanging upside down from the climbing things in the park. Pictures of life going on without her.

She wished she'd never signed up to give blood with Della and Maddalyn. Then she wouldn't have known about her dad not being her dad and her mum having kept the secret that hurt everyone so much. She wouldn't have got so blind with anger that she'd looked for ways to hurt them for being so stupid – her mum for having some sordid shag and her dad for being gullible enough not to recognise that Amy wasn't his.

She dropped her fork and reached for her Aperol Spritz. It was sweet on her tongue as she sucked it through a straw. What would she do if Sofia left? Levi would go soon, because he was just a tourist, then she'd be back to worrying about Davide and his grumpy mother. Noemi and Matteo were going to uni before long. Uni, like Amy had been supposed to do before she binned her exams and went off travelling.

'If I take up Benedetta's offer then I won't be working with you. Not in Il Giardino.'

Amy blinked her way out of her thoughts when she realised Sofia was addressing her again. 'That doesn't matter!' She grasped eagerly at this hint that Sofia might not be dropping out of Amy's life. Her voice had emerged all high and stupid and she sucked more of the Aperol Spritz through the straw. 'We're not always on shift together as it is. But your room would still be next to mine and—' She gulped. 'Please stay, Sofia! I can't trust anybody else, not even my pa-parents!' Her throat contracted, trapping her voice so it couldn't get out.

'Shh, Amy, don't cry.' Sofia reached over the corner of the table and gave her a hug. 'I'll give it a go.'

The relief made Amy feel weak. She knew she was going to blub like a baby because her lips were going all stupid and wavy even though she was trying to smile. Scraping back her chair, she jumped up and dashed back inside in search of the Ladies. Finding that sanctuary, she sat herself on a toilet and cried into ream after ream of toilet paper until her eyes were red and sore.

Levi watched Amy race indoors. He turned to Sofia and saw her eyes shining with tears. 'Don't you start too or I'll join in. She leaps to extremes of emotion and my heart tries to leap with her.' He had to swallow as he passed Sofia a clean napkin.

Sofia didn't lose control like Amy but blotted her eyes once, twice, took a deep breath and a deeper slug from her wine glass. 'That was unexpectedly tricky.'

'But thanks.' He took several gulps from his beer to encourage the heat behind his nose to vanish. 'Really. You don't know how grateful I am. I hope the new job works out OK and that you won't regret it.' Everything about Sofia's manner told him that she wasn't convinced but wasn't sure if there was a better alternative.

'Likewise. I'm not sure what I've done to make her so attached to me.'

As Amy hadn't reappeared, he took Sofia's hand beneath

the table, warm and small in his. 'You were kind to her when she felt as if the whole world was against her. You heard what she said about her parents—' Responsibility felt like a wet, clammy rock in his stomach. He shook his head. 'Fucksake. I was even younger than her when I had the fling that resulted in her. She'd probably hate me if she knew who I was.'

Her hand squeezed his. 'You know that the longer you leave it to tell her, the worse it's going to be?' Her eyes were great dark pools of compassion.

The rock inside him rolled, until it felt as if it was squashing his heart. 'In principle. It's just that, while she doesn't know, I can hang around and see she's OK. Once I tell her . . . If she *does* hate me . . .'

'Let's not even go there.' Sofia took a big breath and blotted her eyes again. 'When she comes back we ought to get another round of drinks to celebrate my "promotion". Along with my smart new uniform I'll have a name badge.'

'Yeah,' he agreed gloomily. 'And you'll be off-limits again.'

'Eh, eh!' she protested in a fair imitation of Davide. 'You promised me a one-night stand. As I won't accept Benedetta's offer until tomorrow I'm still officially sacked and I intend to take advantage of that.'

Lust slithered through him as he looked at her smiling mouth, at the upper slopes of her breasts above the neckline of her top. He was assailed by a vivid memory of his hands and mouth on that silky skin. He felt his body stir. 'I intend to let you,' he replied, dropping his voice as he saw Amy stepping back through the doorway into the garden. He let go of Sofia's hand and prepared to pretend not to notice the red eyes of the troubled daughter who'd so recently set up camp in his heart.

143

Chapter Thirteen

Levi woke Sofia in the morning with hot kisses on the nape of her neck. 'Your appointment with Benedetta isn't until noon so you're still sacked,' he murmured. 'Fancy a one-morning stand?'

Sofia wriggled her bottom languorously against his groin, making him catch his breath. 'You seem to have got to the stand part already.'

He made love to her tenderly, opening the curtains to admire her better in the morning sunlight. Her skin fascinated him, so smooth and fine, and her hair falling across his body whenever she rose above him, stroking his flesh and making him shiver. Would this ever happen again? In case it couldn't, he crushed her against him as she came until he felt like he was part of her, and his own release rushed up to carry him over the edge with her.

Later, they ordered room service and breakfasted on hot croissants and coffee. Levi's new room had no balcony – which was just as well as immediately below stood a collection of bins and crates in an area that Sofia called the utility yard.

They didn't talk about these being their last hours, but Levi saw his own regret reflected in Sofia's unconvincing smile. Not wanting to let the mood darken, after breakfast he took her hand and led her back to the bed. 'I'm going to help you realise another goal. Lie down.'

She climbed onto the bed and settled on her back with an anticipatory expression. 'Is there anything left?'

He picked up his paint palette and poured water into one of his jars, grinning as her eyes widened. 'The tattoo. Personally, I don't think you need any embellishment, but I'm going to let you see how it'd look.' Ignoring her half-hearted protests he wet a fine sable brush and loaded it heavily with Prussian Blue, then arranged himself beside her on the bed, propped on his elbow. 'Hold still.' He began with a lazy swirl across the taut skin of her belly.

'Tickles!' she protested, quivering.

'You'd have to stay stiller than this for a tattoo artist,' he observed, loading his brush again and beginning a series of tiny dots, more to make her wriggle and squirm than to accommodate any painting technique. Then he began long, slow strokes on the undersides of her breasts.

'Mmm. Mmm-*mmm*,' she breathed, eyes half-closing. 'That feels . . . Ooh! It's odd and . . . Mmm, I would never have thought being painted would be so nice. No! Not like that! It *tickles*, Levi!'

'Keep still or you'll smudge.' He laughed, abandoning the tiny flicking strokes he'd just tried. He found he obtained the result he liked with long swirling strokes of a slightly broader brush. Sofia lay still except for the occasional shiver.

Finally, he pulled her up to stand in front of the mirror to admire his handiwork. She pressed back against him, eyes hooded but bright. 'It's back to front.'

145

'Mirror images tend to be. I would have had to plan a little more to write it backwards.' He took a photo of her with his phone so she could see what he'd written in flowing script ornamented with flowers and leaves: *One awesome night ~ Levi Gunn.*

Her smile faded. 'And now it's over.'

They had just enough time to shower before Sofia's meeting with Benedetta. Levi watched the lather he smoothed over her body turn Prussian Blue before washing away.

They didn't say much as they dressed but Levi's mind circled. Amy was frightened at the idea of Sofia not working at Casa Felice. Sofia working at Casa Felice would be jeopardised if she continued to be close to Levi. The most palatable alternative seemed to be Sofia and Amy travelling on together, which would exclude Levi, as his moving on with them was so far-fetched that Amy was bound to start asking a whole shoal of questions. Yet, if he let them go alone, would he ever see his daughter again?

They'd talked around the subject for a while last night, about the chances of Sofia and Amy getting other work with accommodation in Montelibertà, or Levi moving to another hotel to get round Benedetta's irksome rule. He'd checked room availability at the other hotels in the town on his laptop – only four boutique establishments and Gianni Bianchi's much larger Hotel Alba – and struck out in all of them now the tourist season was getting in full swing. And, as Sofia pointed out, he was here to watch over Amy and that could only be done effectively from Casa Felice.

Despite the fatiguing effects of a thorough sexual workout he prowled the room, watching Sofia, seated at the dressing table, brush her hair into a glossy sheet and wind it into a big clip on the back of her head. She dug out a makeup bag from one of her cases and quickly applied eyeliner and mascara.

Done, she rose from the stool. Her eyes, which, for the past twenty-four hours had told him so much of what she was thinking and feeling, were now remote. 'OK to leave my stuff here until I've talked to Benedetta?'

He edged her closer, running his fingers up her arm. 'Sure. I need to catch up on email and talk to Wes so I intend to work from my room anyway. Just come back up when you're ready . . . if you don't think it will cause instant dismissal.'

Her smile was a shadow of its former relaxed and sultry self. 'I won't advertise where I've been and I'm sure Benedetta will realise it's better not to ask. Well.' She smoothed down her dress and for an instant her eyes shone with tears. 'I'm not sure why I feel as if I'm going to the gallows instead of a meeting about a promotion.'

When she would have moved away he stayed her a moment, trying to read her eyes. 'Are you really OK about staying? Is it going to be hard after what happened with your uncle?'

Her shoulders lifted on a sigh. 'Can't deny it was a blow. I suppose I've been harbouring hopes about the wider family I've never had, but I'm OK about staying. What I've never had I'll never miss.' She smiled wryly, touched her lips to his once, twice, then stepped out of his embrace and was gone.

For several moments he gazed at the door that closed behind her. Then, restless, he moved over to the window. Down in the yard a man was moving crates around. Apart from that, Levi could only see the side of the next building and the sky. He took out his phone and examined the photos of Sofia and her 'tattoo' – one up close and one where he'd zoomed out to include her naked breasts and a little of her laughing face.

Unable to settle to work, he paced the room for a few minutes more, then, trying to focus on the reason he was in Montelibertà, rang Freya.

'Is everything OK?' she demanded the moment she picked up. He imagined her as he'd last seen her nearly three weeks ago in Germany. In her forties she was still a striking woman but strain had etched hard lines on her face and stolen away her smile.

'Pretty much. I just wanted to update you.' He proceeded to outline yesterday's chaos, mentioning Sofia only as 'a woman who works here, someone Amy seems to feel safe with', omitting any hint that he'd just spent an amazing night with her. 'I have no idea what to do,' he admitted, as he wound down.

'I don't know either.' Freya's voice wobbled. 'Every few days she sends me a stilted little text to say she's OK. The boys say she communicates with them on social media but I'm forcing myself not to ask for details because I don't want her to stop.'

'I can see that.' He opened his laptop with his free hand.

'She's not talking to Stephen at all,' she burst out. 'He's beside himself that his reaction to – to the news is what sent her off on one. Oh, hell, everything's such a mess! I wish you could just bundle her onto your bike and bring her home again.'

Levi watched his laptop screen as it asked for his password and he tapped it in. 'It would exhibit an insulting lack of concern for Amy's wishes,' he observed. 'She's not likely to react well to that.'

Freya's voice sharpened. 'I do know my own daughter, thank you very much.'

Levi slid his finger across the track pad to move the cursor to the desktop icon that would open his email. 'Whereas I'm only just getting to know mine,' he replied softly as *Loading* appeared on the screen for an instant before a list of emails sprang up, many of them the result of Levi being copied into mail between Wes and the freelancers of The Moron Forum.

Silence.

A layer of frost coated Freya's voice when she spoke again. 'I am aware.'

He sat down on the bed, laptop in hand, kicked the covers to the floor and propped himself comfortably on the pillows. He kept his own voice level. 'Actually, I'm not sure you're thinking about anybody else's feelings in this. It's not about you, Freya. It's not about you wanting her home and seeing for yourself she's OK, you wanting her and Stephen to re-establish their relationship as a first step to you getting your comfortable life back. It's about Amy. It's about keeping her safe, so far as possible, respecting her choices, doing what has the best chance of making her happy. I get that she's only eighteen years old and she's blown off family and education while she goes travelling, but loads of teenagers do. You might also spare a thought for me – the guy you've put in a situation that leaves him no good options.'

'So I don't need to ask if you've identified yourself?'

His eye caught a notification of an email exchange between Wes and Octavia and he clicked on it. 'If I had, I'd have told you. But I don't think it's the right thing to do, because she needs friends right now. That's what I'm trying to be.'

The next silence went on so long that Levi had actually begun to read the email conversation, an innocuous exchange about some overzealous spam protection that was causing glitches behind the scenes of The Moron Forum. Finally, Freya spoke again. 'I do appreciate what you're doing. You've been out there a while now and you must have your own life to get on with.'

'I do.' He opened another email thread between Wes and Octavia. 'But Amy's my priority.' Even if she wasn't always the woman uppermost in his thoughts.

'Don't think she's not mine.' Freya's words were clipped.

Neither of them had much to say after that. Levi dropped the phone on the bed when she'd ended the call, and went onto The Moron Forum and made sure every page was running cleanly, reading threads at random to check the site was still the preserve of sardonic wit without too much input from haters. It was amazing how many people confused satirical comment with an invitation to be a keyboard warrior, picking on some celebrity, politician or social trend to flame without having anything entertaining to add.

After an hour he satisfied himself the moderators were doing their jobs, then went back to wading through emails.

He hadn't quite completed his task when Wes rang. 'Got any coming-home plans yet?' he demanded without preamble.

Levi tried to get the conversation off on the right foot. 'Things are taking longer than I'd hoped. I was just on the site when you rang. It's looking great. You're doing a fantastic job.'

Wes sounded pleased. 'Yeah, things are going OK. I rang to ask your views on starting up a new page.'

Levi was surprised he'd have had time to worry about extra work when he was there on his own. 'What do you have in mind? Wouldn't you rather wait till I get back so there's another pair of hands on deck?'

'Normally. But Octavia's so fast and so competent that I don't see any real reason to wait. It's her idea, actually: *Modern Woman* to balance *Modern Man*.'

Levi felt himself bristling. Was it just the sound of Octavia's name? 'We'd already discussed redressing that imbalance, hadn't we?' It was a bit of a stretch for Wes to present that as 'Octavia's idea'.

Wes swept that detail aside, his voice ringing with enthusiasm. 'Octavia's willing to get it up and running and moderate the forum too. I think it's a fantastic idea because the bias on the site at the moment is definitely towards men – like women are born without a sense of humour. Octavia's just what we need: sassy, irreverent, quick-witted, yet with an underlying intelligence and compassion that will attract women searching for their tribe and men who want to understand women.'

'Right.' Levi could imagine Wes reading that lot off the A4 pad that acted as a mouse mat. He'd either worked on his pitch before he rang or Octavia had given him lots of pointers, because Wes was usually a bit short on opinions regarding what women might want. He frequently referred to himself as 'never having much luck with females'. A homely guy whose friendship groups were exclusively male, in the time Levi had known him Wes had fallen violently in love twice and thrown himself into those relationships in a welter of hours at the gym, new clothes and smart haircuts. On both occasions he'd ended up with gaping wounds in his heart when the girl failed to appreciate his adoration and moved on.

Levi couldn't help recognising, with a sinking heart, the signs that Wes was falling in love once more.

Wes had been part of Levi's life since they met at uni. Stolid by nature, he seemed content to inhabit the background, his motorbike less powerful than Levi's, his enthusiasm for new ventures more moderate. Levi had driven the transformation of The Moron Forum from free-time joke to part-time career to full-on focus then runaway financial success. He was the ideas man, but he relied on Wes's calm good sense to rein him in when he needed it.

Maybe that was why Levi was having trouble with Wes taking the lead in launching a new page? He hadn't tried to trap Wes in the role of Wingman, had he?

'So, you say this initiative's come from Octavia?' he enquired hastily. 'How's it going with you two? Do you think it might get serious?'

'It's going *great*. And yes, I *do*.'

What was it about that emphatic declaration that made Levi uneasy? 'Fantastic. So it's no problem to be involved as well as working together? Some people hate that.'

'Not in the least.' Wes was all earnest enthusiasm. 'She's been using your desk and I value that, to be honest. Working on my own soon got old and Octavia, like me, thrives on a creative pool rather than isolation.'

'She's working from the *office*?' They'd never instigated a 'relationships at work' policy because it was just him and Wes except when Bookkeeper Mary tucked herself in a corner of the office for two days each week. He and Wes didn't need a relationships policy; they needed a whose-turn-is-it-to-buy-doughnuts-on-Fridays policy or a don't-swear-in-front-of-Mary-you-stupid-arse policy.

'That's right.' Something else replaced enthusiasm in Wes's voice now. A hint of warning that he wasn't going to react well to objections? Levi shoved his fingers through his hair. Why did this have to happen just when he was taking uncharacteristically prolonged leave from his desk? It felt off, Octavia coming on to him in a particularly direct manner and then, when he'd politely backed off, approaching his company with a CV of web-wise wizardry and almost instantly falling for Wes. It seemed more like the plot of a psychological thriller than reasonable human behaviour.

He decided to deal with what he could. Blocking manoeuvres and interrogations were likely to piss Wes off and it would prove a challenge on a par with climbing Everest to run the whole site on his own remotely, in between watching over Amy and keeping up his front of being in Montelibertà only to paint pretty pictures. 'OK, talk specifics about the page,' he suggested.

Listening, he paced around the room, finding a path between Sofia's cases, trying to assess the project objectively. He asked a few questions but had to admit to himself that Octavia had thought about her audience and her approach, and even trialled a few thread topics amongst her social media contacts. Apart from a distrust of her, he had no reason not to support her initiative. 'OK, let's give it a go,' he agreed. Then added casually, 'But I'd like a co-moderator on the page, please.'

Wes immediately sounded wary. 'Why should her page be co-moderated? Some of the other pages aren't.'

'True. But some are. And we've never let a moderator go solo that we've known for such a short time. There's no downside to continuing that policy so far as I can see.'

'Oh-kay.' Wes drew the word out as if to indicate it wasn't OK at all.

'Anything else we need to talk about?' Levi asked when he'd waited in vain for Wes to share what was on his mind.

'Nothing from me. See you when you finally make an appearance.'

'Great. Thanks for keeping everything going.' Levi waited. 'Wes?' He removed his phone from his ear and checked the screen. *Call ended*. Had Wes really just turned sulky because Levi wouldn't give his girlfriend sole control of a new page?

He threw the phone on the bed and dropped down after it, skin prickling with the discomfort of not being in his own office at the beating heart of The Moron Forum. Specifically, not being there when Octovia was, and Wes was behaving weirdly.

Then everything that had happened in that bed last night floated into his mind and he wished Sofia's bucket list had included a ten- or twenty-night stand instead of the usual one.

Chapter Fourteen

Sofia plodded down the main staircase as if someone had poured concrete into her shoes. Crossing reception, she glanced out to the sun-splashed Il Giardino and saw Amy speeding towards the kitchen hatch, an empty tray dangling from her hand. Catching sight of her, Amy held up her free hand, fingers firmly crossed, her brow creased apprehensively. Sofia managed a reassuring wave.

'*Ciao,* Sofia!'

She turned to see Aurora behind the reception desk, easily the best of the Morbidellis in Sofia's opinion, but couldn't summon up a smile to match hers. '*Ciao*, Aurora,' she replied, trailing through the door marked *Solo staff*.

She arrived at Benedetta's office reflecting that fulfilling Aldo's request to visit Montelibertà was turning out to be a lot more complicated than she'd expected: Gianni's snottiness; Benedetta's flakiness; Amy tugging at Sofia's heartstrings; and Levi capturing Sofia's attention in a wholly different way. And now she was about to condemn herself to spending her shifts on the front desk when the sunshine of Il Giardino or the terrace was much more what she'd had in mind when she came here. Not responsibility. Not being stuck indoors.

She'd spent way too long incarcerated in the house while Aldo had needed her. Then, it had been worth it. But now?

'*Buon giorno*,' she murmured as she stepped into the brown leatherette dullness of the office and though the door only clicked shut behind her it sounded in her imagination like the clang of a prison cell.

Benedetta was smart and unsmiling in a suit, manicured and made up. A folder lay open before her on the desk, presumably Sofia's staff file as she could see a photocopy of the ID page of her passport, taken when she'd arrived nearly three weeks ago. '*Buon giorno*. Are you to continue working at Casa Felice?'

Sofia took a breath. She thought of the man she'd left in one of Casa Felice's rooms a couple of floors above her head. Then she thought of Amy – red-faced and furious at Davide, white and anxious about being left alone. 'I'd love to.' As Benedetta began to smile and she saw the outside world receding she added desperately, 'but I'd prefer to stay in my current job.'

Benedetta was already shaking her head. 'I am sorry. I've added a local person to the waiting staff. The job I'm offering you is the one we discussed last night. I need another person on the reception roster.'

'Oh,' Sofia said unhappily. 'Then thank you very much. I'll take it.'

'Good!' Benedetta's smile broadened. 'You will be an asset. You know how to talk to people, you are smart and listen to guests' views. You're a team player.' She paused to fold her hands and frown sternly over the top of them. 'There will be no repeat of yesterday's incident in Il Giardino, of course.'

'Of course.'

'I'm making an allowance for your uncle acting unforgivably. I have known Gianni Bianchi for many years and find him a difficult man. Until you let yourself to be goaded into an argument with him you had been cheerful and bright.'

Sofia nodded.

'You must also remember to follow the rules. You understand the importance of the rules. Yes?' Benedetta prompted.

'Yes.' Sofia kissed goodbye to the memories of Levi below her, above her, curled around her, while Benedetta launched into a lecture on attitudes, particularly of those she considered permanent staff, which now included Sofia. Sofia didn't worry too much about the permanency aspect. If there was no time for a simple resignation letter she could work Benedetta up into a rage and get the sack again.

'Yesterday and today will be considered your days off,' Benedetta continued. 'You will join Aurora tomorrow morning at the reception desk at seven. Wear your black dress without the apron to begin with and Aurora will take your sizes and arrange your new uniform.' She hesitated. 'Please note the personal grooming standards of Aurora and me.' Her gaze dropped tellingly to Sofia's neat, unvarnished nails, making Sofia want to curl up her fingers to hide them.

Feeling progressively glummer, she listened to advice on wearing her hair 'neatly' up – 'messy' or 'casual' updos were the preserve of waitresses, apparently – and selecting shoes with a heel. 'I understand,' she acknowledged. The job wasn't sounding any more appealing.

Finally, Benedetta signalled the end of the interview by rising from the desk and opening the door. Sofia escaped, hurrying past the front desk where Aurora was tied up with a guest, and took the lift back up to Levi's floor. His corridor was quiet. Probably most of the guests were out for the day or enjoying a leisurely lunch.

When she reached his room she tapped lightly and he immediately opened the door. He didn't look any more cheerful than she felt. His laptop was open on the bed and his phone beside it.

She paused, suddenly unsure of one-night-stand protocol. 'I took the job.'

'Right.'

They looked at one another.

She spoke first. 'I'd better move my stuff back.'

He glanced at the stacked cases, the top one spilling its contents. 'I'll help you.'

She shook her head. 'Asking for trouble. The luggage has wheels so I can manage.' As he watched, she bundled her things into the top case, fetched her sponge bag from the bathroom and borrowed the bin liner for yesterday's still-damp uniform. She glanced at the tumbled bed and her imagination selected images from last night – and yesterday afternoon and this morning – to set fire to her cheeks.

She fumbled the zipping of her suitcase, feeling ridiculously coy over the sight of his hands and the memory of what they'd done to her. She straightened, yanking both cases upright and pulling out their handles. 'Well—'

He was standing very close. 'Are you reporting for duty straightaway?'

'Not till tomorrow. When I've dumped this lot I'm going to walk into town, I think.'

His hands settled on her waist. 'Fancy lunch?'

Her laugh was breathless. 'We're back to the staff/guest thing.'

He smoothed her hair. 'How about we happen to fancy a walk in the country park at the same time? I'll bring lunch. I want to talk.'

She studied him but his face didn't give any clues as to what he wanted to talk about. 'OK.'

He slid his arms around her and dipped his head so he could kiss her properly, prompting her to abandon the case handles and wind her arms around his neck, closing her eyes as desire swept through her at his body touching hers all the way up.

Finally, she disengaged. 'I'd better go.' But it was only when she was back in her old room and changed into shorts and a T-shirt, her hair brushed into a loose side ponytail, that her heart rate returned to normal. It could have just been the effects of manhandling two heavy cases and a backpack down the steps from the yard to the staff gate, of course. Could have been.

She groaned aloud as she looked around her plain-but-adequate room and began forlornly to restore her possessions to the spots they'd occupied for the past few weeks.

She'd arranged to meet Levi at two-thirty in the same place as before, away from the main trails that linked green clearings between twisted pines and stately oaks. Levi was already seated on the wispy grass swatting away insects when Sofia arrived, out of breath from the trek uphill. Beside him was a lurid blue cool bag. He smiled and rose to kiss her, though the smile was perfunctory and the kiss a tender but almost distracted brush of his lips on hers.

He unzipped the cool bag as he sat himself back down. 'I got the lady at the kiosk down the road to put us together a lunch. Apart from the bottles of wine and water it's all hidden in these little boxes.'

'Intriguing,' she said.

As he was obviously prioritising eating over talking, Sofia joined him in opening boxes of various salads, cubes of pecorino cheese, rolled-up slices of prosciutto and chunks of foccacia bread. Plastic cutlery and glasses were tucked in the corners of the bag. The kiosk lady was evidently adept at supplying packed lunches for tourists.

They sat companionably on the grass, munching glowing red baby tomatoes dressed in olive oil along with crispy green leaves and twirly pasta salad. Levi was quiet, contemplating the tree-clothed slopes of the neighbouring peaks spread out before them as he ate.

'Well, I know why I'm down in the dumps,' Sofia said eventually, wiping her hands on a paper napkin and taking up her wineglass. 'Why don't you tell me why you are?'

He shot her a rueful glance. 'I didn't mean to be bad company but I had a conversation with Wes while you were at your interview and it's left me . . .' He paused to pick up his wine glass and touch it to Sofia's. Because it was plastic it made a pathetic whisper of a sound instead of a *clink*. 'I don't know how to describe how it's left me. Not exactly worried, not exactly anxious, but definitely unsettled. Negative. Feeling I should be there to properly assess what's going on. Wes and I built The Moron Forum out of nothing and a lot of people depend on it for income.'

Sofia listened in silence as he went on to outline how oddly he felt Wes was behaving and how encroaching he found Wes's girlfriend. 'Do you think the site's under threat?'

His shoulders moved in a big sigh. 'I haven't really got any reason to think that. Not a concrete reason. Just . . .'

'A hunch?'

'I suppose that's all it is.' Once again he shifted his gaze to the vista before them.

Heart slipping down to somewhere near her feet, Sofia thought she could hear what he wasn't saying. 'You're going home to Cambridgeshire to sort it out.'

He swatted moodily at a wasp, his smile crooked when he turned to look at her. 'Not immediately, but I've got to go back sometime. Amy might drift around Europe for months and I can't hover like a guardian angel indefinitely.' In the sunlight his eyes were the ice-blue of the topaz Sofia had admired in a jeweller's window in town. 'But the thought of leaving her is tearing at me. I know she's an adult but she seems so vulnerable that I feel sick every time I acknowledge that I've got to leave her – if not right away then soon.' He hesitated, gaze intense. 'I've no right to ask you this, but will you keep in touch with me about Amy?'

Sofia's first instinct was to reply with a prompt 'Yes, of course!' to see relief relax the muscles of his face and know that she'd made his heart lighter. But she paused. Then she spoke slowly, trying to choose the right words. 'Coming here was planned as only the first step in a journey that was meant to take a couple of years. Not just a literal but a metaphorical journey, all about freedom and having only myself to consider after spending half my life as a carer. I've discharged my promises to Dad – except, perhaps the one about being happy. That's been patchy – so, much as I care for Amy, there's an irony in picking up a new responsibility to tie me to her life and schedule. What you're asking is too nebulous and open-ended for me to blithely say yes.

161

'How would it actually work?' she queried. 'What if Amy wants to move on alone? What if she falls in with a bad crowd or gets a boyfriend, will you expect me to report to you? If so, how will she feel if she finds out? What if I decide to move on and it's somewhere Amy doesn't fancy, or can't go, or I just want to be on my own?' She saw disappointment dawning in his eyes but slogged on, needing him to see the whole picture. 'Will you tell Amy that you're her father before you go? It's quite important to acknowledge that if you *don't* then I'm joining in your deception by not telling her. But if you *do*, I can only guess at the effect it might have on her. I don't have any particular skills to see her through it.'

For several seconds he didn't reply. His gaze searched the landscape as if somewhere on a distant grey-green hillside there might be a tree with answers growing on it. Finally, he turned back, brows coming together in a straight line. 'I wonder what it is about you that encourages people to ask you to make promises?'

It wasn't what she'd expected. She'd anticipated a persuasive argument that would allow him to climb on his bike and roar off home to England with a quiet mind. Dismayed at how hollow that mental image made her feel, she sighed. 'Wish I knew.'

'I'm sorry, I had no right to ask. My mind's running in circles, hunting for a way to face the prospect of leaving her here. Frightened of the truth because if I tell her . . . well, everything changes. I can't unsay it. There's no reset button.' His knuckles whitened as his fists tightened. 'I've painted myself into a corner and I don't know how to jump out. I was reeling at the news I had a daughter when Freya asked me to come out here to check she was safe, and what could I do but try to help? I thought Freya would automatically know the best thing to do. Now I know Amy and her somewhat black-and-white view of the world I see that in some ways I've made things worse. No way can I see her reacting well if I let on I've been deceiving her for weeks. And the thought of her refusing to see me again . . .' He shook his head as his words dried up.

Sofia found it hard to offer a positive slant. Amy saw her world as having been rocked by deceit. To learn that one of her newly formed alliances was based on more deceit wasn't going to help her learn to trust again. 'If you could have the time over, how would you handle it?' she asked, trying to come at the problem from another direction.

'I'm not sure how I'd handle Freya's plea for help,' he said tersely, ripping up a handful of wiry grass. 'But, that aside, I suppose I'd write to Amy and introduce myself. Explain things from my perspective and ask if she wanted to meet me. Give her control of the situation instead of rushing in.'

He looked so dejected that Sofia's heart ached. 'But you rushed in to help her. Not to take over.'

'Is that how she'll see it? I'm coming round to the realisation that my first steps have been ill advised and now I'm frightened any next step will be wrong.'

Sofia took his hand – not the one that was ripping up more and more grass as if creating a bald patch was relieving his feelings, but the other one. 'Are you leaving straightaway?'

His hand, hot and dry, tightened around hers. 'I have my room until this time next week – Friday the twenty-second of June – so if nothing else happens at home I'll be here till then. But I can't stay for ever.'

He sounded so bleak that Sofia leaned her cheek against the point of his shoulder, gazing at the hazy pinky beige head of the next peak. 'I'll try and stay with her for a while. And I'll keep your secret because I think telling her the truth right now will only underscore that she can't rely on anybody.'

'Thank you,' he murmured. 'You know—' he paused to swallow '—it's possible that my daughter will never know I'm her father. And if we lose touch this summer and she doesn't return home then I might never see her again.'

The dismay in his voice made Sofia wrap her arms around him and hug him tight. But that was about the only comfort she could offer. Because he was right.

Chapter Fifteen

For Sofia, the next week crawled by. She thought she caught a glimpse of Gianni Bianchi in town and felt irritated when it wasn't him. She would have liked to stick her nose in the air and stalk past.

She began training with Aurora, glad it was her because she was as honest and open as her brother was sly, and as even-tempered as her mother was mercurial. The best thing about her new role was not working with Davide, who now accorded her only the briefest of nods if their paths crossed. Sofia was trying to like him more because Aurora had explained how much her brother had been hurt by their father's departure when Davide had been only ten. Having 'daddy issues' explained a lot about his bad attitude.

The worst thing about her new job proved to be Sofia discovering she had an Achilles heel. She'd comfortably speak Italian in person or on the phone, but when she turned to the wheezy old computer and its booking system she felt as if she barely knew the language at all.

It would have been much easier to read and understand

a paragraph of text with whole sentences and context to aid her but the computer so often proffered single words, short phrases or even abbreviations, and never having used an Italian computer she had no idea of the basic IT terms. Then there was new vocabulary specific to the hotel industry. Check-out sheets with ticks next to headings expressed as initials could be frankly bewildering.

And all the time she was stuck in a suit and heels at a desk instead of outdoors in the sun. Her hair was up in a tight little ball instead of a comfy ponytail. Her nails were painted – though they looked amateur next to Aurora's.

She didn't see much of Levi. Very much aware of Benedetta's beady eye, she didn't seek him out and, as she was no longer waiting on tables, their paths rarely crossed. When they did they smiled and carried on, because Sofia was a member of staff and Levi was a guest. An increasingly solemn guest but still a guest.

Sofia worked a mixture of early and late shifts. Check-in and check-out duties quickly bored her. Guests posed questions that she had to find answers to on the internet, making her feel that they could as easily have done it for themselves on their phones.

The only good thing about taking the job was that Amy seemed reassured by Sofia's continued presence. They managed to arrange a certain amount of time together, to share a meal or a drink or just to sit in the tunnel of greenery outside the staff accommodation. They were spending Thursday evening on the bench outside their rooms when Amy insisted the vine still scraped on the fly screen at her window at night.

'I don't see how it can!' protested Sofia. 'Look! It's tied up like a bondage victim and can't possibly reach your window.'

Though Amy giggled, she insisted she'd heard it just the evening before. 'It always seems to be between one and two in the morning. Maybe that's when I rouse between cycles of sleep. We learned about that last year in school.'

Sofia paused, gazing at Amy's window. 'Really? Every night?'

'Not every. I think I've heard it about three times this week.'

On her next shift Sofia pulled up the staff rotas, to which she now had access. Thoughtfully, she identified three nights recently when Davide had worked the evening shift in Il Giardino, finishing around 1 a.m., while Amy had worked the earlier shift and could have been in bed by then.

Taking up her phone on her next break she texted Levi and explained the situation, receiving an instant reply.

Levi: When is the little shit next on late shift when Amy's not?

Sofia: *Tonight.*

Levi: You and Amy make sure you're safely indoors and don't come out if you hear a noise.

Gleefully, Sofia shared the news with Amy, who was indignant to learn it might be Davide disturbing her sleep and inclined to mutter promises of foul retribution. She readily agreed to leave it to Levi though and huddled up with Sofia at the window with the light out at quarter to one in the morning. Scarcely had they settled when they saw the dark shadow of a man step over the little picket gate and hide behind a handy shrub.

'Levi!' Amy whispered, gripping Sofia's arm so tightly that the circulation almost halted.

Then came twenty-five long and boring minutes before another shadowy figure stepped carefully over the gate and crept towards Amy's window. The scraping noise barely reached Sofia and Amy but it was enough for Levi to shoot out from behind his shrub like a yeti bellowing '*RAAHHHHHH!*'

Davide squealed like a frightened pig, nearly falling to the ground in terror, cursing and swearing in Italian as he slipped and slid his way back to the gate, almost unmanning himself in his haste to scramble over it.

Amy screamed with laughter, snatching open the door to throw herself on Levi with a huge hug. 'That was awesome! Did you see him run? What a wuss.'

Sofia watched from her doorway as Levi returned the hug. 'Confronting him was also an option but this was more fun. You two better get into your own rooms while I disappear,' he whispered, 'just in case Davide tries to get you in trouble by sneaking to his mother that there's a man hanging out near your rooms.'

'But how would he explain having been here to know?' demanded Amy, nevertheless taking a step towards her room.

'He might think of something.' Levi looked at Sofia for a moment, raised a hand in farewell and turned and stepped back over the gate. Sofia waved back before she closed her door, though she couldn't resist peeping out through the window again just in case he reappeared.

He didn't, but a text popped up on her phone.

Levi: Hopefully that will keep the little bastard out of Amy's hair for a bit. x

She sent a reply echoing the sentiment just so she could send a kiss back.

The next day, Friday, Sofia was working the afternoon shift when Levi came to the desk. Aurora stepped forward to greet him and they spent several minutes in deep discussion while Sofia was distracted by what seemed like an ever-ringing phone. After he left, sending Sofia the ghost of a wink, Aurora observed, 'Our English artist must like Casa Felice. He has booked for another week.'

Sofia couldn't help a small hop of her heart but kept her smile no more than politely interested. 'He's lucky you could accommodate him.'

Aurora nodded. 'Today is the twenty-second of June. Once we move into July it will not be possible unless we receive cancellations. All fifty rooms are booked from July the first to September the second.'

'That's good for Casa Felice.' Sofia bent her attention to the check-out sheets spewing from the printer while her heart settled back into what had become its usual state – slow and slightly heavy.

Another week dragged by. Sofia began to feel as if she'd been sewn into her suit and glued behind the reception desk. Once off duty she couldn't wait to get into more comfortable clothes and into the fresh air and sunshine. One afternoon, she strode through town and took the road that wound up between stone houses to the cemetery to leave fresh flowers for her grandparents – more to annoy Gianni if he noticed than because she felt the urge to make it a regular thing. While she was there she gazed down on Hotel Alba and thought sadly of the contrast between her gentle father and his horrible brother. Would her unknown aunt and cousin react in the same way if Sofia dropped in at their hotel and introduced herself?

On her next off-duty day she joined a trip to a local vineyard and learned a little about the fermenting of the richest red wine she'd ever tasted. Aldo would have loved it.

When Sofia and Amy went out for pizza together on Tuesday evening the younger girl reported that Davide was actively avoiding her. No doubt a madman jumping out from behind a bush and roaring at him had struck home as a heavy hint that his behaviour towards the eighteen-year-old was not going unnoticed. Without Davide's unwelcome attentions and with Noemi, Matteo and friends in the town with whom to socialise, Amy looked cheerful and settled.

Sofia asked her casually what her plans were at the end of the summer – whether she'd go to university.

Amy sighed and pulled a variety of faces, a triangle of pizza poised in her hand. 'I didn't finish my baccalaureate exams so uni's out for now.'

'Do you regret binning your exams?' Sofia took a bite of the deliciously crisp pizza crust.

Amy didn't reply directly. 'What about Spain? Aren't we going on together?'

Sofia collected up a string of cheese at the corner of her mouth. 'Still want to?'

Amy replied quickly. 'Don't you?'

'Sounds good to me,' she said easily, concluding that Amy still viewed Sofia as her comfort blanket.

She'd come to other conclusions in the past days. One was that she wasn't cut out to be caught in quandaries. Knowing Levi was Amy's biological father and keeping her in the dark about it felt wrong, but the prospect of sharing the secret that was not hers to share felt 'wronger' and Levi had yet to show signs of wanting to confess his identity to Amy.

Chance sightings of him around Casa Felice taught her

170

that the other thing she wasn't cut out for was one-night stands. She definitely did not possess the gene that would allow her to spend hours in a man's bed and walk away thinking, 'That was nice but let's not be greedy' or 'Can't wait to do that with someone else!'

Instead she found herself missing Levi's conversation and wondering why he was frowning so often and remembering the intensity in his eyes as he'd surrounded her with his heat. Every time he'd entered her she'd felt as if he was stroking her inside. Sex with Levi had not been a wham-bam experience.

Friday had come around again before he reappeared at the reception desk. His had been one of the check-out sheets she'd printed when she came on shift this morning and as she sorted the sheaf into alphabetical order she'd pictured him clearing his room and packing the big black and red bike that had waited silently in the car park all month.

'Hiya,' Sofia said unprofessionally, because she'd been left in sole charge while Aurora attended a meeting in her mother's office and it felt unnatural to say '*Buon giorno*' to him.

Levi leaned his tanned forearms on the counter. His T-shirt was a dark green that brought out the blue of his eyes and it pulled tightly around his biceps. He looked tired, but then he smiled and the fatigue lines vanished. 'What are the chances of me staying for another few days?'

Sofia felt that absurd little hop of the heart again to know he still didn't want to leave. It made no sense to feel that way because his staying made him a guest and being a guest made him untouchable almost as much as his going home to England would. 'I'll look, but I know Aurora said we'd be full from July the first.' She understood the Italian computer now and it didn't take long to bring up the page where each floor had its own plan with crosses through the rooms already reserved. Only one room wasn't booked.

'There's a superior room free tonight.' She began to click forward through the week. 'In fact it's free until Thursday – six nights – so we must have had a cancellation. I could see if there's a less expensive room for part of the period but I don't hold out much hope.'

Levi grunted, propping his chin on his fist. 'What's the rate for the superior?'

'A hundred and seventy-nine euros per night, including breakfast and free wifi.'

'I particularly enjoy breakfast in my room,' he said softly and Sofia felt herself blush hotly to remember them sharing chocolate croissants and hot coffee, the tumbled bed only waiting for them to finish. Judging by the sudden smile in his eyes, that was exactly the memory he'd meant to evoke.

Aware of other guests waiting behind him she returned her gaze to the computer screen, clicking efficiently through floor plans and dates. 'I can't see anything else. I'm afraid the superior room is the only option.'

When she looked back him, his smile had fled. 'I'd better take it. I'm approaching the last chance saloon.'

Ultra-aware that the waiting guests might be following the coded conversation, Sofia sent him a sympathetic look and filled in the dates to reserve room 412. 'Have you decided what to do at the end of your stay?' She tried to make it sound like polite customer-relations chatter as the printer began to whirr out the necessary paperwork.

Silently, he shook his head.

'Here's your check-out for the room you're leaving.'

172

He reached in his back pocket to draw out his wallet. 'I know the drill. I pay for that now and then you check me into the new room.'

'Exactly.' She watched as he slipped his credit card into the machine and tapped out his PIN. The computer updated, and he signed the check-in for the new room. 'You can move your things over. Room 412 has already been serviced.' Then, because the frown had taken charge of his forehead again, asked, 'How's everything going on at home without you?'

He did manage a faint grin at that. 'OK, on the face of it. A couple of things that were worrying me don't seem to have come to anything.'

'Good.' She handed him his paperwork with a bright professional smile. 'I hope you continue to enjoy your visit to Casa Felice.' And because it was what Aurora had told her to say at the end of interaction with a guest, as she handed over his new keycard she added, 'Do let me know if there's anything I can do to improve your stay.'

Laughter flashed through his eyes and he murmured, 'If only it were that easy,' before thanking her at a more usual volume and leaving her to the next guest.

Sofia turned her attention to the elderly English couple waiting patiently for their turn at the counter but all through processing their report that their air conditioning unit was making a noise her head was filled with vivid images of Levi . . . if only things were easy.

It didn't take long for Levi to pack up and change rooms. Being restricted to what would fit in his bike's panniers tended to keep baggage to a minimum, though it had meant making use of the hotel laundry service every few days of this protracted trip.

173

Room 412 was glorious, tucked under the eaves at the back of the hotel and unrolling the whole panorama of the valley at his feet. He leaned on the balcony rail and stared, enjoying the contrast between the hotel's lavender garden and the wild and natural tree-clad slopes and rocky peaks beyond. He fetched his watercolour pad and compared what he could see now to the view he'd painted from the garden and terrace. The rocks looked golden today. The late-morning sun wasn't subtle but it minimised shadows and made the green of the tightly packed woodland unbelievably bright.

He turned to a watercolour sketch of the same view at sunset. He'd taken dozens of pictures, trying to capture the colours at their best but the camera never saw them as intensely as he did, and he'd dashed off this sketch to capture the evening sky as it turned lilac, falling temperatures creating clouds for the sun to paint dusky pink as it slid down behind a crag.

He closed the pad and sighed.

Painting was uncomplicated. The surface of paper was flat and it was only by brushwork and colour that he created the illusion of dimensions. Real life wasn't like that. Sometimes it seemed that what you thought you saw bore no relation to the truth. Stephen Webber had been confident he'd fathered three children until he'd noticed an anomaly in Amy's blood type. The love he felt for Amy hadn't changed, he'd explained to Levi during that awkward meeting at the Webber family home, but everything else had. Stephen felt diminished in Amy's eyes, cheated by his wife not just of exclusivity of sexual access but of his place in the family, out of the happiness he'd thought his. Yet the truth had been there, under the surface, all the time.

Levi had tried to be sympathetic but he hadn't really understood then.

Now he was coming to the end of his odyssey, the weeks when he'd known the privilege of meeting his daughter, he realised why parents were so in love with their kids. Experiencing pleasure in simply watching Amy smile, or feeling leaden when she was unhappy, had taken him by surprise. He'd learned the kind of fear that went with the prospect of losing contact with his child.

Though they'd met only as she leaped into adulthood without a safety net – unless you counted him – he knew her. He might not have changed her nappies or walked the floor with her crying into his neck; he might not have read her school reports or been cross when she'd disappointed him; he hadn't even had the chance to sit in the audience when she sang in the school choir. But on some fundamental level, he connected with her.

It had taken him weeks to realise that Freya, in order to get what she wanted, had ruined his chance of getting the relationship with his daughter off on the right foot. He didn't blame Freya. Not now he knew that being a parent was like wearing blinkers. Sometimes, all you saw was your child. *Your* child. Your *child*.

He turned to the painting of Il Giardino with Amy's figure in the foreground. He was more of a landscape painter but he thought he'd caught that little tilt to her chin that hinted that she'd only be pushed so far.

He flicked through to his only other recent attempt at painting a figure. Sofia lying back on the bed, her arms behind her head, one leg slightly bent, looking out of the picture and laughing. For reference – apart from the images burned in his memory – he was using the photo he'd taken on his phone after he'd 'tattooed' her.

175

He was fully aware of what trust she was reposing in him by letting him take that photo at all. Many girls wouldn't allow anything like that in case the phone somehow got into the wrong hands and they found their nakedness on the internet.

The 'tattooing' had been fun and gently erotic but hadn't made it into the painting. He preferred her silky skin unadorned. It was a shame that their intimacy had been compressed into less than twenty-four hours. He hadn't been anywhere near ready to call a halt.

But he couldn't think of himself or even of Sofia. He had to think about Amy. That's what parents did, put their children first.

His heart lifted as it occurred to him that he shouldn't necessarily view his return to the UK as a full stop to everything. If Sofia and Amy moved on to Spain he could take a quick break in September if Sofia was up for meeting again – and he'd make damned sure he wasn't a guest at the hotel that employed her. Hopefully Amy would accept that they'd formed some kind of connection and wouldn't be uncomfortable with it.

Which would mean he could see Amy again too.

Reluctantly, he turned his mind away from that agreeable scenario and stepped through the sliding doors to put down his pad and pick up his phone to call Freya, more out of a sense of duty than because he thought she'd have anything decisive to offer.

Perhaps because their last conversation had been so scratchy, she answered coolly. 'What's the news?'

'Not much, really. She's made friends amongst the local kids and seems fairly comfortable with things here.' He decided not to tell her about scaring Davide off. He was beginning to get the hang of dealing with Freya's nervous agitation and there was no point upsetting her about a situation he'd already resolved.

'Oh.' Freya was quiet for several moments and Levi guessed she was weighing up whether to be glad for Amy's sake that Amy was surviving happily or thinking that a less positive report might have heralded her daughter returning to the comfortable family home.

He moved on to the main purpose of his call. 'I'll be leaving here on Thursday—'

'But what about Amy?' she butted in sharply.

Levi took a turn about the room, concentrating on not losing patience. 'I'm not going to be able to stay with her for the rest of her life, Freya. I know you feel the way she left home was unfortunate, but she is an adult. This hotel can only offer me a room until Thursday. It's a tourist town and they're choc-a-bloc in July and August.'

'Try other hotels!'

'Amy doesn't work at other hotels. What excuse am I meant to offer for continuing to turn up here? Anyway, I have to return to my own life. I have a business to run. I'm as concerned about Amy as you but there's a limit to what I can do.'

'Damn,' she muttered. 'Didn't you say there's some older waitress she's friendly with? Can you ask her to watch over Amy and report back?'

Considering he'd already secured a promise that Sofia would do almost exactly that for as long as was feasible, Levi was unreasonably nettled. 'I think she'll contact me if there's something really wrong. But she might move on herself at any time. And she's only "older" than Amy,' he found himself adding. 'Early thirties. Younger than you or I.'

He turned to where he'd laid his watercolour pad on

the bed and flipped it open again at the picture of Sofia reclining on his bed, thick dark hair spilling. He was pleased with the way he'd caught the flow of that.

Freya heaved a long sigh. 'I take it you haven't told Amy yet?'

'No.' Gently, he closed his watercolour pad, as if he didn't want Sofia's likeness to witness this part of the conversation.

'It would have been better if you'd told her from the beginning.'

Irritation jumped on his back like a goblin. 'It's a bit late for you to completely change your mind now! Unless I find a Tardis I can't rerun time. Do you have anything more helpful to offer?'

'Not if you're going to leap down my throat,' she replied sulkily.

Levi suggested Freya try texting Amy while he was still around to offer support if Amy's reaction was negative. Freya rejected the idea as too chancy and countered that the only practical way forward was for him to remain at Casa Felice for a few more weeks. 'I've just explained why I can't!' Levi ended the call, frustrated by lack of progress.

He gave himself time to calm down by making a cup of instant coffee with the room's complimentary sachets before ringing Wes to share information on his return to the UK. 'I'll ride back through Italy and France – I don't have to go to Munich this time. All being well I should reach Cambridgeshire at the weekend and be back in the office on Monday. That's the ninth of July,' he added, as Wes didn't respond.

'Yeah. Great.'

Levi tried to draw him out. 'How are things? Anything you need to ask me or tell me?'

'Not much.'

He tried again. 'Octavia OK?'

'Yeah.'

Knowing his friend was often moody and taciturn when upset, Levi made his voice softer. 'Are you OK?'

Wes gave a half laugh. 'I'm always OK, aren't I?'

For the second time in twenty minutes Levi said his goodbyes feeling uncertain and out of sorts. Life used to be simpler. He ran his business, got on well with his friend and business partner, enjoyed his freedom and set his own levels of responsibility. He hadn't felt a black crow of worry settle on his shoulder whenever he thought about his daughter, and Freya had remained safely in the past, where she belonged.

Opening his laptop, he began to plan his route home. Consulting Maps he divided the route into three journeys of roughly six or seven hours and booked a room for Thursday night at Aosta, just before the Italian/French border, then for Friday night at Reims in France. Finally, he booked himself onto the Calais-Est ferry to Dover early on Saturday.

Soon, his trip would be at an end.

He sifted through that idea a few times in his mind and decided he didn't like it. Black crows and blasts from the past not withstanding, he felt hollow at the thought of leaving Montelibertà.

Chapter Sixteen

Phew, July! The first of the month arrived with searing temperatures and solid bookings. Sofia and Aurora were run off their feet on Sunday checking guests in and out, housekeeping staff hustled to service rooms for fresh occupants, and Il Giardino was full to bursting with red-faced, overheated tourists. Sofia could only spare the occasional glance through the doorway to see the wait staff working busy tables under sun-baked parasols as she parroted meal times for what felt like the hundredth guest.

It was towards the end of her shift when she became conscious of two people watching her. She was listening to an elderly lady's story of how her coach broke down on a day trip to Rome but her eyes were drawn from the lady's gently wrinkled face to the watchers. With a shock, she realised it was Gianni Bianchi and a young woman, probably three or four years younger than Sofia. When her gaze rested on her uncle, he scowled.

When the lady went off to browse the leaflet stand in search of more entertainment, Gianni and the young woman approached.

'*Buon giorno*,' Sofia said tonelessly.

Gianni, smart in a suit with a white shirt but no tie, didn't bother to return the greeting. He glared at Sofia. 'So, you have snubbed me. I extended a hand to you but you have shown plainly where your loyalties lie. I would have apologised for my hasty words but now I see there is no point.' He turned upon his highly polished heel and stalked out with his nose an impressive distance in the air.

Blankly, Sofia watched him go. What had just happened? Gianni was obviously furious all over again but she hadn't the least idea why. Seeing Aurora sending her a questioning glance while she stapled a card receipt to a check-out sheet, Sofia shrugged, hoping it looked as if she didn't mind being publicly berated by one of her nearest living relatives. 'Sorry. My uncle.'

Aurora raised an eyebrow. 'I know who Gianni Bianchi is.' Her glance slid to where the young woman still stood gazing at Sofia. The young woman wasn't smiling but she wasn't scowling either. She looked to be about twenty-four.

Sofia had little choice but to acknowledge her. 'May I help you?'

The young woman tilted her head slightly. 'Will you talk to me? I'm Chiara Bianchi. Your cousin.' Chiara didn't look like Gianni. Not only was there was no trace of hostility in her eyes but she had a longer face, a slightly-too-large nose and a firm jaw.

Though she felt a spark of interest that a member of her family was promoting the idea of a normal conversation, Sofia began to say that she needed to get on with her work. But then curiosity took over along with a trickle of excitement. 'My shift ends in fifteen minutes.'

Chiari stepped back to glance through the doorway to the outside. 'I see my father has waited for me. We will meet you in Il Giardino.'

Sofia had to stop herself from rolling her eyes. 'I hope he can control his temper this time.' She made no attempt to simplify her vocabulary. Chiara's English was impeccable.

One corner of Chiara's mouth twitched. 'I'll suggest it.'

Sofia didn't rush to end her shift promptly. She dealt with two keycards that had stopped working – probably through being shoved in the same pocket as a mobile phone – and then became embroiled in helping an American lady who'd come to Montelibertà to meet Italian relatives and had left it to the last minute to decide it would be a good idea to learn the Italian for *yes, no, please, thank you* and *sorry*. Could Sofia please write it down for her?

But, finally, the time came for her to sign out of the computer system and hand over to the next shift. Sofia collected her bag from the back office and, squaring her shoulders, sauntered outside, pausing to let her eyes adjust to the bright sunlight. Thomas, Paolo and Noemi were the wait staff and Gianni and Chiara were seated at a table in Paolo's section. As Sofia joined them she slipped her jacket over the back of her chair and sat down without waiting to be invited. When Chiara courteously asked if she'd like to order a drink she chose tea to make herself seem as English as possible, though she loved all forms of the delicious Italian coffee Chiara and Gianni already had before them.

Paolo pretended to grumble, '*Inglese, Inglese!*' when he took the order but at the same time gave her a big grin and a wink that made her grin back.

Once he'd headed off, Sofia turned to her cousin and

uncle enquiringly. It was they who'd called this meeting so she didn't see why she should begin the conversation.

Chiara spoke first. 'My father and you have made an unfortunate start but we would like to talk to you.' She hesitated. 'We are all family.'

'Of course.' She kept her tone cool. To say that she and Gianni had made 'an unfortunate start' probably qualified for understatement of the decade. Sofia flicked a glance at Gianni and, to her surprise, she saw that he was looking slightly sheepish.

'Perhaps you're aware that we do not often come to Casa Felice,' Chiara went on, fiddling with a sachet of brown sugar that lay in the saucer of her coffee cup. 'We are competitors. My father and Signora Morbidelli are not friends. It's for this reason that my father spoke harshly when he saw you behind the reception desk.'

Sofia looked at Gianni directly. 'You have an objection to me working here? But you saw me working in Il Giardino before.' She didn't blush at the memory of cursing at him. He'd earned it.

Stiffly, he nodded. 'I offer you a job at Hotel Alba, the Bianchi hotel, and you do not even consider.'

Sofia gasped. 'Like f—!' She paused to allow Paolo to place her tea in front of her while she erased the four-lettered response from the tip of her tongue. 'I received no such offer,' she said instead, trying to subdue a fiery lick of temper.

Gianni glanced at Chiara and she took over for him, her voice soothing. 'When Signora Morbidelli ended your employment he was embarrassed about his part in the argument. Later in the day, he returned and asked Signora Morbidelli to tell you to contact him. He would make sure you had a job at Hotel Alba.'

Gaze darting back and forth between two pairs of brown eyes so like her own, Sofia didn't even try to hide her scepticism. 'That seems an odd consequence of an altercation that included my parents and myself being insulted in a variety of ways.'

Gianni glanced at Chiara and said in Italian, 'Perhaps now is the time for me to speak to Sofia alone.'

Chiara hesitated, but then nodded, so Sofia guessed this eventuality had already been discussed. Too curious to do anything but bid her cousin a polite farewell, she sipped her tea while Gianni frowned down at his coffee cup. When he'd checked that his daughter was safely out of earshot he asked, 'Do you mind if we speak in Italian? No? Thank you.' He paused to take a deep breath. 'I apologise. I was rude and harsh. I picked on the subject of money to lash out at you to disguise the real source of my anger and pain. Chiara knows what lies beneath that, what I'm going to tell you, but it's better that she does not have to listen.' He glanced at Sofia and then away. 'Forgive me. This is very difficult.'

Sofia's heart stepped up its beat as she watched his throat working. What on earth could be coming?

'Aldo was my big brother,' he began huskily. 'I loved him. I tried to be like him. He was a good man with many friends. Girls liked him too. But when he fell in love with Dawn . . .' He stopped again, taking up a paper napkin and blowing his nose vigorously.

Realising that Gianni, for all his bluster, was both upset and trying to tell her something important, Sofia murmured, 'Wait one moment,' and hurried to the bar to grab a jug of water and two glasses. Back at the table, she poured a glass and stood it at his elbow.

He drank deeply, murmuring, '*Grazie mille.*' He put

184

down the glass and met Sofia's gaze for seconds before he spoke in a voice filled with pain. 'I loved Dawn first. The beautiful Englishwoman. She came to our house as my girlfriend. I wanted my parents to meet her before I asked her to be my wife. Instead, she and Aldo . . .' He paused to drink again, muttering, 'I'm sorry.'

'Wow,' Sofia breathed, stunned. She watched moisture gather in the crease beneath Gianni's eyes. 'I had no idea. Papà has never told me.'

He tried to smile. 'I loved them both. Aldo tried not to fall in love with her. He was tormented. He said to me, "I have betrayed you" and I said, "Yes, you have." But you cannot choose who you love or I know Aldo would have chosen another woman. But, imagine!' He swallowed hard before beginning again. 'Once Dawn realised her feelings for Aldo she told me the truth – she didn't cheat behind my back. She was very sorry, I know. But I was young and hurt and so angry I thought I might die.' He managed a faint, self-deprecating smile. 'I was even more dramatic then than I am now. Hard to believe, eh?'

Detecting a much greater resemblance to Aldo now in the hint of roguishness in his eyes, Sofia's heart turned over. Tremulously, she managed to summon an answering smile. 'It would be rude of me to call you a liar.'

His smile broadened before fading once more. 'I told Aldo I would never speak to him again as long as I lived. I said I hoped Dawn left him broken-hearted and found a more honest man. I said he didn't deserve her.' He winced, a bleak, faraway expression in his eyes. 'The situation caused great distress in the family. My parents were torn between their sons. Aldo told my parents that he and Dawn would live in England. She had only been passing the summer here in Montelibertà and had a good job waiting for her at an English university.'

'She was a lecturer in biochemistry,' Sofia confirmed numbly. It was all she could do to process the story she was being told, no matter how good her Italian. Little shockwaves were rippling inside her as she tried to imagine her father, the person she'd been closest to in the world, stealing his little brother's girlfriend. She'd never known him do anything that could be described as even vaguely dishonourable but where love was concerned . . . And once Gianni knew, what would have been achieved by giving Dawn up?

'She was an intelligent woman. She wasn't conservative. She dressed in all the fashions, she loved rock music, she put colours in her hair.' He smiled painfully. 'I know there were many tearful letters and telephone calls between my parents and Aldo in the first years he lived in England, especially when—' he paused and cleared his throat '—he married Dawn without telling them, without giving them the opportunity to be at the wedding because he didn't want them to risk upsetting me. He said he was "in the wrong", and every action put him farther outside the family fold. Dawn wrote to me privately and begged me to make the first move. I tore her letter up. I, too, believed Aldo was in the wrong.'

Sofia felt as her eyes were lined with grit they stung so much. 'And what do you believe now?'

Gianni remained silent for several moments. Around them tourists chattered and crockery rattled. The parasol above them flapped in the breeze. Finally, he sighed. 'I think there was no right or wrong. Only sadness. Perhaps if Dawn had lived, or if my parents had, then someone would have found a way for Aldo and me to settle our differences. Dawn had a very big heart.' Carefully, he wiped his eyes on his immaculate white cuffs. 'I will be truthful with you. When I first met you, I saw in you not my beautiful niece, but evidence of Dawn and Aldo's love. After I allowed all that old anger out, I marched out to my car and drove off in a rage. I raced off up into the hilltops and found a quiet spot. I cried to think of Dawn. Then I was hit by remorse to think how appalled she would have felt at my behaviour towards her daughter and that I was still harbouring anger towards my brother. I returned here to ask for you. Signora Morbidelli refused to discuss your whereabouts, which is why I left the message.'

Sofia sipped her water in an effort to ease the lump that had risen in her throat as her uncle shocked her with this story of family turmoil. 'A message I never received. I was surprised when Benedetta offered me a new job, but I didn't want to leave Montelibertà yet so I took it.'

Gianni inclined his head. 'I understand now. But when I saw you working on the front desk, smiling and happy, I felt as if you were doing it to spite me. I apologise, Sofia.'

So-FEE-ya . . . The inflection was exactly as Aldo's had been, as if her father were speaking to her through his brother. The thought turned her voice into a croak that she could barely make heard over the chatter of voices and clatter of crockery around them. 'It's bizarre to think of these things going on, things that have affected me in the most fundamental ways, even that I exist at all – and I've never heard the truth till now.'

Gianni leaned back in his chair. He looked exhausted, sunken. 'Family feuds are terrible. Aldo never returned to see our parents. Dawn—' he swallowed noisily '—had been gone for some time before he told them of her loss.

They began to make plans to visit England but the car accident happened. I've lived with the guilt that if I'd accepted reality in a more mature way they would have seen their eldest son again and met their English grand-daughter. They would have offered Aldo comfort on the death of their daughter-in-law.'

'Ohhhh,' Sofia breathed, heart swelling. 'No wonder Papà was always sad when he talked of his family.'

Gianni wiped his eyes on his cuffs once more. It was a curious, defiant little gesture, as if he was daring anyone to say anything about him crying in public. 'I thought Aldo must contact me after the accident but I was a coward. I left my aunt, my mother's sister, to telephone him with the news. He must have thought I meant it when I said I'd never talk to him again. He stayed away because of me, but I thought we'd have time to meet again. I let time go by. And by.'

'I'm sorry Dad never got back here.' Sofia was half-surprised to realise she meant it for Gianni's sake, not just Aldo's. All her antipathy had drained away as he'd made his confession. 'He couldn't do much as his heart became worse; travel was impossible in later years.'

Gianni clutched his forehead, then his heart. 'I am ashamed.' He paused. 'I must now be candid with you.' He paused again, for longer. 'My wife, Mia, is unsettled by the idea of your presence in Montelibertà, the daughter of the woman I loved before her. She knows the story, of course.' He fidgeted with a napkin, smoothing out the crumples before adding in a low voice: 'It was a scandal at the time. I can understand her anxiety that people will gossip.'

Leaden dismay settled in Sofia's stomach. Gianni had swept aside so many barriers between them during this

188

emotional conversation, and now he was revealing the presence of a new one. She flushed. 'I never gave much thought to how my visit would affect your family. I should have found a way to contact you before I arrived. But I'd made Papà some promises.' She related the story – leaving out her interpretation of behaving as a young single woman should – and he listened keenly, smiling occasionally, sometimes wincing, as if he found the tale bitter-sweet. She took out her phone and showed him photographs of Aldo she kept in a special folder there.

Gianni clucked his tongue and sighed, shaking his head, moved to tears once more to see his brother so weak and wan.

The afternoon wore on and to better enjoy their conversation now they'd cleared the air Gianni ordered a bottle of spumante brut, a dish of olives and a plate of bruschetta, whispering that they were not as good as at those offered at Hotel Alba. Paolo finished his shift and Amy took over, swerving efficiently between the tables with her ponytail swishing, lifting one fair eyebrow at Sofia as if to ask, 'Is that who I think it is?'

Sofia tried to communicate back, 'Tell you later!' as she and Gianni discussed why Benedetta hadn't only failed to pass on Gianni's message but offered Sofia a job herself. Sofia concluded that it must have been that she couldn't resist the opportunity to annoy Gianni.

'She may have hoped you'd report to her what you saw. In which case,' Gianni proclaimed, wiping his fingers as he finished disposing of his share of the bruschetta, 'you must visit us as soon as possible to send Signora Morbidelli quite mad with unsatisfied curiosity.' He sobered as he added, 'I would like very much for you to come. Please, Sofia.'

Sofia's throat tightened. 'I'd like that too. But what about your wife? I wouldn't want her to be uncomfortable.'

Gianni gave another expressive shrug. 'Mia's not your enemy. She is just a little wary.'

He sounded convinced, so, tantalised by real blood ties to Gianni and Chiara, Sofia agreed to lunch at Hotel Alba the next day. She made a silent vow to give Mia no reason to see her as a threat, though she was too pragmatic a person to expect her aunt to love her on sight.

Gianni had, after all, named his hotel Alba, which meant sunrise or daybreak.

Or dawn.

When Amy finished her shift at one in the morning she felt almost as miserable as she had in the first days of being a waitress.

Benedetta was a cow. Amy knew the menu and had learned loads of Italian phrases, but today she'd got in a muddle with the word *caldo*, which meant hot but sounded as if it meant cold. The customer, a local, had been trying to obtain hot milky coffee and she'd taken him cold milk. Why couldn't the stupid man have just ordered latte like everyone else?

Instead, he'd roared with laughter at her mistake and made a huge show of drinking his glass of milk, smacking his lips and rubbing his belly. Davide laughed too, before loudly telling red-faced Amy her mistake. Then, while she rushed to get the man what he'd ordered in the first place, Davide, the knob, had told tales to Mummy. Benedetta had called Amy into her office and made her feel a complete idiot.

Sometimes Casa Felice still felt a hostile place. Amy trailed back in the direction of her room, reading her texts from her brother as she went.

Kris: What's up ur not usually this quiet

That, at least, raised a smile. Amy understood that the message was as much of his soft side as Kris would let show because he was full of teenage-boy BS.

Amy: I'm working! Why don't u try it?

Kris: Pretty sure I wouldn't like it hahaha

She returned an eye-roll emoji and then a selfie of herself pretending to hold her sides laughing. Kris sent her a thumbs-up.

Scrolling through her WhatsApp group with Maddalyn and Della she discovered that while she'd been waiting on tables they'd been having a conversation about wishing they'd gone travelling like Amy instead of bowing to family pressure to go straight to uni. When she got to the end she saw they'd already wished each other *Night hun!* so it was too late for her to join in. She didn't know what she'd contribute anyway. *Don't do it!!!* felt favourite right now. A nice little bedroom in Halls and student parties sounded attractive when compared to whiney customers and moody-cow employers.

As she flicked through Instagram, she trod slowly down the steps and through the picket gate, stopping short as she realised Sofia was sitting on the bench. 'Hey,' she said, but quietly, because Sofia was dangling an empty wine glass from her fingers and frowning at the moths dive-bombing her in the light streaming from the window of her room.

Sofia glanced up and smiled. Amy had got to know most of Sofia's smiles now and this wasn't a real one.

Amy flopped down onto the bench too, glad of a chance to unwind before bed. One of the killing things about the last shift was being dog-tired but too awake to sleep. 'What's up? Was it your uncle I saw you with?

191

Have you made up with him? I saw him kiss your cheeks when he left.'

The smile was a little more natural this time. 'He apologised for before and told me a lot of stuff about Dad.' The frown came back to chase the smile away, though she added, 'Want some wine? Get a glass if you do.'

'OK.' Amy wasn't mad on wine, though at least Sofia had white instead of red. Red tasted like petrol. Even then, she wished she had a bottle of 7up to spritz the wine up. It didn't taste so sour that way.

Sofia didn't say any more about her dad and Amy didn't ask her because she didn't like to see her friend looking so sad. Instead, Amy told her about the man with the cold milk and Benedetta being a bitch. She told it like it was a funny story and Sofia did grin and give Amy a tiny push, saying, 'What are you like? You know that *freddo* means cold!'

'I know. I forgot.' Amy giggled. The wine was beginning to make her feel a bit better. Or maybe that was just being off-shift and hanging out with Sofia. 'Want to have lunch tomorrow? You're on at three, aren't you? I'm off all day, and Tuesday.' She said tomorrow even though it was today really because they all did that, as if acknowledging finishing work after midnight sucked so much that you had to pretend you hadn't.

But Sofia was pulling a face. 'Can't, sorry. I'm going to visit my uncle's hotel. Turns out Benedetta only offered me the reception job to piss Gianni off.' She explained how Benedetta and Gianni didn't like each other and how it led to Sofia working on the front desk. 'So I'm going to Hotel Alba for lunch tomorrow,' she finished.

Amy seized on what she saw as the important part of this rigmarole. 'You're not going to work for your uncle,

192

are you?' She thought of not having Sofia in the next room, not being able to go to her when Davide was knobbish. Her stomach lurched like it did when her mum drove too fast over a bridge.

Sofia sipped her wine listlessly. 'What do you think I should do?'

'You should stay here,' Amy responded instantly. 'I know I'm being selfish but it'll be scary if you're not here. And,' she added, remembering, 'Levi ate in Il Giardino tonight and he says he's going home in a few days.'

'Yes.' Sofia's expression didn't change. 'I handled his last booking. The hotel's full from Thursday but he said he has to go home to his business anyway.' She hesitated. 'He's a nice guy, isn't he?'

'Really nice. Always smiley. It would be horrible here without either of you.' Amy took down her hair from its ponytail and began to comb the strands with her fingers.

Doling out the last of the wine, Sofia's smile made a reappearance. 'I don't think it would pan out, me working at Hotel Alba, even if I wanted a job there. My uncle told me a load of stuff.'

Amy sat, wide-eyed, as Sofia launched into this whole big story about her uncle being in love with her mum in the old days. It was like something off the telly, one of those saddo films her mum liked to watch on cable.

She got so distracted that she almost forgot about Sofia maybe leaving Casa Felice. And before she could bring it up again Sofia was already asking, 'So, what about your family? Have you talked things over with your mum yet?'

Maybe it was that second glass of wine or Sofia confiding in her, but Amy suddenly found words flying from her lips. 'Nothing's changed. My mum's still been keeping her scabby secret all my life, my dad's still not my dad, my brothers are only my half-brothers.'

Silence. Amy looked at Sofia's frozen expression. 'Yeah, I know. I never told you the whole story, did I? I found out my mum had a thing with some bloke just before she married my dad – the man I thought was my dad – and so he's not my dad.' She stopped, heart tripping up just at hearing the words on the air. 'I mean the person I thought was my dad is my stepdad.'

'I get it. That's really crap for you.' Sofia slipped a comforting arm around her. She hesitated. 'And for the dad you've always known. How did he take it?'

Amy felt tears begin to trickle down her cheeks. 'He was ho-horrified. Dead hurt. He shouted at my mum, said she was just like her weird friend that visited from England – a right trollop. She really cried. I just stoo-stood there. I couldn't believe it. Then I had to go and be sick. I got really angry and didn't want to talk to either of them so I left.' She sucked in a breath that caught on a sob. 'I feel as if I don't know who I am. I've lost the old me. It's like when I came round from anaesthetic when I had my tonsils out and was so disoriented I couldn't stop crying.'

Sofia stroked a lock of Amy's hair back from her face. 'Did you never talk that sense of disorientation through with them? Did your mum explain what happened?'

'She just said she got drunk at a friend's hen night and went with some local man. She said she truly thought I was Dad's, not this bloke's.'

'That's probably true.'

'She said she got unlucky.' Amy could hear the hurt in her own voice. She sounded like Louis when he got pissed off with Kris. In a minute she'd say 'THASSNOTFAIR!' all in one word, like Louis did.

194

'Aw.' Sofia clicked her tongue. 'Sweetie, I bet she didn't mean that the way you've just made it sound. How could it be unlucky to have a beautiful, fantastic, clever, kind daughter like you? Probably she meant that the odds were very much against her getting found out.' Sofia hopped up, jogged into her room and reappeared seconds later with a box of tissues.

'Listen,' she said, passing them to Amy. 'If you ever get to a few weeks before your wedding, whenever that might be, without having made a mistake or two with men, I'll be astonished. Just about everybody gets drunk and has sex with the wrong person at some time. Really. Everyone.'

Blowing her nose, Amy gazed at her blearily. 'Have you?'

Sofia rolled her eyes. 'OK, except me, because I didn't go out as much as some people because of Dad. I did nearly do it.' Sofia brought up her hands to cover her eyes. Amy suspected she was over-egging the drama as a distraction technique but was too interested to complain. 'Dad went into hospital for a few days, just when someone dropped out of a trip to London to see *Dirty Dancing* and go on the Eye and all that tourist stuff. A neighbour was the organiser and offered me the place. Dad was really keen I should go – he felt guilty at how much of my time was spent helping him. So I went and after the show we went back to the hotel bar. I got talking to this lanky guy with terrible dress sense and a boring haircut.'

'And you ended up—?'

'Not quite.' Sofia fanned her red cheeks. 'He was too drunk. Mortifying, or what?'

Her grin was so impish that Amy found herself grinning back. Then she sobered. 'At least you didn't end up pregnant with a baby you didn't want.'

Sofia tucked Amy's hair back behind her shoulder so she could look into her face. 'Has your mum ever actually said she didn't want you?'

Amy shrugged.

'I'm sure she did want you. Or she would have terminated the pregnancy, wouldn't she?'

Amy shrugged again. 'Perhaps it was too late by the time she realised.' But, actually, that possibility had never once occurred to her. It did make her feel a teeny bit less crap.

Sofia's voice sank to a murmur. 'You know you could just ring your mum and talk to her, don't you? Explain your feelings.'

'No way!' Amy couldn't even imagine it. Couldn't bear to. When you packed your bags and left home because your mum had acted unacceptably you couldn't just phone up as if it had never happened. 'No,' she repeated more loudly and definitely.

'How about your dad? Did you ever speak to him? I feel a bit sorry for him, being the innocent party.'

Studying her fingernails, Amy frowned. 'But he's not my dad. He used to be, but now I can't even call him that.'

'Oh, come on.' Sofia gave her a gentle squeeze. 'He is your dad. Not biologically, apparently, but he's the one who loved you all your life. I'll bet he did all the dad-things, didn't he? Looking after you, driving you places, playing in the garden, helping you learn to ride your bike—'

'But he's not my dad! Some loser I don't even know is.'

Sofia screwed up her forehead as if she were thinking. 'Just because you don't know your natural dad doesn't mean he's a loser. He might be a decent guy.'

Amy was suddenly angry that Sofia was questioning

196

her opinions. It seemed a touch too close to picking sides and, moreover, picking the one that didn't have Amy on it. She wriggled out from under Sofia's arm. 'I don't care what he's like or who he is!'

Sofia didn't seem to take offence at Amy's snapping. She brought her knees up to loop her arms around them and laid her cheek against her knees. 'Perhaps I'm just feeling sorry for your poor dad because I was so close to mine for so long.'

'Probably.' Amy got up. 'I'm going to bed now.'

'Night.' Sofia didn't move. Her voice sounded a bit strained. But it wasn't until Amy was lying in bed that she thought about how Sofia's voice had wobbled and wondered whether she'd been trying not to cry about losing her dad.

However angry and filled with justifiable outrage Amy was, the idea of her dad dying filled her with terror. She was sure she'd never live through anything so crippling.

In the end, she picked up her phone from where it was charging on the little table near her narrow bed with the wonky headboard and flicked to her messages, reading back some of those under 'Dad'. She'd once gone to her contacts list with the intention of pressing 'edit' and changing 'Dad' to 'Stephen' but she hadn't quite had the heart to do it. His last, ordinary, before-the-end-of-Amy's-world texts swam before her eyes, asking what time she wanted picking up from her friend's house and whether she wanted pizza when she got home. He hadn't texted her at all since she left.

But she'd told them that if they did try to contact her she'd disappear . . .

Her stomach gave a great lurch of remorse. She wished

Sofia hadn't said anything about Stephen being innocent in all this because now Amy couldn't summon up why she'd felt anger towards him. Being stupid enough to be cheated on no longer seemed much of a crime.

Maybe it was the wine making her brave but she got up and crept to the window to peep out. Sofia had gone. Amy opened the door quietly and went outside to pick up the signal.

Amy: *I'm sorry if I was crappy to you. Its not ur fault. x*

Before she could go back inside her phone began ringing in her hand.

'Amy!' her dad's voice said hoarsely. 'Amy, none of it's your fault either. Come home, darling. We love you. Are you managing OK? Are you safe? Do you have enough money?'

'I'm fine.' Amy's voice went wobbly at the sound of the voice of the man she'd loved all her life. She swallowed hard and they talked for ages. She told him about Montelibertà and that she did get homesick sometimes but she wanted to be on her own at the moment. He told her that he'd wanted to bite his tongue out every day since she'd left because he blamed himself for not considering her feelings, just thinking about himself and what the devastating news meant to him.

'It's all right,' she said bravely. 'I only thought of me, so we're even.' They even managed small, strangled laughs at that.

'Can I tell Mum we've spoken?' he asked hesitantly.

Amy considered. 'Yes. But I'm not ready to talk to her yet.' When the call was over she went back inside her room to lie awake staring into the darkness, realising that Dad being able to ring her as quickly as he did without

Mum trying to butt in from the background might mean that Dad and Mum weren't in the same bedroom.

She sighed. It was a totally shit situation. And if Sofia left Montelibertà that would be total shit too.

Chapter Seventeen

The next day, Sofia set out down the hill to visit Gianni at Hotel Alba, butterflies doing aerobics in her stomach and Via Virgilio's crawling traffic loud in her ear. Her thoughts were on what lay ahead – getting to know her uncle's family. Her family, in fact.

At the beginning of her journey she could see Hotel Alba on the facing slope but it was hidden from her view by a multitude of other buildings as she got down into the centre of Montelibertà. Traversing both Piazza Roma and Piazza Santa Lucia, busy with tourists and loud with as many English and American voices as Italian, she followed the route she'd memorised up Corso Musica, a street that, once past the theatre with a sort of bandstand outside, quickly narrowed. It wasn't until she branched into Corso Sant'Angelo and rounded a sharp bend that Hotel Alba popped into view again.

Sofia paused to drink it in. Tall and white with the ubiquitous terracotta tiled roof, it was probably twice the size and twice the age of Casa Felice, and looked as if it was a cut above. Stonework framed the windows and arched like eyebrows over the doorways. Imposing urns set at intervals around the building were extravagantly planted with red, white and purple petunias. The road and pavement leading up to the hotel were cobbled, and the main doors stood welcomingly ajar.

Subduing an urge to retreat, if only to the nearest large window to check her appearance after a twenty-minute walk, Sofia strolled through the imposing doors, hoping her attack of nerves didn't show. In the vaulted reception area, the ceiling was hung with impressive glass chandeliers. Walls and ceilings were painted white but the floor was glossy black marble, and the sofas dotted about were black too. Bureaus and side tables were painted a dull pewter. Paintings depicting busy market places and teeming cafés dotted the walls, bold splashes of colour standing out against the otherwise monochrome elegance.

Several guests sat around with either phones or tablets in their hands. Sofia guessed that the best free wifi was in this area.

Behind an imposing reception desk faced in more black marble, an impeccably turned out young man smiled as he wished her 'Buon giorno.'

In the distance Sofia could hear voices, closing doors, the *ting* of a lift. She swallowed. 'Buon giorno. I'm here to meet Gianni Bianchi. I'm Sofia Bianchi.'

The man's smile didn't waver, though interest flashed for an instant in his eyes. 'Please, take a seat. I'll let him know you're here.' He picked up a black telephone.

Too restless to sit, Sofia wandered over to inspect one of the largest of the artworks, a view down the slope of a cobbled street depicting colourful shops and people gazing into their windows. It was painted in broad

201

brushstrokes and was definitely best viewed from a distance. Wondering vaguely whether the artist had long arms or had to keep jumping back several yards to view a work in progress, she decided she preferred Levi's smaller-scale and more delicately executed watercolours. An image of him in the lavender gardens flashed into her mind, leg drawn up as a prop for his pad, eyes narrowed, hair blowing back from his forehead as the brush in his hand moved across a page of greens, blues and purples.

Levi. She felt apprehension slither down her spine as she revisited the uncomfortable reality of being confidante to both him and Amy. She'd never before been in the position where she felt simultaneously on the same side as, and betraying, two people.

'*Sofia, benvenuta all'Hotel Alba.*'

She swung around from the painting to find Gianni smiling quizzically, his suit crisp and not a hair out of place. He came forward to kiss each of her cheeks, his cologne wafting over her as she pulled herself back into the moment and thanked him for his welcome.

With a brief nod at the staff member on reception, Gianni ushered Sofia courteously around the desk and through an arch, taking a small corridor to the right and unlocking a door that led into what proved to be a delightful apartment, airy but well lived in. 'This is our home. Chiara has an apartment in the town so Mia and I have plenty of room here.'

'It's beautiful,' said Sofia truthfully, looking through a wide arch into a sitting room. In the apartment, as in the reception area, plain walls were hung with many pictures. There the similarity ended. Here the furniture was informal and well-loved, cosy fabric armchairs nudging up against tapestry sofas and faded velvet stools, blues, pinks, golds, browns and greens jumbled happily together. As if to emphasise that this was a place to be comfortable, Gianni shed his jacket and tie and hung them on the curly arm of a coat rack, removed his shoes and slid his feet into backless slippers.

Ceiling fans stirred the air as he led Sofia through the sitting room and then another arch. 'Mia! Chiara! Sofia is here.'

Chiara appeared in a green embroidered summer dress that hinted at this not being a workday for her, her shoulders rising prettily from the peasant-style neckline. She beamed. 'Sofia!' They, too, exchanged kisses, though they'd met so briefly before. Sofia supposed that as they were family kissing felt more natural than not kissing. 'Please come and sit down.' Chiara led Sofia between billowing voile curtains out into a courtyard with pots of startlingly red geraniums around the perimeter like a handkerchief embroidered at the edges.

At a table sat a woman who turned to watch them approach.

Chiara took Sofia's arm. 'Let me introduce you to my mother. Mamma, here's my English cousin, Sofia. Sofia, my mother, Mia Bianchi.'

Sofia had a moment to appreciate that Chiara making the introduction must have been planned as being more palatable than Gianni doing so. Simultaneously, she was swamped by the oddness of so many people sharing her surname when for so long she'd known only herself and Aldo, and was momentarily stuck for words.

Mia rose. Her dark hair was styled in a neat bob, greying at the front, and, like Gianni, she looked to be wearing a suit without a jacket. '*Benvenuta all'Hotel Alba.*' She shook Sofia's hand, extending her arm a long way as if discouraging Sofia from any idea that they would exchange kisses. She smiled, but it was a mask, devoid of warmth.

Sofia murmured polite thanks for inviting her into their hotel and their home. The resemblance between Chiara and Mia was marked, although friendliness emanated only from Chiara. Both women were groomed and poised, making Sofia glad she'd bothered with makeup and wrangling the top of her hair into a fishtail braid to hang over the loose layer below.

Mia reseated herself and Gianni held out a chair for Sofia while Chiara vanished back into the apartment in search of coffee.

Sofia made every effort to make herself agreeable to Mia. She spoke only Italian; she praised the apartment, the courtyard and the hotel. Mia's smile remained firmly in place as she quietly thanked Sofia, but she made not the least attempt to develop the conversation, even when Gianni and Chiara tried to draw Mia in as they asked Sofia about life in the UK.

When this had gone on awkwardly for ten minutes, Sofia addressed a direct question to Mia. 'Has Gianni mentioned to you that I work at Casa Felice?'

Mia nodded. 'It's good,' she murmured. 'You have a job already.' She shot Gianni a faintly triumphant look and he sent her one of exasperation in reply.

Sofia let the subject drop.

Lunch began with soup served by a quiet, middle-aged lady in leggings and a T-shirt, garb for 'the help' that seemed out of keeping with the boutique elegance of Hotel Alba, but in keeping with the comfy family apartment within it. White and red wine arrived in stylish carafes.

Mia retreated again from the conversation except when Gianni was telling Sofia all about the hotel and she joined in with a firm, 'Gianni named the hotel "Alba" because it's one of the first buildings in Montelibertà to see the sun rise, you know.'

'How interesting.' Smiling and nodding politely, Sofia gazed at her hostess as if she genuinely found Mia's contribution fascinating, though actually she was in little doubt that what her aunt actually meant was *he absolutely didn't name it after Dawn, your mother, so don't think it for a moment!* And, probably, *Dawn has been gone so long that I'm quite displeased you've turned up to unsettle Gianni by reminding him about his youthful tragedy.* Mia's glacial smile seemed designed to observe the niceties but disguise whatever was going on behind and Sofia found herself reflecting that at least you knew where you were with Benedetta because whatever her mood, she showed it.

As the soup was removed, replaced with fish and a rainbow of roasted vegetables, Gianni began describing Hotel Alba to Sofia in greater detail, its rooms, its clientele, even the general structure of employment. Sofia served herself with asparagus, carrots, baby tomatoes and sauté potatoes and passed the vegetables to Mia on her left.

Mia took minute portions of everything and passed the platter to Chiara, waiting for Gianni to take a breath before inserting smoothly, 'I think you're forgetting that our guest works for the opposition, Gianni.' Her tone was light enough but Sofia was left in no doubt that Mia genuinely didn't want Gianni to share too much. If Gianni had begun to feel warmth towards his niece, Mia was trying hard to stop him acting upon it.

Chiara began to ask Sofia about her childhood and Sofia responded brightly, sharing the few memories she had of her mother but mainly the lovely relationship she'd known with Aldo. She described their Edwardian house close to the railway station in Bedford and the grassy river embankment where Aldo had loved to walk when he was well enough, admiring the flowerbeds or finding a bench where he could watch the boats. It didn't exactly make her feel homesick but she was abruptly reminded of how much she missed Aldo, and tears sprang to her eyes. Chiara murmured sympathetically and Gianni's eyes grew wet.

Mia, though, maintained her air of separation. She might as well have been encased in ice.

When lunch had been rounded off with figs, watermelon and more coffee, Sofia glanced at her watch, thanked her uncle, aunt and cousin for their hospitality and explained that she had to be on duty in an hour.

Gianni immediately jumped up. 'But I haven't shown you the hotel.'

Sofia didn't have to look at Mia to know that she'd be arching her eyebrows. She seemed to have more expressions of displeasure than any three other people put together but Sofia could understand her defensiveness. If you knew your husband had once been deeply in love with another woman, and that other woman's daughter came along and was also an inconveniently close relation to your husband and daughter, it probably felt quite a threat.

So she just gave him a smile. 'I can't stay longer. Benedetta will sack me again.'

'That may not be a bad thing.' He laughed and prepared to walk her out, donning his tie, jacket and shoes at the front door like armour before stepping into the hotel. Once in the public areas he persuaded her to at least leave Hotel Alba by the side exit so he could show her the dining room and terrace. Both were beautifully kept. Sofia hadn't checked out the star rating for her uncle's hotel but she was pretty sure it would be at least one above Casa Felice's, even though the terrace had only a side-on slice of the magnificent view into the valley. 'You have a beautiful place.'

Gianni took her hands and kissed each of her cheeks. 'Now that you have seen our hotel, how do you feel about working here? I'd enjoy having another member of the family on board. Why not return on your next day off? I can show you the hotel properly and we can discuss what role you might like.'

Sofia freed her hands in order to give her uncle an impulsive hug. 'I'd love to see you again, but I won't stay in Montelibertà after the summer so it's not fair to take you up on that offer, however kind.' Stretching the truth a bit she added, 'I have plans to move to Spain with a friend.'

His smile became wistful. 'I hope you don't hold our first meeting against me. I was over-emotional and irrational.'

'Of course I don't.' Sofia gave Gianni a cheerful wave and turned away, glad she'd visited her family's hotel . . . but, also, quite glad to leave it. However much Sofia would like to be closer to Gianni and Chiara, Mia had made her feel as if Sofia was there on sufferance, which was not a pleasant feeling.

Corso Sant'Angelo was steep enough to propel her into a swinging stride across the cobbles and into Corso Musica. Before long she was crossing between the elegant buildings surrounding Piazza Santa Lucia, pausing when she recognised the burly figure, bountiful eyebrows and moustache of Ernesto Milani at one of the pavement cafés. 'Ciao, Ernesto!' She thanked him for passing her message to Gianni and explained that she'd just been to visit the hotel.

'I hope you were made welcome,' responded Ernesto in a tone that hinted that he wouldn't be surprised if she weren't.

'It was interesting,' she said evasively, bearing in mind Mia's fears of gossip. After passing the time of day with him, she was obliged to hurry through Piazza Roma to Via Virgilio to avoid being late for her shift. Rushing up the hill in the stultifying afternoon sunshine even made her think favourably, for once, of the air-conditioned coolness of reception.

She was halfway to Casa Felice when she realised that one of the figures strolling ahead of her was Levi Gunn, T-shirt clinging to his shoulders. She halted, taking a wistful moment to notice his tight rear view in cargo shorts, once again wishing life was simpler where he was concerned. She *could* motor past, tapping her watch and laughing about Benedetta having her hide if she was late – but that was no way to treat someone who'd shared his bed and body with her. Then again, if she fell in beside him she'd have to make a decision about whether to pass on Amy's confidences. Another option was to hang back, but she now had only twenty minutes to get to her room, shower, dry, dress, put up her hair and log on at reception.

Then he turned, as if feeling her eyes on him.

'Hey,' she said, as she caught up.

The Italian sun had bronzed his skin and bleached his hair and his teeth looked very white as he grinned. 'Day off?'

'No, I've been to visit my uncle and I'm hurrying because I'm on at three,' she explained apologetically.

He speeded up to keep pace with her. 'Really? The same uncle who you swore at?'

She grinned. 'Long story! No time right now.'

Levi proved he had something else on his mind anyway. 'Have you seen Amy? She seemed a bit quiet when I saw her in Il Giardino earlier.'

'Not since we both got off shift last night,' Sofia replied. 'Why was she in Il Giardino? It was supposed to be her day off. If she was called in to do a shift, that could have made her down, I suppose.'

'True.' He paced beside her, his limbs moving easily but none of them touching her. He began to tell her about his lunch in town and that he'd forgotten how salty pecorino was when he'd ordered it and had had to drink two pints of beer to compensate. They reached the hotel and he raised a casual hand in farewell as he turned into Il Giardino in the direction of the main doors. Sofia hurried around towards the yard.

But just as she reached the gate he suddenly appeared again before her, breathless. He must have veered off his course and sprinted along the edge of the car park to intercept her in the tiny space between the corner of the hotel and the fence to the yard. 'Oh!' she gasped as he whirled her into his arms.

His eyes blazed with laughter. 'Nobody can see us here,' he whispered and stooped to kiss her quickly but thoroughly, his hands settling comfortably on her buttocks to pull her close against him. 'Having trouble keeping my hands off you. You look fantastic,' he murmured. Then dropped a last kiss beside her mouth and released her, vanishing back around the corner, leaving Sofia to race down to her accommodation, heart hammering. But at least she had a smile on her face.

Luckily, once dressed in her uniform, she found it possible to pull all her loose hair back into a bun and wrap the fishtail braid around it in a stylish way she thought even Benedetta and Aurora would approve of. If she'd had to unravel the whole damned thing and brush it into a new style she would definitely have been late.

As it was, she slid into the space behind the reception desk bang on time, gasping, '*Ciao*!' to Aurora. Aurora looked away from whatever she was doing only long enough to murmur, 'Before you log on, my mother would like to see you in her office.'

Sofia thought, *Oh, crap. Now what?* but she said, 'Thanks, Aurora,' and made her way calmly to the staff area. She was soon knocking on Benedetta's office door and hearing '*Entra*' before going in.

Benedetta didn't offer her a seat. With one hand on her computer mouse she looked away from the screen only long enough to say, 'You're dating a guest again? I have just seen you with Signore Gunn.'

Shock grabbing the nape of her neck, Sofia stuttered, 'No.' Then decided, mutinously, not to elaborate. Walking up the hill with a guest was definitely not 'dating' and probably no other boss in the world would pretend that it was.

Benedetta clicked her mouse a couple of times and glanced up once more. 'I saw you.'

'I caught up with him just before he reached the hotel and he began a conversation. It would have been rude not to reply.'

'And it would have been rude not to let him kiss you? Put his hands on you? I was at a window above and could see you plainly.'

Oh.

Sofia stared, dumb with dismay. Benedetta was wearing the same dark, simmering expression as when she'd sacked her before. But Sofia was damned if she was going to be sacked again now, just when she'd done all the freaking training for the job she didn't want and Levi was leaving. She gathered her wits quickly. 'I had lunch with my uncle, aunt and cousin at Hotel Alba.'

Benedetta's mouse clicking paused as she looked up, eyes narrowing as she waited for more. Sofia couldn't think where to go from there and was already wishing she'd thought of another conversational gambit to distract Benedetta from her mean-minded complaints, but then Benedetta sat back, folding her hands and summoning a smile. 'And how is the Bianchi family?'

'Well, thank you.'

Benedetta nodded encouragingly. 'I hope your uncle didn't try to coax you away from us?'

Anger at the question stirred inside Sofia but a wish to avoid getting herself sacked again kept the escape valves closed tight. 'In fact he did.'

Benedetta waited.

Sofia let her.

Benedetta weakened first. 'Are you going to take it?'

'No.'

'You seem upset.' Belatedly, Benedetta waved Sofia to a seat, leaving her own chair in order to pour two cups of coffee from the filter jug in the corner of the room and place one before Sofia.

Sofia added the cream Benedetta offered but not sugar. 'I'm not upset,' she replied, feeling very upset at finding herself caught in other people's personal and political crossfire when all she'd wanted to do was come to Montelibertà and be free.

For several moments Benedetta sipped her coffee, assessing Sofia with her gaze. 'Perhaps you were shown around Hotel Alba?'

So Benedetta *was* hoping Sofia was a spy in the camp. Deciding that this conversation was heading downhill fast and the best she could hope for was to keep a hand on the steering wheel, Sofia settled back in her chair. 'I was shown a little. It's a beautiful hotel.' She paused delicately. 'I've been invited back . . .'

Eyes widening in excitement, Benedetta almost spilt her coffee. 'Really? Would you perhaps be able to . . . learn about the hotel?'

Sipping her coffee and licking her lips as if taking a moment to consider, Sofia let her voice drop conspiratorially. 'I think so. Would you want me to?'

Benedetta's eyes nearly popped from her head. 'Very much.'

'Details that aren't available on the Internet?'

'Exactly.' Benedetta had let her voice drop to match Sofia's. 'Key staff . . . would they be interested in an approach from another hotelier? Deals and discounts with suppliers. Details of regular affluent customers perhaps?'

Sofia drained her cup, replaced it on its saucer and rose, smoothing down her skirt. She neither agreed nor refused but smiled as she moved towards the door. 'Shall I return to reception and log on now?'

'Yes, yes!' Benedetta was positively beaming. 'I would like to know when you've visited Hotel Alba again.'

'I understand.' Sofia shut the door softly behind her as she left and returned to her post on the front desk, disappointed at what people would do in an all's-fair-in-love-and-business kind of way; knowing she was just as bad for deliberately creating the impression she'd pass information to make Benedetta forget about seeing Sofia in a clinch with a guest.

Aurora looked at her enquiringly as she logged on to the computer. Sofia mumbled something about everything being sorted out so Aurora returned her attention to the guest she was helping.

Sofia's eye was caught by the sight of Levi, his lower half clad in biker gear, powering his way down the main stairs two at a time, crash helmet and jacket hooked over his arm. He grinned in her direction with a small lift of his eyebrows.

Sofia returned a businesslike smile before turning to answer the phone, definitely not up to telegraphing that Benedetta had somehow seen him kiss her.

By the time she'd taken the call Levi had gone and she settled down to alphabetising the check-in forms for guests expected after 6 p.m., imagining that he was taking his bike for a run to check it over before he began his long trek back across the continent in three days' time. Presumably bikes had to have their fluids topped up just like cars so maybe he'd take it to a garage.

Soon he'd be gone for good. Back to his life in England, his business, his family, his home.

The screen blurred and she had to blink hard to clear her vision. Once Levi had left, Sofia would be able to assess her situation depending on whether he'd told Amy he was her father and what Amy's reaction had been. The more she thought about it, as she shuffled the tedious paperwork the hotel generated every day, the more convinced she became that he'd go without telling Amy the truth. Maintaining the status quo kept his options open.

And then . . .? She definitely didn't feel as if she could leave Amy on her own if she didn't want to be left. Amy had tied a little string around Sofia's heart despite her best intentions to keep that heart pristine for her couple of years travelling or, at least, for this one summer in Italy. With sudden resolve, Sofia decided she really would suggest that they begin looking for somewhere else. Maybe Spain or maybe just elsewhere in Italy? She didn't feel as if she'd finished with her father's homeland yet, but Montelibertà, without Levi, didn't attract her. Better to be somewhere fresh, without all those memories looping more and more strings around her heart.

Then she forced herself back to thinking about check-in forms because everybody knew that string didn't stretch. Certainly not right across Europe.

Chapter Eighteen

When Levi returned to the hotel three hours after he'd left, he pulled the bike back onto its stand. He couldn't wait to drag off his helmet and Joe Rocket jacket. He wiped the sweat off his face and ran his fingers through his hair to lift it from his scalp. A ride usually helped him order his thoughts, leaning with the bike as it cornered, opening it up on the motorways – *autostrade* here – for the thrill of seeing the scenery flash by.

But this ride hadn't provided him with any such comfort.

It had made him feel baked into his gear; it had made him angry at himself for not being able to make a decision; and it had made him sad he was leaving this beautiful place behind him. Leaving his daughter. His *daughter*. He'd almost got used to the idea that he had a daughter . . . but not to the fact that she didn't know that he was her father. And he was leaving bright, breezy, smiling, caring, practical, incredibly hot Sofia, a woman to whom he'd formed a connection on all kinds of levels.

Carrying his jacket and sweaty crash helmet, he was glad to gain the cool interior of the hotel reception area.

As if magnetised, his eyes swivelled towards the front desk to see if Sofia was there. She was, smiling professionally, dealing with some hipster with a man-bun and a beard. When she turned to search for something in a set of drawers Levi saw the hipster altering position so he could check out Sofia's rear view.

Levi whipped his gaze away as if he'd been caught in a lecherous moment himself. In fact it was an unwelcome flash of jealousy that made him look away. He didn't want to watch another bloke eyeing Sofia up. He frowned despondently as he trudged up the stairs. Not only did he not have exclusivity with Sofia, on Thursday he'd be leaving Casa Felice and Montelibertà and might never see her again. Bedford was only an hour from his home in Bettsbrough but, from what she said, whether she returned to the UK at all was up in the air. She was travelling. Physically and emotionally exploring, learning, stretching. Being free.

Later, up in his room, when he'd showered and pulled on clean shorts, he sent Sofia a text for her to pick up on her break.

Levi: Can we talk? Maybe you could ring me from your room when you get off tonight if you don't have other plans.

Before he could put the phone down and decide what to do with himself for the evening the phone rang, but it was Wes's name that flashed onto the screen. Automatically, Levi opened his laptop as he answered so he could get online to work with Wes if he needed to. 'Hey.'

'Are you still coming back at the weekend?' Wes was obviously not in the mood for greetings.

'Yes, it's all booked.' And then, when Wes didn't immediately reply, 'How's everything your end?'

216

A hesitation. Then, 'OK. Just thought I ought to report in that Octavia's gone and I've revoked her access privileges because there's something off about her.'

Levi's heart turned over with a heavy thud. 'What happened?' With swift movements he switched his phone to speaker and set his fingers to racing over the keyboard of his laptop to access the server. 'Wes?' he prompted, when the silence had gone on for a few seconds. He glanced at his phone.

The call had ended.

Swearing at the instability of the local mobile signal he gave Wes a few minutes to call back while he accessed the server log, able to see where only an hour ago Wes had revoked all user privileges for Octavia Hawthorn, deleting her username and password, the usual practice when anyone left. Relieved and anxious in equal measures he snatched up his phone and tried to ring Wes back.

The call went directly to voicemail. He cursed at technology that was only any good when it worked and tried to get Wes via the office landline. Then Facetime, Skype and Facebook calling and WhatsApp's call facility, all without success.

Wes had gone offline, if not off the grid – at least so far as Levi was concerned.

He snatched up his phone again and rang his brother, Tyrone, who answered immediately. 'Hello, stranger! You've been a bit quiet. Mum's been worrying about you taking off on some painting odyssey at no notice then staying so long.'

'I'm fine, and I called her last weekend and told her I was fine,' Levi answered impatiently.

'Must be her mum-radar working overtime. She thinks you're behaving oddly. I said, "What's new?"'

Levi broke into his smartarsery. 'Ty, are you still at the garage? Can you do me a favour and whiz upstairs to see if Wes's there? I need to talk to him.'

Tyrone sounded unperturbed. 'Don't think there's much point. He left a while ago. I watched him drive away. He said he was working from home for the next few days.'

'Did he say why?' Levi's heart began a slow descent to his boots. There was no reason for Wes *not* to work at home. The advantage of working solely in virtual products was that a laptop and internet access to the server and the networked Mac Pros were all you needed. Wes didn't bother with a landline at home and his mobile could easily be switched off, which was great when he wanted to concentrate but crap if you wanted to get hold of him. And Levi did.

He snapped back to the present when Tyrone spoke again. 'That girl he's had working with him's OK, isn't she?'

'Octavia?' Levi said numbly. 'I think she's his girlfriend.'

'Looked like it.' Tyrone chuckled. 'He looks as proud as a dog with two doodahs, walking around holding her hand and kissing her. Have you met her? Hot or what? Wes's wearing the dazed look of a bloke in love.'

'Yes. They met through me. She's the girl who found my phone that time.'

'Really?' Tyrone gave an elaborate sigh. 'Maybe you should have snaffled her for yourself. Even for a happily married man she's a distraction, wafting around the place.'

'Not my type.' And perhaps about to get less so.

He got off the phone with his brother as soon as he could, after enquiring as to the welfare of Tyrone's wife Beth and toddler twins Grace and Serena. Then he settled on the bed to spend the evening combing through the server files – but without being able to find a thing wrong.

218

He searched every page on the site and still couldn't find anything. In fact, the site looked fantastic and the stats showed it was attracting more traffic than ever, including the *Modern Woman* page that Octavia had instigated. She'd been logged in as a moderator as recently as yesterday and appeared to have been fulfilling that role with humour, accuracy and diplomacy, exactly as the notes to moderators requested.

WTF? Levi sat back.

He'd expected to find something. His uneasiness at Octavia being involved in his business hadn't gone away, even while he'd been absorbed in what might happen here in Italy. As if to remind him of unfinished business, his phone beeped and Sofia's answer to his earlier text flashed onto the screen.

Sofia: It'll have to be from the garden because phones don't work under the terrace, so no guarantee of privacy. Don't get off till 11 though.

Levi: That's fine.

He rolled off the bed and stretched, suddenly conscious of an uncomfortable emptiness in his stomach. It was after eight, when he checked the time, so it looked as if Sofia had taken her break a bit late. He'd walk into town for dinner. Maybe it would clear some of his bafflement over Wes and/or Octavia. He pulled on a clean T-shirt and grabbed his wallet.

As he mooched through reception he was able to catch a glimpse of Sofia's head, phone clamped to her ear as she gazed at the computer screen, rubbing her temples as if to soothe an ache. He paused to try and catch a snatch of her speaking in Italian because she always sounded alluring. When they'd been in bed together he'd asked her to speak Italian to him and she'd laughed as she complied, later admitting she'd said he had a nice arse. He'd liked her speaking Italian to him even more after that.

She was doing more listening than speaking now though, frowning in concentration, so Levi stepped out into the warm, soft evening air, catching the perfume of the oleander bushes as he skirted Il Giardino and set off down the hill to town where the lights were just beginning to show in the dusk.

By the time he let himself back into his room just before eleven to catch Sofia's call, his mood had been lifted by a couple of beers. He'd have infinitely preferred to be having the conversation in person but things had conspired against them.

It was nearly eleven-thirty by the time his phone rang and *Sofia* appeared on the screen. 'I'd begun to think you'd forgotten and fallen asleep,' he joked as he answered.

'Sorry. It's been a long day.' She sounded tired and flat. He could imagine her on the bench outside her room, dragging her arms from her jacket and kicking off her shoes. In the same colourless tone – and maybe because she didn't want to talk about her day – she posed a string of questions. 'Did you enjoy your bike ride? Did you fill up ready for your mammoth journey to the UK? Is everybody at home excited about seeing you again? How's Wes coping?'

He hadn't intended to focus on his leaving but he related his concerns about Wes's odd phone call and the unease that persisted even though The Moron Forum was running like a well-oiled machine.

'It sounds as if it's definitely time for you to return to real life,' she responded. 'We've got each other's contact details so I can . . . keep you up to date. Unless you've made some decision that will affect things?'

He got up to pace the room, reading her coded questions and appreciating her discretion. 'I can't tell her. There's just too much to lose if she reacts as she did when she first found out. At least this way I've still got a link with her, which I feel I owe Freya too.'

'I've never been called a link before.' If anything, Sofia's voice was flatter. 'Well, if I don't get the chance to talk to you before you go, have a good journey.'

That sounded so much like a sign-off that he tried swiftly to get the call heading where he'd meant it to. 'Hang on! I'm hoping we'll get time to talk. In fact—' he took a breath '—when I was out on the bike I happened upon a little guest house about five miles away and I've booked a room for Tuesday night.'

'Why's that?'

Troubled by her lack of emotion he stopped pacing and sat on the corner of the bed, dropping his voice to an intimate murmur. 'I was hoping you'd like to . . . be there with me.' When she didn't immediately answer he added, 'To say goodbye properly.' More silence. 'Just overnight, Tuesday/Wednesday. You'd be back ready for whatever shift you're working on Thursday.' *When you stay and I go.*

She was silent for so long that he wondered if she'd fallen asleep with the phone in her hand. Then she sighed. 'I got another bollocking from Benedetta this afternoon. She saw us kissing. To distract her I told her I'd been to Hotel Alba and let her think I was going to spy for her. I met my aunt today and spying for the opposition is so exactly what she suspects I'm going to do so I feel a scumbag, even though I was only trying to keep my job until I can talk to Amy about moving on, because it might take a while to organise. I've been thinking of heading to the coast.'

It was as if chilly hands had stroked up his arms. He found himself strangely reluctant to address the idea of her moving out of Montelibertà, existing in a space he'd never seen. Beach and sea instead of mountains. 'Hell. I shouldn't have surprised you with that kiss but you looked so amazing that I couldn't resist. I'm sorry it dropped you in it and I understand that must have been uncomfortable. But Tuesday and Wednesday are your days off this week, right? We'd be right away from here so I don't think Benedetta could have her spies out.'

The silence was even longer this time. 'Levi—' She paused. 'I'm going to say no.' Another pause while she seemed to struggle to speak, and the word 'no' reverberated in his head like a death knell. At length she went on. 'I keep thinking of the title one of Dad's favourite Leonard Cohen songs, "Hey, That's no Way to Say Goodbye". What you're suggesting sounds no way to say goodbye – getting closer just to get farther apart. It's brutal. I think I'd rather leave things as they are.'

'Oh.' He rolled back on the bed and gazed sightlessly at the ceiling, his stomach plummeting as if he'd lurched into the depths of his own disappointment. He hadn't realised how much he'd been relying on her saying yes, looking forward to arranging a taxi to the little guest house tucked away up a winding road beside an olive grove. Spending the evening and night with her.

He tried to think. She sounded as if she was saying she was protecting herself, which was positive in a distorted sort of way because it meant she had feelings for him. But positive wasn't much comfort if it meant he'd never be with Sofia again. Suddenly he was exhausted and empty and as if, in 'returning to real life' as Sofia put it, he was ripping off bits of his heart to leave in Monteibertà.

'You've presented a confusing perspective on things,' he said eventually, his voice now as flat as hers. 'But—' He ran out of argument before he could finish the sentence. 'OK.'

A sniff reached him down the phone line. 'Sorry. I just think it best.'

'OK. You sound shattered. I'll let you go.'

He ended the call and practised ceiling staring for a few minutes, then found the Leonard Cohen song on YouTube and listened to the words. They were about distances, love going and love staying, and not wanting to create ties that couldn't be untied. It spoke to him of goodbye being the best option.

He hadn't anticipated Sofia thinking that way.

In the hot midnight garden Sofia pulled herself up wearily from the bench and went into her room, which was stuffy from being shut up. Hanging up her jacket and skirt ready for her shift on Thursday, she fought off the urge to ring Levi and reverse her decision. Her head told her she was right but the rest of her thought she was as mad as a box of frogs. She could have spent another night with Levi.

She opened the shutters on the inside of the window to let air circulate. There was no point wearing anything to bed. She cleaned her teeth and switched off the light, lying on the cool sheet for a while, the only light from her e-reader as she tried to lose herself in a book.

Her mind was too busy to get lost.

Switching the e-reader off, she tried to sleep.

Her mind was too busy to fall asleep.

Hearing Amy come in from her shift, she got up again, pulled on a camisole and a pair of shorts, opened her door and stepped back out into the strip of garden, hoping there weren't too many bitey bugs on the wing tonight because she didn't have the energy to start squirting herself with repellent, even though she didn't want to wake up in the morning covered with big itchy lumps.

Hardly had she settled herself on the bench, which was at least cool beneath her thighs, when Amy's door opened and she appeared, looking young in an oversized nightshirt with a picture of a cute dragon on the front. Her phone was in her hand as if glued there. Sofia smiled a greeting.

'I heard your door go.' Amy perched on the bench alongside her, sticking her lower lip out and puffing damp tendrils of hair from her face. 'It's like an oven in my room.'

'Same. With all these bushes and the vine out here there's no breeze to our rooms and the summer's really heating up.'

Amy bundled up her hair and kept it off her neck by resting her head back against the wall and trapping it. 'I always thought servants were hidden away in attics, not under terraces.'

'At least live-in jobs have their compensations. If you have to find an apartment or house share somewhere it's a pain. Especially if you suddenly decide to leave, because you have to give notice and get your deposit back.'

When Amy turned to look at Sofia her fine blonde hair all fell down onto her neck again. Her eyes were massive. 'So you are thinking of leaving?'

'A bit,' she answered unguardedly, needing to blow off steam. 'I'm sick of Benedetta's moods. I like my uncle and cousin now we've talked properly about the past but my aunt's definitely against me getting too close to them. I'm beginning to feel a bit done with Montelibertà.' She couldn't explain that there was no reason to stay after Thursday because what was tying her to the job was Amy and what Levi needed was to be near Amy as long as he could. But once he'd gone . . . 'I've fulfilled most of my promises to Dad. I can be young and free anywhere. I've barely scratched the surface of that one.'

'So what are you thinking?' Amy looked like an uncertain twelve-year-old in her dragon nightwear and her fine eyebrows curling apprehensively.

Sofia gave her a grin. 'I'm thinking about looking for a job at a seaside resort. I hope you don't mind though – not Spain, not yet. I want to see other parts of Dad's country and speaking the language here is a definite advantage. Would—'

The phone in Amy's hand began to ring and she frowned down at it. 'Oh. It's my little brother Louis. Since I talked to Dad the other night both my brothers have called. I think Louis is missing me.'

'He must be to ring you this late. Answer! I'll go in to give you privacy.'

'But what—?' Then Amy sighed and put her phone to her ear, saying, 'Are you all right? Why are you up at this time? No, I can't sleep either but Mum will stress if she knows you're awake. Is it really hot at home? Yeah, boiling here.'

Sofia patted Amy's arm and slipped off to her room. She felt sleepy now. Maybe it was because she'd taken the first tiny step to moving on. She meant to wait until Amy's call was over and pop out again to ask what Amy thought about moving to a coastal resort in Italy rather than Spain, but lost her battle with her heavy eyelids and plunged into sleep instead.

Sofia began her two days off. She tried hard to catch up with Amy again to conclude their conversation but the younger woman seemed to be either working or asleep. As the season heightened Benedetta had the wait staff working split shifts or longer hours. It was a touch maddening when Sofia wanted to talk.

Frustrated, she went out alone on Tuesday. It was easier to avoid temptation if she kept out of Levi's way. The temptation of spending tonight with him. She caught sight of him once, frowning and grim as he did something to his motorbike in the car park. It was an awkward place for him to be hanging out if Sofia wanted to leave Casa Felice without encountering him, but she hit on the idea of departing via reception with the excuse of checking whether she'd left a pen behind last night. Benedetta was manning the desk and was obliging enough to search under all the paperwork while Sofia checked the floor but neither of them was able to locate her pen.

Unsurprising, really, as Sofia hadn't actually lost it.

After a few minutes of the fruitless searching she was able to shrug off the supposed mystery and exit via the front door and around the far edge of Il Giardino, so avoiding the car park.

Strolling down the hill, the sun pressing on the top of her head and exhaust fumes from the traffic drowning out the scents of lavender and oleander, she visited a few shops to gaze at gaily painted ceramics and useful items made of olive wood. Drifting into Piazza Santa Lucia she spotted Ernesto at one of the open-air cafés, reading a newspaper, an empty coffee cup at his elbow. She threaded her way through the tables and asked if she could join him.

Folding up his newspaper, Ernesto proclaimed loudly, 'Of course! Of course!' Over more coffee, and later lunch and wine, Ernesto shared his many stories of Montelibertà and whatever he could dredge from his memory about Aldo and his family.

'And now you've met your Uncle Gianni.' His kind eyes twinkled.

'I have,' she agreed. 'I think Dad would be glad he's done well. Hotel Alba is very grand and impressive.' She deliberately didn't mention their inauspicious first meeting, feeling it didn't reflect well on either of them. 'I expect my grandparents were proud of his head for business.'

Ernesto rumbled into an anecdote about Gianni's entrepreneurship that involved brokering a deal to sell the olives from his parents' olive grove when he was fourteen. 'Unfortunately,' he ended on a roaring laugh. 'The olives were not his to sell and Agnello had already made a deal of his own.'

Though Sofia laughed she felt the hot prickle of tears more than once as Ernesto's rich baritone hit all the same rolls and peaks as she'd heard from Aldo for so many years.

At two-thirty Ernesto consulted his watch and declared he had an appointment at the registry in fifteen minutes and regretfully took his leave with two smacking kisses to Sofia's cheeks.

Feeling as if she were mentally checking out from Montelibertà, even if she could easily be here for a couple of weeks yet, she bought a bottle of water and toiled up the slope to call again at Hotel Alba. The afternoon heat had really taken hold and some of the smaller businesses had closed their shutters for siesta but Sofia had an urge to revisit the gracious building and perhaps tie another of those little strings on her heart.

This time to her family.

As Sofia neared the open area at the front of Hotel

Alba she saw her cousin. In a smart business suit, Chiara was evidently taking her leave of a man outside the hotel. Though Sofia hung back, unwilling to intrude, Chiara swung round with a big grin as the man hefted his briefcase and headed off towards the nearby public car park.

'Sofia!'

They kissed cheeks, Sofia feeling overheated and scruffy next to Chiara's business chic.

'You're just in time for coffee,' Chiara exclaimed. 'My parents are away for the day, taking some well-earned time off. Let's sit on the terrace. It will be pleasant beneath the pergola.' She chattered about the hotel as she led the way to a wooden table on a curved stretch of paving edged with tubs of clipped box to separate it from a formal garden. The pergola, roofed with split bamboo, filtered the sun without closing it out entirely.

Chiara's hair was swept up into a topknot. She looked much more at ease in her dark business suit than Sofia ever felt in her similar-but-the-cheap-version uniform.

They ordered drinks from a waiter then Chiara turned to Sofia expectantly. 'So. Have you come to talk about joining us at Hotel Alba?'

Certain that even had she wanted to join the Montelibertà Bianchi empire, discussing it while her uncle – and particularly her aunt – were away would not have gone down well, she tried not to commit herself. 'I thought it would be nice to call again. It was a spur-of-the-moment thing.'

Chiara looked happy enough to hear it. 'It's lovely to have the opportunity to get to know my English cousin. I'm just sorry I never met Uncle Aldo. But I have something to show to you if you have the time?'

228

Sofia's curiosity was piqued. 'I do. I'm not working today.'

Chiara jumped up and vanished in the depths of the hotel, and Sofia had time to admire her surroundings. The garden was symmetrical and well kept with geometric flowerbeds and an ornate marble fountain burbling in the centre of a grassy lawn.

It was only moments before Chiara returned, a dusty blue volume in her hands, faded tassels hanging from an equally faded chord. 'Look!' she urged. 'This is an old photograph album. It belonged to my grandmother. *Our* grandmother,' she corrected herself.

Sofia's stomach turned over as Chiara placed the album on her lap. 'Wow,' she breathed, running her hand over the faded brocade cover before opening it up, inhaling the scent of aged paper. The pages were thick and black, the photographs held in place with shiny black triangles at the corners. She gazed down at a faded monochrome wedding photo, the bride's eyes glowing, a huge veil frothing back from dramatically waved hair, the groom beaming from above a tall collar and a dark suit. 'Is that them? Our grandparents?' she whispered.

'It is. More than fifty years ago.' Chiara squeezed Sofia's arm. 'They look so happy. But how Nonna ever moved in that enormous dress, I don't know. And Nonno looks as if his collar and tie will choke him.'

They turned the pages together. Chiara was able to point out great-grandparents and great-aunts and uncles and Sofia had to wipe her eyes. 'I feel as if the missing part of me is in this album.'

Soon a baby appeared in Maria's arms in a picture, Agnello beaming beside them.

'Baby Aldo,' Chiara murmured.

Sofia had to wipe her eyes again, gazing into the cherubic face. 'The missing part of him's in this album too.'

Every page brought a chapter in Maria and Agnello's lives, a chapter of Sofia's unknown family history. Another baby joined the family, Gianni; family snaps of picnics and footballs and bikes mixed with the occasional studio portraits. Colour photos became more common than black-and-white.

Chiara and Sofia laughed together over outmoded clothes and cheeky grins, bikes in the garden and birthday cakes in the middle of a polished dining table. 'This table is in our apartment now,' Chiara said. 'My father kept it.'

'I must have seen it.' Sofia turned another stiff page.

Chiara tapped a faded colour photograph of a birthday party that depicted Gianni posing with a cake iced with a big 10, children gathered around him. 'Do you know who that is?' Her polished fingernail came to rest beside the thin, excited face of a girl who looked a couple of years younger than Gianni.

'No idea. Should I know?' Sofia prepared to turn to a fresh set of prints.

'It's my mother.'

'Really?' Sofia returned to the photo, examining it carefully. 'Your parents knew each other as children?'

Chiara laughed. 'Almost all their lives. The families were friends and attended the same church.'

'I didn't know.' Sofia began to turn the pages with a fresh eye, looking for that same little girl at other parties, at picnics, riding a bike that was too big for her, wearing an expression of intense concentration. 'Is this our grandparents' garden?'

'But yes, it is on Via Salvatore.'

'Of course.' Sofia turned more pages, studying the stone

house and its many windows. She worked through the album, pausing for a long time at a photo of teenage Aldo and Gianni in football kit, arms slung around each other's necks and beaming. 'It's nice to see there was affection between them once.'

It was when she reached the pages relating to when Aldo and Gianni were young men that her heart began to beat harder. Not all the photographs were uniform squares or rectangles; some were smaller, as if scissors had been taken to them.

Once or twice an elbow or shoulder intruded at the cut edge.

Someone had been cut off. Sofia had to drag in a deep breath to counteract the drumming of her blood in her ears, realising that one missing part of her was *not* in these pages – her mother, Dawn. Had someone methodically excised her from the family history? A heartbroken Gianni? A jealous Mia? A sensitive grandparent keen to avoid further hurt?

Chiara had fallen silent as if she were seeing the album through Sofia's eyes now and feeling uncomfortable.

To alleviate the awkwardness Sofia said, 'Here's your mother as a young woman. You look like her.' The early-twenties Mia in the picture stared at Gianni with her heart in her eyes. Sofia turned page after page. In one of the cut-down images, Mia, Aldo and Gianni were looking towards the cut edge of the photo. Aldo and Gianni were smiling, eyes alight. Mia's expression was more of a glare.

Very soon, Aldo disappeared from the photos. The snap-shots were once again of a uniform size and, after many more pages, Gianni and Mia's wedding photograph appeared to round the album off.

With a sigh, Sofia closed the volume and handed it back.

Though it had given her a wonderful insight into the early life of Aldo with his family, it had also left her sad, as if she'd lived through that turbulent time in the Bianchi family herself.

Chiara smoothed the cover regretfully. 'I'm sorry. I wanted to share the pictures of your father as a boy. I didn't think of . . . the old story.' A cleft had dug itself between her brows and she looked sincerely upset.

Sofia summoned a smile. 'It was nothing to do with us.' Except if Gianni had married his first love, Dawn, neither Sofia nor Chiara would be here. It made her reflect on the randomness of life and relationships. Of her links to her family so tenuous; of Amy's being not what she thought; and Levi's including a child he didn't know he had.

Chiara's voice broke into her thoughts. 'I'm afraid I have work I must attend to, but please stay for as long as you like. Perhaps a glass of wine?' She glanced around as if ready to summon a waiter.

Sofia jumped up. 'Thank you, but I think I'll walk up the hill to look at our grandparents' old house. You don't have time to come with me?'

'I wish I did.' Chiara put down the album in order to embrace Sofia fiercely. 'I hope to see you again soon. I'm intrigued by my English cousin.' She laughed. 'Papà was so astonished to learn you spoke good Italian. It was the first thing he said to my mother after he'd met you. He said he could imagine you staying in Montelibertà for a long time. It was then he began to talk of offering you a role at Hotel Alba.'

Sofia felt torn. Whatever happened in the future, whether Mia ever treated her with anything other than cold courtesy and whether Gianni could look at her without feeling a double dose of pain, here was one clear and clean link to her bloodline. Her cousin. 'In some ways, I wish I could. But I don't think I'll be in Montelibertà for long.'

'Oh.' Chiara looked downcast. 'I was hoping we would get to know each other better.' She hesitated, trouble clouding her eyes. 'You won't leave without saying goodbye, will you?'

'Of course not!' Sofia gave her cousin a spontaneous hug.

They exchanged contact details and Chiara issued directions to their grandparents' old house and promised to tell her parents that Sofia was sorry to have missed them.

Then Sofia was free to set off further up the hill, negotiating the twists and turns of the streets to a broad thoroughfare in a comfortable neighbourhood of houses gazing out over the town. She found the house she was looking for easily. Being of stone it had changed very little in the thirty-odd years since the photographs in her grandparents' album.

She stood for several minutes, gazing into the gardens and imagining her father using trees for goalposts as he played football with his little brother. Then, in their twenties, Gianni bringing home the English girl he'd fallen in love with . . .

Tears pricked her eyes. It was a very strange feeling to know herself to be the result of the love of her parents but the pain of her wider family. It was no wonder Gianni had exhibited such mixed feelings towards her and Mia had greeted her so coolly.

She only emerged from her dark thoughts when she received a text.

Levi: *Are you avoiding me?*

It didn't lift her mood but the code between people

who'd slept together demanded honesty, in her view. She sighed as she replied.

Sofia: I thought it would be easier all round if I spent my days off away from Casa Felice. I'm sure you understand.
Levi: Not really.

She wasn't sure she understood herself. Self-preservation had prompted her to decline his invitation. She was suffering from a strong sense of how much she was going to miss him and spending another night with him would only make her miss him a hell of a lot more.

With a last look at Via Salvatore 58, Sofia turned and wandered back down into the town, found a quiet corner in a pavement café and ordered Orvieto Classico.

She hadn't come to Montelibertà with the expectation of representing safety to an eighteen-year-old, she thought, but nobody with half a heart could leave Amy to fend for herself. The younger girl stood at a crossroads and Sofia had the ability and knowledge to act like a benign human satnav. Heart and soul, she knew that.

On her phone she opened a new browser window and went to the same website where she'd found her original job at Casa Felice to begin researching openings at Italian coastal resorts like Rimini and Sorrento. She liked what she saw. High season meant a lot of live-in jobs for experienced wait staff. The listings for multiple openings were all with huge hotels but the advantages of Amy and her being together outweighed the impersonal aspect of working for a big chain.

Sofia changed to her messages app and sent Amy a text for when she came off shift to see if she would be free any time tomorrow, Wednesday, thinking they could look at the website together then.

Aware of time dragging, of being alone, she prepared

to while away the early part of the evening over a bowl of pasta while she checked out Città della Pieve on her phone as a good place to take herself the next day.

Then, with a distinct feeling that being a young and free woman ought to be more fun than this, she wandered back to her accommodation to spend the last of the evening reading.

The next day, after talking sternly to herself about life being what you make it, and telling herself that if she felt down during a long hot summer in a country she'd longed to visit all her life then she ought to be ashamed, she strode down the hill to catch the bus from where Via Virgilio passed Piazza Roma. She bought a couple of pastries and a takeout cup of coffee and breakfasted gazing through the bus window at alternating woodland, farmland and vineyards until she saw the golds, pinks and browns of Città della Pieve rising above the trees.

Her research had told her that parts of Città della Pieve dated back to medieval times and, as she strolled beside the wall dating back to the twelfth century, she tried to breathe in the atmosphere of permanence and serenity. People had been living out their lives here, perched up on a hill, since Roman times. As a travel site had informed her importantly, Colin Firth was a resident, although she didn't catch a glimpse of him as she wandered the narrow streets, trying not to wonder how Levi was filling his time today. She lunched on salad and a glass of wine while she watched the world go by from a table outside a trattoria: groups of old men argued and laughed; small children were chivvied by harassed mothers. The sun was particularly strong within the walls on the hilltop and after lunch Mr and Mrs Tourist seemed to be in the majority, sweating and frowning and turning pink.

Finally, Sofia gave up trying to pretend she was enjoying herself and took the bus back to Montelibertà. Her object had been achieved – to while away Levi's last day without giving in to the temptation of phoning him. In less than twelve hours he'd roar off on his motorbike. The only contact they'd have would be the occasional message about Amy, unless Sofia was going to take the giant stride of not only forgetting and forgoing her two-year single-person-travelling plan but presenting herself un-invited on Levi's doorstep in England to see if he was up for an extension to their one-afternoon-night-morning stand.

Ignoring the heaviness she felt inside, she showered and changed. She tried ringing Amy but the call went to voice-mail so she decided to grab herself something to eat.

As Levi's motorbike was absent from the car park, she decided there would be little risk of running into him if she ordered something from Il Giardino to take back to her room. She'd just given her order to Thomas when she spotted Amy emerging from the gate to the yard.

'There you are! I was beginning to think you'd been abducted by aliens.' Sofia hurried to the edge of Il Giardino to intercept the younger girl as she gained the pavement and turned towards town.

'Oh. Hello.' Amy looked pale and unhappy, just as she had when she first arrived.

Sofia was concerned. 'You OK?'

'Yes.' Amy began to edge round her. 'I'm going to meet Noemi.'

If she wanted to pursue the conversation Sofia found she had to rotate on the spot. 'I texted you. I was hoping we could talk—'

''Course.' But Amy didn't pause to firm up arrangements.

She hurried on down the hill, her blonde hair flying behind her.

Left alone, Sofia glanced across at Davide, who was picking up an order at the kitchen hatch. Had he started bothering Amy again? Why hadn't Amy told Sofia or Levi if so? Or had Levi told Amy he was her father and that was what was making her look so woebegone? But surely Levi would have sent Sofia a message to put her in the picture?

The evening was warm and Sofia took a couple of bottles of cold beer to go with her calzone and set off for her own quarters, exchanging friendly goodnights with Thomas and Matteo and offhand nods with Davide.

Levi's motorbike still wasn't back in its usual space and she tried to be glad, but the thought that she'd probably already seen him for the last time made her throat ache.

Head drooping, she scuffed across the utility yard and descended the steps to the staff gate.

And then a voice came from the shadows. 'I hate this. It's as if we're parting on bad terms.'

Heart hammering, she halted.

Levi stepped out of the shadows, his brows drawn together in a horizontal line. 'Are we on bad terms?' he asked.

She shook her head. 'I thought it might be easier not to make a thing about saying goodbye.' Like ripping off a plaster in one go instead of peeling it away slowly.

'It's not.' He sounded flat. 'It feels wrong. Rude. Inappropriate. Hurtful. Dismissive.' And then, as if she hadn't got the message the first time: '*Wrong.*'

The box containing the calzone was warm in her hands. She'd been looking forward to eating it but now just its smell was making her feel queasy. 'Your motorbike's not in the car park.'

'I parked around the corner.'

'Oh. Have you sorted out what's going on at home with your business? Your friend Wes and Octavia?'

'No.'

'Have you told Amy the truth?'

'No. But what the fuck have these things got to do with you refusing to see me for the last two days of my stay? If you ask me, *that's* no way to say goodbye.' He moved in until he could rest his hands lightly on her bare arms.

In a moment of weakness she let herself lean into him and his face moved close to hers. He began to drop kisses on her forehead, her cheeks, her eyelids, the corner of her mouth and then her lips, caressing her with his tongue, his hands moving to cradle the back of her head and the small of her back. She could feel the calzone box squashing against her stomach. The beer bottles chinked.

'Your life's in England,' she managed, when he let her up for breath.

He groaned as he laid his cheek against her hair. 'And yours isn't. I get that. But I still wish . . .'

'That?'

'That things were different.' Finally he released her, leaving her with lips tingling. 'I'll be in touch.'

'OK.' Aware of his gaze on her she turned and fumbled her way through the staff gate and into her room. But, somehow, the knowledge that she had to get up before six tomorrow wasn't enough to let her sleep. The room was hot and airless, bugs buzzed outside and Sofia's mind wouldn't rest, constantly reminding her that she was living her dream as well as fulfilling her promises to Aldo to travel and live like a single woman. It would be ridiculous to swap that for pursuing a relationship in England that had never even had a chance to get going and might never live up to hope or expectation.

She'd known Levi Gunn such a short time and in the morning he'd be gone, back to his own life. And out of Sofia's.

Chapter Nineteen

Since the conversation on Monday night when Sofia had said she didn't want to go to Spain, everything had turned to crap all over again, Amy thought as she climbed up Via Virgilio as if it were Everest. She felt as if there was a big stone in her stomach. Sofia hadn't said that Amy was invited to go with her wherever she did go.

What was it with people? Did the whole world have to let her down? Amy had begun feeling OK about Montelibertà and Casa Felice when first Levi, then Sofia, had said they were moving on.

Levi wasn't unexpected. It was a shame because it had been good to have a man who kept asking, dad-like, if she was OK. She was pretty sure Davide wouldn't have shit himself half so much if it had been her or Sofia who'd jumped out in the dark and bellowed 'Rah!' at him that night by the staff accommodation – that had been so cool – but Levi was a punter, a tourist, and all guests checked out sooner or later.

Sofia, though. Amy had tried to tell herself about the age difference . . . but she knew in her heart she'd expected

Sofia to keep her word because she'd provided Amy with something that felt like solid ground when her life had turned to shifting sands. Noemi and Matteo would be off to uni in the autumn. What would Amy do then? She only expected to remain at Casa Felice until mid-September.

She passed the kiosk, all shut for the night. A cat on a wall mewed at her as if to beg for fuss. When Amy stopped and put out her hand the cat jumped down and vanished into the darkness.

Amy resumed her trek, blinking back babyish tears that a cat had rejected her along with everyone else.

The backs of her calves began to ache. She'd worked the lunch shift extended by two hours, which was like an eight-hour power walk balancing heavy weights, then trekked into town only to stand up all night in a bar because it was packed and she hadn't wanted to be the dweeb who whined, 'Can't we go somewhere where they have chairs?'

Now she had to walk back again and the uphill slog wasn't made any easier by her carting along a sackload of negative thoughts. She tried to do what her dad – Stephen – always suggested and think positively.

She could go to Germany or the UK, where she knew the language, and get a proper job. That was positive. She had money because she'd been paid in euros all the time she was here and she was almost shocked at how much was in her account.

Or she could even go home, wait for the resits and finish her exams. The thought crept into her head like a puppy hopeful of a fond reception. She was homesick again. It was gnawing at her stomach, hanging from her heart, burning behind her eyes. Sometimes she wanted nothing more than to go back to the sturdy family home

241

in Neufahrn. She could almost imagine the train journey back, changing twice, then in ten hours or so pulling into München Hauptbahnhof. She could be home in Neufahrn an hour later. She thought about ringing Stephen or Kris – Louis would probably already be in bed.

Even . . . well, she could even ring her mum, couldn't she?

She'd been so angry for so many weeks but now she'd talked to Dad the thought had been nagging at her that never forgiving her mum meant never seeing her mum. Deep inside herself she knew she couldn't do that, especially as it would probably mean not seeing Kris or Louis either, or at least not until they were old enough to travel independently. And Louis was only twelve now.

As if reading her mind, her phone rang. She scrabbled for it in the tiny bag she wore crosswise across her body. *Kris* the screen said. A tiny warm feeling began in her heart as she answered. 'Hey. What you up to?' There was a bench nearby and she dropped down on it, lifting her hair off her neck as a light breeze stirred the warm air.

'Umm, yeah.' Kris seemed to be having trouble deciding what to say.

Amy could imagine him rubbing his fingers through his hair, which grew in a cowlick at the front. He'd always tried to flatten until recently, when he'd had his hair shaved at the sides and spiked up at the front.

'Yeah, what?' She laughed. 'What's up?' Then her stomach twisted into a little knot of misgiving. 'Are you OK?' Kris was only usually tongue-tied if he had to confess to a broken window or getting caught out at school.

'Umm, yeah,' he said again. Then in a rush, 'Mum and Dad were having this crazy argument tonight. Really loud, so I could hear what they said.' He paused.

'That's crap,' Amy said, making her voice encouraging.

Stepping back into her role of big sister made her feel a surprising amount better. Until the day the truth had boiled over her family, removing layers of skin, she'd rarely heard her parents argue. Certainly not in the bellows-of-rage way. 'Was it, like, dead upsetting? Was Louis upset?'

'He's on a sleepover.' The words seemed to be coming to Kris more easily now. 'Thing is, Dad was really angry all over again and Mum started shouting back. And . . . well . . .'

'What?' Amy's hair tickled her face as the breeze tried to get it to play. She swept it back.

Kris took an audible breath. 'Umm, yeah. Dad said it was driving him insane, that Mum had lied all this time. They were talking about your . . . umm, like, you know, your real . . .'

An icy hand grabbed at Amy's insides. She tried to keep her voice steady. 'My real dad?' Just saying it hurt like hell, reminding her that she wasn't who she thought she was, that she didn't really have any right to call Stephen Webber 'Dad' at all. She wasn't even 'Webber' herself, when you thought about it.

'Yeah.' Probably relieved to have her put it into words first, Kris went on all in a rush. 'And you know what, Amy? He came *here* to this house!'

'*What*? When? How could he?' Amy felt frozen with horror. 'He couldn't. Mum had a thing with him before her and Dad got married, before we moved to Germany.'

'But he's been here and talked to Mum and Dad, not long after you left,' Kris insisted. His voice had become hoarse as if he was trying to talk loudly for emphasis at the same time as staying quiet because he didn't want to be overheard. 'Dad told Mum that he knew why she'd invited him but it had been torture. He asked her if she'd been in touch with him all these years and she denied it.'

'But she's *in touch with him now*?' Amy's voice had dwindled to a whisper. She tried to throw her mind back. Hadn't she demanded to know who her real father was? And her mum had just said he was someone she barely knew. Some bloke she'd met on a hen night.

'She must be. But she said she'd never had a thing to do with him until you'd left. Not since . . .'

'Since he got her pregnant with me?' she said numbly.

'I guess.' Kris had a lot of American friends at the international school and was always saying 'I guess' or 'I figure'. 'Dad said it was bloody funny how easily she'd been able to find him as soon as the shit hit the fan. And Mum said—' Kris cleared his throat, '—Mum said, "Look, it's simple. When I went to Bettsbrough on that hen weekend everyone was teasing him because his dad had a garage and if anyone tried to take a shortcut across the forecourt his dad used to shoot out and shout at them to get off, that their surname was Gunn and everyone called his dad Bullet." She just had to look up Gunn, garage and Bettsbrough on the internet then she could click their contact button and say she was an old friend trying to get in touch with him. Your real dad, I mean. Turns out he even works at the garage.'

Amy pulled in a long shuddering breath. Her biological father's surname was Gunn. Suddenly he didn't seem so shadowy. 'So what's his first name?'

'I didn't get it, if they said.' Kris sounded sympathetic.

'So my dad's name is Something Gunn and he lives in a place called Bettsbrough.' Tears began to splash down hotly onto her bare arm. 'Mum knew all this and didn't tell me?' Fresh anger began to tighten her skin. 'And this man's been to see Mum *and Dad* and nobody told me that either?' Her voice began to shake so hard she could scarcely get out the words. 'And he knows about me and hasn't been in touch?'

Kris's voice had gone all tight and small too. 'I guess.'

'So where were you and Louis while this man came to our house?' Now Amy couldn't bring herself to call him 'my real dad'.

'Don't know. We could have already been in bed or it could have been when we were both out. After—' he made a gulping noise '—after you'd gone, me and Louis went to an adventure park thing in the forest with Sean and Eddie and their parents for three days. They, like, asked us all of a sudden and I thought it was Mum and Dad wanting to get us out of the way for a bit. Louis kept asking me whether I thought they were going to split up while we were away. He kept crying. Maybe it was then.'

Crying all the harder at the thought of Louis crying, Amy tried to think what to do. Rage washed through and through her at the thought that people kept knowing things about *her* life all the fucking time and not fucking telling her. Amy rarely said the F-word, even in her head. But some fucking people! She even thought again about going home to Neufahrn solely to rage into their house and scream in her mum's face that she had to just *stop* hiding things. That she had to tell Amy everything there was to know about *Amy's life*.

Then she thought of Louis and Kris and how shitty another huge row would be for them, and that they were having a rough ride anyway because of Amy and her inconvenient parentage. She wouldn't willingly put them through more crap. 'Right,' she choked. 'This man knows

I exist, he's been to see Mum and Dad and then just dropped out of sight, has he? Decided he doesn't want to know me? Right? Well, what about if I want to know him? Let's see how he likes that.'

'What do you mean?' whispered Kris apprehensively.

'I'm going to go and find him.' Amy reassured Kris that he'd done the right thing in telling her and ended the call. She wiped her cheeks on the backs of her hands, sniffing hard. There weren't many people traversing the hill now but a kindly, plump, middle-aged woman stopped to ask Amy if she was OK, while the woman's husband looked on.

Amy managed a tremulous smile. 'Just homesick. I was talking to my family.'

'Aw, bless. Here, lovie, have a few tissues.'

Thanking her, Amy wiped her face and blew her nose then assured the couple that she was OK now and when they'd started back on their journey up the hill she called up the web on her phone.

It wasn't hard to follow the route her mother had already taken, though at first she misspelled the place name and Google told her it was *Showing results for Bettsbrough* to set her right. It sounded vaguely familiar but there were so many places with 'brough' or 'borough' that they all sounded alike to a girl who'd lived in Bavarian Germany for half her life. She typed into the search engine 'bettsbrough' 'gun' and 'garage' and . . . abracadabra! There was the link to the Gunn's Motors website. Still sniffing angrily she bookmarked it and then put *monteliberta to bettsbrough* in the search engine and went to a travel site that worked out the whole trip for her.

She had her debit card in her bag and with a succession of angry little stabs at her phone screen booked her entire passage from here to the UK, stalling only when she didn't have her passport number so couldn't complete check-in. Tucking phone and card away she stormed up the hill to her room to grab her passport and finish the process.

She remembered saying to Sofia 'I've lost the old me.' Maybe when she found her real dad she'd get some inkling of who the new her was. For a start, she was someone who was going to confront the man who wasn't even brave enough to get in contact with her once he knew he was her dad. What a cowardly tosser.

Chapter Twenty

When Sofia began her shift on Thursday at 7 a.m. the first guest she had to deal with was Levi. Aurora wasn't around, as she'd begun to leave Sofia alone on the front desk during quiet periods.

'Bike's all packed. I'm ready to check out,' he said, waving his key card. He waited in silence while Sofia printed his check-out sheet, forearms resting on the marble next to his red motor cycle helmet.

Glancing through the printout before passing it to him she summarised the contents. 'You prepaid your room and there are no extras.'

'Agreed.' He gave her his key card in exchange, warm from his hand, and his eyes locked with hers. 'I hope things go well for you.'

'And for you.' Sofia's thoughts flew back to the way he'd held her last night as he'd kissed her. Having already said goodbye like that, this clinical exchange felt incongruous.

He sighed and straightened up. Sofia could hear from the solid *thunks* as he shifted his feet that he was wearing his biking boots. 'Will you say goodbye to Amy for me? I saw her yesterday evening but she was in a rush. It was all a bit . . . awkward and unsatisfactory.'

'I'll tell her when I see her.' And as there was nobody else in reception so early in the morning she added, 'Try not to worry about her. I'll let you know she's OK for as long as we're together.' She felt tender inside, as if his pain and perplexity were contagious.

'Thank you.' He hesitated, nearly spoke, didn't, then turned and strode across the marble floor and out of the doors, his jacket over one shoulder.

Sofia stared after him until she heard his bike roar to life, the engine drop to a gentle grumble and then roar again before it diminished down the hill. She imagined him slowing through town then picking up speed as he headed for the *autostrade* that would take him on today's leg of his journey.

She turned back to the computer and worked steadily through the morning, switching on a smile whenever one was needed. She checked out other guests and printed the sheets ready for when those checking in began to arrive. Eleven o'clock came and went and she glanced through the doors to the sunlight of Il Giardino several times, hoping to catch sight of Amy as she knew she was on early shift today. She took phone calls, gave out maps and information and soothed guests who were ruffled by inefficient towel changing or breakfast ending before they'd heaved themselves out of bed.

It was nearly three and the end of the shift when Aurora arrived to replace her. 'My mother would like to see you in her office, please.'

Sofia looked up, startled. 'Now?' The summons, unfortunately familiar, usually signalled her getting sacked.

Benedetta hadn't seen her kissing Levi in the dark of the gardens last night . . . had she? The woman must have night-vision goggles if so. Well, what the hell. If she had, she had. Sofia could always put in motion her plans to leave, though it would be complicated by not having talked to Amy yet and Levi's room not being available for her to retreat to while Amy worked her one-week notice. Maybe Chiara would give her a bed. It probably wouldn't please Mia if she threw herself on the charity of her uncle.

'Yes, please.' Aurora turned to greet an approaching guest.

Sofia was left to make her way to Benedetta's office and tap on the partly opened door. Benedetta beckoned her in with rapid, agitated movements. 'Where's Amy? Do you know where she's gone?'

Coming to an abrupt halt, Sofia gazed at her in astonishment. 'Gone?'

Benedetta jumped up and began to pace. 'She didn't arrive for work at eleven so I sent Noemi down to knock. When she received no answer she tried the door and it was unlocked. All Amy's things have gone and the room key was on the bed.'

Benedetta's office seemed to shift around Sofia in a slow swoop, making her grope behind herself for a chair to fall into.

'You don't know?' Benedetta demanded.

'No.' Sofia's voice sounded distant. 'I saw her yesterday evening. She didn't seem particularly happy but she didn't say why.' She wanted to ply Benedetta with questions about what time Amy left, and how, but Benedetta was very obviously in the dark. Where the hell had Amy gone? What was she running away from this time? Guilt stole over her. Why hadn't she tried to detain Amy yesterday evening and make greater efforts to see why she was being so distant? Because she was too absorbed in her own worries, she answered herself. She'd thought about Amy only as a consideration, an influence on what she, Sofia, did next.

She moistened her lips. 'I take it you've tried to ring her?'

'She's not answering.'

Panic painted a broad stripe of sweat down Sofia's back. Amy was still reeling from the shock of what had happened to make her flee her home. True, she'd got herself to Montelibertà and Casa Felice but Sofia knew that wolves like Davide were drawn to her, scenting a lamb that had strayed from the flock.

She realised that Benedetta was putting a cup of coffee before her on the desk and encouraging her to drink. Automatically, Sofia did so. 'Have you asked Matteo and Noemi whether they know anything? She made friends with their group. Maybe she met someone there that she's gone off with?' But she knew she was grasping at straws.

Benedetta paced a couple of steps to and fro once more, if not wringing her hands then clasping them so tightly that the knuckles gleamed. 'Noemi is on duty in Il Giardino and Davide has talked to her already. She says Amy left them after eleven last night. Matteo is on his rest day so I'll phone him now.' She suited her action to her words but, although Matteo answered straightaway, he had no light to shed on Amy's whereabouts.

Benedetta took another turn about the room. 'I don't like such a young girl vanishing from my hotel.' She spoiled this laudable comment by adding, 'If anything's happened to her and the word gets out, it could be very bad for Casa Felice.'

Disregarding Benedetta's not exactly unselfish slant, Sofia wiped her sweating palms on her skirt. 'I'll get my phone and try her myself. She might pick up for me when she wouldn't for you.' She jumped up and hurried off to grab her bag from the back office. Her first call went to voicemail and she left a message. 'Amy, are you OK? Everyone's wondering where you are. Ring me back!' The second and third attempts went straight to voicemail too. By then, she was back in Benedetta's office where Benedetta was still doing her pacing thing again.

'Why doesn't she answer?' Benedetta snapped. 'You're her friend.'

Just in case Amy was refusing to answer on purpose, Sofia began to text, thumbs flying across her screen at the adrenalin crashing around her body. She decided that a white lie was called for in the current situation.

Sofia: Amy, if you get this text ring me. Benedetta is talking about contacting your parents to say you've disappeared and asking if they want to involve the police.

Thirty seconds later, Amy rang. Sofia fumbled to answer. Before she could speak Amy said, 'Tell her not to be so stupid. She's got no right to call my parents. She's just being a horrible stressy witch as usual.'

Sofia pressed the phone to her ear, hoping Benedetta couldn't overhear sufficiently well to translate Amy's English. She decided not to waste time with explaining that the mention of her parents had only been a ruse. 'Are you OK? Benedetta called me in to say you'd taken off and I've been frantic ever since.'

'Have you?' Amy's voice sounded suddenly small and unsure.

Sofia let some of her exasperation filter into her voice. 'Why wouldn't I be frantic at you leaving without a word? Especially as I've spent most of the past couple of days trying to pin you down to a conversation about us moving on together.' She disregarded the frostily raised eyebrows with which Benedetta greeted this news.

'Did you? I thought—' Amy's voice was smaller than ever. She paused and in the hush Sofia caught the unmistakeable sound of a public announcement system.

Her heart bounced off the pit of her stomach. 'Where are you?'

A hesitation, then Amy answered. 'Roma-Ciampino airport.'

'Holy shit. Where the hell are you off to?'

Another pause. Then Amy spoke with more determination. 'OK, I'll tell you but I don't want you to tell anyone else.'

'Benedetta's extremely concerned too. I'm in her office,' Sofia said, to make it plain that Amy might be overheard.

Immediately, the younger girl became flustered. 'Just tell her sorry, that I got some news and I'm on my way to . . .' She paused, obviously trying to come up with something. 'On my way to see some of my family.'

'Hang on.' Sofia passed the message on to Benedetta, who muttered about a 'silly English girl' and told Sofia in Italian to pass on to Amy in English that she'd forfeit wages in lieu of notice. Sofia stopped and glared. 'I'm sure you don't mean that. You're going to pay her for the hours she's worked. *Aren't* you? Because she's a seasonal worker, so you can't demand notice.'

Benedetta's face darkened but she reluctantly conceded, flapping her hands at Sofia. 'I've wasted too much time on that girl. She should be back with her family. She's too young.' Evidently her concern was over now she knew Amy hadn't been coerced or abducted from Casa Felice.

Sofia was glad to leave the office, getting Amy to hang on while she hurried through the hotel, across the terrace and into the staff garden. Dropping down onto the bench she and Amy had shared so often, she panted, 'What's going on?'

A long sigh came down the phone line. 'I'm sorry I went without telling you. I thought . . . Well, I thought you were going on to a seaside hotel on your own, so you didn't want to be bothered with me any more.'

'*What*?' Sofia was dumbfounded. 'I was trying to discuss us going on together on Monday evening, but we were interrupted by you getting a call from your little brother. I've been trying to get to talk to you about it ever since.'

'Oh. You didn't say anything about me – just you leaving.' Amy sounded more sheepish than ever. 'I've been feeling really shit.'

'Amy! We'd already agreed—! Look, let's not worry about that now. Tell me why you're at the airport.'

Another public address announcement came down the line making Sofia grip the phone impatiently. Amy spoke again, sounding doubtful. 'I think they might have just called my flight. Hang on.' Sofia sat through shuffling and scratching. Then Amy came back on the line. 'No, that was Heathrow not Stansted. I've moved seats now so I can see the screen.'

'So you're going to the UK?' Sofia took a deep breath to prevent herself adding '*Why would you do that?*' and tried to sound relaxed. 'What time's your flight?'

'Seventeen thirty-five. I've been through security.'

Amy really was on her way. Sofia mentally apologised

for doubting her travel capabilities. 'So what's taking you to the UK? Are you going to your grandparents?'

'No!' Amy sounded hurt and angry. 'I'm going to England to find my real dad and tell him what a shit he is.'

For a couple of seconds Sofia was too shocked to speak. Then, 'I didn't think you knew who—'

'My brother Kris rang and told me he'd heard Mum and Dad – Stephen-Dad, I mean – having a row. That man, my real dad, has been to our house in Munich.' And the whole story of how Freya had got in touch with Levi came tumbling out, caked with outrage and hurt, the same story Sofia had already heard from Levi's perspective. 'So I did the same as Mum and found this garage on the internet and I'm going to go find him and tell him he might be too cowardly to face me but I'm not too cowardly to face him. He hasn't made any attempt to get in touch with me. I can't get over the fact that *Mum* knew who he was, *Dad* knew who he was, he'd been *to our house*, and nobody told me!' Amy was sobbing now. 'I honestly don't know who I can trust any more. Everybody just lies!'

Sofia listened with rising alarm, thinking frantically. Despite her promise to Levi, should she tell Amy now that she actually knew her read dad pretty well? It might prevent the news being such a massive shock than if she turned up at Gunn's Motors and heard it there. But once Amy knew that Sofia had been perpetuating the deceit . . . Sofia had a strong feeling that Amy would instantly cut ties between them. All the younger girl's hot-headed behaviour to date pointed to that result.

Levi's secret had never seemed both harder to keep and more impossible to reveal.

She cast around for a way to talk Amy out of her precipitate exit. 'The thing to remember is that nobody's actually done what they've done to hurt you. Maybe they've been a bit ill-advised but—'

Amy indicated her contempt for that viewpoint by snapping uncharacteristically, 'Oh, balls!' Then, 'I think I just heard my flight being called. Bye, Sofia. I'm going to have to turn my phone off now.'

'Keep in touch, Amy!' Sofia half yelled . . . just as the line went dead in her ear. Stunned by the turn events had taken she stared at her phone, mind working furiously. Even if Amy's flight had been called a good two hours prior to take-off, she wouldn't have to switch her phone off yet. She was obviously in the grip of a tumult of emotions and being irrationally defiant to anyone and everyone and, whilst Sofia couldn't entirely blame her, someone needed to keep a cool head to try and sort out as much of this mess as could be sorted.

Levi needed to know what Amy was up to. Quickly, she opened her contacts list and selected *Levi*. She got the ringing tone and then voicemail. 'Levi, it's Sofia,' she said. 'Ring me as soon as you get this message. Amy's found out her real dad's connection to your dad's garage and she's on her way there.'

Leaving the phone on the bench so she'd hear when he rang back, she hurried into her room, threw off her uniform suit, which felt as if it were choking her with its formal jacket and high collar, and wriggled into shorts and a top. She made herself coffee in the biggest mug she could find and went back into the garden, the heat hitting her as she stepped out of the comparative cool of her room.

She glanced at the phone. Nothing.

Crap. Probably Levi was hammering along on his motor-bike and there would, obviously, be no chance of hearing the phone ring. Hoping she might get him when he was

256

making a pit stop she rang at ten-minute intervals for the next two hours, pacing restlessly in and out of her room between times. Then she decided to try texting, as everyone saw texts as soon as they looked at their phones and it wouldn't rely on catching him at just at the right moment in the same way that a call would.

Sofia: Ring me as soon as you get this message. It's really important.

Then she texted Amy.

Sofia: Travel safely. Keep in touch. Remember that I'm always on your side. xxx

After she'd pressed *send* she hovered for ten minutes, just in case Amy had calmed down and rang back. Then she hovered for another ten minutes wondering whether she should ring Amy again – but would that be disrespectful of the boundary she'd drawn by saying she had to turn her phone off, even if Sofia knew she'd been telling porkies?

Time dragged by. Sofia prowled restlessly, folding the clothes she'd left in the tumble dryer, making coffee and checking her phone was still showing a good signal and hadn't somehow put itself on silent or 'do not disturb'.

By seven she knew she had to do something or burst. She tried three more times to ring Levi, leaving a couple more messages, as if he might unaccountably have not realised from her earlier messages and texts that something had occurred that warranted his attention.

Eventually, driven by a gnawing emptiness and the knowledge that she'd hardly eaten today, she went up to Il Giardino, phone in the pocket of her cut-off denim shorts and ringer volume up full. Feeling the need for comfort food she chose from what she thought of as the tourists' part of the menu – a bowl of chips and a couple of sachets of tomato ketchup with a mug of tea. Noemi, whose section she was in, served her amidst muttered questions about Amy. Benedetta had apparently told her that Amy was off on her travels and Noemi repeated several times that Amy hadn't said a word about it the evening before.

Sofia nodded and shook her head at the right points and added in a couple of shrugs to indicate that it was all a mystery to her too.

Her phone didn't ring.

She left half the chips and ordered a beer.

Her phone still didn't ring.

She tried Levi again then, in desperation, went into reception. Elise was on duty, whom Sofia only knew from handing over the front desk at the end of a shift. Despite knowing that she must be contravening at least two of Benedetta's rules by being in the wrong clothes in the wrong place and logging on when she should be logged off, Sofia just smiled and said, 'Need to check something.' She went into the recent guest records on the computer and checked that Mr Levi Gunn's mobile number in their records corresponded with the one in her phone. It did, of course. She'd known it would because hadn't Levi messaged and called her from that number while he'd been here?

But she was clutching at straws. That's what people did when they didn't know where to turn. They checked things they already knew to be correct and repeated fruitless tasks like ringing the same number over and over even when there was no reply.

Just as she was about to turn away from the computer she noticed a red star next to Levi's name to denote a 'live' note concerning this guest. She clicked through to the relevant entry and saw:

258

Caricabatterie trovato nella stanza di questo ospite dopo il check-out e la partenza.

She almost swore aloud, until she remembered herself. *Telephone charger found in the room of this guest after check-out and departure.* No wonder Levi wasn't answering his phone. It was probably out of charge.

Sofia shut down the record automatically and with a parting smile for Elise trailed back out to Il Giardino. She nearly ordered another beer but then, deciding she must keep a clear head, ordered espresso instead.

Dusk was falling. Lights coming on. It was nearly eight-thirty.

Amy should have reached England, presumably en route to this small town called Bettsbrough in Cambridgeshire, a neighbouring county to Bedfordshire, where Sofia had grown up.

She knew Levi expected to take at least three days to travel home and had left that morning, Thursday. That meant he wouldn't get back until Saturday at the earliest.

To make sure that she hadn't had a change of heart and stayed in Italy, gone home to Germany or hitched a ride to Timbuktu, Sofia rang Amy again, inexplicably reassured when the ringtone she heard was the good old British double ring. Amy didn't pick up but Sofia felt she'd at least reached her destination country.

Presumably Amy wouldn't be able to raise anybody at the Gunn garage until it opened tomorrow, Friday. A cold feeling stole over Sofia. Where would Amy spend the night? Did she have enough money to stay in a hotel? Did she have her grandparents' contact details if she found she needed someone to turn to in the UK? Kids often relied on the generation in between for details like

259

that and she was pretty sure that in her present state of mind it would be a cold day in hell before Amy rang her mum or dad.

Putting aside that worry for a moment she tried to envisage Amy approaching a member of Levi's family and finding out the truth . . .

She should have told her while she had her on the phone. This new conviction hit her like a bucket of iced water. OK, it wasn't her secret, it wasn't her business but, clearly, the chances of Amy discovering Levi's identity from his family were now high, and it would be a much greater blow than if she heard the truth from someone who could explain Levi's thinking behind withholding the truth, and highlight the purity of his intentions. Did Levi's family even know that Amy existed? They might snub her or call her a liar. They might be angry with her.

Where the hell would Amy go then?

Amy needed a friend to turn to. Sofia jumped up, threw a twenty-euro note on the table and hurried across Il Giardino and the yard and down the steps to the staff accommodation.

Fumbling as she unlocked her room, she fell in, yanked her cases from beneath the bed and began to fling in her possessions.

Then she paused for thought. Idiot! What was she going to do? Sit in the garden and wait for a magic carpet to arrive? She raced back outside, dropped on the bench and took a calming breath while she got online and searched for the fastest way to get to England. In twenty minutes she'd booked the 23.09 train to Roma Termini. It got in too late for her to get the shuttle bus or train to Roma-Ciampino airport so she'd have to get a taxi. But that would allow her to be at the airport in bags of time to catch the 06.30 from Rome on Friday morning, landing at Stansted at 08.15. She got out her credit card and booked each ticket for the Italian leg of the journey.

Trains ran directly between Stansted and Peterborough and she could buy that ticket at Stansted Airport. She was bound to be able to get local transport between Peterborough and Bettsbrough once on the ground.

She went back indoors to finish her packing.

On the way through the hotel, dragging her suitcases one at a time up the steps, she stopped at reception and scribbled a note for Benedetta.

Sorry to leave you in the lurch, Benedetta, but I'm going to the UK and won't be available for shifts. Best wishes, Sofia Bianchi.

She even smiled, imagining vividly the expression on Benedetta's face when she discovered that another silly English girl had done a runner.

Chapter Twenty-one

Amy perched on a wall across the road from Gunn's Motors, watching the comings and goings of the place, her heart crashing about her chest with the enormity of what she was here to do.

It had been a drizzly Friday morning but now the sun was popping in and out of the clouds and Amy wished it would stay out all the time. British summertime didn't seem very summery after Italy. She'd asked for an extra blanket at the Airbnb she stayed at last night and the lady who owned the house, Jean, had said, 'Gosh, you must be a cold mortal.' She was round and middle-aged and used words like 'gosh' and 'crikey' a lot. She reminded Amy of her grandmother in Hendon, comforting in a way as during the years Amy had lived in Germany, England had slowly slipped into unfamiliarity.

The forecourt Amy was watching was curved to follow the line of the corner it stood on and had room for about ten cars with their prices on the windscreens. Behind them stood a few vehicles without prices. A man in navy blue overalls had come out, started one up and driven it inside the building. The car was now on a ramp in the air with the man working underneath it. He wasn't her father. He only looked about ten years older than Amy herself.

The two-storey building stood diagonally on the plot, the woodwork painted white and the windows made of that kind of crinkly glass you couldn't see through properly. Apart from the entrance to the repair shop the building had another pair of doors and a few people had been and gone through them. A man with grey wavy hair and gold-framed glasses emerged with two of the callers as if chatting while he saw them out. He probably wasn't her father. He was old. . . . *'his dad had a garage . . .'* He could be her grandfather. Another man came out and handed the older man a cordless phone, said something with a grin and went back inside. He had dark blond hair. . . . *'Your real dad. Turns out he even works at the garage.'*

He could be her father!

After they went in, another figure emerged in navy blue mechanic's overalls. He carried a bucket and began washing one of the cars that was for sale, a white one. He was only about Amy's age. It made him seem approachable. Screwing up her courage, she crossed the road in what she hoped was the kind of saunter the confident girls at school had used. She wished she had gum to chew because they'd done a lot of that too.

A chain was looped from post to post around the edges of the forecourt about a foot from the ground. Amy stopped just short of it and tossed back her hair.

The boy in the overalls looked up. He carried on looking at her though his hand was still moving a soapy sponge in circles over the side of the car. 'Hello,' he said.

Amy pushed back her hair again. It kept blowing into her face in the wind. 'Is the market down this road?' She already knew it was. She'd walked through it to the bank ATM to withdraw cash from the English account she'd opened ready for uni. Her mum had put £200 in it and Amy had withdrawn fifty of that. Another £56 had already been showing as a withdrawal for the Airbnb so she'd gone inside the bank and talked to someone about how to move money from her euro account. She might go back and do that later, depending what happened at Gunn's Motors.

The boy nodded, his hand still busy with the sponge. 'Yep. Straight down. You can't see the stalls from here but they're just round the corner. Don't you live in Bettsbrough?'

'Not at the moment.' She decided not to get into that. 'You?'

'Yep.' He dipped his sponge in the bucket and moved a bit closer to wash the next bit. Then he picked up a hose and rinsed it all off.

The conversation lagged and Amy realised she was in danger of standing there like a dork. Inspiration struck. 'I've got family in Bettsbrough though and I was just wondering if Bullet still works here.'

The boy looked up with a grin. 'Don't let him catch you calling him that. We're all supposed to call him Bryan. Yes, it's still his place.'

Excitement and nerves made Amy's voice shake. 'And what about his son? I can't remember his name.'

Picking up the bucket and sponge again the boy moved closer to her to begin on the bonnet. 'Tyrone works here too.' He glanced across at the double doors. 'I think they're both in there. Just ask inside. Val's probably on the front desk. She's Bryan's wife.'

'Thanks.' Amy's voice was definitely shaking now. The boy looked at her with curiosity and opened his mouth

264

as if to speak again but Amy cut him off with a quick 'Bye!' as she turned away.

The journey along the pavement and in through the break in the chain fence to the double doors seemed endless. Amy's legs felt three times their normal weight and the tremor in her voice had filtered into her entire body. The double doors finally loomed, then she was past them and into an open area painted white, with an L of grey seating on one side and a desk on the other. A lady sitting behind the desk gave Amy a smile as she looked up from her computer. 'What can I do for you today?' Her dark hair was threaded with grey and cut in a fringe that seemed to rest along the top of her glasses.

Amy clenched her hands in her pockets as if holding onto something so she didn't run away, trying to recall the anger and purpose that had fuelled her epic trip to Bettsbrough yesterday. She cleared her throat and spoke loudly so her voice wouldn't shake. 'Are Bryan and Tyrone Gunn here, please?'

The lady's eyebrows lifted. 'They are. Did you want to see them?' Curiosity was written all over her face.

'Yes, please.'

The lady took her name and disappeared into some back area. After a minute of a muffled conversation she reappeared. 'Would you like to come through, dear?'

Amy had to force her heavy legs to transport her and her pounding heart around the desk, down a short corridor and into an office containing two untidy desks. The two men she'd caught sight of outside, the grey-haired one and the blond, occupied a desk each.

The grey-haired man smiled comfortably. 'Good morning. Amy, is it? I'm Bryan Gunn. Come and sit down and tell me what I can help you with.' But once she'd halted Amy's legs became so heavy they took root. She swivelled her head to look at the blond man, who was regarding her with a puzzled smile in his hazel eyes. He looked . . . he looked *familiar*. Was it possible for a child to recognise its father on some level, even if they'd never met?

'Are you all right?' she heard Bryan Gunn say, but Amy couldn't stop staring at the blond man.

'This is my son, Tyrone,' Bryan added, sounding half-puzzled, half-amused at Amy's dumb gawking.

So it was him. Bullet Gunn's son. Amy opened her mouth but no words came.

'Hello, Amy,' Tyrone said encouragingly.

Amy suddenly wished she'd taken the chair when it was offered to her because her legs began to shake and tingle. She drew in an enormous breath and held it before letting it out as a teacher had once suggested she do at the start of an exam to calm her nerves. She swallowed hard. 'I think you're my dad,' she blurted out.

Tyrone's eyebrows flew up. 'What?'

'I think you're my dad,' she repeated, her voice gaining strength now the point of no return had been reached. She turned to look at Bryan Gunn. 'Which makes you my granddad.'

The silence in the room could be felt. Tyrone's face was a picture of shock and Amy's mind began to leap crazily from conclusion to conclusion. He was going to say he didn't want anything to do with her. He was going to throw her out. Call her a liar.

It was Bryan who spoke first, rising from his seat and coming around the desk to bring the chair he'd first offered her up close behind her knees. 'Sit down, Amy,' he said gently. 'And tell us what makes you think Tyrone's your dad.'

Weakly, Amy sank onto the seat. Its covering was slightly

itchy. She kept her eyes on Tyrone. 'You came to our house in Germany a few weeks ago, didn't you? You knew about me but you went off again without making any contact. So I decided to find you.'

But even as she said the words, Tyrone was shaking his head. His cheeks had flushed. With relief? 'That's not me.' His voice wasn't as soft as his father's, but it wasn't unkind. 'I haven't been to Germany for years.'

'He works here every day with me,' Bryan chipped in. 'It seems unlikely he made a dash to Germany and back in the last few weeks without me knowing.'

Confusion made Amy's head spin. Her throat felt coated in dust. 'My mother's name is Freya. Freya Williams she was.'

Tyrone shrugged and shook his head again. 'I'm sorry. I'm pretty sure I've never known a Freya Williams. What year were you born?' When Amy told him he looked no wiser. 'I would have been around twenty when you were conceived. I was at university then.'

Amy wanted to put her head between her knees to stop it spinning. 'I think it happened here, in Bettsbrough. My mum said the man was Bullet Gunn's son from this garage—'

Bryan and Tyrone both said, 'Oh!' at the same time. From the corridor came a fainter echo. After a moment, the lady from the front desk stepped into view. She'd obviously been hanging about in the corridor, listening. Now she was hanging onto the doorjamb as if she needed to.

She stared at Amy. 'We've got two sons,' she quavered. 'And the other one has been away all summer in Europe on his motorbike.' She took a deep breath and exchanged glances with Bryan over Amy's head. 'But his name's not Tyrone. It's Levi.'

'Levi? *Levi*?' Amy felt as if she was going to faint and actually did have to put her head down to her knees for a moment. Voices swam in and out of her ears. The lady – if she was Bryan's wife then it looked as if she was Amy's grandmother – crouched down beside Amy and patted her shoulder.

Tyrone went off somewhere and came back with a glass of cold water. 'Can you sit up? Have a few sips.'

Amy did. It seemed to stop her skin from pumping out sweat. She looked around at the three concerned faces. *Levi*. It had to be the same Levi from Casa Felice, the nice guest who'd helped Amy out with Davide. The guest who stayed ages at the hotel, painting watercolours and who had such an obvious liking for Sofia. She looked at Tyrone again. That's why he'd seemed familiar! Not because she'd recognised her father but because of the resemblance he bore to Levi. She sipped from the glass until it was empty, than she put it down. Her hands clenched into fists so tight that her nails dug into her palms. 'Sorry,' Amy managed to say to Tyrone. 'But I was told he worked here and the boy outside told me that you did.'

He nodded, comprehension in his eyes. 'I work in the garage with Dad but Levi has an office in the building, too. Upstairs. For his own business.'

The lady glanced at Bryan. 'It would explain why Levi made such sudden plans to spend time in Europe.'

Bryan heaved a great sigh as he gazed at Amy. 'You've just beaten him here by a day or so. He's due back tomorrow. I think you'd better talk to him then.'

At the idea of facing Levi, the Levi she'd known for weeks, the Levi who'd kept it secret who he was, Amy's anger reared up again full force. Talk to him? *Talk* to him? The man who was too cowardly and deceitful to

268

admit to being her dad but put on a pretence of being a kind stranger instead?

Suddenly the power came back to her legs and she jumped up, making the older couple – her grandparents – shuffle back from their crouched positions on the floor before her. 'That won't be necessary!' she barked, like her mum did when she was outraged. Then she blundered past everybody, uncaring if she bowled anybody off their feet. Her legs told her to run.

And so she ran.

Unaware of her feet touching the floor she ran out of the building and onto the pavement outside, past the boy still working on the white car. Behind her she could hear a man's voice shouting, 'Amy? Amy!' She thought it was Tyrone but she closed her ears and pushed her legs faster until she almost tripped.

When she finally stopped, her breath like fire in her throat and her chest aching, she was in an unfamiliar part of town where black iron benches were artistically arranged amidst flower tubs on a paved area, a refuge from the road running alongside. As if in stark counterpoint to the prettiness, she saw a young man hunched on a sleeping bag in a shop doorway, hair tied back and clothes grubby. Amy sank down onto one of the benches, legs like rubber. Her hair slid down to shield her face while she tried to make sense of her once-pleasant-and-predictable life.

Her thoughts raced even faster than her heart.

What the hell had Levi been playing at? She felt stupid, humiliated, that he'd known who she was when she hadn't had a clue about him. Even if she couldn't summon a coherent argument to support it, her overwhelming feeling was one of betrayal. She closed her eyes, adrenalin draining from her system so fast it made her light-headed.

What the hell should she do next? Jean had told her she could reserve the room at the Airbnb again tonight if she texted by noon. Soon, she promised herself. Soon. Once she knew the answer to 'What the hell should she do next?'

It was disorienting to realise she'd nothing to stay in England for, but she had nothing to go anywhere else for either and the mere idea of making decisions, going on the internet and paying for things, made her feel sick with anxiety. Should she return to Italy? The idea of her still having a job at Casa Felice was laughable and finding another would take time. Back to the secrets and betrayals of home? That made her feel as if sadness had set like concrete inside her. Then again . . . the prospect of never seeing her family made tears slip down her face.

When it came to it, she had no more direction than the homeless guy over there. He looked to be about her own age and she didn't want to end up sharing his doorway.

She could contact her grandparents in Hendon, but the fact that there hadn't been a stream of calls and texts from Nana this summer told her that Amy's mum hadn't rushed to share the news of the family upset with her own parents. Wearily drawing up her knees and resting her forehead on them she supposed that it didn't matter how old you were, your parents always thought they could poke their noses into your life and Mum probably wasn't super-keen to hear Nana's thoughts on what had happened.

The bench turned cold beneath her as the sun went in and the wind sharpened its edge. She stopped trying to think. Everything was too difficult. The world was too tough a place to live in. She felt empty and drawn in.

After a few moments, she recognised the feeling as hunger. When had she last eaten? She'd been too nervous to eat breakfast at the Airbnb and had drunk orange juice instead; Jean had been jokingly exasperated with her turning down Full English.

Sitting up, she noticed the homeless guy watching her from his doorway. He didn't look away when he saw her looking at him. Maybe living on the street made him immune to the usual conventions. Or maybe he was so used to people hurrying by without catching his eye that he thought he'd become invisible.

But not invisible to everyone, it seemed, because at that moment an old Ford Fiesta slowed at the point where the road met the paving and young men hung out of every window pointing and hooting at the homeless guy, jeering, shouting things Amy didn't catch. The homeless guy gave a roar of rage and leaped to his feet, kicking away the sleeping bag and racing fruitlessly at the car as it accelerated just enough to keep ahead of him as he screamed, 'Fucking bastards!' after it.

Giving up the unequal race, he returned to his doorway with slow, beaten-down steps, wiping his eyes on the cuffs of his hoody. He dropped back down to the ground and glanced around to see whether anyone had taken any notice. When nobody showed a sign of it, his shoulders heaved on a sigh and he returned to just sitting, gazing down the street with a distant stare.

Shaken by the casual cruelty of what she'd just witnessed, Amy stumbled to her feet and hurried across the paving towards a nearby McDonalds. Inside, she chose at the touch-screen, having to concentrate as she was used to the German version. When the order was ready to collect she asked for a separate bag for each of the meals.

Outside again, the two warm bags clutched against her and the aroma of fresh fries wafting up to her, the task

271

she'd set herself seemed suddenly enormous. But she looked at her destination doorway, squared her shoulders and began to walk. This wasn't even the hardest thing she'd had to do this morning.

The homeless guy looked up as she approached, his eyes on her bags of food but without any hope or expectation. He didn't raise his eyes to her face until Amy stopped a step away from him. She cleared her throat. 'Chicken McSandwich or Big Mac?'

His eyes widened. 'Me? Why?'

'Because,' Amy shrugged weakly, not really knowing how to explain the urge to feed him just like she'd fed that dog in Montelibertà.

'Oh. Um, Mac, please.'

'Tea or coffee?'

'Coffee. Please.'

His expression turned from disbelief to delight as she checked she had the right drink before handing it to him along with one of the brown paper bags, wishing him 'Guten appetit.'

'Thank you! Thank you so much, that's really kind!' he called after her as she went over to one of the black benches to begin her own meal, cringing inside that she'd wished him *guten appetit*. Could she have said anything more likely to highlight the differences between them, she from her solidly middle-class family and well-travelled background, he from a doorway of a charity shop that had closed down? Why hadn't she just served his McDonald's up with a linen napkin and on a silver tray?

She snorted with unexpected laughter at the thought that Benedetta would no doubt have snapped at her to carry her tray up on her shoulder as she'd been taught.

Then suddenly she was aware of the homeless guy

approaching her, casting a look back at his sleeping bag as if to check nobody was going to steal it while his back was turned, cradling his McDonald's to his chest. Hesitantly, he sat down on the bench beside hers, a move that seemed to be calculated to be close enough to talk while showing her he wasn't about to encroach on her space.

'That was so nice of you,' he said. 'I don't know what to say.' Everything about him was just less than clean and very worn. Though his hair was tied back it looked unbrushed.

Amy felt shy. 'I felt bad for you. Those guys in the car . . .'

He laughed bitterly. 'Yeah. They were the bullies at my school and they think it's funny. My name's Matt and I live in a doorway so they call me "Doormat". Hilarious, eh?'

She suddenly realised that that was what the horrible men had been shouting. 'Hey, Doormat!' 'I hope they crash their shitty car!' she declared.

He laughed again, properly this time. 'Me, too. Well, thanks again.' He rose and returned to his doorway, settling again onto his sleeping bag to eat fries as if savouring every one.

And that was when Amy realised the difference between her and him. *She had choices*.

She stopped feeling defeated and, flushing with mortification at her recent pity party, acknowledged that the number of her choices was magnified by having money and someone to turn to.

'Stop snivelling,' she told herself aloud. She took out her phone and scrolled down her contacts list until she could tap on *Sofia Bianchi*.

Chapter Twenty-two

After only snatches of sleep overnight on the train and plane as she tried to make up Amy's half-day head start, Sofia climbed aboard the Peterborough to Bettsbrough bus just before midday, dragging along her suitcases and a giant headache. Having booked online for two nights at the Bettsbrough Travelodge, she was grateful to a kind lady bus-seat partner who told her when it was her stop and ensured the driver gave her time to heave all her luggage onto the pavement. By the time Sofia had lugged herself and her belongings to her room all she wanted to do was sleep.

She threw off her clothes and dropped into bed, not even having the energy to unpack a nightie. Cool sheets. Soft pillows. Bliss . . .

She dreamed she was back in Italy, trying to talk to Levi on the sun-soaked terrace of Casa Felice. Benedetta bore down on them, but a familiar tune was emerging from her pursed lips instead of angry words. It was just like the jingle of Sophia's phone when it rang.

Waking with a start, she realised the noise actually was

the ringing of her phone. Groaning because she felt as if she'd hardly slept at all, she scrabbled to pick up her handset. Then, reading the name on the screen, she blinked herself to full consciousness. 'Amy?'

'Hello,' said a flat little voice.

'Are you OK?'

'Suppose. Why is everything so crap?'

'Life does get a bit like that sometimes.' Sofia rubbed her eyes, hoping she was sounding sympathetic and philosophical but also truthful. She pulled herself into a sitting position. 'Where are you?'

'In Bettsbrough.'

Sofia laughed. 'Me, too.'

For the first time in the conversation Amy sounded something other than dreary and lost. 'Seriously? Why?'

'Well . . .' Sofia screwed up her eyes and crossed the fingers of the hand not holding the phone. 'I hope you don't mind but I wanted to see you were all right. I promised . . . you that we'd move on together.' She'd nearly said *promised Levi I'd look out for you.* 'So I followed you over. You seemed to have a lot on your plate.' She waited, apprehensive in case Amy took umbrage.

But Amy choked, 'Mind? Of course I don't mind! You're so fantastic, Sofia. Have you really come all this way just to be with me? When everybody else in my life is feeding me shit it's you, someone I've only known a couple of months, that's there for me. I found out today . . .' Her voice wobbled piteously. 'I found out today that my real dad's Levi! That's why he was at Casa Felice! He knew who I was all the time and ne-ever said a thing.' Then Amy burst into tears.

Shoving guilt aside, Sofia swallowed hard. 'How did you find *that* out?' she demanded in what she hoped was

275

an astonished tone. Her shame at having been in possession of this knowledge for ages brought tears prickling to her eyes but she recognised that if there was ever a time to come clean with Amy, this definitely was not it. If Sofia had been cast in the role of 'only friend' or even 'only hope' then what was best for Amy was for Sofia to live up to expectations.

Amy launched into a story of imperfect research and mistaken identity, sniffing all the while, as Sofia tried to get the gist of this latest episode of the younger girl's recently chaotic life. 'It all sounds incredibly upsetting for everybody,' she concluded. Then, just to put something positive out there, 'He must have been at Casa Felice for some reason though, don't you think?'

'Mum sent him to spy on me, obviously!' Amy all but snarled.

OK, so Amy was not yet open to positives and as, actually, she wasn't too far from the truth, Sofia decided to focus on what she hoped would be the most immediate and practical help. 'Give me some idea of where you are and I'll come and find you.'

'I'm on some seats in a pedestrian area near McDonald's in the town centre,' Amy said with a loud sniff.

'I'll head your way now. Sit tight until I get there.' Having received the necessary assurances, Sofia ended the call and stumbled out of bed. Knowing she was no good to Amy shambling around like a zombie, she staggered into the bathroom and switched on the shower. While she waited for it to heat up she typed the meeting-place details into her Notes app and saw from her phone's home screen that it was 13.47 on Friday 6th July. No wonder she felt as if she'd hardly had any sleep.

She'd hardly had any sleep.

276

'Less than one hour,' she moaned piteously. Nevertheless, she forced herself to stagger into the shower. She had to go and find Amy.

It was another hour, following directions kindly furnished to her by the desk clerk, before she passed McDonald's, homed in on the nearby benches and spotted Amy's blonde head with a heart-thump of relief.

As Sofia hurried over she realised Amy was talking to someone on the next bench. 'There you are!' she sang gaily, as she arrived, trying not to look too askance at the shabby young man Amy was talking to.

Breaking off the conversation, Amy leaped to her feet and flung her arms around Sofia's neck. 'I can't believe you came back to England just for me! It must have cost tons.'

Gladly, Sofia returned Amy's hug. The thin shoulders within her embrace made Amy seem newly vulnerable. 'Are you OK? Did you find somewhere to stay?' The scruffy guy had risen too and was watching them with a wary expression. He glanced over his shoulder at where a sleeping bag lay in a shop doorway.

Amy disengaged, wiping the corner of her eyes with her fingers but beaming through her tears. 'I Googled "cheap places to stay in Bettsbrough" and got an Airbnb. It used to be a granny annexe at the side of a house.' She half-turned, including the scruffy guy in the conversation. 'This is Matt. We've been swapping hard-luck stories.' Amy's smile faded and worry clouded her blue eyes instead.

'I just came over because she seemed upset,' Matt put in swiftly, shuffling back as if he expected Sofia to object. He glanced at the sleeping bag again.

Bemused, Sofia smiled politely at Matt, taking in his possessions in the doorway and his dishevelment. Amy had befriended him? Most people confined their contact with the homeless to the occasional purchase of *The Big Issue*.

Matt looked still less comfortable. 'Right, well, good to meet you, Amy. I hope things work out. Thanks again.' He backed away a few steps then headed back to the doorway, scooped up his sleeping bag and backpack and hurried off.

Amy watched him go. She sighed as she turned back to Sofia. 'Poor Matt. He's in a fix because his stepdad told the council that he'd left home of his own accord, even though it was his stepdad who actually told him to leave because he was eighteen and it was time he looked after himself. So the council have to decide whether Matt's intentionally homeless and he's not getting much help while it gets sorted out. He sleeps on his friends' floor once a week so he can at least get a shower and put his clothes through their washing machine so he doesn't stink too much. They say he can stay more but he knows they've hardly got any money and they're looking for someone else to move in. He thinks no one would agree to live there and share rent if he was dossing in the sitting room. It's really shitty. He's scared of the hostels so he's roughing it on the streets for the summer and crossing his fingers that the council will have offered him something by the time the cold weather comes. He hates the idea of going to one of the homeless charities. He desperately needs a job but it's not as easy as you think.'

'Wow, I hope he gets sorted out,' Sofia said inadequately, gazing after the diminishing figure sympathetically. She waited to see if Amy had more to say, and when she remained silent, suggested, 'Shall we chat over coffee? I'm parched.'

Amy nodded immediately. 'Yeah, McDonald's, because I've had an idea about them.'

Sofia decided not to ask.

A few minutes later, over coffee for her and Sprite for Amy, Sofia learnt what had befallen Amy at Gunn's Motors.

'I couldn't believe it when they said the name of Levi and that he'd been in Europe for weeks,' Amy declared indignantly. 'I never heard his surname, I suppose.'

'Working in Il Giardino you'd never have to know it.' Sofia watched Amy squeaking her straw in and out of her Sprite before asking gently, 'Any ideas of your next step?'

'Not really.' Amy frowned.

'What about the Gunn family? Were they nice people?' Sofia felt a little shock of realisation. Levi had never replied to any of her texts or voicemail messages! The fact had flitted in and out of her mind while she'd been travelling but she'd told herself she'd sort it out when she got to her destination. Instead, she'd fallen into bed.

She eased her phone out of the pocket of her jeans to check it. Still no new messages.

Amy slurped again. 'Yes, they were kind. But when I realised who Levi was I got really upset and angry and ran out.' Her blue eyes were gloomy. 'I suppose it was a bit crap for them, me turning up then running away.'

Sofia sipped her coffee. After the Italian stuff it tasted very . . . English. 'If he hadn't told them about you then it would have been a bombshell, I expect. But Levi—' She hesitated.

'What?' Amy demanded.

Sofia flushed. She'd been about to say he'd acted out of the best of motives, lurching over the boundary of what

279

she was supposed to know and what she was not supposed to know.

'Sorry,' she prevaricated, rubbing her eyes. 'I'm zoning out because I haven't had much sleep. I think I was going to say that the Gunns will probably want to get to know you now they know you exist.'

'Oh.' Amy's fair eyebrows almost disappeared into her hair. 'I hadn't thought of that.'

'And Levi.'

'Levi!' Amy jerked upright. 'He can fuck off!'

Sofia held up a hand, using the other to rub her temples. 'Don't shout. I know you're upset he didn't tell you who he was, but if I were you I'd be gagging to know his reason.'

The entire situation was a mess. Sofia was no longer even trying to form an opinion on whether Levi should have explained, but at least she could try and steer Amy into thinking more deeply than her knee-jerk reaction had so far suggested.

'Why?' Amy punctuated her question with a truculent slurp of her drink.

'Because it's intriguing. Why did he visit your home in Germany? And why didn't he explain who he was? Why did he stick up for you when you were going to be sacked the day he arrived? Why did he hang out in the garden in the early hours of the morning to frighten Davide off?'

'No idea. He sucks, anyway.' Moodily, Amy twirled her straw.

'I thought he was nice.' And she thought about him pretty often.

Amy's eyes slid around to peep at Sofia. 'I think you *liked* him quite a bit, didn't you?'

'Yes,' Sofia answered honestly. 'Partly because of the ways he helped you. Maybe I have a hero complex.'

Amy turned her gaze to the window, evidently nowhere near ready to dismount from her high horse.

Sofia blinked eyes gritty with fatigue. Through the window she could see the Friday comings and going of the small market town around a few national chain shops, building societies, banks and a bingo hall. She knew there was a shopping mall nearby because she'd passed its entrance further up the street. Bettsbrough looked an OK sort of place. Smallish. Ordinary. Average. Smaller than Bedford, but not that different.

It wasn't that far from Bedford, come to that, near enough for the accent to fall comfortably on Sofia's ear. The journey would take an hour by car but she didn't have one . . . and though she'd definitely make time to visit her parents' graves before leaving the UK again she shrank from seeing her old home in the hands of someone else with no Aldo watching through the window from his bed for her to walk up the path.

She shook herself. What she needed to think about was Amy, not about the place she couldn't wait to leave a couple of months ago. But when she turned back to Amy she discovered only an empty seat.

Then she caught sight of her. She blinked. Amy was going through the McDonald's recycling bin.

Bemused, Sofia crossed to join her. 'Sudden urge to count the cups?' she asked mildly.

Amy glanced up. 'I'm collecting the beans for Matt.'

'Beans?'

Amy tapped the side of a coffee cup. 'See? Every hot drink cup has a coffee bean sticker. When you stick six on one of these little cards you can exchange it for a free cuppa. Lots of people throw theirs away so I'm collecting them. I can give the full cards to Matt and he can use them to get hot drinks.'

'Enterprising.' Sofia watched her work for a few seconds, remembering the defeated slump to Matt's shoulders as he'd hurried away from them. 'Are you sure you'll see him again?'

Shrugging, Amy shook her head. 'Not completely.'

Retiring to the table and the last of her coffee, Sofia watched her young friend. Amy was an interesting case. Much of the time she was quiet and even timid, but she obviously felt things deeply and took little prompting to fly into action.

Amy being preoccupied with her task, Sofia took the opportunity to text Levi once more. She had no way of knowing when he'd surface but she was feeling at sea over how to deal with Amy, not to mention increasingly dubious about the corner she was being backed into by the situation.

By the time Amy eventually returned to the table, flushed with success that she'd filled three and a half cards, Sofia was torn between returning to the Travelodge to sleep or just putting her head down and sleeping where she sat. Her yawns felt as if they were stretching her mouth past its natural size. 'Are you staying at the Airbnb tonight?' She yawned.

Amy muttered, 'Crap,' and quickly made a phone call, apprehension in the defensive curve of her shoulders. She sighed when she ended the call, blue eyes doleful. 'I didn't text by twelve as I was supposed to and Jean's let the room to someone else. I've got to go and clear out my stuff.'

Sofia tried to force her sluggish brain to work. 'There's a sofa-bed thingy in my room at the Travelodge. Want that?'

282

Relief rolled off Amy in waves. 'Do you mind?'

'Not as long as you let me get some sleep when we get there. I'll even see the desk clerk and book you in legitimately so you have sheets and a quilt.'

'Thank you-oo!' Amy gave Sofia a big hug, clinging to her as if scared she'd disappear if she let go.

Sofia's eyes grew moist as she returned the hug. Poor Amy. Nothing was going easily for her at the moment. '*If*,' she amended belatedly, hoping fervently that she wasn't overplaying her hand, 'you'll agree to stay in Bettsbrough long enough for Levi to get here and talk to you himself.'

Amy tensed. Then her narrow shoulders heaved on the biggest sigh yet. 'Suppose so.'

Chapter Twenty-three

Levi arrived at his home in Bettsbrough on Saturday evening exhausted and sodden.

The heat of Italy had gradually given way to intermittent thunderstorms as he'd ridden north into in the Grand Est region of France and the band of wet weather had followed him right into England. He'd had to cope with spray soaking his boots, car drivers impatient with his desire not to ride through the road-edge puddles, and decreased grip and visibility. His pace had dropped and he was half a day later than he'd hoped.

And he was really, totally, royally pissed off.

Right from his first overnight stay at Aosta, north of Turin, he'd been aware of the absence of his phone charger, though he'd spent half an hour in the car park grimly going through his panniers.

His phone was already dead and though he consoled himself that at least he hadn't lost the phone itself this time the annoyance had set the tone for the whole journey. During the night the motel fire alarm had gone off twice, leaving him outside in the dark instead of snug in bed.

The next day, continuing his journey, he crossed the border into France and the police at the toll booths had pulled him over and checked through his panniers before letting him repack and waving him on. Accidents on the *autoroute* had led to the A5 coming to a standstill and by the time he reached the hotel in Reims the last thing he'd felt like doing was riding into town to locate a phone charger and cable. It wasn't as if he felt chatty. In fact, he decided not to power up his laptop either. If there was all hell breaking loose on The Moron Forum or amongst its contributors then trying to sort things out via email would frustrate him and delay his return to his office where all he'd need would be at his fingertips.

On Saturday he pressed on when the bad weather hit, only to be caught up in chaos at Calais-Est as a host of Brits with caravans, roof racks or trailers decided to go home because it was raining. When he finally got across to Dover he headed north before anything else could go wrong.

At last!

It was still raining but at least he was here.

He wheeled the bike into his triple garage beside his Aston Martin – which had taken up more of the money The Moron Forum had accumulated for him than he cared to think about – and his quad bike, pressed the remote to lower the garage door, and let himself into the house via the kitchen to avoid not just more rain but the mountain of mail he expected to be awaiting him inside the porch.

The air inside the house smelled musty and he opened a couple of windows even before he began to strip off his protective gear. His plan was to take a shower and get into dry clothes before phoning out for takeaway and

285

opening a beer. Then, and not before, he'd think about firing up his laptop and phone and connecting with the world once more. He was tired to the bone and weighed down by doubts. His time in Italy had proved so . . . inconclusive. Not a failure but certainly not a success. He'd assured himself that Amy was capable of surviving outside the family home in Munich but ridden away without revealing himself as her father. Now he was so far from her the decision was beginning to feel sickeningly wrong. He sighed as he hung up his gear.

It felt strange to be back in this detached house he'd had built on the edge of town, a very comfortable five bedrooms with en-suites, the master taking up most of the very top floor, up in the roof. It was overlarge for just one person but it had seemed like a good investment. After the constant noise of living in a hotel, then three days of the bike's roar, his house seemed incredibly quiet. It was restful but it was also . . . empty.

He'd got as far as his bedroom, and drawn the curtains on a view of a copse and farmland rather than the glorious mountains and beautiful valley he'd become used to, when his landline rang. He closed his eyes for an instant in protest at the fates conspiring to stop him getting warm and comfortable, then grudgingly picked up the cordless handset from beside his bed.

And wow, that bed looked inviting. Maybe he should forgo the takeaway and just fall into bed after his shower . . .

'Levi?' said his brother's voice, from the phone.

Levi moved the handset closer to his mouth. 'Hey, Ty. How are you doing?'

'Where the hell have you been? I've been trying to get you since yesterday.'

'Sorry. I must have left my phone charger in Italy so the

phone died on me.' Belatedly, he became aware of the tension in Ty's voice. 'Anything the matter?'

Tyrone drew in a long audible breath and blew it out again. 'Where to start? We had a visitor at the garage yesterday. A girl called Amy Webber.'

Levi froze. 'Amy? At the *garage*? She was in Italy when I left. Why's she in England?'

'Looking for her father – who she at first thought was me.'

'Why?' Levi demanded blankly.

The snort of exasperation that came at him down the line almost perforated his eardrum. 'The only information she had was that her father was Bullet Gunn's son. Someone pointed me out and it didn't seem to occur to her that there would be more than one of us. But don't you think we ought to start with the basics? It seems as if she has reason to believe she's your daughter. Care to comment?'

Slowly, Levi sank down onto the carpet, his back against the bed. 'I was going to tell you all when I got back.'

'She *is* your daughter?' Ty's voice almost shot off the scale.

'I haven't had a DNA test but yes.' Economically Levi related the story, ending with, 'I didn't want to explain to Mum and Dad until I'd seen Freya and checked out whether what she said was true. Then I thought I'd just be in Italy a week or so and would come straight back. But things kept cropping up.'

Tyrone turned flinty. 'Ever heard of the phone?'

'Don't pull that big-brother crap.' Levi scowled, though Tyrone couldn't see it. 'Do you seriously think it's the kind of news best broken by phone? It was going to be a difficult conversation and I wanted to face my family while we had it.'

'OK,' Tyrone allowed grudgingly. 'But she beat you home, man. When we explained it wasn't possible I was her dad Mum chirped up that she had another son, one who'd been away in Europe. When Amy heard your name she totally flipped. Jumped up and made a break for it. I tried to go after her but she's quick and I couldn't really go chasing a young woman through the town centre unless I wanted to be arrested.'

Groaning, Levi sank his head in his hand. 'Where is she now?'

'No idea.'

'Oh, shit.'

'Indeed. I think you'd better go and see Mum and Dad.' Tyrone began to sound more sympathetic. 'Good luck.'

'Mum and Dad, much as I love them, will have to get in the queue. It's more important I find Amy and make sure she's OK. There's someone I can contact who might be in the know.' As he spoke, Levi rolled to his feet, grabbed his mobile phone and a charger from the drawer beside his bed and plugged his phone in. 'Thanks for letting me know, Ty. I can't just leave Amy running around town or even heading off somewhere else. What if she hasn't got enough money? What if some creep hits on her? I have to make her safety my first priority.' In the bathroom he switched on the shower and yanked a towel from the stack.

'OK. I'll tell Mum and Dad you're safe and well, at least.' Tyrone sounded as if he might be trying not to laugh.

'What?' Levi demanded impatiently. 'What's funny?'

Tyrone did laugh then. 'You sounded just like a dad.'

'Oh. Well. I'm trying.' Levi said his goodbyes and stepped into the deluge of hot water. As he washed his hair and rapidly soaped his body he could hear his mobile phone message tone repeating so frenetically he thought it must be malfunctioning. He grabbed the towel and dried himself as he made his way back to where he'd left the handset. As if in defiance, as he picked it up it gave one final beep and fell silent.

'No wonder my freakin' battery died so quickly,' he muttered to himself. There were more than twenty texts and almost as many voicemails. He tapped on the text message icon first. A whole slew of them were from Sofia. Deciding to cut to the chase, he went for the most recent text first.

Sofia: *I met up with her OK. She's introduced herself to your family – I'm sure you'll hear all about that! She's calmed down a bit, but I'm afraid she's angry with you for not explaining who you were. SHE STILL DOESN'T KNOW I KNOW. I feel bad about it but what Amy needs most is a friend so I'm trying to be that. We're in the Travelodge on a big roundabout near a pub called The Chequers. When you finally get this message DON'T RING ME, in case she hears your voice, because we're sharing a room. Text me ASAP.*

Wincing at the part about Amy being angry, Levi scrolled back to the beginning of the messages from *Amy's going to England!* through *Damn, your charger's been found in your room. Might explain why you're not answering* and then brief step-by-step updates as Sofia made the decision to follow on, landed in the UK and headed towards his home town. Though Amy was at the forefront of his mind it gave him a hot flood of pleasure to realise Sofia had not been left behind in Montelibertà but was within a ten-minute drive of where he stood.

289

He replied:

Levi: I'm back in Bettsbrough and just got my phone working again. You don't know how relieved I am to know you're with Amy. My brother rang to tell me about her visit to the garage but had no idea where she'd run off to. Phew! THANK YOU for coming over to be with her. You are amazing.

That was the easy bit. He sat on the bed, pushing his pillows up against the headboard to sink into. After several minutes of watching through the window as dusk stole across the sky, he continued:

Levi: My primary aim is to see Amy and explain/apologise in such a way that she doesn't react by vanishing, and which leads to me having some kind of dad/daughter relationship with her. I realise it would be subject to where she's living but I can't bear the thought of her hating me. As you've done so much already I suppose I should hesitate to ask you but . . . What do YOU think's the best way of getting her and me together?

And then, because it was true and he was hyper-aware that he might see Sofia again soon he sent another text – well, hell, she'd sent him about two dozen!

Levi: I've missed you. x

Then he began on his voicemail, smiling as he listened to Sofia sounding urgent, then fed up, then quite irritated, actually saying 'Argh!' at one point. Next came several messages from Tyrone asking him to get in touch ASAP. He sounded irritated too, but he wasn't so cute.

And finally . . . a quite unexpected voice.

Levi was so nonplussed he more or less missed what was said first time around and had to listen to the message again. 'Hiya, Levi, it's Octavia! Welcome home. You've been away so *long*. You'll call me as soon as you get this, yes? I'll be *waiiiiiting*.' The message ended with multiple kissing sounds.

'What the fuck?' he asked his phone, stupefied. 'What's wrong with that woman?' She sounded for all the world as if they were in a relationship and that he'd simply ring her back the instant he heard her voice. Instead, he grimaced and deleted her message.

Back at the Travelodge, Sofia had slept for a few hours. Now, refreshed, she was sitting on the bed with her phone conveniently nearby while Amy engrossed herself in Saturday early evening TV on the BBC.

Finally, Sofia's patience was rewarded when her phone buzzed and her heart hopped as she saw that finally, *finally* Levi had sent a text. She read it twice before replying, all too aware that the relationship between Levi and Amy hung in the balance and anything Sofia felt about Levi was presently secondary to that.

Sofia: Welcome home! Phew, indeed. I feel as if Amy needs a bodyguard. When I caught up with her she'd just made friends with a guy her age who seems to be homeless so now she's sighing over his bad luck. Re. her feelings towards you, she's a teenager and an underconfident one in many ways. Therefore she acts with hostility if anyone does anything unexpected. But it's a front. She's scared and angry and she needs support. Let me think for a few minutes . . .

She sent that and then saw his second text and her heart skipped. In fact, she found she was thinking more about the fact that Levi missed her than about what she was meant to be thinking about – how to get Levi together with Amy.

While Amy laughed at an ancient episode of *Dad's*

Army, Sofia tried to work through the options. Should they meet Levi by 'accident'? She could suggest to Amy they eat at the nearby pub and let Levi know so he could 'happen along'? No, she felt instinctively that this would be wrong, and the same went for Levi turning up at the Travelodge unannounced. If Amy were to smell a setup then she could easily stop trusting Sofia and the longer Sofia remained the good guy the more support she could be.

Finally, she picked up her phone again.

Sofia: I think we should be as truthful as possible. I'll tell her you've messaged me, give the gist and ask Amy if she'll agree to meet you so you can explain the reasons behind not telling her your identity in Italy. I'll emphasise that you're upset and want to see her. What do you think? x

Levi: Agree. It's good of you to take on the intermediary role and I'm grateful. I feel really nervous. x

Sofia: Now you're making me feel nervous! I'm going to offer her time to think about her response so she doesn't feel under pressure.

Sofia waited until the credits rolled on Captain Mainwaring and his platoon. Then she cleared her throat. 'Levi messaged to ask if I'd heard from you. He's arrived home to a phone call from his brother telling him what happened earlier and he's frantic that you've vanished.'

Amy sent her a wary look from beneath her lashes. 'Oh?'

'I've told him I'm with you and he's dead relieved. But he wants to know if you'll meet him so he can explain.' She paused to try and gauge from Amy's expression how that idea was going down.

Amy wasn't giving much away, however. She picked up the TV remote and flipped to the on-screen menu as if more concerned with what else she could find to watch than whether to allow her natural father into her life.

Sofia added, 'Look, you don't have to decide right away. In fact, I think you shouldn't. It's a big deal. I'm hungry. Why don't we go get something to eat? You can think about what you want to do. That pub next door looks good and—'

'I'd rather go back to McDonald's.' Amy kept her eyes on the TV screen while her thumb worked the remote. 'I want to see if Matt's about.'

'OK. Let's do that,' Sofia agreed, trying to convey an equanimity she didn't feel at the prospect of having to walk back into the town centre, still feeling washed out from minimal sleep. Also, it was typical of Amy's tender-heartedness to want to help Matt, who was so obviously in need of a helping hand, but Amy needed support herself.

Amy's needs weren't as evident as Aldo's had been but something about the mixture of uncertainty, shyness, vulnerability and grim determination had awoken a response in Sofia from the first. Maybe she'd become entrenched in the role of caring while she'd been looking after her dad? Whatever, it seemed natural to locate her bag and jacket and fall in step beside Amy as they headed back towards the town centre.

It took them just over twenty minutes on foot, passing a couple of pubs and a clubs. Judging by the groups of girls in tall shoes and high hems, Bettsbrough's Saturday nightlife was stirring.

It wasn't actually raining but the July sky was still as grey as if it had fast-forwarded to October. As they stepped onto the beginning of the pedestrian zone Amy asked with what Sofia recognised as carefully contrived indifference,

'Suppose I do meet Levi, where's he hoping things will go from there?'

Wary of being underqualified for such an important conversation, Sofia chose her words carefully. 'I expect that's one of the things he wants to discuss. My impression is that he wants to be in your life, but I suppose you ought to hear that directly from him.'

She was congratulating herself on carrying that off quite well until Amy answered grumpily, 'I've done OK without him so far. Had to, haven't I?' She pointed to her left as they passed Market Square, presently untenanted except for a banner advertising a farmers' market on Tuesday. 'If you go up there and follow the road at the top, Gunn's Motors is just round the curve. Apparently Levi has his own business in the same building.'

'Yes, he runs—'

'Look, there's Matt!' Amy interrupted, beaming and waving in the other direction.

Sofia hovered in the background as Amy hurried to meet Matt, who detached himself from a group of three other lads and came forward tentatively, hands in pockets. Amy pulled out her collection of coffee bean cards, which Matt, nodding enthusiastically, accepted. Amy, looking a few degrees more relaxed, shrugged and gave a half-laugh. One of the other lads came over and spoke to Amy too, and she smiled shyly from behind her hair.

The boy clapped Matt on the shoulder. Matt nodded and waited until he'd moved off before speaking to Amy again. Amy replied and twice Matt shook his head. Then he backed off with a smile and a hand lifted in farewell, turned and jogged off in the wake of the rest of his group.

Sofia moved up to Amy's shoulder. 'OK?'

Amy shrugged disconsolately. 'I offered Matt a

McDonald's but tonight's the night he gets to stay at his mates' place and they've got food for him.'

Sofia patted her arm comfortingly, feeling her friend's confused emotions at not having her offering accepted. 'Do you still want to eat at McDonald's? Because I can see an Italian on the other side of the market place. We could check out whether it's as good as the real thing.'

Amy smiled faintly as she sent a last look after Matt before turning away. 'Pizza Margherita sounds wicked.'

Sofia tried to chat brightly as they covered the distance to the restaurant, Bella Bella, which promised *an authentic taste of Italy* in large gold letters across the top of its window. The aromas issuing forth as they opened the door certainly gave the right impression and they hung up their jackets, took a table near the window and prepared to let others wait on them for once.

Amy was mainly silent. Sofia, feeling the need for the bracing qualities of alcohol, ordered a glass of Frascati. Amy went for pear cider but played with the glass more than drinking its contents, staring out of the window at the people coming and going across the square.

When they'd shared a pizza and side salads she sat back. 'What do you think Levi means about being in my life? I know you said I should ask him. But what do you think?'

Acutely aware that her opinion might sway things, Sofia considered. 'Nothing negative. He's not looking to tell you off for not getting your homework in on time or anything like that.' Amy's blue-eyed gaze didn't waver so Sofia knew she wasn't going to get away with anything that superficial. 'I assume he wants to continue to get to know you. To be in your life in some form. He's very focused on knowing you're OK and stepping up if you need him. But you know that, right? Because that's what he did in Montelibertà.'

Amy gave combined nod and shrug, as if her agreement was reluctant.

'And have you heard of The Moron Forum?' Sofia added, hoping to impress. 'He owns it. Or shares owner-ship with a friend, anyway.'

'Seriously? That's cool. It's on the list of stuff we can't access at school but I've read it on my phone. Is he, like, seriously rich then?'

'He said he's doing OK.'

Amy fiddled with her napkin, frowning again. She peeped up at Sofia. 'Were you sort of . . . seeing him?'

There was nothing to gain from lying. 'Sort of.' Sofia flushed. 'If you decide not to meet him, you wouldn't mind if I did, would you?'

Amy shrugged again but this time looked faintly surprised, as if it was dawning on her that there was more involved here than just her feelings and needs.

They ordered coffee. Sofia floated the subject of the future. Amy looked uncertain. 'What about us going on somewhere together?'

Sofia was surprised how relieved she felt that Amy was still thinking of them as a unit. She was beginning to realise that her desire to help Amy weather her storm was stronger than her wish to be free from ties and cares. In fact, after the past few weeks of companionship she wondered how much she'd enjoy going solo. 'I don't go back on my word. But the summer's passing by and we'll probably only get opportunities in Europe until the end of September. After that we'd have to follow the sun and the tourists and look further afield. Or wait it out until we can go to a snow resort and be chalet girls to the skiing fraternity in the Dolomites or the Alps.'

Amy looked interested. 'I've done skiing at home.

Germany gets a lot of snow and you don't have to go that far from Munich to find ski schools.'

As if wanting to join in with their conversation Sofia's phone began to vibrate in her pocket. She would have declined the call but when she glanced at the screen Chiara's name flashed up. 'It's my cousin in Montelibertà, I'd better answer.' She did so, speaking quietly in the hopes of not offending anyone's idea of restaurant/phone etiquette.

Chiara greeted her enthusiastically. 'Do you know your shifts next weekend yet? We're having a little party in the hotel gardens for my parents' wedding anniversary and I wondered if you could come.' She laughed. 'I have to be honest, I have an ulterior motive. I hoped that if you were here to help celebrate then Mamma might thaw, and you might find you like Hotel Alba—'

'Oh, Chiara, I'm sorry,' Sofia broke in awkwardly, wishing she'd thought to ring her cousin before this. 'I'm afraid I'm back in the UK at the moment. Something came up and I had to come home.' Her cheeks heated up.

It was Chiara's turn to say, 'Oh.' Then she sighed. 'But you said you wouldn't leave without saying goodbye.'

'I know, I am sorry,' Sofia repeated wretchedly.

'Will you return?' Chiara sounded hopeful now. 'Papà still has hopes you might—'

'I'm sure I'll come back some time,' Sofia said brightly, wilfully misunderstanding her. 'I loved Montelibertà. And I'll keep in touch, I promise.' She ended the call after a few moments more, conscious of her cousin's disappointment and Amy's narrow gaze.

'You're going back?' Amy said.

Sofia shrugged, deliberately downplaying how sorry she was to have disappointed Chiara and making a mental note to call her again soon to apologise again for doing a disappearing act. 'Sooner or later, I expect.' Never again seeing Montelibertà gave her a hollow feeling but it seemed unlikely that there would be a job for Amy at Hotel Alba and now was not the time to be drawn into any plans that would exclude her.

But Amy wasn't fooled. 'Go if you want. They're your family,' she murmured, though her anxious expression said that Sofia going was the last thing Amy wanted.

Tinkling piano music began to swirl from speakers in the corners of the restaurant. It was almost full now, lots of couples out on date night or groups of friends forgetting the working week for a while. Sofia made her voice very soft so occupants of neighbouring tables wouldn't hear. 'You actually can trust me, Amy. I said we'd go on together and we will – unless you decide you'd want to go home or something.'

But Amy was shaking her head even as the words hit the air. 'Not yet. I don't feel . . . safe. I need to get my head round things on my own. My mum, she's quite bossy. If I went home she'd be all right for a few days then gradually start taking over again. And I'd think, like, what gives her the right? If she could keep something incredibly important from me for my whole life?'

A waiter came and lit the tea light on their table, checking whether they'd like to order anything more. Sofia asked him for another latte to justify continuing to occupy the table. 'Everybody makes mistakes,' she went on when the waiter had gone, quite glad to have turned the conversation from Chiara's call because there was no point letting it unsettle Amy. 'I don't mean to sound like I'm taking your mum's side, or Levi's side, but I think one of the hardest things about becoming an adult is accepting the fallibility of other adults.'

Amy looked struck. 'Did you have that with your dad?'

'Of course!' The waiter returned with the latte and Sofia waited for the cup to be set before her with a little pot of sugar lumps, breathing in the aroma and thinking of Aldo's love for milky coffee before continuing. 'I loved my dad to bits but he could be stubborn. Sometimes he refused to follow doctor's orders so either hurt himself or went through a bad health patch as a consequence. That had a direct impact on me as his carer. He'd do something he wasn't supposed to and fall and gash his head for example, which would then become infected and he'd be poorly with a fever.

'Sometimes it made me angry and there would be a heated exchange of views. It took me a while to accept that he was just making a decision based on his wish not to be such an invalid, to do things for himself. In time I became more capable of seeing things from Dad's point of view. One of those coming-of-age things, I guess.'

Amy's eyes widened. 'I thought you and your dad had this fantastic relationship and you'd been like that Florence Nightingale woman.'

'Life's rarely that simple,' Sofia admitted sadly.

'Why does everything have to be so hard?' A tear gathered at the corner of Amy's eye. 'Matt said I'm lucky because he'd like a dad who wanted a relationship with him, rather than a stepdad who chucked him out when he was eighteen. His real dad moved away and lost touch with Matt when he was only little.'

Sofia's heart went out to both Matt and Amy, struggling with such serious issues in their young lives. She passed over a clean napkin and stroked Amy's arm consolingly until she'd finished blotting her eyes, leaving little crescent moons of mascara across the napkin's white surface.

Just as Sofia was about to suggest they wander back towards the Travelodge Amy heaved a sigh almost big enough to blow over the pepper grinder. 'OK. You can tell Levi I'll meet him.'

Only just preventing herself from laughing at Amy's martyred air, Sofia smiled understandingly instead and took out her phone. 'I'll send you his number and you can arrange it with him direct.'

Panic raced across Amy's features. 'But you'll be there with me, won't you?'

Wrong-footed, Sofa paused. 'I hadn't thought of it. I can be, if you want.'

'I do. And please can you be the one to text him, as well? I don't know what to say. And I don't want to meet him tonight.'

Amy sat back and folded her arms as if throwing up a fence but, beginning to feel the effects of fragmented sleep over the past couple of days, Sofia was quite glad to hear they weren't instantly plunging into another drama. 'OK. I'll try to arrange it for tomorrow.'

Amy screwed up her face in thought. 'Can it be Monday? At McDonald's for lunch?'

Sofia gazed at her friend, wondering whether Matt was going to get an invitation to join them, but she didn't want to derail the peacemaking process by questioning Amy too closely. 'OK. The motel doesn't seem full so I presume we can stay a bit longer.' Any way that got Levi and Amy talking was a good way.

And it meant that Sofia would see Levi again.

Chapter Twenty-four

Levi endured an uncomfortable Saturday evening. Once he'd received reassurance that Amy was safe but he had to wait for her ruling on the matter of meeting up, he decided he'd better visit his parents at home and clear the air.

It was surreal to sit in the lounge of the house in which he'd been brought up and talk to them about the existence of his daughter of eighteen. They were understandably concerned about what had befallen her since she scarpered from Gunn's Motors but to say they were stunned by the whole episode and disappointed in the way he'd handled it was an understatement.

'Why didn't you just tell us?' they kept demanding, his mum slightly tearful and his dad showing signs of the pugnacity that had earned him his nickname.

Levi lost count of the number of times he went over it. 'I wanted to be certain of the facts before I told you, and then I wanted to give you the news in person.'

Val instantly moved on to 'Why didn't you tell her who you were?'

At the same instant, Bryan demanded, 'But are you certain? What about a DNA test?'

'Don't be silly!' Val countered. 'He doesn't need a DNA test, you only have to look at her. Her eyes are exactly the colour mine were when I was younger, and she's got the Gunn chin.'

Bryan stuck out the chin in question. 'That's not very scientific.'

'She's mine,' Levi put in quietly. 'I've known from the moment I saw her. I'm sorry you're shocked but I had no idea until Freya got in touch with me in May.'

Bryan shook his head and took his glasses off to polish them on his shirt. 'May? But it's July! Why didn't you just tell us? It's been a funny summer. I feel as if I hardly know my own son. And that Octavia woman Wes took up with. Do you know her?'

'Of course he does,' Val interrupted. 'She's the one who found his phone when he lost it, just before he went away. But she's very odd, Levi.'

Warily, he nodded. 'I thought so too. But why bring her up now?'

Bryan put his glasses back on. 'She was supposed to be working in your office upstairs but she hung around downstairs all the time.'

'There's no Ladies upstairs,' Val pointed out.

'She had to come down for that,' Bryan allowed. 'But she didn't have to hang round asking twenty questions about Levi, did she?'

Focusing abruptly, Levi gazed at his dad. 'What the fu— hell for?'

'I thought you might be able to tell us. Maybe she's another little surprise you've been storing up for us. Another secret.'

302

Levi rubbed his face, his stubble rasping. 'No, she damned well isn't. She's left the business anyway. I'll have to try and catch up with Wes tomorrow and find out what went on. When I was in Italy things got a bit strained because he employed Octavia without discussing it with me.'

'Wes's been odd too,' Val put in. 'When he was first with that Octavia he was pleased as punch, wasn't he Bry? Then he turned sulky.'

'I think she ended things.' Levi was about to make his excuses to his parents and go home to bed when his phone beeped to alert him to a new text message.

Sofia: Amy wants to meet you on Monday. She's having a bit of a hard time emotionally so I don't know how things will work out but she's asked me to be there too. Are you OK with that?

Levi almost dropped his phone in his haste to type in *YES!!!* Hopefully Amy would be calmed by Sofia's presence. He'd be calmed by it himself, come to that, and something inside him lit up just at the prospect of seeing her. The only slight disappointment was that Amy wanted to wait until Monday.

Sofia: Amy suggests McDonald's. It's near where the unfortunate homeless kid hangs around. I think she's quite absorbed in his situation. It seems to be making her pensive.

Levi: OK, let's go with what she wants then worry about her motivation if and when we need to. Thank you. Tell Amy I'm looking forward to seeing her again. x

After bringing his parents up to date with a brief 'Sofia's got Amy to agree to meet me on Monday so I hope I can sort things out with her then. I'll let you know,' Levi kissed his mother, gave his dad a man-hug, and escaped home in the hope of a bit of peace and quiet.

So when, after the short ride through the dark streets, his bike's headlight picked up Octavia sitting on his doorstep as he rumbled up the drive, he was deeply pissed off.

Crossly, he pulled up, switched off the bike and heaved the machine back onto its stand, before releasing himself from his crash helmet.

'Yes?' he said, treating Octavia to a cold stare.

Octavia had jumped to her feet and now she spread her arms wide and gave him a beaming smile. 'That's not much of a greeting after you've been running around goodness-knows-where for weeks.'

Levi took several deliberate steps back in case she had any plans to wrap those arms around him. Being cool and remote would be challenging with her clinging to him like a monkey shinning a tree. 'What do you want, Octavia?'

Pouting, she let her arms fall. 'I thought we could get together and—'

'Well, we can't.'

The pout vanished and her lips thinned. 'You might as well know this about me. I usually get what I want.' Then she turned and stalked away into the darkness. He saw her silhouetted briefly at the end of the drive as the motion-detector security light came on. Then she was gone.

Unsettled by Octavia's weirdness considering he'd never had a relationship with her and had politely blocked any attempt she made to start one, he opened the front door to his house and tripped over the mountain of mail he'd ignored earlier. Swearing horribly, he scooped up the collection of envelopes and leaflets and carried them through the hall to drop on the kitchen table. Though yawning and dead beat he riffled through the haul in case it contained anything that seemed more important than dragging himself upstairs to bed.

It was then he found Wes's letter of resignation.

Sunday was not a good day. After trying to ring Wes and getting only voicemail, Levi had dropped into bed on Saturday night thinking a good night's sleep would help him cope with life's tricks, only to toss and turn, his mind refusing to stop thinking about Amy, Sofia, Wes and Octavia.

He gave his car a run to Wes's house on Sunday morning. It was a neat, plain house in the midst of a neat, plain estate built of yellow brick, not ostentatious but not cheap. It suited Wes. He liked to keep his lawn mowed and flowerbeds weeded but he wasn't out in the garden today, and he didn't respond when Levi knocked at the door.

Frustrated and worried, he gave the knocker an extra hefty flip as he turned away. To his surprise, the door suddenly opened and there was Wes, hair sticking up, looking bleary.

Levi almost took a step back from this uncharacteristically dishevelled version of his friend. 'There you are! Are you OK? Did I get you out of bed?'

Wes shrugged. 'It's Sunday, isn't it?'

As he said no more, Levi came straight to the point. 'What's up, Wes? I only found your resignation last night. I was stunned.'

After several moments of treating Levi to a narrow-eyed stare, Wes stepped back and waved him into the house. Levi tried to ignore the empty pizza box on the hall floor that he had to step over, and, when he entered the sitting room, several empty beer cans on the coffee table – if nine could be considered several.

Wes made no attempt to either clear up or offer a hospitable cup of coffee. He just plumped down in a chair and waited for Levi to do the same.

Levi tried to keep the anxiety and tension he was feeling from his voice. Wes didn't look like Wes and that worried him. 'What's wrong? I can't believe you've resigned, obviously, but I'm more worried about you. Have you had bad news? Are you ill? I haven't seen you in this state this since we were students.'

Gaze falling contemplatively to the row of beer cans on the table as if someone was going to come along with an air gun and use them for target practice, Wes shrugged. 'What state?'

Levi gazed at him, puzzled. 'Messy,' he answered succinctly. Then, softening his voice, 'Do you need help? I've no idea what's going on. When I went away we were best mates running a business together. You seemed perfectly OK with me going off to see what was happening with the daughter I never knew I had and were your usual composed and competent self. I come back and you act like you're in darkest depression.'

For a second Wes's lips tightened as if he were physically struggling to keep words in his mouth. Then he raised his hands and pressed the heels of them against his eyes. 'I suppose I am,' he said, sounding muffled. He let his hands drop back into his lap. 'I know it's not really your fault.'

Levi sank back in his chair, mind churning but coming up with no answers. 'So, if it's not "really" my fault, is it *kind of* my fault? Something I've done? Do you feel I was away an unreasonable length of time? What?'

'It's all made me really unhappy,' Wes replied morosely.

'Me being away?' Levi repeated. The answers Wes was

giving didn't seem to go with the questions Levi was asking.

'Not as such.' Wes propped his elbow on the chair arm and covered his eyes as if he didn't want to see Levi's face. His breath shuddered. 'When I found out – I just felt like shit. Utter shit. Lower than dirt. I thought she was really into me but *of course* she wasn't. Why would she be? Plain, homely Wes, two stone overweight. Always in Levi Gunn's shadow. I got to really resenting you.'

Ice began to form in Levi's gut. 'She?'

Wes swallowed hard before saying hoarsely, 'Octavia.' Another of those shuddering breaths, only one step removed from crying. 'She was only with me because she wanted to keep track of you. She was quite open about it when she dumped me. She's got a thing for you. You slid off her radar so she came to the office to search you out. When I said you were away for an unspecified length of time she seemed to shrug it off. But then she got flirty with me and we started seeing each other. I thought we really had something.' He heaved in another breath.

Horror washed over Levi. He had to force his words past an obstruction in his throat. 'Wes, I am so fucking sorry. I had no idea. Well,' he amended truthfully, 'I did think it was odd that she seemed to have struck up something heavy with you so quickly and I wanted to warn you off her but you seemed so defensive. If I'd realised she was doing anything so cold as using you I would have said it anyway.'

Wes's breathing began to quiet. Wearily, he let his hand drop from his face. 'I suppose so. But I'm not going to be able to see you guys together. Hence the resignation.'

Levi almost leaped from his chair his blood boiled so high. '*Together*?' he thundered. 'We're not together! Not now, not ever. Her behaviour's not normal. I barely know her. I didn't know her at all before she found my phone, when she made it obvious that she was interested and I tried to make it equally obvious that I wasn't. I thought it had ended there, I promise you.'

Wes's eyes chilled. 'So she wasn't at your house last night like she texted and told me.'

'She texted to tell you?' Levi could scarcely speak for fury. 'She called at my place uninvited and I immediately sent her on her way. That was it. What a bitch!'

After a long moment Wes nodded, as if accepting Levi was telling the truth. 'Seems like I'm not even good enough to get your leavings. That's how pathetic I am.' He retreated behind his closed eyelids once more.

Levi stayed with him for an hour, unsure whether Wes actually wanted him there but with a strong reluctance to simply leave him in this state. He made coffee, he talked about how Wes was definitely worth more than a scheming flake with no conscience. He loaded the dishwasher and took out the rubbish.

He tried hard, but in vain, to get Wes to take his resignation back. Eventually, bitter with the knowledge that his best friend might truly be too unsettled to stick around, he went home when Wes asked him to. Intellectually he knew he was blameless in the whole episode . . . but it still felt like his fault. He cursed Octavia for managing to mess up his friendship and affect his business. He'd heard of people having unwanted admirers and the havoc their irrational obsessions could cause, but he still felt incredulous at finding himself a victim.

Thinking angry thoughts about Octavia and her loose screws he drove to his office. Gunn's Motors was closed on Sundays but he had his own set of keys, of course.

Everything looked normal as he shut off the burglar alarm at the panel and took the stairs two at a time. In the office, the Mac Pros stood dark-screened and silent on the island of desks amidst the usual detritus of work – pads, pens, trays and phones. The coat hooks were bare of Wes's jackets. Everything felt strange. Levi had left it all behind nearly six weeks ago and, it being Sunday, that there was no backing track of doors closing, cars starting and people talking downstairs in the garage.

Powering up his machine, he logged on to once again spend hours going through every page and all its files . . .

. . . to find everything exactly as it should be.

He sat back, brows knitted. In a way, he would have welcomed evidence that Octavia had somehow got herself root user privileges and done something to their server, proof for Wes that Octavia hadn't only worked for The Moron Forum in an elaborate, bald-faced ruse to keep tabs on Levi.

Falling back on the solace of methodical work, he emailed everyone responsible for pages to tell them he was back in the country . . . and, by the way, here's your fresh password. It never hurt to safeguard security, he thought grimly, as he listed each password and updated the server.

Everything else he left for Monday.

Monday. Anticipation and apprehension shivered through him. He'd see Amy again. And Sofia. His heart missed its step and he took out his phone, wanting to ring Sofia and hear her voice. Then, realising there was, for once, no reason not to do exactly that, dialled.

Sofia picked up on the second ring. 'Hey.' She sounded relaxed and happy – her default, now he thought of it.

His voice seemed to drop two notes just because he was talking to her. 'How are you? What are you up to?'

She laughed. 'We're in London at Amy's request, looking at clothes in Camden Market. We got the train from Peterborough.' Her voice dropped. 'I think she wanted to get out of Bettsbrough for a bit. She wanted to mull.'

He was conscious of a swoop of disappointment. Probably it was Amy's need to 'mull' that had prompted her to choose tomorrow instead of today for their meeting but it had left Levi restless, in limbo. He'd hoped Sofia would be nearby so he could see her.

'What time are you coming back?' he asked experimentally. 'I could pick you up to save you getting the bus back from Peterborough to Bettsbrough. They're probably a bit slow on a Sunday evening.'

'Is there room on your motorbike for three people?'

The laughter in her voice made him smile. 'I have a car too.' Quite an expensive car, even if he had bought it second-hand.

'Hang on. I'll ask.' Sound became muffled, as if Sofia had covered the mic while she consulted with Amy. Then she came back. 'I think we'll stick with the bus.' Was that regret in her voice?

He made sure to keep his own voice even. 'OK, I'll see you both tomorrow as planned.'

He closed the office and headed off towards the supermarket to stock up his fridge, conscious of Sunday opening hours, then drove home, feeling as if the day was dragging.

A parcel awaited him on his doorstep. His name, in upright, angular handwriting. No address. It rattled when he shook it. He didn't even take it indoors to open it, just ripped off the paper to find inside a box of chocolates in the shape of erotically entwined couples.

He could think of only one person likely to send him

310

something like that and, sure enough, when he found the card it said, *Thinking of you, Octavia x.*

He didn't know her address to send them back and he had a feeling that contacting her, even if it was to ask her not to send gifts, would count as engaging with her. With a growl, he tossed the box in the bin unopened and took himself and his shopping indoors vowing to never let his phone out of his sight again if losing it led to this carry-on.

Chapter Twenty-five

Levi drove to the office bright and early on Monday morning. He needed to get back in the swing of things, and it would pass the time before meeting Amy and Sofia at lunchtime.

Wes had left no task half done except the creation of new emoji for the forum, which he'd begun for the fun of it but not completed. If Levi couldn't persuade Wes to rescind his resignation then he'd outsource the rest to a graphic artist. He could think of few jobs he felt less like attempting himself, especially as Wes had used quirky animation software Levi had no desire to learn.

He felt sick every time he thought of how bleak Wes was over Octavia. He couldn't believe what a freaking user she was and the knowledge that he, Levi, had brought this on Wes, however unwittingly, made him feel unclean.

He slogged through his work, including spending half an hour with Bookkeeper Mary to go through recent accounts, still half-expecting to find something Octavia had been up to.

Finally the clock crawled towards noon and he rose unsteadily from his desk, heart thumping.

What if Amy told him she never wanted to see him again? Although he'd known his child such a short time the mere possibility caused his stomach to leap as if he'd swallowed a frog. He trod downstairs, hardly feeling the steps beneath his feet. When he passed his mum's workstation she held up a pair of crossed fingers to him, well aware of his errand.

It took only a few minutes to reach McDonald's and take a booth near the window. The final minutes ticked past and he wondered, with a feeling of near panic, what he'd do if Amy and Sofia just didn't turn up and he never saw either of them again.

He checked his phone for messages. Nothing. He wiped his palms down his black jeans.

Then suddenly they were just inside the door, looking in his direction, Amy pale, Sofia dark, Amy apprehensive, Sofia beaming, an encouraging arm around Amy's shoulders.

He jumped to his feet, relief making him grin like a clown.

But Amy wasn't smiling. She was staring at him as if he was likely to change into a monster any moment. It took several moments before she began to move towards him.

'Hiya!' Sofia said brightly, as they drew near.

Levi returned the greeting, wishing it felt appropriate to add a kiss. Amy slid into the booth opposite Levi and Sofia followed. He wanted to say, 'Well, this is awkward!' to make them laugh but he was too worried that Amy would think he didn't see the situation as something to be taken seriously. He cleared his throat. 'Shall I order? Or do you want to . . . talk first?'

Amy muttered, 'I'm hungry,' so he took their order and

went to the counter. He wished Amy had nominated some-where else for lunch, somewhere where they had wait staff so he didn't have to turn his back.

Amy hadn't vanished by the time the food was ready, however, and he returned to the table with a laden tray. Amy muttered her thanks and concentrated on opening packaging and using a straw to pierce the lid of her drink. Levi waited. Eventually she flicked him a glance.

'I'm sorry,' he said immediately. 'I'm sorry I couldn't tell you who I am. Your mum told me about the message you'd left that if anyone came after you you'd vanish. I agreed that your safety was paramount and, in completely uncharted waters as a parent, did as they asked. She and Stephen were terrified of losing touch with you altogether. None of us knew you were going to do such a great job of getting employment and how hard you'd work to keep the position. We didn't know you were going to make a friend like Sofia, who could speak Italian and help you out if things went wrong. We just knew we wanted to keep you safe.' Unexpectedly, his throat tried to close up on him at the thought of all the things that could have happened to this fragile-looking girl in front of him. He had to take a couple of gulps of coffee before continuing.

'As I got to know you, I agonised over whether and when I should tell you. I really did. I lay awake at nights worrying, coming back over and over to the fact that once I told you, I couldn't take it back. As long as you *didn't* know, you wouldn't take flight. I had the opportunity of sticking with you.' As she remained silent, he added, 'Do you want to ask me anything? Go ahead.'

Amy swished her straw, making the ice cubes rattle. Finally, she started to speak. 'Do you have other kids?'

314

'No.'

'Not that you know of,' she corrected him – unanswerably, in the circumstances. 'Do you feel like my dad?'

He went for absolute honesty. 'I don't know. The news that I had a daughter, that she was already eighteen and I'd missed everything about her childhood, her school, her friends, was a massive shock. But the first moment I saw you I felt a connection.'

She frowned. 'I didn't feel anything like that. I just thought you were a nice man.'

He felt a tiny smile tug at the corner of his mouth. 'That's a start.' He glanced at Sofia, whose brown eyes were soft with compassion. He would have given a great deal to slide an arm around her and take comfort from her warmth and softness. As if she'd read his mind he felt her leg press stealthily on his beneath the table, sending a tremor right through him. This meeting was all about Amy though, and he returned his focus to her as she began to burrow into his memories of the hen party weekend when she'd been conceived, even rolling her eyes at him when she found out he'd been younger than she was now. Eventually, she propped her chin on her hand and met his gaze squarely. 'Sofia thinks I'm lucky to have found you while I'm still so young because we've got a lot of time to get to know each other if we want to.'

Gratitude to Sofia set off a tiny explosion of warmth inside him. 'I want to.'

She withheld her vote. 'And if I decide not to keep in touch with you, she said that's my choice, but she thinks it's a waste of a dad.'

This served as a reminder of how few people Sofia had in the world and his voice emerged more huskily than he'd meant it to. 'I can see why she'd feel like that, can't you?'

'Yeah.' Amy fidgeted with her straw again, the shutters coming down on her expression. 'Have you got a house here?'

'I have.' Impulsively, he added, 'Sofia texted that you two are staying at the Travelodge. You could both come and stay with me instead if you want. My house is a reasonable size.' He ignored the flicker of surprise on Sofia's face.

Amy turned to Sofia, eyebrows raised. 'I suppose we could, couldn't we?' She shot a glance at Levi. 'I mean, until we decide what to do next.' Sofia shrugged and nodded, shooting Levi a quick glance of her own as if to say, 'Didn't see that one coming'.

Amy sat up straighter. 'Can I see where you work? Sofia says you own The Moron Forum.'

It was Levi's turn to be taken by surprise but something in Amy's eyes told him she was putting him through a test. 'I own most of it. Of course you can see where I work. As you've already discovered, other members of your family work in the building so you'll probably see them too. They'll want to meet you properly. Mum's already given me a right ear-bashing for not telling her about you earlier. My brother Tyrone and his wife Beth have given Mum and Dad two granddaughters, Grace and Serena, and they definitely like being grandparents.'

'Oh.' Amy looked taken aback but also intrigued as he sprang family members on her. As usual, she touched base with Sofia. 'You'll come, won't you?'

'If you want me to.' Sofia gave her a quick, comforting squeeze, flashing Levi a smile at the same time. He wondered who felt more reassured – himself or Amy.

Nobody ate much of their food. Levi led them outside, ready to shepherd them across the market square and up the road to Gunn's Motors, but Amy stopped and looked right instead, where a figure sat in the doorway of an empty shop. She glanced up at Levi. 'There's my friend Matt. Come and meet him.'

This must be the one Sofia had told him about. Levi wished he'd paid a bit more attention because he had a hunch that Freya would freak if she knew. However, he replied, 'Sure,' and let Amy usher him over.

Matt scrambled to his feet with a big grin for Amy. Then, checking Levi out, grin fading, his expression became anxious.

Amy waved a vague hand. 'This is Levi I told you about. My real dad.'

'Yeah?' The look Matt sent Levi seemed half-friendly, half-apprehensive. 'Hello.' He nodded and smiled at Sofia too.

'Good to meet you.' Levi extended his hand and Matt hesitated before he put his own none-too-clean one into it.

Amy asked him a few questions about how things were going and whether he'd heard from the council.

Matt looked agonisingly embarrassed. 'I went down and they said I missed an appointment. I miscounted the days. I used to use my phone for my calendar and clock but once the contract ran out I sold it so I could get food.' He hunched his shoulders and managed a smile. 'I've made another appointment and my mate's set up an alert on his phone for the day before. He's going to come and get me then I'll sleep at his place so I can shower.'

Levi, listening to Amy replying earnestly, 'I hope the council can house you soon,' made a mental note to talk to his dad about the young homeless in Bettsbrough and what could be done to help them. Bryan was a leading light in the Rotary Club as well as the Chamber of Trade.

317

Matt grimaced. 'I hope so, too, but apparently I did everything wrong. I hated the idea of handouts so I didn't claim benefits and stuff . . . but then I didn't get a job either, so I'm stuffed while they assess me. I've sold nearly all my things except for a few clothes. I think the lady at the council's trying to help though.' He gave a half-laugh. 'I thought about being a *Big Issue* seller but I don't even know where to start signing up for that.'

Levi wasn't sure whether Matt really thought it was much of a joke. None of them joined in his laughter, anyway.

They said goodbye and left Matt to his doorway as they turned towards Market Square. Amy sighed as soon as they were out of Matt's view. 'I feel really bad for him.' She told Levi about how his stepdad had told him to leave the family home and his mum hadn't stuck up for him.

'I feel bad for anyone that kind of thing happens to,' Levi said. He'd read about the infamous 'downward spiral' of homelessness some people got caught in through no fault of their own. Then the forecourt of Gunn's Motors came into view and he was hit by the realisation that he had another surreal situation to face – watching the family he'd known all his life get to know his daughter.

At the thought of 'family' another thought flashed across his mind. He glanced at Amy, keeping pacing between him and Sofia. 'Is there any chance of you phoning your mum? She's distraught.'

A mulish look crossed Amy's face. 'I don't think I'm ready.'

Levi almost let it go. But then he found himself saying quietly, 'I have faith that you're mature enough to cope with a strained phone call if it comforts the person who has loved you and cared for you all your life. I know you're angry with her but she never meant you to be hurt.'

Amy halted to frown at him. 'So now I know you're my dad I have to put up with you being on my case?'

Levi thought he detected a smile lurking beneath her cross expression. 'Isn't that my job?'

'Jeez,' she grumbled. 'Next you'll start with the "Do it for me" emotional blackmail crap.'

'Family do do things for each other.' Awkwardly, he gave her shoulder a pat and though she didn't look as if she welcomed it particularly, neither did she pull away.

Chapter Twenty-six

Sofia had no idea how Levi had kept himself together during his crucial meeting with Amy. It had been so emotional that Sofia had almost lost it a couple of times herself. Amy had looked so lost and wary until she seemed to realise he was the same Levi she'd known in Italy and had begun to relax.

For Sofia the meeting had been unsettling. Though both she and Levi had been focused on what Amy was going through, Sofia had felt as if the air crackled every time Levi caught her gaze; that his eyes were making suggestions and promises. Most of his focus was on Amy – he'd travelled halfway across Europe and spent weeks with his own life on hold so he could watch out for her, so that was unsurprising – but still she was frustrated to be with him again in such circumstances. It was like someone putting a lush chocolate brownie in front of her then tying her hands so she couldn't reach out and take it.

When they reached the premises of the Gunn family's business, a prosperous-looking sales and repair garage, she hung back.

The lady on the front desk ended her phone call abruptly when she saw them and hurried shiny-eyed from behind the desk, her smile warm and eager. Sofia wasn't surprised to hear Levi address her as 'Mum', and the two men who appeared like greyhounds from their traps were easy to identify as Levi's dad and brother.

Everyone wanted to talk to Amy, warmth and curiosity combining as they tried to make her welcome and set her at her ease. How odd it was, Sofia thought, feeling quite misty-eyed at witnessing Amy's hesitant smile, that Sofia had travelled to Italy to find the missing half of her family and Amy had travelled to the UK to find hers.

As if aware of Sofia's thoughts, Amy and Levi looked back for her at the same moment. 'This is Sofia.' Levi introduced her to each family member in turn, using his parents' given names of Val and Bryan.

Sofia smiled and murmured politely.

Everyone seemed to have some idea of where she fitted into things, judging by the fact that they didn't ask. Levi calmly moved things along. 'Amy and I are still talking stuff through so we'll go on upstairs.'

Val grabbed Levi's arm in sudden anxiety. 'Wait! That Octavia's up there! She arrived about twenty minutes ago. When I said you were out she said she'd wait and swept up there before I could say yes or no. I've been up twice to say I didn't know how long you'd be but she just said she didn't mind waiting. I didn't know what to do.'

Levi's expression changed as if at a flick of a switch, anger blazing in his eyes. 'How convenient. I want a little word with her.' He turned to Amy. 'This person has been causing me a bit of irritation behind the scenes and I need to set her right on a few things. It'll probably be best if you wait down here.'

321

Amy shot a wary look at Val. 'Well . . .'

Val beamed. 'Granddad's got a stash of Crunchies in his desk he doesn't think I know about. Shall we stage a raid?'

A smile flickered on Amy's face. 'Well . . .' And she allowed herself to be steered down a corridor with Bryan mock-grumbling and Tyrone laughing in their wake.

As Sofia hadn't been invited on the Crunchie raid she followed Levi out of the foyer and up a staircase, reaching the first floor slightly behind him.

'Hello!' said a female voice ultra-brightly the instant Levi gained the landing.

Levi stepped into the room that was obviously his office, his response clipped and unfriendly. 'What are you doing here?'

By crowding in behind him and peering around Levi's broad shoulders Sofia was able to catch a glimpse of a tall, willowy blonde woman wearing a lot of makeup, her hair coiffed into an elegant up-do, her white cotton top simple but well cut. She was attractive in an over-groomed way, though at least ten years older than Sofia.

Octavia didn't look over-thrilled when she caught sight of Sofia. 'I wanted to see to unfinished business, Levi, but I see you're not alone.' She gave Sofia a chilly smile. 'If you could leave us to have a private chat—'

'Why did you dump Wes?' Levi stuck in, putting out an arm to stop Sofia leaving, while not budging from where he stood.

Octavia wrinkled her nose, smiling coyly. 'Oh, Wes.' She waved her hand dismissively. 'I just wanted to make it clear to him that once you were back—'

'My being back doesn't affect you in the slightest.' Levi stepped aside and indicated the way down. 'It's time you were going.'

'But Levi—' Octavia made her mouth a little O of disbelief. Sofia wondered if she practised her expressions in front of the mirror.

'Out,' Levi snapped.

As her pout hadn't worked, Octavia turned her glittering gaze on Sofia. 'Is it her? You've got a thing for little brown mice all of a sudden? I assumed you'd leave her safely behind in Italy.'

Sofia had already begun an indignant gasp at being referred to as a brown mouse when, catching her by surprise, Octavia reached out and yanked up Sofia's top to leave her stomach bare. 'Oh, you're not the same person. I thought you were the one with the tattoo.'

Hot with outrage, Sofia leaped back, snatching the fabric from Octavia's hand. 'What are you on about?'

Octavia folded her arms. 'When he was in Italy he took pictures of someone I thought was you but she had this tattoo—'

Levi's voice was suddenly low and dangerous. 'You have some way of accessing the *photographs on my phone*?'

Sofia felt faint. 'What?'

Octavia halted, looking caught out, her lips parted as if ready to bring out some defence . . . if she could only think of one. Then she made a grab for her handbag from a nearby desk and whisked around as if to make a dash for it.

Like lightning, Levi jumped into the doorway to block her escape route. 'You either explain what you've been up to or I inform the police you've been invading my privacy and maybe even stealing my identity.'

Octavia puffed up her chest in indignation. 'I haven't used your identity.'

'I'd want it checked out though, because it sounds as

if you might have the opportunity and you've certainly been up to something. As you've had a certain amount of access to my data and software, I'm sure there'd be enough suspicion for me to file a report.'

She scowled at him.

Levi scowled back.

Then Octavia heaved an exaggerated sigh. 'You're blowing everything up out of proportion. I only borrowed one of the passwords you had listed on your phone. It didn't do any harm.'

'The password to the server, I assume. So that's how you got Dick fired! You signed in as him and screwed up his page,' Levi stormed. 'There's an identity theft offence right there and—' He halted and turned as running foot-steps pounded up the stairs towards the landing.

Amy swung around the banister looking happier than she had since arriving in the UK. 'Granny said— Oh! It's *Auntie* Octavia! I didn't know you knew her. Hello, Auntie Octavia.'

Levi's eyes almost bulged from his head as he stared at his daughter. 'Auntie?'

'She's one of Mum's friends, not my real auntie. She's been to visit us in Germany though. She caused havoc.' Amy sent Sofia a conspiratorial look. 'I told you about her once. She's the one—' She halted and looked from Levi to Octavia and back. 'What's up?'

Sofia watched consternation form on Octavia's face before she straightened her features into a semblance of an indulgent smile. 'Amy? I didn't realise you'd nearly grown up.'

Amy obviously didn't appreciate being patronised. 'I'm all the way grown up.'

Moving swiftly, Levi shepherded Amy into the room

then shut the door and leaned on it. 'OK, Octavia. Spill.' His lips were a thin, uncompromising line. Octavia pouted. Her eyes flickered from Levi to Amy as if hunting for where to gain traction in the argument. Inspiration must have been in short supply because after several moments of silence her shoulders heaved on a sigh. 'Oh, all right!' she snapped. 'Freya asked me to check you out. You know why.' She looked meaningfully at Amy.

Amy breathed a shocked, 'Ohhh!' at this casually revealed evidence that at least one more person knew about the truth that had slunk out of the family closet.

'She wanted to contact you to see if you'd go after Amy,' Octavia carried on blithely, 'but she thought she'd better look into your circumstances beforehand. If you'd been married with a bunch of kids I doubt she'd have bothered because you probably wouldn't have been able to go. She'd been able to establish your people still owned the garage and, as I'm local, asked me to see what I could find out. It's not hard to get information by falling into conversation with the right people. I flirted a little bit with Tyrone then pretended to see his wedding ring and said I thought someone had told me Levi Gunn was single. He said no, Levi's my brother, who works upstairs. All I had to do was hang around outside until you came out – and follow.' She looked at Levi beneath her lashes. 'I fell a little bit in lust I suppose.'

Sofia could scarcely believe her ears. 'It sounds more like a giant obsession then "falling a little bit in lust".'

'There was no harm in it,' Octavia added sulkily. 'It's not as if he's married or anything.'

'So how did you get my phone?' Levi's expression was forbidding, his voice like steel.

It was his turn to be treated to Octavia's sulky look. 'It

was a spur-of-the-moment thing because you made it so easy. I was sitting just behind you in that coffee shop. I watched you type your access code in twice – you held the phone so just about anyone could see! Then you put it down right on the edge of the table while you did something with your laptop and I just sort of . . . picked it up as I went by. I added myself to your Dropbox where your photos upload to automatically.'

Slowly, Levi shook his head. 'Brazen.' He took out his phone and looked at it as if it had personally betrayed him.

'Wow,' Sofia marvelled, glaring at Octavia. 'You're shameless. I feel sorry for you if you don't even know how wrong it is to do what you did.'

Amy butted in. 'She did something odd when she visited us in Germany a couple of years ago. My parents didn't really discuss it with us kids but it had something to do with one of Dad's blokes at work and Mum telling her off. That was when Mum said she was a right trollop.'

Octavia sent Amy a poisonous look. 'That was a simple misunderstanding blown up out of all proportion.'

'None of her marriages have worked out, Mum says,' Amy added.

Levi frowned blackly at Octavia. 'I ought to call the police in case you've tampered with anything that's going to affect my business.'

For the first time, Octavia looked seriously alarmed. 'You're deliberately making it out to be more than it was! It was just a bit of a game, that was all.' She calmed herself with an obvious effort. 'Look, I didn't do anything to harm you.' Unexpectedly, her voice choked with tears. 'I wanted you. I only came here to work because it would get me closer to you.'

'And poor Wes,' Levi pointed out dryly.

Again, Octavia shrugged off Wes's plight. 'It's not my fault if he misread.'

For a long, long silent moment, Levi contemplated the tall woman who somehow looked childish, standing before him, twisting her fingers while she waited to see what he'd do.

Abruptly, he stepped aside and opened the door. 'Get out.'

Relief flashing across her face, Octavia swung her bag onto her shoulder and got.

Chapter Twenty-seven

After Octavia had gone – after shuddering at the memory of Octavia flipping up her top to look at her bare stomach as if personal space and privacy were not issues – Sofia made instant coffee. Levi's office was all set up with cardboard cups and sachets of milk and sugar. Meanwhile, Levi talked earnestly with Amy. 'I hope you don't hate this too much – but I have to ring your mum and talk to her. Octavia's behaviour shouldn't just be brushed off, and I feel I deserve an explanation from your mother too.'

Amy heaved a long-suffering sigh. Levi's gaze didn't waver so, begrudgingly, she snorted, 'Oh, go on then.'

Sofia hesitated in her task, then put back one of the cups, poured water into the other two and stirred. It gave her a really odd sensation in her stomach to hear Levi say into the phone, 'Freya? Why the hell did you send that bloody lunatic Octavia to spy on me? I don't care if she is the only person you know in Bettsbrough,' he went on cuttingly. 'I understand from Amy that you know full well she can act unacceptably. Do you know how much trouble she's caused?'

Moving quietly, Sofia put the full coffee cups down in front of Levi and Amy.

Levi gave her a quick smile but then returned his attention to his conversation. 'Hang on.' He put his hand over the mouthpiece of the phone to talk to Amy. 'Your mum says asking Octavia to be a pair of eyes on the ground didn't come from a bad motivation. She wanted some idea of how I'd be affected before she spilled the beans so feels she was trying to save me trouble rather than cause it. I can accept that.'

Amy was a bit pale but at least she seemed to have fallen back into her old easy way with Levi. 'I feel weird Mum was talking to Auntie Octavia behind my back though.'

Levi gave her a reassuring smile. 'But you'd taken off and were refusing to talk to her, weren't you? Maybe now's the perfect time to change that because she's asking to talk to you. What do you think? You've probably got to do it some time.'

After several seconds of fulminating silence, Amy heaved a sigh. 'OK.'

Levi held out the phone. 'I think you'll feel better.'

'Yeah.' Amy squared her shoulders and took the phone. She looked at it without moving.

Sofia drifted towards the door. 'I'll go off for a walk for a bit. Give you privacy.'

For once Amy didn't demand she stay. Sofia ran lightly downstairs, glad that Val wasn't at her desk and so she could get out into the fresh air without feeling obliged to chat.

She felt so strange.

It was great to see Levi and Amy redefining their relationship but it left her role in things so high up in the air she felt giddy.

Once outside, instead of taking the road to the market square she chose the one at right angles to it, passing bus shelters arranged in a neat line. Walking briskly, she passed the local college, a pub and a furniture shop. The road took her downhill and curved right. Within five minutes she was at the pedestrian zone, which meant she could walk through it and be back at Gunn's Motors in no time. Not feeling a sufficient period had elapsed for Amy to have what promised to be a difficult conversation or, for that matter, for Sofia to sort through her own jumbled feelings, she turned left into the indoor shopping area. And went right around it in ten minutes.

Bettsbrough was the original 'small town'.

Moving more slowly now, she stepped back outside again and, with a small wave in Matt's direction, sat down on a bench to try and absorb all that had happened in a handful of days. It seemed amazing that she'd missed only a few shifts on Casa Felice's reception in the hated suit, because she felt a long way from Montelibertà.

Next time, she'd get a job with plenty of access to the outdoors.

Whatever 'next time' proved to mean. Maybe Amy would go home to Germany now. Maybe Sofia should return to Italy? Had she been too quick to dismiss the idea of working at Hotel Alba?

Gianni and Chiara, and even Mia, were the only family she had.

Going back to Italy would mean leaving Levi, because he was so obviously part of Bettsbrough. His home was here. His family, his business. His life. She thought about that for a long time, letting the July sunshine bathe her as she watched the people of his town go about their Monday business, hurrying, laughing, talking, shopping or making phone calls.

With slow steps she returned the Gunn's Motors building half an hour later, passing Val with a smile but heading straight for the stairs. Levi and Amy were sitting together at the desk, their coffee cups empty now. Amy's eyes were red but she smiled tremulously and got up to give Sofia a hug. 'Mum and I have made up.'

Sofia felt her own eyes burn. 'That's so great!' She hugged the slight figure hard, concentrating on what a wonderful thing this was for her friend and trying not to wonder what it meant for Sofia herself.

'And,' Amy went on after they'd disentangled themselves, 'Mum's really cross at Auntie Octavia. She's going to call her and make sure she's got the message to butt out of Levi's life. She thinks Octavia might need help because she's been so weird.'

'You've missed out an important detail,' Levi prompted. He looked more relaxed now.

'Oh, yes!' Amy opened her eyes wide. 'Octavia was the *bride*! You know, when Mum and Levi . . . it was a hen weekend? It was Octavia's. Mum and her were at flight attendant school together and so Levi met Octavia then but he didn't remember.'

'Being expected to remember some girl you met eighteen years ago for a few minutes in a club when she was dressed in cowboy gear, a Lone Ranger mask and a net curtain veil is a big ask,' Levi remarked dryly.

Amy giggled. 'Anyway, Mum's going to sort Octavia out.'

Levi pretended to mop his brow, making Amy giggle again. Sofia grinned.

'So what now?' Levi looked at Sofia and Amy expectantly. 'Shall I drive you to the Travelodge and grab your stuff to take back to my place?'

331

Sofia's heart tossed itself like a pancake. It would be sensible to say no. Her head was screaming, *'Don't! The more involved you get with him the harder it will be when you leave.'* But her heart and her libido were bellowing, *'Go for it! Have a few lovely days with him before you have to go back to your own life!'*

Amy got in before Sofia could decide which part of her to answer with. 'Can that wait a bit?' The youngster's gaze had become solemn. She looked at Levi. 'I want to talk to you about something important.' She took such a deep breath that her shoulders hunched. Then blurted out, 'Please will you give Matt a job?'

Levi sighed, a small frown pleating his brow. 'I'm not sure—'

'No, listen,' Amy broke in. Her voice trembled. 'It's really hard to get a job when you don't have a place to live. He can use his mates' address but he's got no phone number to arrange interviews. He's got no degree, and no work record because he's only just finished sixth form.'

She had to clear her throat before she could go on. 'I know the homeless seem scary to some people. They think they're all addicts but Matt's not. He just needs to eat and somewhere to sleep.'

Levi didn't speak. Sofia, seeing the brightness of his eyes, suspected that he was suffering a lump in his throat as Amy pinned him with her earnest gaze, her hands clenched on the desk in front of her.

And she hadn't finished tugging at his heartstrings yet. 'I'm asking you to do it for me. You can train him for something, can't you? He's a good person. He didn't wake up one day and think, "I know, I'll live in a doorway." It happened because he didn't know what to do when his stepdad chucked him out and he's only just finding out about benefits and things, but it's all taking so long. And there are these boys who used to bully him at school and they drive past and laugh at him and call him Doormat.' Her voice broke, a tiny sob escaping into the still air of the office.

'All right,' Levi said gruffly. 'Go get him and I'll talk to him and see what his IT skills are like. There will be some routine jobs I can give him, I expect, if he seems all right.'

'*Yes!*' Amy leaped off her chair, punching the air, beaming smiles chasing away her tears. 'Thank you! Thank you! I'll go find him. We can move in with you later. Thanks. Oh, *thank you*!' Amy threw her arms around Levi and hugged him tight, then released him and ran out through the door.

Sofia gazed at Levi, who looked as stunned as if a summer nymph had just appeared and granted his dearest wish. She tried to joke but her voice came out all wobbly. 'Congratulations. I think you just became a father.'

He laughed shakily. 'I was incapable of saying no to her. It was like she was drawing my guts out when she cried. Is it always going to be like that?'

'So I've heard.'

Levi shook his head and rubbed his palms over his face. Then his eyes appeared above his hands and fixed on Sofia. He leaped up, strode around the desk and yanked her into his arms, making her say 'Oof!' at the suddenness. He crushed her against him so she could hardly breathe, ribs hard against hers, her cheekbone mashed against his collarbone. They stood, entwined, bodies silently communicating.

It was one of the best hugs she'd ever had.

'I've missed you,' he murmured. 'Even though we've been together today I still missed you because it wasn't the right time to do this.' He slackened his hold just enough to allow him to dip his head and touch his mouth to hers, softly questing, his tongue stroking its way into her mouth, making her close her eyes to savour the sensation, the heat.

And a voice said, 'Oops! Sorry, I should have coughed or something.' Amy stood in the doorway, eyes like saucers.

Sofia tried to spring away but Levi kept his arm around her. 'It's all right, come in.'

Amy hunched her shoulders, shooting Sofia a look of amused disbelief as if to say, *I can't leave you alone for a minute.* 'There's another thing,' she said to Levi. Matt doesn't have anywhere to live and it's not just the rent people need, is it? They need to pay a deposit and for their electricity and everything. Did you say your house is quite big?'

'Quite,' Levi said faintly.

'OK, good.' Amy swung back out of the room again.

Sofia began to shake with laughter. 'Did you just get a lodger?'

He groaned and shut his eyes. 'I'm going to have to go into training for this parenthood thing. I need courses on "Learning how to say no" and "How not to fall into traps that are only obvious once you've crashed to the bottom of the hole."'

Sofia, though laughing, hugged him to her more tightly than ever.

Chapter Twenty-eight

The next fortnight was the most bittersweet of Sofia's life.

Levi took Matt on under the title of 'trainee'. Trainee what, he didn't seem too sure, but Matt had taken an A level in Computer Science and IT so, although he wouldn't get his results for several weeks, there was a foundation to build on.

Sofia knew Levi had been secretly impressed that when Amy told Matt he had a chance of a job he'd insisted on running all the way to his mates' place to beg a shower and borrow a clean shirt before running on to Gunn's Motors and presenting himself, panting, for his interview.

Levi hadn't gone so far as to give him a room in his own house but accompanied him to his mother and stepfather's place and suggested coldly that they help towards a deposit. The stepfather scowled every time Levi turned his baleful gaze on him but Matt's mother, with a noticeable unwillingness to meet Matt's eye, gave him two hundred pounds she'd just taken out from a cash machine. Shocked that Matt's parents were pretty middle-class so you couldn't even excuse their behaviour on the grounds of being hard up, Levi contacted an estate agent he knew – probably someone he'd been to school with: he seemed to have an entire portfolio of useful contacts from that source – and got Matt a room in a house of multiple occupancy, putting up the rest of the deposit himself and standing as guarantor for the rent, telling Matt he'd better work hard so he could pay his living expenses. Matt hadn't been able to speak and had to bite his lips hard as he wrung Levi's hand in inarticulate gratitude.

Amy got to know her grandparents, her Uncle Tyrone, Aunt Beth and two toddler cousins Grace and Serena over family meals and even a family day out to a park. Sofia resolutely excused herself from these events, no matter how many times Levi invited or even cajoled.

Instead, she hung around Levi's house to surf the net, looking through the dwindling summer jobs in Europe and beginning to think that she might as well go straight to the Canary Islands . . . if she didn't return to Montelibertà. She'd telephoned Hotel Alba on Gianni and Mia's wedding anniversary to offer congratulations. She'd got Mia first, who'd seemed first touched and then pleased at Sofia's good wishes. Gianni had come on the line and told Sofia once again that there was a job waiting for her. When Sofia, encouraged by the slight thaw in Mia, tentatively mentioned Amy he'd sighed apologetically, that, although something might come up, he didn't presently have anything to offer someone so young and inexperienced.

Sofia still hadn't discussed onward plans with Amy properly because there always seemed to be something

Amy wanted to sort out first, like deferring her conditional university place, talking to her family in Germany and thrashing out painfully thorny questions such as whether she could continue to address Stephen Webber as 'Dad' now she knew he hadn't been there at the conception.

It was Levi who'd clarified that for her, slinging an arm across her shoulders as he said, 'Think how gutted he'll be if you start calling him "Stephen". Things have been bad enough for him, haven't they?'

Amy pulled a face of anguish and said, 'I know, right?' And that was another matter sorted.

More in the 'bitter' column than the 'sweet', on a Friday when Levi was at work and Amy spending time with Grace and Serena, who'd really taken to having an older cousin, Sofia set off for her once home town of Bedford. A time-consuming mixture of bus and train journeys took her eventually to Norse Road Cemetery. She stood before the pale grey marble headstone where now the name of Aldo Agnello Bianchi was inscribed below that of Dawn Bianchi née Hill. Echoing her actions in Montelibertà a couple of months ago, she crouched on the grass and arranged fresh flowers in the vase – jolly red Sweet Williams this time. Then she laid a hand on the cold marble and murmured, 'I've managed most of the promises, Dad. Montelibertà is a wonderful place and I'm sure I'll visit again. The happiness thing's a bit more complicated.' After a few minutes thinking about her parents, she walked back to the station, though it took an hour, feeling unsettlingly in limbo, unable to imagine herself living once again in Bedford but not knowing exactly what place was in her immediate future.

The sweetness of her stay in Bettsbrough was mainly centred around the nights, when Sofia shared Levi's room at the top of the house. His bed sometimes felt like the centre of her world, where he sank into her body every night. She'd wind her arms around him and pull him harder and deeper, as if that way she could keep him.

Because with every passing day something seemed to hook Levi and bind him to Bettsbrough and his life without her. Wes requested a couple of months' sabbatical before making a decision about The Moron Forum so there was only Levi to manage the remote workers, fix problems and train Matt, even without any innovation or development of the site. Amy came to Levi for advice. His family was all over him, involving him, enjoying having him home.

When Sofia broached the subject of researching jobs with Levi before raising it with Amy, he kissed her and said, 'Can you wait a few days before talking to Amy? I think my family would be gutted if she left right away.' Sofia was happy not to have to end her visit yet so she kissed him back and decided to live in the moment for a few days longer.

When she brought it up the next time he pulled her close and murmured, 'I still think Amy needs more time.' Sofia didn't disagree as she met his kisses with some of her own, but she was becoming more and more aware that the longer she stayed with Levi the harder it was going to be to say goodbye.

It was at the end of the two weeks that Sofia approached Levi the third time. They were together in his bed, cotton sheets cool against their naked skin, Sofia's head on Levi's chest and his heartbeat steady and strong in her ear. 'July will soon be over. If Amy and I are going to move on then

338

I think it's got to be soon.' She said it experimentally, making it an opportunity for Levi to suggest Sofia didn't leave at all.

He didn't take the opportunity.

He stroked her hair, threading his fingers through until he reached the skin on her back and sighed. 'I think,' he said, sounding as if he were choosing his words carefully, 'that Amy might be getting around to asking me if she can stay here, at least for now.'

'Oh.' Sofia processed this. 'I suppose she hasn't said anything to me because we sort of had an arrangement and so she feels awkward – she's still not a big fan of difficult conversations.'

'Possibly.'

Sofia became aware of a sinking sensation in her chest. 'If I'm not waiting for Amy then I could leave any time. I could talk to my uncle about doing a spell in Hotel Alba.'

'I suppose so.' He shifted restlessly. 'They're your only family and I wouldn't want to stop you going back to Montelibertà or having other travel adventures. But don't feel you have to rush.'

'Thank you,' she responded politely, feeling as if he was being nice because she'd helped him above and beyond the call of duty with Amy and he didn't want to seem as if he was kicking Sofia out.

She let the beginning of another week pass by, feeling vaguely depressed and unsettled, then on Wednesday decided to give Amy a nudge, catching her coming in from meeting Matt during his lunch hour.

Amy was all smiles as she swept in, bringing with her the scent of the garden. 'Hey!' She looked a different kid from the frightened and angry waif Sofia had befriended back in May. Matt was definitely good for Amy, a nice guy with a sense of humour and a sense of decency, and Sofia had no idea why his mum had allowed the stepdad to act with such meanness towards him.

'Got a second?' Sofia asked casually. 'Let's go into the conservatory.'

Once they were seated in rattan chairs, looking out into a large garden Levi seemed to treat mainly as a meadow, Sofia got straight to the point. 'I get the impression from Levi that you're thinking of staying here for a bit.'

Amy coloured hotly. 'I'm thinking about it,' she admitted cautiously, her fingers pleating the front of her top. 'But I'll travel on with you if you want. I know you want to be out of the UK for at least two years.'

On edge, Sofia wanted to close her hand over Amy's to still her fidgeting fingers. 'It's OK, honestly. I understand that things have changed for you. You've straightened everything out with your family in Germany and you've found this great family in England too. I think it's terrific, Amy, honestly. I would hate you to think even for a minute that you have to come with me.'

Tears began to form on Amy's eyelashes. 'I'm sorry, Sofia. You've done so much for me, following me to England and everything, I feel really shitty for bailing on you. But it's just that I like it here at the moment.'

'I know.' Sofia was so anxious to soothe Amy's fears that she left her chair and knelt beside the younger girl so she could slide her arms around her. And at least focusing on Amy gave her a chance to ignore the slimy sick feeling inside herself as she saw her departure from this little market town drawing inexorably near. An insistent phrase began to hammer around her skull. *This means it's time to say goodbye to Levi. Time to say goodbye to Levi*. To distract herself, she pulled Amy closer into her embrace and searched for words of comfort. 'I began my travelling on my own, didn't I? I'll carry on that way. I'll miss you, of course, because we've become real friends. That's why I promised Levi I'd stick with you when he had to come back here.'

Amy sniffed dolefully. 'I don't think I would have survived—' She halted.

Sofia's stomach turned over as she realised what she'd said. Numbly, she sat back on her heels, wanting to bite back the words. But it was too late.

Another still moment, then Amy yanked herself free, turning on Sofia a fierce and red-rimmed glare. 'When he had to come back here? That means you knew he was my real dad!' Amy's face, aside from those accusing eyes, was dead white. '*That's* why you followed me to the UK! Not because we were friends, not because you were frightened I wouldn't be OK, it was because you knew!' Her eyes glittered. 'And now, lucky you, you're sleeping with Levi and hasn't that worked out well? For *you*!'

Then she leaped to her feet, spun around and made a dash for the door. She was halfway across the hall and headed straight as an arrow for the front entrance when Sofia put a spurt on and was able to grab her arm. 'Amy!'

Amy had to pause or race out of the door towing Sofia behind her like a water skier. 'Get off!' she hissed, eyes flashing, all sign of the shy, quiet Amy lost in the raging teenager who'd taken her place.

Sofia only tightened her grip. 'Wait! Listen!'

Grudgingly, Amy paused.

Sofia released her hold. 'I'll go,' she said quietly. 'This is your home. It has to be me who goes.'

Amy stared resolutely in the other direction.

Heart aching, Sofia turned towards the stairs. It cost her enormous effort to lift her feet from one step to another but she managed it.

They were, after all, the first steps on her next journey.

Chapter Twenty-nine

Packing sucked. Sofia felt as alone as she ever had. As alone as when Aldo died. More alone than when she'd packed up and sold their house. More alone than when she'd stepped onto the plane to Italy. More alone than when Levi had roared out of Montelibertà on his Ducati.

Automatically, she tossed clothes into her suitcases and swept personal things into her backpack. She grabbed her toiletries from Levi's bathroom and fished her shoes from the bottom of his wardrobe.

It took a bit of doing to haul the suitcases down two flights from the top of the house to the hall, but she managed it. She leaned her backpack against them then sat on the bottom step to wait for Levi to come home from his office, which he usually did between five and six. The shit hitting Amy's fan didn't mean Sofia was prepared to cheapen the brief but intense affair she'd had with him by leaving without saying goodbye. That wasn't any way to do it.

The time crawled by. She used her phone to book a room in the Travelodge for tonight. Then she followed her heart towards where, if she couldn't be right here, she wanted to be.

She rang Gianni. She had to wait till he was located and her call redirected to him and he replied, '*Pronto.*'

'*Ciao, Gianni,*' she began. 'It's Sofia. Is—' She had to draw in an unsteady breath and swallow before she went on. 'Is the job offer still open? I'm thinking of returning to Montelibertà.'

'Come,' he said instantly. 'We'll talk when you get here. We'll arrange things.'

Another of those unsteady breaths. 'Will Mia—'

'The past is past,' he said softly. 'She knows that.' They talked for several more minutes, even discussing the possibilities of formal education in hotel management as part of Sofia's development, and she ended the call feeling reasonably sure she could make a life for herself with or near her Italian family, especially when Chiara called within a minute to celebrate the news, burbling joyfully about introducing her to all her friends.

When she'd ended that call too, Sofia could hear Amy moving around in her room and wondered whether to go up and try to apologise again. Even more than being obliged to leave Levi now, practically this minute – she glanced at the clock and saw it was turned five already – she hated knowing Amy thought she'd been a false friend. It added several extra chunks of lead to her already weighty heart.

Before she could fully make up her mind whether to go up, the sound of a key in the door set apprehension walking its cold fingers down her spine.

Levi stepped into the hall and grinned at her, eyes alight, hair falling over his forehead. 'What are you—?' Then his gaze fell on the suitcases and he stopped short, the grin falling from his face. 'You're leaving.' Disbelief laced his voice.

Heart beating up in her throat, Sofia climbed to her feet, trying to smile. 'I'm afraid it's time.'

His eyes fixed on her. 'You must really want to get on with your next adventure.'

She knew he was referring to their discussion when he'd told her there was no rush. Was it only last night? The hours had trickled through her hands like sand. While she'd waited on the step she'd had time to consider this farewell and, as if she could hear Aldo singing, *Hey, That's No Way to Say Goodbye*, had decided not to tell him about the harsh words Amy had flung at her. What purpose would it serve? Levi's relationship with his daughter was too new and fragile for Sofia to want to threaten it.

So she held onto her smile. 'The summer's getting away from me.'

He nodded. He didn't come any closer, just shoved his hands in his pockets and frowned. 'Where are you going?'

'Montelibertà. I decided to give Gianni's offer of a job a try. Hope Mia can live with it.'

Slowly, Levi nodded. 'I can see why you'd want to return. It's just that I thought we'd have more time than this.' He cleared his throat. 'Would it be OK if I came over sometime?'

For some reason, Sofia had talked herself out of the possibility that Levi would want to carry things on, even on an occasional basis. *Did* she want to see him again? Just as when he was leaving Montelibertà, she suspected the crumbs of comfort from a few flying visits might damage her more than being brave and ending it now, while things were so good. And the way Amy felt about her would make things awkward too. A lump formed in her throat.

As she stood silently struggling, Amy's voice came from the top of the stairs. 'She let the cat out of the bag,' she said flatly. 'She admitted she knew about you being my bio-dad. I thought she was my friend but she was just keeping a promise to you to keep an eye on me. And we know what she's like about promises.'

Levi's gaze sharpened as it flitted to Amy, but his voice was gentle. 'I see. Could you come down here a minute?'

A moment's pause, when Sofia thought maybe Amy would refuse, then Amy ran lightly down, Sofia drawing aside to let her past.

Levi lifted his arm invitingly and Amy stepped close so he could loop it lightly around her shoulders. 'Tell me what happened.'

Amy recounted the afternoon's spat, Levi nodding as he listened. At the end of the slightly garbled story of how Amy concluded that Sofia had probably followed her to England so he could sleep with Levi again he nodded very slowly. 'So you asked Sofia to leave?'

'No!'

'So I wonder why she's going right now, today?'

Amy frowned in thought. Then she shot Sofia a guilty look before dropping her gaze to the floor. 'I was upset and I was going to leave but she chased after me and said she'd go instead.'

Levi reached out a hand and tipped up Amy's chin. 'You're an adult, Amy, and I don't want to come the heavy-handed dad on you – I'm not even sure I know how – but I'm worried that constant running away is going to cause you problems sooner or later.' He paused, his gaze never wavering from Amy as he added carefully, 'I understood what drove you to leave home in the first place, and even what sent you chasing off to the UK, but are you beginning to use flying off in a strop as a legitimate way of punishing people? Sofia's been good to me as well as you, and I'm afraid I put her on the spot. I told her I'm your father out of my need for a listening ear. Then I asked her not to tell you in case you did another disappearing act.'

'But—'

Levi gave Amy's shoulders a gentle squeeze. 'I put her in an awkward position and she did the best she could. It wasn't Sofia's secret, it wasn't her problem and it wasn't her responsibility, but she did her best to come through for us.'

Amy stared at the floor again, a red tide creeping up her neck.

But Levi wasn't finished yet. 'I'm not sure why you're angry with her about this but not angry with me.'

The red tide became darker.

Levi was inexorable. 'I notice she was going to leave without telling me about your part in what happened.' He waited, but Amy still made no reply. Sofia began to feel sorry for her.

'Will you do something for me?' Levi continued, his face grooved and drawn. 'Will you go up to your room to give me some privacy to say goodbye properly to Sofia?'

At the strain in his voice Amy's eyes flew to his in horror. 'But you told me you didn't want her to— Oh, no! Look what I've done!' she gasped. Then she swung round and grabbed Sofia's hands. 'I'm sorry! I'm sorry I lost my temper. Neither of us wants you to go but Levi said we had to let you do the travelling and have the adventures you've always wanted. He said even if we love you, we have to. You don't really have to go tonight, do you? I'm truly sorry I was such a bitch.'

347

Sofia simply couldn't speak. Amy's words twirled dizzingly her mind. *Neither of us wants you to go . . . even if we love you . . .* Dimly, she was aware of Levi gently detaching Amy from Sofia, murmuring that she should leave him to try and sort things out now.

Then suddenly it was just Sofia and Levi standing in the hall together with her suitcases between them and the sound of Amy's closing bedroom door echoing down the stairs.

She gazed at him, her eyes swimming with tears. 'You told Amy you don't want me to go?' she whispered.

Levi smiled a lopsided smile and took her hand. 'Do you think you could come out from behind your wall of suitcases for this conversation?'

When they were standing toe-to-toe, he laced his fingers with hers. 'For the record, if you had only come to England in order to sleep with me, I would be sublimely happy. And, no, I don't want you to leave, though I recognise the selfishness of that. Even had my darling newly-discovered-and-occasionally-bratty daughter not decided to have a tantrum and then in an effort to make amends start tossing around words like "love", I had intended to have a long and serious conversation with you.'

'What were you going to say?' Sofia felt the lead weights beginning to drop from her heart one by one as what might be happening began to dawn on her.

He dipped his head to brush her lips with his. 'That I love you and would like a future with you. That it might be possible, in a few months, for me to travel with you, if I can coax Wes back and once I know what Amy's doing. You could go on ahead until I could join you. That is, of course—' he kissed her again, more deeply this time '—if you have feelings for me too.'

Heart soaring, Sofia raised herself up on tiptoes and pressed her body all along his as she returned his kiss. 'Really deep feelings, actually.' She felt some of the tension leave him at her words. 'And,' she murmured against his lips, 'it seems to me I could sort everything . . . by staying here with you.'

Instantly he pulled back to look into her face. A huge smile curved his mouth. 'What? Here in little ole Bettsbrough?'

'Here.' She kissed him. 'There.' She kissed him again. 'Anywhere you are.'

Epilogue

One year later
Promise #6: Be happy, Sofia.

'Here? Seriously?' Sofia, pulling off her crash helmet, shook out her hair, laughing in delight as she dismounted from her perch on the pillion of Levi's motorbike. She gazed up at the building in front of her. 'This is where we're spending our honeymoon?'

Levi pulled off his own crash helmet and gazed up at Hotel Alba in satisfaction. 'I thought you might like it.' He began to unfasten his jacket in deference to the July sunshine and Sofia quickly followed suit.

The double doors to reception stood open invitingly and Gianni stood there smiling, hand in hand with Mia as if to give his wife reassurance that the arrival of Sofia would mean no lessening of Gianni's affection, as Chiara dashed forward to fling her arms around her cousin. 'You came!'

Sofia laughed, though she had to wipe her eyes with the backs of her hands. 'Did you know about this when

351

you all came to England for the wedding? It was only two days ago and you said nothing!'

'It was a big secret, all planned by your husband. For months we've held a reservation for Mr Levi Gunn and Mrs Sofia Gunn.'

Then Gianni was effusively kissing each of Sofia's cheeks, an example followed, with more reserve, by Mia. 'Welcome,' she said, 'though we're not at all convinced by what your husband has planned for this evening.' She smiled when she said it though.

Sofia turned to Levi. 'You've planned something else?'

Levi shrugged, grinning lazily. 'Let's get checked in. The evening will look after itself.'

When evening came Sofia hadn't been able to get him to divulge the secret but she put on a summer dress – the kind that didn't crease easily as it had had to travel in her backpack – and let Levi lead her from Hotel Alba. 'Come on, you've got to tell me now! Where is this special place where you've booked dinner?'

'I'll show you.' They walked down into the town, through Piazza Santa Lucia and Piazza Roma to . . . Via Virgilio.

Sofia gurgled with laughter. 'Are we going to eat at Il Giardino?'

His eyes shimmered with amusement. 'I have to admit I kind of like the idea of Davide having to serve you drinks with a smile but, no, I've booked the terrace. I thought you might enjoy the fact that Benedetta's rules don't apply to you now.'

Laughing, she reached up to press a kiss on his cheek. 'Got to admit it will be fun to be a punter when I was never allowed there unless on duty.' She began to tow him up the hill in her eagerness to go.

A table had been reserved for them with snowy linen and gleaming silver. They drank Orvieto Classico and laughed when Benedetta suddenly appeared and greeted Sofia with an acerbic 'I hope you're here to work your notice!' But she smiled and wished them both well, proving that she had a human side, even if she hid it well sometimes.

'We are *so* going to have to come back with Amy,' Sofia hissed, as Benedetta departed for the dining room, probably to give some poor server a hard time about how they held their tray. 'She would adore having Benedetta be nice to her. And Davide!'

Levi raised his glass to clink with hers. 'If we could get her attention between her volunteering for worthy causes all over Bettsbrough and finding excuses not to go to university.'

They were halfway down their second bottle of Orvieto Classico, replete from wonderful tortellini followed by rich tartufo, when Levi became suddenly serious. He took Sofia's hand. The darkness had dropped softly around them, lights springing up all over the terrace, and Sofia felt as if they were enclosed in their own enchanted grotto.

'What would your father think of me, do you think?' His voice was gentle.

Instantly, Sofia's eyes brimmed, though she smiled tremulously. 'He'd think you were perfect. He'd say, "Promise me, Sofia, you will remain as happy as this man has made you today."' She laughed. 'And he'd probably demand you promise to make me happy and he'd have a lot of ideas of how you should do that because he always had plenty of opinions.'

His eyes filled with heat. 'I have quite a few ideas

353

of my own about how to make you happy but I certainly wouldn't have wanted to share them with your dad.'

Sofia giggled. 'He would have been thrilled that we came back to Montelibertà for our honeymoon.'

Levi's gaze was suddenly intent. 'We could come back here to live, if you want. Now Wes is back on board at The Moron Forum I could work from here – I've already talked to him about the possibility and now Octavia's found some other poor mug to haunt he's up for it. You could work with your family.'

'Are you serious?' Sofia could scarcely believe her ears. She felt as if her heart was galloping all over the terrace, whooping with joy. 'But what about your own family? And Bettsbrough?'

'I've talked to my lot. They understand. It will take a big adjustment for them but they'll visit. Probably quite a lot, if I know my mum and daughter. You've no idea the trouble I've had making Amy keep the possibility to herself! She's nearly given it away a hundred times but I wanted to suggest it to you here, back where it all began.'

'Wow.' Sofia could hardly breathe for joy. She gazed across the valley and took a moment to savour the pleasure of being back. Then she turned to Levi, the man who had changed all her plans but now was offering to give them back to her. 'How about we try it for two years? The two years away from the UK I promised myself? Then we can talk about where to base ourselves permanently.'

'Here, there, wherever you are,' Levi repeated her words of a year ago, raising his glass. 'To Aldo. The man who, by demanding promises from his daughter, sent her to Italy. And to me.'

Sofia touched his glass with hers, then raised it to the sky, eyes turned to the blue deepening to lavender. 'I kept

354

all my promises. Especially the one about being happy. *Salute, Papà.*'

Leaning across the table to give her new husband a kiss, she didn't think she could get much happier. It just wasn't possible.

Acknowledgements

This book has seen me shamelessly hitting up friends old and new to help me bring you the story of what happened *One Summer in Italy*, and I welcome this opportunity to express my gratitude. Neil Hesman, who runs my website www.suemoorcroft.com, advised me on all things website-related, especially The Moron Forum, whilst Paul Matthews gave me The Moron Forum's name. Sara and David Moody of Arte Umbria, the little patch of Italy where I have run many happy courses and writing retreats, provided information on local matters and seasonal employment; unlike Benedetta, they have a fair and responsible attitude to their summer workers! Angela Petch kindly supplied me with other information Italian; Ross Warren answered my questions relating to hotels and hotel staff; Gilli Allan on watercolour painting; and Kev Moorcroft on Germany and the ex-pat family.

Mark West, brilliantly supportive fellow writer and entertaining conference buddy, read an early draft of *One Summer in Italy* and provided his usual perceptive feedback.

Emanuela Anechoum generously read the manuscript to correct the Italian. I so appreciate the input of both. Pia Fenton/Christina Courtenay and Myra Kersner/Maggie Sullivan were perfect sounding boards on our writing retreat at Pia's house.

The amazing support for my books from the members of Team Sue Moorcroft is a joy. Credit for naming characters and places to Susan Baker (Beth), Sue Sharp (Grace), Tracy Shelley Stokes (Serena) and Neil Slade (Via Virgilio).

It's a joy and a pleasure to work with my wonderful agent Juliet Pickering of Blake Friedmann Literary, TV and Film Agency and Team Avon at HarperCollins. You power my books to new heights!

Heartfelt thanks to you all.

No acknowledgements would be complete without also expressing my appreciation of the Facebook friends and Twitter followers who enter into fascinating conversations on research matters; all the wonderful book bloggers who review my books, join in my blog tours or invite me onto their blogs; and, most of all, my fabulous readers. Thank you.

In theory, nothing could be better than a summer spent basking in the French sun. That is, until you add in three teenagers, two love interests, one divorcing couple, and a *very* unexpected pregnancy . . .

Escape with Sue Moorcroft in this glorious summer read! Perfect for fans of Katie Fforde, Carole Matthews and Trisha Ashley.

Win a luxury trip to Italy*

Thanks to the wonderful people at Kuoni, you can have an adventure just like Sofia Bianchi and win a four-night stay for two at the five-star Lefay Resort & SPA on the shores of Lake Garda in Italy.

Enter on http://books.harpercollins.co.uk/campaigns/ win-a-luxury-trip-to-italy

The prize is for two people and includes flights from London Gatwick, four nights in a Prestige Junior suite, breakfast at restaurant La Granda Limonaia and access to Lefay SPA World.

Discover Lefay Resort & SPA Lago Di Garda: https://lagodigarda.lefayresorts.com/eng

Book your own holiday with Kuoni: http://www.kuoni.co.uk

*Terms and conditions apply. Visit http://books.harpercollins.co.uk/campaigns/ win-a-luxury-trip-to-italy